Hannibal's Niece
As Part of the Defining Karma™ Grant Program

The firm GABE Advisors, LLC, founded by author and creative entrepreneur G. A. Beller, established the Defining Karma™ Grant Program to identify unique literary, television, and film projects. Over a period of eighteen months, the team reviewed numerous submissions from aspiring writers. A number of the stories were well written, but were not the right fit. When asked what exactly they were seeking, Beller replied, "We'll know it when we find it."

Hannibal's Niece was written over fifteen years ago, only to be relegated to the author's back shelf to gather dust when it had been rejected by agents and publishers. Author Anthony R. Licata had given up hope that it would ever get published until, through a series of seemingly unrelated events, he discovered the startup grant program Defining Karma™, dusted off his manuscript, and submitted *Hannibal's Niece* for consideration. Beller and the team knew immediately they had found their first author.

The circumstances that brought Licata and the publishing participants together characterize the very definition of karma.

GABE Advisors is proud to award their Defining Karma™ Grant for Literature to Anthony R. Licata for his outstanding novel, *Hannibal's Niece*, and hope to see more from this talented author in the future.

GABE Advisors, LLC
Defining Karma™ Grant Committee

www.definingkarma.com

Hannibal's Niece

*A Tale of Love, Murder, and Deceit
in Ancient Rome*

Hannibal Meets Scipio at Zama

Anthony R. Licata

DISCLAIMER:

This book is not a work of fiction. Names, characters, places, and incidents were inspired by true events, though many are the product of the author's imagination and are used fictitiously to build a believable historical world. For story purposes, the author altered the timeline of some historical events, names, and relationships, while attempting to maintain much of actual history as possible.

Cover Design: Vivian Craig
Cover Images: *Portrait of Vibiana*, Matthew James Collins, 2016; *The Fight Between Scipio Africanus and Hannibal*, c. 1616-1618, by Cesari, Bernardino (1565-1621), Heritage Image Partnership Ltd/Alamy Stock Photo.
Maps and Battle Diagrams: James Swanson

ISBN 978-0-9966799-4-7 Hardcover
ISBN 978-0-9966799-3-0 Paperback
ISBN 978-0-9966799-5-4 ebook

G. ANTON
Publisher
Chicago

HANNIBAL'S NIECE

For Jack and Betty Licata,
without whose sacrifices
none of this would have been possible.

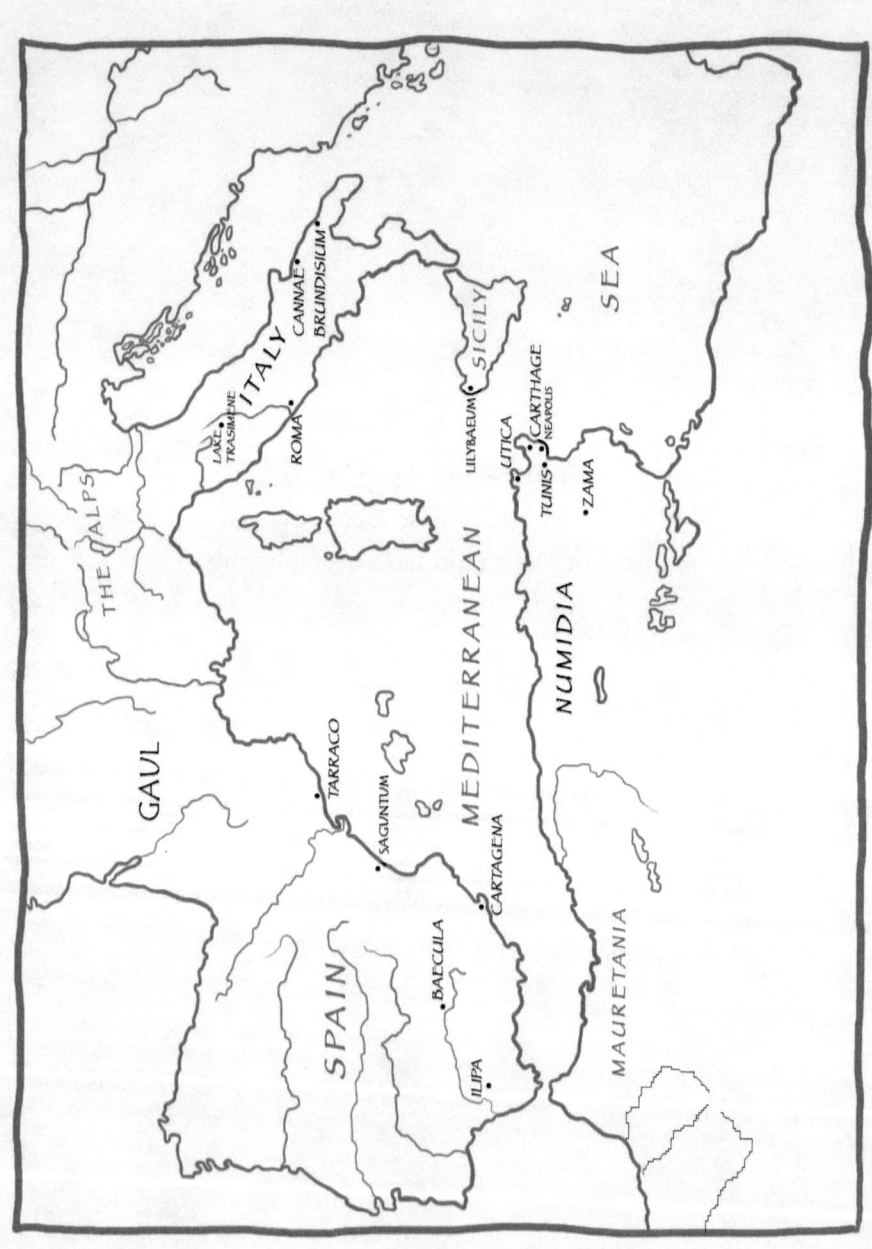

GAUL

THE ALPS

ITALY

CANNAE
BRUNDISILIM
LAKE
TRASIMENE
ROMA

SICILY

LILYBAEUM
CARTHAGE
UTICA
NEAPOLIS
TUNIS
ZAMA

SEA

MEDITERRANEAN

NUMIDIA

MAURETANIA

SPAIN

TARRACO
SAGUNTUM
CARTAGENA
BAECULA
ILIPA

INTRODUCTION

GREAT RIVALS MAKE GREAT nations. In the history of the world, no rivalry was more intense than that of Rome and Carthage.

After the collapse of the vast empire assembled by Alexander the Great, the Roman people embarked upon a relentless expansion of their influence, first throughout Italy, and then abroad. Eventually, Roman ambitions came into stark conflict with the similar designs of Carthage, the powerful city-state located on the mainland of Africa, just across from Sicily. Carthage was the world's first huge maritime power. She used her navy to extend her holdings across the Mediterranean, into Spain and Sicily. Roman visionaries understood full well that with the riches of Spain at her disposal, Carthage would build massive armies to augment her fleet. Even worse, the Carthaginian presence in Sicily amounted to a dagger aimed at the heart of their fledgling Roman Republic.

Hostilities were inevitable. In the first of the Punic Wars, fought from 264 BC to 241 BC, Rome defeated Carthage. A harsh peace was imposed: Spain was divided between the two powers at the River Ebro, Carthage was forced to pay tribute, and the Carthaginian presence in Sicily was reduced to a mere toehold.

But no peace can long withstand the greedy desire for conquest. After a mere twenty-three years, upon the most trifling of pretenses, Carthage moved north of the Ebro and captured the city of Saguntum, committing horrible atrocities in the process.

Outraged, the Roman Senate dispatched a delegation to Carthage to ascertain her intentions. "We bring you peace or war," said the Roman envoy. "Take which you will."

In reply, the proud answer rang out, "Whichever you please, we do not care."

Came the famous Roman response: "We give you war."

Hannibal, Carthage's brilliant champion, struck first. He marched from Spain into Gaul and to the Alps. These towering peaks, peopled with hostile tribes, stood as Rome's natural barrier to any invader. Incredibly, against all odds, Hannibal brought his entire army through the mountains, and the territory of Italy lay open before him.

In addition to his guile and military genius, Hannibal possessed a profound advantage: trained war elephants, the mere sight of which would create panic in his foes. With these animals leading his deadly charges, Hannibal routed the Romans at every turn.

Hannibal further benefitted from a peculiarity of the Roman republican system of government. Control of the military was vested in two consuls, elected annually. This system, designed to prevent a tyrant from seizing power, assured a lack of continuity in the chain of command and led to the appointment of generals who were more accomplished at politics than soldiering. The Roman consul Sempronius was beaten at the Trebia River, with a loss of over ten thousand men; the consul Flaminius and four legions were slaughtered at Lake Trasimene. And at the Battle of Cannae in 216 BC, Hannibal defeated the consul Varro, killing fifty thousand Romans and capturing ten thousand more. It was the worst disaster in Roman history.

After Cannae, numerous towns and cities in the Italian peninsula renounced their allegiance to Rome and converted their loyalty to Hannibal and Carthage. Lacking sufficient supplies to undertake a siege of Rome, Hannibal decided against a strike against the city. Instead, he embarked on a campaign of terror throughout Italy, thus inducing more territories to defect from Rome, which clearly could not protect them from the raider.

In the panic following Cannae, the Roman Senate appointed Quintus Fabius Maximus as dictator to take charge of the defense of the Italian peninsula. Faced with Hannibal's aura of invincibility, Fabius made it the policy of the Roman Army to withdraw whenever Hannibal and his elephants approached, refusing to become embroiled in a general engagement. Roman offensive actions were limited to blockading Hannibal's lines of supply and ruthlessly re-acquiring the various territories that had defected. The war thus degenerated into a long series of raids by Hannibal against the Roman countryside.

A great nation in crisis will find a champion, and eventually a young Roman stepped forward to challenge Carthage.

This is the story of the life, and the love, of the Roman who conquered Hannibal.

◧ BOOK ONE ◧

GAUL

SPAIN

TARRACO

SAGUNTUM

BAECULA

ILIPA

CARTAGENA

MEDITERRANEAN SEA

MAURETANIA

NUMIDIA

I

Baecula, Spain
208 BC

A FINE MIST SHIMMERED IN the cool morning air, catching the first bits of orange light. The sun hit the massed gray metal armament as it pulsed slowly forward, throwing a harsh glare across the rolling Spanish plain.

From his vantage point on a steep ridge east of the assembled armies, young Publius Cornelius Scipio leaned forward in his finely tooled saddle. He squinted hard, trying to make out the enemy formation. Beneath him, sensing his master's determination, the stout white warhorse Bucephalus canted slightly under the shifting weight.

Scipio was pleased with his choice of a site for the battle, just east of the small town of Baecula. The two armies had been skirmishing for days as they groped for advantage of terrain. The Romans had gotten the better of this preliminary duel and now stood lined on a pronounced rise in the mossy plain, the easterly approach to the nearby Silver Mountains, named for the rich lodes buried there. The range towered in the distance, offering vast wealth to any who might take and hold the territory. But money was not on Scipio's mind. Of more immediate importance: his position gave the attackers the added burden of marching uphill with the sun in their eyes. There was a spring-fed stream near the Roman lines, so if the fight should drag on, his soldiers could be refreshed. On either side of the plain stood a dense forest, which Scipio had thoroughly scouted for signs of enemy soldiers. There appeared to be none, but he had maintained continual surveillance to avoid a nasty surprise against his flanks.

"How many, Laelius?" he asked quietly.

Beside him, on a smaller chestnut stallion, sat the senior legate, Garibus Paullus Laelius, in effect Scipio's second in command. He was much older and far more experienced than his commanding general. Laelius shook his head slowly, conscious of the heavy ornamental brass helmet he was wearing. "I would say twenty-five thousand men, perhaps even thirty thousand."

"And what do you make of their formation?"

Again the officer paused for several moments, allowing the swarming mass to come into clearer view. "Hasdrubal Barca is cautious," Laelius replied evenly. "He apparently is not a disciple of his brother Hannibal's tactics—he brings forward a standard balanced line against you."

Scipio sat back, pleased that this analysis matched his own. "Good," he grunted. "We're ready for them."

The young leader was proud of the army—*his* army now—that stretched out below him. There were five legions, nearly twenty-five thousand men in all, with two thousand cavalry, ablaze with scarlet-and-gold standards, each with its own distinctive insignia and flags. Formed up for battle, each infantryman wore a *galea*, a pot-shaped steel helmet, and a heavy mail shirt fitted over a dull red tunic that fell to mid-thigh. His feet were sheathed in special military sandals, strong and well ventilated, and fitted on the underside with iron hobnails for traction. Each carried a broad wooden shield, equipped with a metal cover over the central handle; two long wooden spears called *pilum*, tipped with deadly narrow metal points remarkably effective at piercing shields and armor; a short sword; and a side dagger. The short sword was a design the Romans had copied from the Spaniards, a vicious weapon capable of inflicting terrible stabbing wounds, yet short enough to wield easily in the close confines of a crushed battle. But the equipment was not as important as attitude, and here the armies of the Roman Republic were unique. Every soldier was a landowner, a free Roman citizen fighting for his family and fortune. No paid mercenaries or allies of dubious loyalty! Each had pledged his life and fidelity to the others. There was no fighting force in the world quite the equivalent of a well-trained Roman army, if strongly led.

Scipio waved for two messengers to come forward.

"It appears that the enemy intends to attack across our entire front," he told the men. "You go to the tribune Lucellus"—motioning at one, and then at another—"and you to the tribune Marius. Tell them to stand fast when the battle is joined. Upon my signal, they should employ their reserve to flank the enemy. Not a moment sooner. Now repeat the message."

Scipio listened patiently as each man repeated his orders, then watched as they galloped off to their respective wings.

"Permission to speak frankly, Scipio?" Laelius requested.

Curious, Scipio turned to regard his adjutant. Long a loyal retainer of Scipio's family, the older man was small in stature and compact in build, but possessed strong features. His hair, black as a moonless night, matched his shining eyes, which radiated an alert, intelligent passion. Laelius had never married, and Scipio's late father had informed him before his death that Laelius' tastes ran toward what was delicately referred to in polite Roman society as "the Greek habit." Scipio was quite tolerant in dealing with the personal preferences of his officers—so long as they did not interfere with duty. Scipio respected Laelius' judgment, and if the older man wanted to speak, Scipio would listen.

"Always, my dear Laelius," he said.

"Your strategy, while innovative, puts the army at considerable risk."

Scipio considered his deployment, which thinned the front ranks in order to create a force in reserve. The men of Lucellus on the left wing and Marius on the right were spread in an unorthodox fashion.

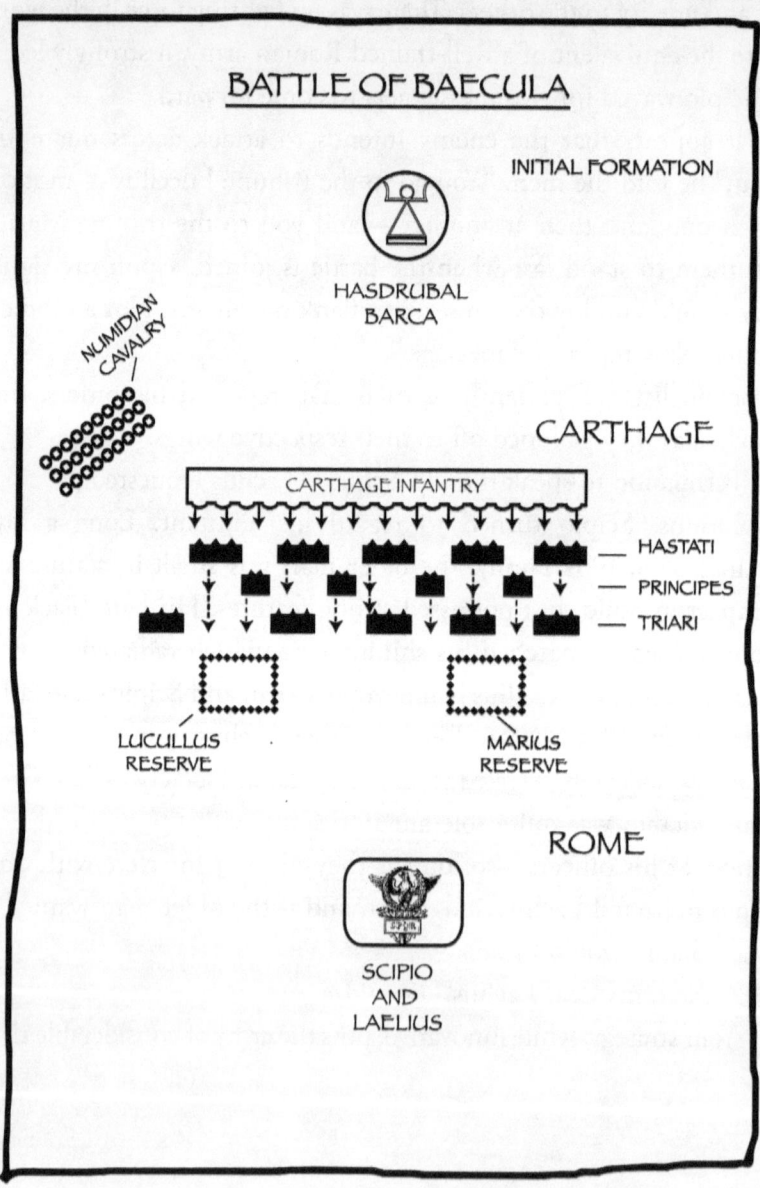

BATTLE OF BAECULA

INITIAL FORMATION

HASDRUBAL
BARCA

NUMIDIAN
CAVALRY

CARTHAGE

CARTHAGE INFANTRY

—— HASTATI

—— PRINCIPES

—— TRIARI

LUCULLUS
RESERVE

MARIUS
RESERVE

ROME

SCIPIO
AND
LAELIUS

Typically, Roman infantrymen formed up in three long lines, shoulder to shoulder, so as to allow no gaps. Scipio had directed that the first rank, the *hastati*, should spread out, allowing a spear's length between men. The second rank, the *principes*, were two spears' lengths back and staggered so as to fill in the gaps in the front rank. The pattern was repeated with the third rank, the *triari*. Scipio hoped to create a defensive perimeter that would make up in depth what it lacked in front-line strength. And by so stripping the ranks, he had established two bodies of two thousand men, half a legion each, held in reserve behind the center, both capable of deployment as the tide of battle dictated.

"We have the bravest men on the front lines, Laelius. Each man has been told precisely what is expected of him and drilled rigorously. They will hold until the reserve is deployed."

Laelius bowed slightly, not wishing further to test his commander's patience. He had done his duty by pointing out the risk to which Scipio's newfangled tactics exposed the army. The outcome of the battle, and Scipio's career, were in the hands of the gods.

The leading elements of Hasdrubal's infantry had been closing cautiously for some time, pausing at regular intervals to see if the Romans would break out of their defensive formation and attack. The anxiety created by this test of nerves was exhausting, but the Romans held fast.

Closer and closer the enemy drew, tension growing palpably, until finally they were within fifty yards of the Roman lines. As they crept ever nearer, the indistinguishable mass of men began to change to individual faces. Like the Romans, the foot soldiers in the Carthaginian Army wore belts hung with brass barb–studded leather strips. The metal studs made a clinking sound as the men marched, amplifying the menace of their approach. This was the worst time, Laelius knew: those dreadful last few moments just before the actual outbreak of fighting. One never knew for sure whether the exposed men facing almost certain death on the front lines would do their duty—or break and run. Tactics? Strategy? Battles turned on the raw courage of the men who defended against the first assault.

Laelius tilted his head slightly and appraised his commander. He had seen Young Scipio more animated during a chariot race than he seemed to be now. If he felt any concern over the first battle to be fought under his command, he certainly wasn't letting it show. Oh, he was a Cornelius, all right! The same broad forehead and piercing blue eyes, aquiline nose, and full, sensuous lips. And his manner: so calm, almost passive in the face of the imminent danger, supremely confident. So very *Roman*.

And so much like his father.

———

Far to the north of Rome, the Arnus River formed the boundary between the Italian Peninsula and the region known as Italian Gaul. From its source high in the Apennine Mountains, the repeated flooding of the river over the centuries had given rise to a fertile delta that flanked its banks all the way west to the Mediterranean. To this naturally rich soil the gods added the blessing of hospitable weather, and so the territory surrounding the town of Florentia became a prosperous agricultural region, yielding bumper crops of wheat and all nature of vegetables. The residents were mainly small farmers who tilled their own lands.

At about the time the city-state of Rome was beginning to expand its influence throughout Italy, to this territory came a clever and ambitious settler, one Publius Cornelius. Publius Cornelius was not particularly good with a plow, but he was a forward-looking man. Laboring one afternoon under a hot sun, he realized that a man's wealth, if limited to what his own personal labor could produce on a farm, was going to be restrained by the bounds of his own energy. He began using slaves to till his lands. Through shrewd business practices and exploitation, Publius Cornelius managed to assemble a considerable agricultural estate. As his land holdings grew, so did his influence and prestige. He took a wife, a rather heavy and simple Florentine girl who just so happened to be the only child of her father, one of the largest livestock farmers in the territory. Naturally, when his father-in-law expired, Publius Cornelius inherited the entire estate, more than doubling his holdings and giving him an entrée into a whole new business. He grew older and wealthier.

Publius Cornelius was able to see clearly that the various territories of Italy sooner or later must come under the domination of the rapidly expanding metropolis located on the Tiber River. Accordingly, he used his influence to cause Florentia to ally herself with Rome, assuring the benefits of Roman citizenship for himself and his bloodline. Old Publius was still a quick learner, and, after making a number of well-placed "gifts" to influential Romans, he managed to get himself elected to the Senate. He served with some distinction, obtaining funds for the construction of a proper Roman road connecting Florentia to Rome: the Via Cassia.

Thus established, the Cornelli became one of the most noble patrician families in the hierarchy of Roman society. Their wealth and influence had been handed down through five generations. In accordance with Roman custom, each firstborn son inherited all of his father's property. As the Cornelli passed along their Florentine estates, their wealth eventually proved sufficient to elect Publius Cornelius Aemelius, great-grandson of the founder of the line, as a consul of Rome.

Aemilius' record as a consul was generally unremarkable, his year in office distinguished by no bold campaigns or serious threats to the safety of the city-state. Indeed, his chief accomplishment in life was the production of an heir, Publius Cornelius Scipio, and a younger son, Gnaeus. As a Cornelius, Scipio was raised to follow in his father's footsteps, to strive for the zenith of Roman society. A disciplined and pious man, Scipio took the woman Pomponia, daughter of the highly influential Metullus Pomponius Agro, as his wife. It was a politically astute match; love was of little interest to members of elite Roman society. Scipio was a young man on the rise, and as he climbed the rungs of the Roman political structure, the business of the state kept him away from Rome during much of his career. During his occasional visits home, he managed to produce two offspring: Young Scipio and, years later, Lucius.

Young Scipio had enjoyed a completely ordinary boyhood, taking in the pleasures of privileged Roman life, playing and growing, always trying to win approval from his strict father—until Carthage broke the peace, crossing the River Ebro and sacking Saguntum. The outbreak of the war split the Cornelius household: Scipio the Elder once again felt the call of duty, and Young Scipio, only thirteen at the time, begged his father to take him along. Oh, he promised a hundred times not to make trouble in the camp! And how his mother protested. But in the end, *paterfamilias*, the Roman custom of absolute rule by the male head of household, won out. The father took the boy with him.

They went first on an unsuccessful mission to intercept Hannibal in Gaul. They arrived in Marseilles, missing the clever Semite by a mere three days. The general pondered his next move: should he pursue Hannibal, hoping to make the Carthaginian turn and give battle? Or should they await instructions from Rome?

It was Young Scipio who came up with the solution. Why not move the army east into Spain, thereby cutting Hannibal off from his base? This would reduce him to the status of a mere raider, and surely the Romans left in Italy could deal with him. Without saying so, Scipio the Elder was impressed with the strategic wisdom of his son's recommendation. He followed Young Scipio's suggestion and dispatched his army to Spain, under the command of his brother, Gnaeus.

Scipio the Elder and his son then returned to Northern Italy to take up the campaign against Hannibal. The decision to bring Young Scipio along turned out to be a good thing after all. When he finally caught up with Hannibal at the Ticinus, a tributary of the River Po, Scipio the Elder was wounded and cut off by the enemy. Seeing his father's distress, the boy assembled a contingent of cavalry and charged forward, saving his father and the other Romans.

After recovering from the battle, Scipio the Elder decided to rejoin his legions in Spain. The father had recognized in his young son the signs of potential greatness: a proud, classically Roman bearing; bold courage that occasionally touched on rashness; and a refreshingly direct manner of dealing with people—unusual for a nobleman. But the boy needed seasoning, a foundation in the wiles of politics. Scipio knew that his son would benefit from remaining close to the seat of power in Rome. And so, at his father's suggestion, Young Scipio stayed with the Roman Army in Italy rather than joining his father and uncle in Spain.

Young Scipio had been brought up to observe the religious rites, and it soon appeared that he was a favorite of the gods. The young man survived the catastrophe against Hannibal at Cannae, even earning distinction by fighting his way to safety in relentless hand-to-hand combat. And after Cannae, he gained more fame. Shortly after the disaster, several men of patrician stock debated fleeing the country and seeking refuge in some foreign land. Upon hearing of their meeting, Young Scipio burst in upon their wicked conspiracy, sword drawn. He swore an oath never to desert his country or permit any other citizen to betray her. He made them swear it, too. After this story made the rounds, Scipio was elected *aedile*, or public magistrate. Only eighteen, he was the youngest man in the history of Rome to hold the office.

His term as aedile was nearly over when terrible news arrived from Spain: the brothers Cornelius had wound up in a battle with Hannibal's brother, Hasdrubal. Things had gone badly. The Carthaginian cavalry, led by a Numidian prince named Massinissa, had outflanked the Romans and crushed them. Scipio the Elder sought to rally his troops and rode into the fray. He was lanced in the side by the spear of a Carthaginian foot soldier. Gnaeus, seeing his brother fall, attempted to rush forward to save him, and he too was cut down. As word spread that the Roman commanders had been killed, panic seized the ranks, and the legionnaires began to break and run. The engagement quickly degenerated into a massacre.

Barca's men then did something that ignited the flames of hatred in Young Scipio, after which he would find no peace until he had his revenge. The Carthaginians stripped Scipio the Elder of his general's armor and brutally castrated the body. The naked and filthy corpse, battered nearly beyond recognition, was tied to a donkey that was then sent wandering into the Roman lines. It was said that Hasdrubal had made a gift of the father's armor to the Numidian horseman Massinissa, who had played such a critical role in the struggle.

Young Scipio was crushed. He chastised himself for remaining in Italy instead of staying at his father's side: perhaps if he had been there, he could have saved him, just like at the Ticinus. Scipio could not come to grips with his father's death—was it guilt for not being there, or a simple inability to accept the fact? Or was it the disrespect the Carthaginians had visited upon his father's corpse? Whatever the cause, he burned with the desire for vengeance.

The wisdom of his father's suggestion that he remain in Italy now became evident. When word arrived that his father had been killed, Scipio hurried to the family estate in Florentia to console his mother and brother, and to cope with his own grief. But the Senate was unable to settle upon a successor to command the Spanish Campaign, and so referred the matter of selecting a new general to the People's Assembly. This became something of an embarrassment, insofar as the likely candidates were exchanging nervous glances, none daring to seek the Spanish command that had proven fatal to such an eminent general as Scipio the Elder. In the silence, Scipio stepped forward to offer himself as a candidate. He emphasized his military record, his election as aedile, and his right to seek revenge for his father's defeat.

There being no other takers, the Assembly unanimously approved his candidacy.

And then Quintus Fabius Maximus, dictator and commander in chief of the Roman Army—"Fabius the Delayer"—tried to overturn the decision. Scipio was too young for this large responsibility, he told the Senate.

So said Fabius, who had sat on his hands for years while Hannibal stampeded through Italy, burning and plundering? Fabius, who always encamped on high ground so as to be safe from attack, thus obtaining a splendid seat to witness Hannibal's wasting of the countryside?

Fortunately, the memory of Scipio the Elder was held fondly by a majority of senators, and they refused to overturn the People's Assembly. Scipio had won his command.

He'd brought five thousand men with him into Spain, a full legion. He had recruited his men carefully and trained them hard. These men he blended into the shattered remnants of the defeated army that had survived his father. The men could see his determination, and were invigorated by it. Scipio was confident of their training and morale, but only this day's events would prove whether he had the rare gift of generalship, the innate ability to lead men to victory. He had not been dreading this battle—indeed, he was hungry for it.

———

Up and down the enemy ranks, the morning air was shattered by the blare of trumpetry. With a shout, the enemy host surged forward.

In response, the Romans hurled their pilum, filling the air with deadly missiles. Many of the spears found targets, taking a heavy toll before the swarming Carthaginians closed and engaged Scipio's front line. These brave Romans absorbed the brunt of the assault and fought hard, if briefly. Almost immediately, the men began to fall back under the sheer weight of the greater Carthaginian numbers at the point of attack. But the long hours of training showed results. The second-line hastati did not panic and flee, but rather gave ground grudgingly, continuing to engage the enemy and slowing its advance while dropping back in formation to the second rank.

The fighting intensified as the more heavily armed principes were engaged. All too soon, however, this line also began to give way, although again the retreat to the triari was orderly and had the effect of filling the gaps in that line. Thus, while the Romans might have appeared to be losing ground, in truth they were strengthening their defensive position, all the while taking a bloody toll on the attacking force, which began to fragment as the engagement wore on.

Pleased with his men's valor, Scipio watched the unfolding battle from a distance. The clash of metal and the screams of the dying were barely audible from his post. Laelius continued to be impressed with the young man's demeanor: if things were in fact going badly for the army, Scipio showed no sign of concern.

"Where is their cavalry?" Scipio asked.

"Judging from that cloud of dust off to the south, I would say that Barca is now employing his horses against your left wing."

The Carthaginian horsemen were warriors from the African territory of Numidia. These lean, strong Africans were skilled riders, fearless in combat, and formidable opponents. It was Hannibal's Numidian horsemen who had turned the tide of battle at Cannae. A horde of them now stormed across the moist plain, apparently intent on sweeping around the left flank of the Roman force while their infantry colleagues concentrated on caving it in.

Scipio waved forward an aide. "Unfurl the flag now for Lucellus," he ordered.

The man raised a large red flag and waved it in broad strokes.

Down on the field of battle, the tribune Lucellus was pacing back and forth behind his rows of engaged soldiers, shouting encouragement to the hard-pressed troops and desperately hoping Scipio would release the reserve to shore up the line. A centurion caught the signal from atop the ridge and pointed it out to Lucellus.

"Is he crazy?" Lucellus grunted. "The reserve is needed to bolster the line!"

Nonetheless, Lucellus the tribune was a Roman, after all. Orders were orders. He shouted to the reserve force of two thousand men assembled near the center, "Now, Romans! Follow me!" As quickly as a man encumbered with armor could move, Lucellus trotted around the far end of the left wing, followed by the main body of the reserve force. Clearing the end of the line and breaking out into the open, Lucellus was shocked to see that his path of advance was taking him directly into the horde of cavalry swooping down on the army.

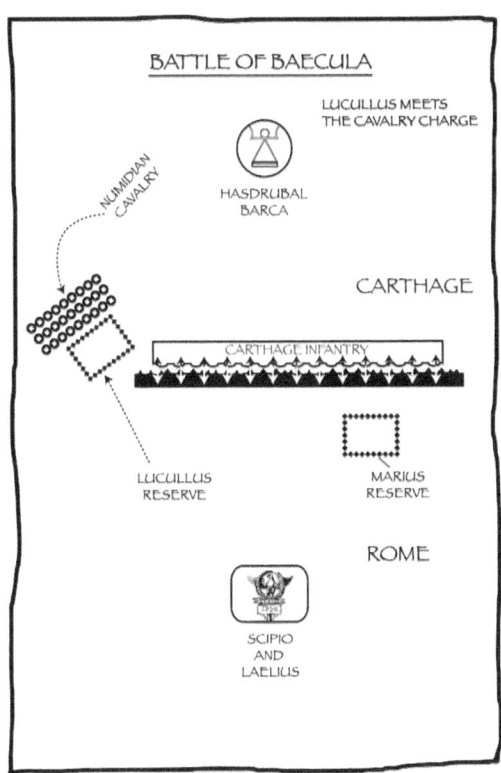

"Lucellus will be cut up!" Laelius said through clenched teeth. "You must do something."

"Patience, Laelius, patience." Scipio waited until the Carthaginian cavalry had plowed into Lucellus' force, then waved forward yet another messenger. "Quickly now, go to Silanus and tell him the entire cavalry is released. He must turn back the enemy cavalry. Hurry!"

On the battlefield, surrounded by the brutal gore of hand-to-hand combat, Lucellus vaguely appreciated that Scipio's deployment of his reserve had indeed blunted the Carthaginian cavalry strike at the main force. But he also understood that his position was desperate. Even the most courageous infantry could not hold off skillful cavalry for long, given the horsemen's advantages of strength, height, and mobility. Watching his men fall all about him, Lucellus rallied his troops and waited for help or death.

His fear was lifted by the crash of Silanus' trumpets behind him. Lucellus turned to see the Roman cavalry charging to his relief.

"Courage, Romans, courage!" he shouted, trying to make himself heard above the din. Once again the Roman foot soldiers stiffened, closing their bloody ranks.

Silanus' cavalry of two thousand riders struck the Numidian horsemen with the force of a thunderbolt, chopping them to pieces with deadly short swords. The enemy was resolute and held for a few moments, taking terrible losses, before beginning to falter and fall back under the crush of the counterattack. Silanus sensed the kill and pressed his riders into a frenzy. The Carthaginian retreat turned into a panic.

As he watched the battle on the left degenerate into a ruthless slaughter, Scipio became animated for the first time. He summoned another man, this one holding a rolled blue flag.

"Now, damn you, now! Give the signal for Marius to move!"

Marius saw the blue flag instantly and wasted no time in putting his reserve force into motion. He double-timed them around the end of his line and struck the enemy flank. Marius had been at Cannae with Scipio, serving as his centurion. He hated the Carthaginians with a fury born of the humiliation Rome had suffered that day. He had instilled this hatred in his troops. They struck with a vengeance.

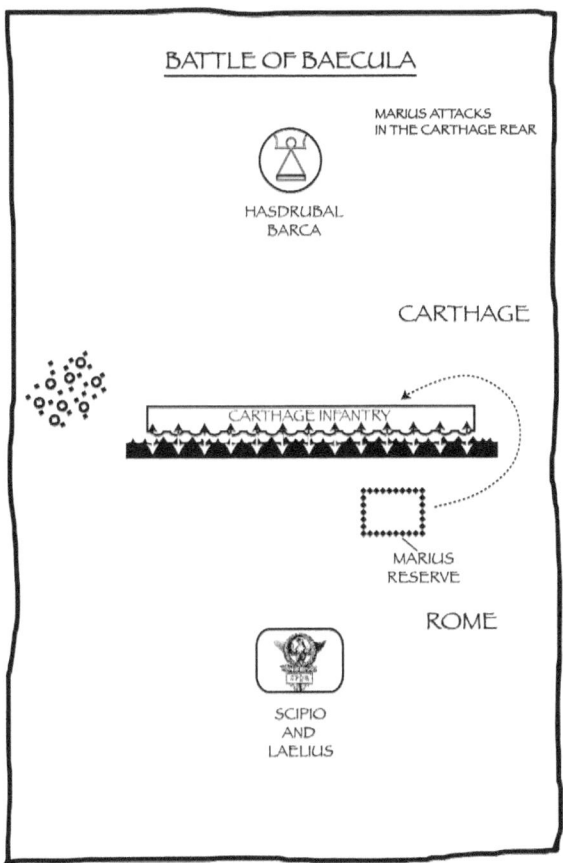

Marius' pressure from the right, coupled with the collapse on the left, was too much for the Carthaginian horde. Within minutes, the bloodletting had become a rout.

Back atop the ridge, Laelius was startled at the sudden apparent failure of Barca's discipline. Could this be the same general who had defeated Scipio the Elder, a man Laelius had revered like a god? Briefly, Laelius considered whether this was some type of trap. Was the clever Barca lurking off on the horizon with some reserve force of his own? Indeed, at Cannae Hannibal had utilized a planned retreat to draw the attacking Roman forces deep into his rear and then closed his flanks upon them. Watching this carnage, however, Laelius shortly rejected that idea. The rout was too brutal, too convincing. Not even the dreaded Hannibal himself would be able to regroup this wild rabble running for its life before the Roman scythe.

"It appears that you have won a glorious victory, Scipio." Laelius' admiration showed a new regard for his young commanding general.

Scipio flared, "I care not for glory. It's Barca I want!" And with that, he summoned forth a final messenger.

"Circulate a message to the men in the ranks. I will pay ten thousand sesterces to the man who brings me the head of Hasdrubal Barca."

II

BAECULA, SPAIN
208 BC

ALONE IN HIS TENT, Scipio restlessly awaited word of Barca's fate from his field commanders. The spacious gray tent, woven from heavy wool, was divided into two sections by a long leather flap that hung from the ridgepole and attached to the wooden end poles. Over the flap hung Scipio's personal banner, a crimson flag embroidered with gold about the border. The Cornelius family insignia, a sword wrapped in ivy, was embossed in the center. Customarily, the commanding general occupied the back half of the tent, with the front reserved for his staff. Tonight, however, he had released the staff to join in the revelry celebrating the victory. The party sounded raucous, and Scipio was certain he would have a spate of disciplinary matters to address the next morning.

Let them have their fun, he thought. *They earned it.*

He swelled with pride, reminiscing about his army's performance. A complete rout! Casualties had been light, except for the carnage inflicted on Lucellus' reserve before Silanus arrived with the cavalry.

Scipio was seated at a large camp table established in the middle of his quarters. In one corner sat a brass stylus and several wax tablets, his official report of the day's events not even half finished. He had grown weary midway through his dictation and dismissed the scribe. On the other corner was a list of awards and commendations he intended to grant for valor in battle. And in the center, a platter bearing bread, olives, and sausages kept company with a silver flask of wine. But he had not touched the food. Scipio hungered solely for revenge, and the lack of information weighed on him.

Barca's command elements had been seen fleeing the battlefield, and Silanus had dispatched a squadron of his best riders to give chase. That had been in the middle of the morning, when the outcome of the battle was already clear. Most of the day had been spent rounding up the fleeing Carthaginians, putting the wounded enemy soldiers out of their misery, and tending to the Roman wounded and dead. Not far from the command tent, a group of surgeons attached to the Roman Army—every one of them a Greek—had been kept busy. An enormous pile of severed limbs was stacked behind their grisly tent. The sawing and cauterizing was still going on, filling the air with horrible screams. No wonder the soldiers had such disrespect for the surgeons, calling them butchers and making grim jokes about their abysmal trade.

And there were uncounted scores of captured soldiers. Scipio was still awaiting a precise number. The prisoners would bring a sizeable haul when they were sold into slavery. By custom, proceeds from the sale of captured enemy soldiers were the sole booty of the commanding general. But Scipio, by way of inheritance, already had more than enough money—and besides, he had no interest in it. He therefore intended to alter the custom and distribute the proceeds of victory to the men of his army. He had big plans for this army, and sharing the prizes of war with them would help to finance their extended absence from their farms.

Scipio's concentration was broken by the clatter of hooves approaching the tent, and he stepped out of his quarters to investigate.

The chilly night air bore the hint of approaching winter, and he drew his crimson cloak tight about him, glad for its weight and warmth.

"Well, Silanus, what news?" he asked of his cavalry commander after the man had clambered down from his mount.

The man was clearly tired from a long day in the saddle, and he was caked with dust. Scipio noticed a blood-soaked cloth wrapped about Silanus' left biceps, a wound from the battle. Silanus drew in a long, deep breath, and Scipio knew at once that the officer was searching for words he did not want to speak.

Scipio relieved him of the burden. "He got away, didn't he?"

"I'm afraid so, Scipio." Silanus lowered his head, steeling himself for the expected rebuke.

Scipio could not hide his disappointment. "You spared no effort in making the chase?" he demanded.

Silanus shook his head. "You can't fault the men. Barca and his entourage had too much of a head start. We finally had to give up the chase. We just returned to camp a few minutes ago."

The general set his jaw. "There's quite a celebration brewing in the camp," he said dismissively. "Go and enjoy yourself."

Silanus was relieved that Scipio would not be issuing reprimands for the unsuccessful mission. He gave his leader a sidelong look and grinned.

"Well, we didn't exactly come back empty-handed," he said.

Scipio did not smile. "What trophy of war could you possibly have brought me that would make up for the loss of Hasdrubal Barca?"

"Come with me," Silanus said, laughing cryptically.

Silanus remounted, and Scipio climbed onto one of the horses that were always kept tethered at the ready outside his tent.

As the two men rode through the camp, Scipio acknowledged the cheers of his men along the route. They may have been drunk, but they were fully aware that their general had led them to a historic—and lucrative—victory with mercifully few losses. This was something new: a commander more intent on slaughtering the enemy than his own men.

The cavalry was bivouacked at the far end of the camp, just inside the stockade wall, so horses could be dispatched efficiently in the event of a surprise attack. The horsemen were assembled in a crowd, and they let loose with yet another cheer as Scipio approached. And, thanks to the light of a dozen torches ringing a makeshift platform, he saw at once the solution to Silanus' mystery.

The men had gathered to ogle a group of eight nude women standing, heads down, on display in the center of the stage. They shivered in the night air, hands tied behind them. A single rope tethered them at the neck.

Silanus dismounted and climbed onto the platform. He motioned for silence, but it took several moments for the lewd catcalls and shouts to die down.

"My general," he said in a voice loud enough for all to hear, "you asked of your cavalry two things today. One we delivered: a smashing blow that sent the enemy running!"

The men gave a roar of approval, and Scipio bowed, acknowledging his appreciation of their service.

"Unfortunately," Silanus continued when the noise abated, "we could not grant your second request, the head of Hasdrubal Barca. But your cavalry pledges this to you now—if you will but bring us to battle with him again, we will not disappoint you a second time!"

There was another round of cheering. Scipio felt his displeasure with this officer ease a bit—Silanus had a superb ability to motivate the men.

Silanus held up his hand, and the men quieted again. "We may not have captured Barca, but we did take the next best thing: his harem!"

This time, the roar nearly caused Scipio's horse to panic. Scipio brought the animal under control, then dismounted and handed the reins to a nearby soldier. He walked over to the platform and took a helping hand from Silanus to step up.

Scipio moved slowly down the line of the humiliated and miserable women, making a big show of inspecting each one, pinching and poking, allowing the men their fill of ribald comments and laughter. Barca, he had to admit, certainly had a fine taste for female flesh. The women were no older than twenty, and remarkably nubile. Barca apparently had a preference for lush bodies, with particular emphasis on spectacular breasts. All but one were clearly of Spanish descent, with rich brown skin, dark eyes, and deep black hair. Any of these seven would be a handful in bed.

The one odd member was a tall redhead, trembling at the end of the line. Lightly freckled, the girl's tense, angular body was lean and hard, with well-defined muscles in the calves, thighs, and belly, whereas the others had a softness giving just the slightest hint that in later years they could grow fat. She was a marvelous specimen, with thick, shoulder-length tresses more orange than red, and the same ice-blue eyes that Scipio himself possessed. The eyes alone would have clinched it for him, but she also carried perhaps the most incredible breasts of the entire lot—firm and full, high and perfectly round. The taut nipples were peculiar, however, jutting out brazenly but with little or no areolae.

Unlike the others, this long-legged redhead struggled to retain some measure of pride despite her nudity. She did not meet his gaze, but neither did she look away. He resolved to have her.

"No general can win a battle without brave soldiers, and I was fortunate today to have you," he told his troops. "And so, I choose to take only one of these women for myself." He pointed at the redhead and nodded at the murmurs of approval. "The rest I give to you."

After another roar, he continued. "Silanus will have his pick, and then distribute the rest to the men who showed particular valor on the field today. I commend you for your service to Rome. A grateful Rome salutes you!"

He waited until the applause receded and then turned to Silanus. "Do not forget Lucellus and Marius when you hand out these prizes."

Knowing of Laelius' tastes, Scipio did not include his second in command in the awarding of this particular booty. He then pointed to his own trophy. "Have someone take her to my sleeping tent. Summon a surgeon, and have her inspected thoroughly for any sign of disease. See to it that she is washed and fed. And use someone reliable—this one belongs to me. I'll be there shortly."

Silanus held his face impassively. He had wanted the redhead for himself! A plebeian, Silanus had for his entire life chafed at the privileges taken for granted by patricians such as his young general. Would not the redhead have been a small enough reward for his services in sweeping the Carthaginian cavalry from the field? It was always the same: the patricians took the best for themselves, leaving only chaff for the most deserving. He struck his breast with the customary salute and set about the task.

Scipio, oblivious to his officer's resentment, bounded from the stage and waded into the group, congratulating each man and giving words of encouragement for the battles he hoped lay ahead.

———

The point of a spear pressed against the small of her back, providing all the encouragement the redhead needed to move along. She did not know where they were taking her, nor what they had in mind, but she was more angry than shamed at the rude treatment she was receiving at the hands of her captors. All along the route, the coarse Roman soldiers guffawed and made crude jokes at her expense. She brazenly shook her breasts at some of them, daring them to touch her.

The guard behind her grabbed her by the arm, roughly jerking her to a halt before a tent, larger by far than any of the others. The standards mounted outside the tent confirmed her suspicions: this must be the dwelling of the Roman commander, that savage who had made such a show of her on the platform. And with a shudder, she realized why she had been brought here.

"What are you doing?" she heard one of the soldiers say to her guard.

"The general said to give her a bath. Now, how am I supposed to do that?"

"I know," said the first. "Bring her over here."

The woman felt herself being pushed again, and she stumbled, falling onto her face. She looked up, and found herself staring at a long wooden trough, used for watering horses.

"No!" she screamed as they picked her up and dropped her onto her buttocks in the frigid, brackish water. She emerged, spluttering, teeth chattering, furious. Her hands were still bound behind her, but she struggled to her feet. As the Roman came alongside her at the trough, she kicked at the water with all her might, causing a large splash. The soldier was enraged at being doused with the cold water, and he slapped her hard on the side of the head, making her ears ring. The force of the blow knocked her backward into the water, and before she could scramble up, she felt a strong hand on her head.

"No!" she screamed again, to no avail.

The soldier pushed her head into the black water and held it there, watching as her struggles became violent. He released her, and she surfaced, gasping for air and crying.

"Here, use this," the first soldier said, handing something to her tormentor. She felt something hard and rough against her sides and recognized the pungent smell at once. Saddle soap! They were scrubbing her as though she were some piece of leather!

She spat at the soldier with a cold fury. The man responded by dunking her again, and this time holding her under until she began to turn blue.

When she got her breath again, he asked her simply, "Are you ready to behave, or do you want some more?"

Her hair was soaked and completely disheveled, and drops of water fell as she shook her head.

"All right then, let's get this over with," the soldier said.

He washed her from top to bottom, lingering for a few moments at her genitals. He resisted the temptation to penetrate her with his hand for fear of what her new owner might do if he found her damaged. Realizing that she was shaking violently from the chill, the soldier helped her out of the trough and wrapped her in a blanket. He unsheathed his sword and cut her bonds, then took her inside the tent, where the surgeon waited.

———

The sentry posted outside Scipio's sleeping tent was conversing with Demosthenes, a short, swarthy Greek with a massive nose who was the chief surgeon of the army. Scipio had a grudging measure of respect for the Greek, for when he had first arrived in Spain, his feet had broken out in a terrible rash, large red pustules covering both members. Demosthenes pronounced him the victim of a fungus and applied a poultice made from ground roots of some indigenous plant. The cure took, and he had not since been troubled with the ailment. It was a rare success for the doctor.

"How do you find her?" Scipio asked as he paused at the entrance to the tent.

"Clean. You will not contract anything from her," Demosthenes said, a mischievous grin on his face. "Except perhaps the loss of your heart."

Scipio ignored the Greek and stepped past the guard into the darkened tent. The tent was smaller than the command tent but still roomy compared to the typical hut in which the men were housed, eight to a tent. Two small candles, set on his trunk in one corner, threw off the only light in the confined space.

The girl was sitting on his cot and was startled by his sudden presence. Edgy, she jumped to her feet. Scipio looked her over, noting that her eyes were red and puffy—she probably had been crying while waiting for him. The mud on her feet had been washed away, and her bonds had been removed, but her slender wrists were bruised and welted from the coarse ropes. She clutched a blanket.

Scipio went to her and gently but firmly removed the blanket. As if somehow more shy now than when on display before hundreds of men, she looked away and crossed her thin arms before her breasts, seeking to obtain some measure of cover from his discerning inspection. But he took her wrists in his hands and put them at her sides, so he could look at her, unobstructed by any impediments. She bore the strong scent of saddle soap, which amused him. Lit by the gentle glow of candles, her lines seemed softer and even more lovely than they had when he'd admired her on the platform. Away from the garish glare of the torches, her hair, still damp from the dousing she had received, now seemed more auburn than bright red. Her face was long and oval, dominated by elegant cheekbones holding sway over a straight, slender nose. Her lips, pale like the rest of her skin, were folded in a thin line with a hint of a downturn at the corners, just above a slightly dimpled chin. Running his eyes down her frame, he noticed a small mole on the swell of her belly, above the dense orange triangle at the apex of her thighs. He felt himself stirring.

"What is your name?" he asked, in Spanish. Silence.

"Insolent slave girls who do not answer their master may find themselves without a tongue," he said.

There was fear in those bright blue eyes, and she struggled to hold back tears.

"You need not be afraid," Scipio said with tenderness. "I'll take nothing from you that your master Hasdrubal Barca has not had a hundred times."

With that, the girl broke into uncontrollable sobs.

Scipio, surprised, was suddenly unsure of himself. This was certainly peculiar behavior from a pleasure slave. He waited until the girl regained control of herself, then pushed her back onto the cot.

"Please," she whispered in Latin, "don't hurt me."

He was shocked. "You speak Latin?"

She nodded.

There was more to this slave girl than met the eye, he decided. He reached out and tried to cup her firm breast in his hand, but she jumped away at his touch.

"Surely," he said sternly, "you are not a virgin!"

The girl again was overcome by a fit of tears and Scipio was at a total loss. How could Barca have such a beautiful woman in his harem and not have used her? Perhaps he was saving her for some special occasion, or maybe he intended to make a gift of her.

He took her hands in his own. Surprisingly, they were rough and hard, quite unlike the typical harem girl's. "That's enough. Stop that crying or I shall really give you cause to weep."

Gradually her fight for self-control was successful.

Scipio put his finger under her chin and lifted her head so that her gaze met his. "All right, now, let's have it. What were you doing in Hasdrubal Barca's love harem?"

"I am no pleasure slave of Hasdrubal Barca," she said hotly. "I am Vibiana, his daughter."

Scipio staggered at this news. His head reeled with the possibilities. Barca's own daughter—Hannibal's niece—naked, in his tent! Imagine the ransom that Carthage might pay for the return of a nobleman's daughter! Perhaps he could even construct a trap for his hated enemy, with this morsel as the lure!

Finally, he brought himself to ask, "What were you doing in a military camp?"

"My mother was a Spaniard," she explained between sobs. "She was the daughter of Allucius, chieftain of the Celtiberian people.

Hannibal arranged for my father to marry her in order to seal an alliance with Carthage. She died giving birth to me. I would not have been born, but they cut her open to save me—they probably were hoping I was a boy," she said, an unmistakable note of bitterness in her voice. "I have been at my father's side all of my life. I was there when my uncle took Saguntum. I can ride as well as any man—I was taught by Massinissa himself—and can handle a sword nearly as well."

Scipio said nothing, trying to absorb everything she had related.

"You seem speechless—a rare thing for a Roman!" she observed. "Surely you cannot say that there are no women in your camp."

It was true. A Roman army, as it traveled, acquired many camp followers, insofar as the soldiers were propertied men and entitled to bring along anyone they pleased. Many of the men were accompanied by personal servants of all types, including women.

"But you were in the harem!" he finally managed to say.

"I wasn't taken with the harem," she explained. "I was captured separately by two of your brutes before I could get to a horse. If I had, they'd never have caught me. Instead, they put me on display with those whores."

Scipio crossed over to a small table in a corner of the tent that held his toilet items and a pitcher of wine. It was an exceedingly sour vintage, approved for army use only because its bitter flavor might discourage overconsumption. He poured some into a ceramic goblet and brought it back to the girl.

Reluctantly, she took the proffered cup and sipped from it. The strong brew instantly brought color to her pale cheeks, further enhancing her looks.

The liquor also seemed to fortify her courage, for she said with some haughtiness, "I shall expect to be treated as a noblewoman of Carthage. And that does not include being washed in the cold water of a horse trough by some common thug of a Roman soldier. Or having my privates inspected by some charlatan who passes for a

Roman army doctor. My father and the people of Carthage will pay a substantial ransom for me."

Scipio stroked his chin for a moment, studying this Vibiana, who seemed now to be giving orders. He was completely captivated by her body, those perfect breasts pendent before him. And she was fiery, befitting that red hair. A thought occurred to him.

"Do you believe the ransom will be any less if you are no longer a virgin?"

This point gave her pause, but she remained resolute. "I am not a common field whore to service the carnal appetites of Romans, no matter what their rank. I demand to be treated properly. If I am not, you will answer to my uncle, Hannibal, for whom no Roman is a match."

Scipio struggled to control his emotions at her threat. Here, before him, was the only person he had ever met who had actually been in the presence of his nemesis.

"Tell me about your uncle," he said, anxious to know more about the man he hated so vehemently.

"I haven't seen him since he took Saguntum," she answered, pondering the implications of the question. "I was only a child, and can barely remember him. He left with his army after that, and I haven't been with him since. But even if I had any useful information, I certainly wouldn't give it to you," she said defiantly.

Scipio, now angry, grabbed the cup from her and threw it across the tent. "Watch how you speak to me! I alone will decide your fate. And I care not for money, so your promises are of no interest to me."

"Then you are unlike the Romans I have always heard about," she said tartly. She considered the man standing before her, a man in control of her destiny. Until today, she had never seen a Roman up close. This one was of medium height, solid build, and rugged handsomeness—and very near her own age. Beneath a thick cap of light brown curls, his face was square and masculine, with classic strong features: his broad forehead was typical of nobility, but the nose was just a shade too prominent. She was moved by the thick, full lips that dominated his square jaw and pronounced chin. And those eyes! Clear and cold, masking his thoughts, and bright blue, just as her own. He radiated leadership and power, and at once she understood how he could have led an army to victory over her father. Soldiers would follow this man, even to their own deaths. And women surely would be pleased to be possessed by him.

She pushed the thought from her mind. This man was a Roman, a plunderer of the helpless, enslaver of children, killer of innocents. All she had ever been told was of the evil and suffering that his race had perpetrated on her people. She must hate him! And yet, he was so handsome. . . .

Scipio retrieved the blanket and handed it to her.

She happily took it and wrapped it about herself.

"Guard!" he called out sharply, jolting her with his firmness.

Seconds later, a brawny Legionnaire stepped into the dim light of the tent. "Sir?"

"This woman stays with us," Scipio said to the soldier, without removing his gaze from her. "Establish her in a tent across from mine, keep a sentry with her at all times, and let no one touch her."

Feeling sweet relief flood through her, Vibiana mustered up her most defiant look.

Scipio sensed himself being captivated by this firebrand of a woman, and he struggled to maintain his harsh command demeanor. "Send someone out to the civilians who are traveling with the army," he said, turning his head a bit to the other man. "Find her some suitable clothes. Something befitting her loveliness. Pay for the clothes and obtain reimbursement from the senior legate."

Vibiana, pleased by this kindness, gave him a slight nod of her head, and stepped past him to follow the guard out of the tent.

Just as she reached the entrance, she paused and decided to push her luck just a bit further.

"Sir," she asked softly, "may I ask you a question?"

Scipio, who by now had begun studying a scroll with the casualty counts from the battle, looked up. "You may."

"Do you know if my father survived the battle?"

"He did," Scipio replied in a rueful tone. "It appears he has escaped."

For the second time in only a few minutes, Vibiana again felt herself deeply relieved.

"We will face him again," Scipio said with a smile. "But he will fare no better next time."

"We shall see," Vibiana said, her tone just a touch sharper than she wanted it to be.

She followed the guard out of the tent.

Not so bad, she thought as she walked in the cool night air. *Better than I could have hoped . . .*

———

Inured to the camp routine, Scipio awoke at the first hint of sunlight brushing the sides of the tent. He rose and pulled on a clean white tunic, ringed with the crimson and gold of his rank, then went to the flap. The guard was still posted outside, and Scipio told the man to fetch the girl and some breakfast. A tray heaped with honey cakes, fresh fruit, and two bowls of porridge arrived before Vibiana did. The porridge was standard army fare: a thick soup made from milk, bread, lard, and just enough vinegar to assure a vile taste. Scipio sniffed at it lovingly, convinced that he had acquired an affection for it.

Minutes later, Vibiana appeared, clad in a simple woolen shift and in a pair of ill-fitting sandals. She looked nervous, wondering why she had been summoned back to the command tent.

"I thought you might join me for some breakfast," he said in a welcoming tone.

Unsure of what else to say, she replied cautiously, "As you wish, General."

He motioned toward a camp stool and said in an airy tone, "You are under no obligation. If you cannot tolerate the presence of a Roman officer while dining, you may return to your tent."

Vibiana blushed. "No, no," she replied. "I'd be happy to join you."

As she took her seat, he scrutinized her attire. "Is that the best he could find for you?"

Vibiana looked down at herself, realizing how dowdy she appeared, and laughed. "Well, he said it was late; it was hard to find anything."

Scipio shook his head as he put some fruit and a honey cake on a platter, and then poured wine—selected from his personal collection rather than the bitter army issue—into a goblet for her. "Well, this *is* an army camp," he said, "but we will get you something better."

"I appreciate your kindness," she said. And then, noting he had not given her any of the porridge, she suggested, "I am a veteran of camp life. I can handle that, too."

Scipio gave her a sidelong look. She was fabulous, even in those most humble clothes, her hair still in tangles, and without any cosmetics. He tried to imagine how she might look properly attired.

She took a sip of the porridge, and made a horrible face, at which he burst out laughing.

"Ha!" he exulted. "Too strong for you?"

She reached for the wine, and slugged down a deep swallow.

"Thank the gods you have given me better wine than last night," she said, clearing her throat, the wretched taste of the porridge still overpowering her senses.

"The Roman Army will conquer the world because of that porridge!" Scipio said, slipping back into his haughty demeanor.

Vibiana pursed her lips. "My uncle thinks differently."

Scipio sat bolt upright. "Enjoy your breakfast," he said icily, rising from the table. "My duties require my attention."

Watching him go, she realized she had made a huge mistake.

"Sir?"

He turned to face her.

"I did not mean to upset you. I am sorry."

Gazing at her, taking in her radiance, he realized he could not be angry with her.

"I wish to dispense with formality in this relationship. You may call me Scipio," he said with a smile.

And it melted her, that smile.

———

After making a brief inspection of the camp, Scipio returned to his now-empty command tent. His thoughts ranged back to the events of the previous day. *There are lessons here,* he thought. *Maneuvers, communication, flexibility, concealment—these are the critical elements of battle. I must not simply line the men up and march them to their deaths in a heavy-handed frontal assault: defensive tactics take less of a toll. Better to allow the enemy to commit to the attack, and rely on timing and execution for a successful counterattack.*

Hannibal himself was a practitioner of these tactics. Scipio felt certain that Hannibal's continuing successes were due less to his own innovation than to the obstinate refusal of Roman generals to adapt their techniques to meet his trickery—Scipio's own father included.

And, even more important, the combined striking power and mobility of a cavalry was absolutely essential. Hannibal's superiority in cavalry had defeated Scipio's father at the Ticinus and had won the day at Cannae. Indeed, his father had been killed by the Numidian horsemen under Massinissa. He resolved always to treat his cavalry as a priority—and someday, he would persuade the powers that be in Rome to increase the size of the cavalry complement accompanying the legions.

The thought of the Roman bureaucracy soured his mood. The Senate was terrified of Hannibal, and Fabius, whom Scipio considered a base coward, had done nothing but manipulate the Senate's fear so as to hang on to his position. *If Fabius were as good at soldiering as he is at politics,* Scipio thought wryly, *Hannibal would have been sent packing back to Carthage years ago.*

Hannibal! How the distant specter of that man had shaped the contours of Scipio's life, separating his family and depriving him of his father. And it was not just the fate of his family, of course, that had been altered by the Semite. The course of history had been changed by Hannibal's invasion. The Carthaginian had visited epic suffering on the people of Italy, and the Roman who finally defeated him would be famous through the ages. Scipio brought his hands together in a loud clap: he would be that Roman!

Scipio took up a brass stylus and a wax tablet and began to write:

My Dearest Mother Pomponia,

It pleases me greatly to report that the gods have blessed our family again. My army has won a victory against Hasdrubal Barca, and Father is avenged. As I have suspected all along, Barca proved himself a coward, fleeing the field when it became clear our forces would prevail. Even now, our search parties are looking for him, and if they are successful, I shall have the satisfaction that I have for so long awaited. I only hope that seeing Barca dead will finally put to rest my troubled mind and quench the ambition that seems to give me no rest or peace.

I know you will be concerned to learn that I have seen battle, but fear not. The men performed magnificently, and not a hair on my head was ever in danger—certainly not like my service at Cannae, where I was lucky to survive the generalship of that idiot Varro.

Dearest Mother, rest assured that I carry with me every day the heavy burden of being a Cornelius. We are a great family of Rome, and our honor imposes a high duty. Two generations of Cornelli have been elected consul of Rome. With the blessings of the gods, I shall be the third.

I understand from my brother Lucius that you are doing your part to curry favor with the gods. He has written to tell me that you journey each month from Florentia to visit the temples in Rome with offerings for our good fortune. I urge you to continue your effort, for this undertaking is enormous—Spain is such a vast territory—and I can certainly use all the help your entreaties to the gods may provide. For my part, I too have observed the religious formalities, offering sacrifices and prayers daily.

You should know that Lucius has been urging me to allow him to join our camp. I know your feelings regarding this matter, and have been stalling him. But someday soon you must accept the fact that he, too, is a Cornelius and will be drawn to follow his destiny, take him where it will. Until then, he is a loyal son, and you should be proud of him.

Your devoted and loving son,
Publius Cornelius Scipio

Satisfied with his letter, Scipio stepped out of the tent and arranged for Vibiana to be made comfortable with a suitable bath and proper clothing. He also warned the guard that the girl claimed to be a proficient rider and that under no circumstances should she be allowed near a horse.

Waiting outside the tent was Narcussa, a slightly frail, ancient Ligurian slave who served Scipio as his personal valet. He had inherited Narcussa with the rest of the army from his father. Narcussa had fallen into slavery due not to any misfortune of arms, but because of money, or rather, the lack of it. Narcussa's father had run up debts, and when he was unable to pay, the entire family had been sold into slavery to satisfy his creditors. Narcussa still bore the painful memory of that day when, though a mere boy, he had been thrust naked onto the auctioneer's block and sold to Scipio's grandfather, the consul Publius Cornelius Aemelius, for ten sesterces. That was the last day he ever saw his parents or his siblings, all of whom had preceded him on the block.

Aided by the old man, Scipio attended to the details of his grooming. He bathed in a large brass tub, decorated with the likeness of a lion at one end and a bear at the other. Narcussa rubbed his body with scented oil, then watched as Scipio scraped himself clean with the strigil, a curved metal instrument. After the valet shaved him, Scipio went to a small altar where a half dozen doves and a ceremonial knife with an ornately carved ivory handle awaited him. He offered his prayers to the gods and slew each of the birds. He then kindled a small fire and threw their remains into the blaze, again offering prayers for the continued success of his mission.

Finished with his daily rites, Scipio went to his command tent and reviewed several communications he had received from scouting parties during the night. Troubled by one such missive, he summoned his senior officers to a meeting.

While he was waiting for his officers to gather, a slender young black man, clad in the brightly patterned garb of the Numidian cavalry, was led in, accompanied by a coarse-looking centurion. Scipio admired the skill that had produced the intricate pattern of shapes on the young African's cloak.

"In the course of arranging the sale of the prisoners, we found this one," said the stern centurion. "You may find him to be of particular interest."

The youngster carried himself with noble bearing, despite the bonds that held his hands behind his back. He was handsome, with fine features atop a slender frame.

"What is your name?" Scipio asked, speaking in Greek.

"I am Massiva, a Numidian. My father is dead, and I have been raised by his brother, Massinissa, my uncle." The youth's Greek was flawless, delivered by a deep, rich voice.

Scipio sighed. "It seems we have better luck at taking the relatives of our enemies than in catching our enemies themselves."

The young man looked at him blankly.

"You appear young to be serving with the Numidian horse. What is your age?"

"I am fourteen."

"Are the Carthaginians so desperate that they must press children into service against us?" Scipio did not bother to point out that he had served in his father's camp at the same age.

"My uncle Massinissa forbade my participation in combat because of my age. The day we fought the Romans I stole a horse and armor without my uncle's knowledge, and I went into the line. My horse fell, and I was thrown. The Romans took me prisoner."

Scipio picked up a small iron seal from his desk and handled it delicately, passing it from his left hand to his right and back again as he mulled what to do with this youngster.

"Do you know what became of your uncle in the battle?" Scipio asked.

The finely sculpted black head shook slowly. "No. He was part of Hasdrubal's command group. I did not see him after our cavalry charged."

"Tell me about your uncle."

"He is heir to the throne of Gala, king of the Numidians, my grandfather. He is a brave fighter, wise and generous. He has been like a father to me. Someday he will rule all of Numidia."

Scipio stroked his chin thoughtfully. "And why does he fight with the Carthaginians against Rome?"

The youth gave him an odd look, as if his question were elementary. "Carthage is the most powerful city in the world. Our territory adjoins hers, and while our land is vast, we are not nearly so well populated. If we were not allied with Carthage, they would conquer us. I have heard my uncle say that it is better to be a partner than a slave."

There was a knock at the post holding the tent flap, and Scipio called out his permission to enter.

He greeted Laelius warmly and repeated the substance of the progress of his interview with the youth. Laelius slowly looked the captive over with a skilled eye, and Scipio blushed when he realized what was on Laelius' mind.

"No, my friend," he said, putting his hand on Laelius' shoulder. "This one's too valuable to sell, not even to you."

Laelius was disappointed but accepted the edict. "His uncle holds your father's armor. Perhaps we could arrange a trade," he suggested.

Scipio considered the idea for a moment, then turned to the youngster. "Do you wish to rejoin your uncle?"

Tears welled up in the boy's eyes. "Do not be cruel to me. I know full well the fate that awaits me as a captured prisoner of war."

Scipio leaned back in his chair. "Then let this serve as a lesson to you and your uncle. Someday he may find it in his interest to side with us, rather than Carthage." He turned to the centurion and said authoritatively, "Release him."

While the soldier was freeing Massiva's hands, Scipio walked over to a large chest in the corner of the tent and returned with several items. "This gold ring bears the Cornelius signet. It was a gift to me from my father, before he fell on the field of battle here in Spain at the hands of your uncle. I make a gift of it to you now. And also, this fine tunic, which should keep you warm on your ride to rejoin your uncle. I hope you find him."

Massiva was too overcome to respond.

"Centurion," Scipio said, "equip this man with a horse and provisions. Give him an escort to accompany him for as long as he wishes."

The soldier nodded, his ruddy face impassive.

Scipio put his arm around the youth's shoulders and walked him out of the tent. "That gold ring is a symbol of my authority throughout any territory controlled by Rome. You may make such use of it as you may find helpful. And in the future, I would suggest that you obey your uncle's instructions. Next time you may fall prisoner to a commander less generous than myself."

When Massiva was gone, Laelius looked at his general patiently, waiting for him to explain his actions.

Scipio shrugged. "I may someday find it expedient to enlist the support of the king of Numidia," he said simply. "Better to have him already indebted to me."

Laelius nodded. "I had a soldier in to see me this morning. He wanted payment for some clothes that he bought for a captured harem girl. Said you ordered it. What is that all about?"

Scipio laughed, and a thought occurred to him. There could be all kinds of trouble if the woman Vibiana's relationship to Hannibal became known. Better to keep that detail to himself. "I'll tell you later," he replied to Laelius.

By now, the tribunes Lucellus, Marius, and Silanus had arrived, and they were admitted to the headquarters. Scipio greeted them with a knowing look, asking each man as he arrived if he had slept well. And of course, each man averred that indeed he had, exchanging ribald grins with their leader.

Scipio settled onto a camp stool and pointed at a large map of the known world affixed to the side of the tent. "I have received information this morning that Hasdrubal Barca has departed for Italy. It is thought that he intends to join up with his brother Hannibal."

The officers accepted this news stoically. What was their general up to?

"Perhaps we should follow him."

They thought him mad, but only Laelius was senior enough to give voice to their concerns. "Scipio, one victory—impressive though it was, to be certain—does not establish your qualifications to take the field against Hannibal himself."

"I can see that you suffer from the same disease that afflicts our dear senior consul and dictator, Fabius the Delayer," Scipio replied, his voice dripping with contempt.

Laelius retained his temper, knowing that Scipio certainly did not mean to insult him but sought to initiate a lively discussion. "I do not think you mean to question my courage, insofar as you have had ample evidence of it during the tenure of your command," the older man said formally. "I was merely giving voice to the criticism that you would face in the Senate. Even you will have to admit that you have your enemies there."

Scipio clapped his fist into his cupped left hand. "The people desire a commander who can beat Hannibal. I am that man. The Senate will have to submit to the will of the people."

They all looked at him again as if he had lost his mind. Scipio's family line was thoroughly patrician, as blue-blooded as could be found in Rome. His ancestors certainly would have been shocked by his suggestion to submit military decisions to the masses.

Seeing their displeasure, he warmed to his theme. "It should come as no surprise that we cannot find a general to beat Hannibal. The Senate selects our consuls each year and entrusts them with discharge of the war. But look at whom they select! Men who may know politics, but couldn't tell a moat from a latrine unless a centurion told them. And Fabius—he's too afraid of his shadow to ever launch an attack!"

"My dear Scipio, the system of electing new consuls every year has preserved our liberty while producing great men in the past—your own father among them," Laelius pointed out. "And Varro, who nearly cost you your life, was a plebeian, so the masses have not proven any more adept at providing leaders than the Senate."

Marius spoke up. "Scipio, I agree with you about Fabius. I for one happen to believe that story about why Hannibal spared his estates from destruction. They must have made a deal. Hannibal ravaged everything around Fabius' property, but didn't touch a single blade of grass on Fabius' land."

Laelius shook his head. "Now, gentlemen, surely you do not believe that Fabius is guilty of treason, whatever you may think of his shortcomings as a general. True, Hannibal spared his estates, but I think that may have been due to Hannibal's own shrewd desire to sow this very kind of dissent among our ranks rather than any prearranged agreement between Hannibal and Fabius."

"Scipio, you know that I will follow you anywhere," said Lucellus, a strapping physical specimen who had a standing offer that he would hand over his command to any man under his service who might best him in a wrestling match. So far, no one had challenged him. "But Hasdrubal is not the general that Hannibal is—that bastard whipped us badly at Cannae. You were there."

"At Cannae we were poorly led," Scipio retorted.

"But those elephants!" Lucellus said.

"I have given considerable thought to that problem," Scipio snapped. "And I have a solution. I know what must be done to beat them—and Hannibal."

Lucellus held his ground. "Still, I doubt that any army under Hannibal's command would break and run the way Barca's men did yesterday."

Laelius moved to the map. "There is one other matter," he said, indicating their current location in Spain. "Your imperium from the Senate is to subjugate this country. And I submit that one victory does not accomplish that mission. There are still substantial Carthaginian forces near Ilipa." He pointed to an icon on the map. "And not far away is Cartagena, a heavily defended fortress. If you move against the army at Ilipa, we will face a full army probably determined to avenge the beating you gave them yesterday, Scipio. Even after you defeat it, you'll still have the problem of a complex siege to take

Cartagena. It may hold out for years. All these problems must be resolved before you can even think about taking on Hannibal."

The others nodded, relieved that any confrontation with Hannibal was years away.

Scipio was not so easily distracted. "Rome cannot win this war with Carthage by taking Spain, for all its riches. Not while Hannibal romps throughout our home peninsula."

"Of course not," Laelius replied, his tone even. "But no one yet has beaten Hannibal, and until you enhance your stature, the Senate will not allow you to try. The conquest of Spain will give you a reputation that will make it impossible for the Senate to deny you a chance against Hannibal, if that's what you wish for."

"Even you admit that our campaign here could take years," Scipio retorted. "That's what Fabius wants. His strategy is to wait for Hannibal to die of old age!"

The tribunes laughed at this, and the laughter relaxed the mood in the room a bit.

Scipio rose from the stool and walked over to the map. "Since you all seem to be convinced that no Roman army—not even one led by me—can beat Hannibal, suppose I tell you I have a plan to drive Hannibal from the peninsula without fighting him. What would you say to that?"

"I would say that you've been drinking too much army wine," Lucellus put in, drawing laughter from the other two tribunes.

Scipio smiled and studied the map. "The way to get Hannibal out of Italy is not to attack him. Instead, the thing to do is *attack Carthage itself*." He paused to let this sink in. "I want to mount an offensive against Hannibal's homeland, carrying the war to those pirates' own backyard. I would go on a campaign of bloodletting and terror to rival Hannibal himself, and before our march reached the city, they'd be screaming for Hannibal to hurry home to save them."

The men were dazzled at this possibility. With Hannibal out of

Italy, the legions could quickly restore Roman control over the entire peninsula. There was only one problem with the plan, and it was Marius who worked up the courage to expose it.

"But, Scipio, then that army would have to face Hannibal in battle."

"Perhaps by then I will have found tribunes who have the courage to take on a legend." Scipio sniffed in disgust, and the tribunes stiffened noticeably. He was delighted to have stung their vanity. "If it makes you feel better, the Roman army facing Hannibal in Africa need not give battle to this 'invincible' general. We can follow Fabian tactics: we'll simply withdraw to safety."

"Not a bad plan," Laelius said finally, acknowledging the obvious.

Scipio settled back onto his perch. "Damning with faint praise, eh, Laelius?" He sighed. "No, my friend, I'm afraid you're right. They'll never let me employ such a strategy until we prove our success here in Spain. So enough of this idle talk. Let's get on with the business of conquering this country and making ourselves rich."

Laelius watched as Scipio unfurled a map of Spain, smaller than the world map posted on the tent wall but far more detailed as to the territory in question, and began laying out his plans. Listening to the outline of the coming campaign, he understood that Scipio's heart was elsewhere: somehow, the young man would find a way to work his will and bring Hannibal within reach of his sword. And, he realized with a terrible sense of dread, when this confrontation finally occurred, "withdraw to safety" was the last thing Scipio intended to do.

III

Toriorum, Italy

207 BC

THE SHEPHERD VENATIUS STRETCHED out on a large rock out-cropping and relished the warm midday sun, feeling its heat on his bald pate. He had long since cast off the heavy cloak he had brought with him at dawn into the pastures. Now, as perspiration trickled down his back, he loosened his coarse brown homespun garment.

After the wet and frigid winter that had punished southern Italy, it was a relief to feel the turn of the season. In the purple distance, he could see the snow-capped tips of the Apennine Mountains, a sign that the cold winds could return in a sudden snap although the valley was clearly showing the signs of spring. All about him the vegetation exploded with lush greenery, and farther down the valley where the land was tillable, plowing farmers were already struggling against the soggy fields.

Spread out on the gently sloping hills before him were nearly sixty fine sheep, grazing nonchalantly on the sweet, thick grass. The flock had come through the winter in fine shape, with no outbreak of disease or loss to the ever-dangerous wolves that lurked about the fringes of the valley.

Venatius studied his flock carefully. They were nearly ready, he decided, for delivery to the market in the town of Toriorum, not far off. Thinking of his likely profit, he turned slightly toward the town. The outline of the buildings was clearly discernable at this relatively short distance. Venatius' small farmhouse was situated between his location on the hill and the town, and he could see smoke wafting from the chimney of his dwelling.

Theresa would no doubt at this time of day be baking bread for their supper, he thought. She might even surprise him and fry up a bit of bacon so that he could dip the fresh dark bread in the grease, his favorite treat. She was a strong, stout woman, a bit plain perhaps, with dingy brown hair and unremarkable features, but ideal for the burdens of agrarian life and childrearing. At this latter activity, she had proven especially proficient. So far, she had borne him four boys, three of whom had survived the hazards of peasant infanthood. The oldest, Tiboninus, played within earshot of his father, not far from the grazing flock.

Tibby, as his father was fond of calling him, was splashing about in a shallow brook that bubbled through the meadow. Venatius leased the ground for his humble sheep-raising operation from the nobleman Marcinius, a senator of Rome. Venatius, of course, had never met the senator, dealing instead with the appointed local overseer. It was said that Marcinius and others of his class had profited greatly from Hannibal's tactics since so many landholders had abandoned the countryside for the safety of Rome. Wealthy men like Marcinius had been buying up the vacated land at a fraction of its value before Hannibal's invasion.

Watching his towheaded, slightly scrawny son at play, Venatius felt a calm glow of contentment: if he was not rich, neither was he poor. Theresa and Venatius had established a comfortable, secure life for themselves and their children, and the proceeds from the sale of this herd might even enable them to buy a plot of land for themselves while the prices were depressed.

"Tiboninus," he called to the child playing in the cold stream, "that's enough. You'll catch your death if you stay in there much longer."

Like any ten-year-old, Tiboninus chose to ignore his father's instructions and kept splashing about in the clear, cold water.

Irritated, Venatius climbed onto the rock to yell at his son. But an ominous rumbling just beyond the ridge caught his attention. When he saw the source of the noise, his voice froze in his throat.

Bearing down on him, riding at full gallop, was a column of armed marauders. There could be no mistaking their colors. It was a Carthaginian raiding party.

The intruders were clad in full battle gear, topped with hideous black helmets adorned with serpents and dragons. They brandished swords and spears and shrieked frightfully.

His heart beating wildly, Venatius leaped from the rock and ran frantically toward his son, struggling to find the ability to shout.

"Run . . . Tibby . . . run! Run for your life!" he beseeched.

Bewildered, the boy looked up and watched as his father scrambled toward him, the horde of horsemen rapidly closing the gap. Even pushed by panic, the shepherd was no match for the Carthaginian ponies. They trampled him, did the same to the boy, and continued their charge toward the town.

Two riders broke off to inspect the small stucco farmhouse. Theresa had heard the rumble of hooves, and by the time she stepped outside to inspect, the two men were within the compound, scattering the chickens and ducks as their horses stomped about. Her two younger boys had been playing in the barn and were drawn out into the yard by the ruckus. Theresa screamed as one man ran his spear through her youngest. Her middle son, only seven, fell to a slashing blow from the heavy sword of the other man.

In the kitchen was a large knife that she used to slice the family's bread, and Theresa bolted for it as the men dismounted. They found her waiting for them in the little farmhouse, brandishing the knife, a wild look in her eyes.

"Well, Sammodius, what do you make of this?" the larger of the two asked his companion.

"Too ugly for the slave blocks," the other replied. "There's nothing here of any value. Finish her off and let's rejoin the others."

The first man leveled his sword at the woman. She lunged at him in a pathetic attempt to strike a blow. The soldier, an experienced swordsman, blunted her jab easily and plunged his sword deep into her belly, then thrust upward, gutting her. They left her to die alone, writhing as her blood turned the dirt floor of her home into scarlet mud.

By now, the leading elements of the force—it was more than a mere raiding party, numbering five hundred men—had reached the outskirts of Toriorum. The town was an obscure rural post, hardly more than a widening along the path that marked the route between Thurii and Heraclea. Home to a few artisans and various middlemen engaged in forwarding livestock and produce onward to the hungry markets of Rome, it was no different from any of the hundreds of other farming communities in the Italian hinterland, completely unnoteworthy and not even shown on many maps. As such, it had no garrison or fortifications. Some of the residents, veterans of service in the legions, possessed weapons. The few who realized what was happening and managed to get to a sword were nonetheless quickly cut down in the murderous rampage.

There were perhaps eight hundred or so people in the town, and the ferocious raiders killed at least several hundred in their first swath through. Before doubling back, they lit torches and set fire to every house to flush out the rest. Given their lack of effort to search any of the residences before burning them, they seemed disinterested in plunder; terror was their apparent mission. With the skill of cattle drivers, the armed riders took only a few minutes to round up the survivors in the meadow.

The Carthaginian riders formed a large circle around the terrified and weeping townspeople, numbering perhaps four hundred in all. Acrid smoke from the burning buildings hung thick in the air. One horseman, who, from his regal bearing and handsome charcoal stallion, clearly seemed to be the leader, trotted forward and looked over the crowd. He was a rather slight and diminutive man, and oddly, the only rider not wearing a helmet. His only notable feature was a thick beard that, like the bushy hair on his head and arms, was streaked with gray.

"Separate yourselves," he shouted to them in Latin. He possessed a clear, booming voice that seemed to belie his small stature. "Women on the left, men on the right."

There was a chaotic scramble as the frightened citizens tried to obey his command, but eventually some semblance of order was restored as the two groups sorted themselves out. The rider dismounted and sauntered toward the women. He walked with a slight limp, a constant reminder of an old javelin wound. He wandered casually through the females, pointing out several of the younger and more attractive ones. Amid cries of anguish and outrage, these women were taken by other Carthaginian soldiers to a wagon that had been brought from the town and posted outside the ring of steel.

The man paused aside one young woman who carried a small, squalling baby in her arms. She was lovely, with a supple body and flaxen hair. Realizing the child was drawing attention to her, the woman frantically tried to shush the caterwauling infant. The raider turned his head slightly as if to get a better look. She saw that a long, jagged scar ran from his forehead just above his left eye down over the eyelid, extending to the middle of his cheek. She realized that the man was blind in his left eye. A frightful look—the look of death itself—passed over his face as his cold gray eye settled on her.

"Is this your child?" he asked the woman. She did not respond.

He motioned for her to give him the child, but she clutched the infant even tighter to her bosom and pleaded with him to leave them alone. Angry, he tried to wrest the child from her, but the mother's grip was tenacious. Two soldiers came over and pinioned the woman's arms, finally enabling the man to separate mother from child. He stood holding the youngster while the screaming and kicking woman was dragged off. Without a word, he passed the child to an elderly woman standing nearby, who reluctantly took the bundle. Hatred for this terrible invader was evident in her face.

Soon enough, the officer had finished with his grim selection and returned to his waiting warhorse. He remounted and rode out of the circle.

Once he was clear, the soldiers drew their swords and fell upon the crowd in a brutal, bloody frenzy. After a few minutes of wild melee, the screams and moans fell silent. The people of Toriorum lay slaughtered, their blood soaking the trampled turf.

The leader rode over to the cart, the handful of women confined there too shocked by the massacre even to weep.

"A miserable catch, eh, General?" said the soldier who was busy clapping irons about the ankles of each captive. The women would be marched back to the main camp, and made available to the common soldiers, part of their reward for a seemingly endless campaign in hostile, foreign territory.

"All Romans are miserable," said Hannibal without emotion.

"Aye, my lord, there's no denying that. How long do you think we'll keep this up?"

Hannibal was amused at the boldness of this grunt, for he was not accustomed to disclosing his plans to common cavalrymen.

"That, my friend, is simple. We keep at it until all the Romans are dead."

And with that, Hannibal dug his spurs into the horse and galloped off, in search of more prey.

Rome

The Temple of Cybele was not the most ornate house of worship in Rome, but because the goddess represented motherhood, the structure was always populated with supplicants. Her temple was located on the Aventine, one of the Seven Hills of Rome, and faced south toward the convenient landmark peaks of the Alban Hills, to aid her priests in studying the sky for omens. The structure's elevation on a relatively high podium of stone necessitated a long, narrow stairway to the entrance. The sanctuary was comprised of a single large room housing an immense likeness of the goddess. She was a serene beauty, with a head of curly hair piled high beneath a tall ceremonial veil. Not even the modest draping of the typical matronly dress favored by the Romans could conceal her ample bosom, symbolically suitable for the suckling of Roman infants. She held in both arms a round-faced baby of each sex. The size of the statue required a high, arched ceiling, supported by rows of tall stone Corinthian columns. Above all this was a tiled roof, with sculptured chariots drawn by lions at each of the four corners and upon the apex. The gilded ornamentation around the frieze and on the entablature above the entrance all contributed to the resplendent appearance of the temple.

Inside the temple was a veritable storehouse of treasures, all donated to the goddess in the hope of procuring a blessing upon an impending pregnancy or the prosperity of a favored child. Marvelous jewelry, embroideries, furniture, cups, vases, vast quantities of gold and silver, bronzes, and statues had been piled up over the years at the finely carved altar established at the feet of the goddess and maintained under the watchful eyes of the priests, or augurs.

Only the week before, the festival of Cybele had been a raucous affair in which the priests had carried a likeness of the goddess in a parade, marching to the beat of drums, cymbals, and trumpets along a route strewn with coins and flowers. All along the route, expectant mothers would break into the retinue and offer gifts of roses. The parade terminated at a pit dug near the temple. There, a priest clad in magnificent vestments descended. A covering was placed over the pit, onto which other priests led a bull, whose horns had been gilded and flanks thickly garlanded with colorful flowers. The beast was slain with the sacrificial knife, and the blood flowed freely into the pit through a small opening left for such purpose. The priest underneath took care not to let a drop of blood touch the ground, making sure that his ears, eyes, lips, and the whole of his body was steeped in it. When he reappeared, streaming with the "life-giving rain," he was revered and regarded as regenerated for eternity.

A sturdy woman wearing a pale blue dress stood before the altar and heaped incense into the brazier. As the rich aroma began wafting toward the ceiling, Pomponia, widow of Scipio the Elder and daughter of the late Metullus Pomponius Agro, stepped back. She extended her arms outward, palms up, in supplication to the goddess. She reminded the goddess of the pain she had borne in her life: rendered motherless at the age of seven by an outbreak of scarlet fever, she had been raised on a rural estate by a stern father more concerned with advancing the careers of his sons than with her needs. He had betrothed her, in the Roman custom, when she was only fourteen, to the equally stern Publius Cornelius Scipio, now remembered as Scipio the Elder. It was her duty, her father told her, to be the best wife she could be. She had tried hard to live up to her father's expectations.

Fortunately, her fears of an unhappy marriage had proven groundless. Scipio was a considerate man, gentle with her and accommodating of her wishes. Theirs had been a pleasant and fruitful marriage, reasonably happy until the war with Carthage erupted. The war had taken both her husband and her oldest son away from her and widowed her. Then, only two months later, her father had passed away, taken in the night by a stroke. So much suffering, in so short a time! Now, she begged Cybele, as a mother, to bring her son Scipio safely through the conflict in faraway Spain. Her husband, she reminded the goddess, already had given his life in this terrible war—to lose a son would be more than she could bear. She trembled slightly, overcome with the intensity of her prayer. Then, her supplication finished, she turned and made a motion to a boy at the rear of the sanctuary.

Lucius Cornelius Scipio, her younger son, took a spotless white dove from the cage he held and brought it forward to her. A eunuch priest swathed in a white linen robe hurried forward with a golden platter and a sacred knife. The dove's throat was deftly sliced, and the living entrails quickly cut out.

The priest pored over the liver and the other organs and looked up at Pomponia. She handed him a golden coin, and a sweet smile swept across his face.

"The auspices are favorable," he said. "The goddess has heard your prayers."

Pomponia sighed with relief and took another coin from her still-open purse. She handed it to the priest. "Thank you," she said as the man carried the remains away.

She took her son by the hand, and together they left the temple. The bright sun momentarily blinded them as they stepped out of the building.

"Where now?" young Lucius asked.

"Now, we must go to the Temple of Apollo," she replied.

Lucius made a face. "Really, Mother, is it necessary to say prayers to *all* the gods every time we come down from Florentia? Surely the prayers we have already said will be sufficient."

Pomponia gave him an extremely cross look. "Your father already has fallen in this war, and your brother is on campaign. I will not leave his fate to chance."

Their sandals crunching on the gravel roadway, they headed down the Via Apulia, toward the Temple of Apollo. The narrow street was congested with people of every class, from noblemen hurrying about their business to abject beggars pleading for coins. Pomponia kept a watchful eye on the shuttered windows of the tenements flanking their path, as the occupants routinely pitched their slop out the window in careless disregard of passersby. Scores of women stood in line at a public fountain, the only source of fresh water for the poorer residents of the city. They walked past dozens of shops wherein bakers, barbers, and craftsmen of every sort plied their trades. Pomponia paused to buy several candles made from tallow fat rolled around a thin papyrus wick. She cast about a butcher shop and found the sausages not to her liking, but in the next stall was delighted to seize a large, fresh tuna, which she determined to have broiled for their supper.

Lucius pulled her to a stop before a small booth that housed a metalsmith. "Look, Mother," he said. "What a fine set of armor!"

Inside the booth, the smith looked up and smiled at this compliment. His gnarled hands held up his work for the boy to admire: it was a finely detailed cuirass, with intricately inlaid silver and gold ornamentation molded into ivory fittings. The handiwork depicted two stout bulls, their thick horns locked as if in mortal combat. Atop their intertwined horns perched the imperial eagle, symbol of Rome, wings outstretched, talons extended. The breastplate was nearly finished, and the craftsman was installing a felt lining to cushion the metal and prevent it from chafing its wearer.

"It is fit for a consul," Lucius said admiringly.

"Indeed," responded a voice from the corner of the booth, "it is for a consul, or a former consul, at any rate. This cuirass is for me."

Pomponia recognized the familiar voice at once and stiffened as its owner stepped into view. "Greetings, Quintus Fabius Maximus," she said respectfully, but with no trace of warmth in her voice.

Fabius stepped forward. "Well, well. The widow of our dear

departed colleague, Scipio the Elder. I trust that you are well, Pomponia, and recovering from your double loss?"

"As much as one can expect," she said, wary of the man who had opposed giving the Spanish expedition to her son.

"We all were saddened by the unexpected death of your father," Fabius said gently. "It was a stroke, I understand?"

She nodded.

"A pity. They are vicious, those strokes. But better that it took him quickly, and in his sleep, for those who survive find that their lives are not worth living." Then, changing the subject, he added, "You must be proud of the accomplishments of Scipio the Younger."

"I do not consider the feats of war to be a source of pride," she said tartly. "I only pray for the safe return of all our soldiers."

"As do we all," Fabius agreed. He regarded the boy Lucius for a moment, then said, "And this is your younger son? He grows tall and strong. There is a definite likeness to the father; I can see it."

He smiled at the boy. "Soon you too will take up arms in the cause of our people."

The boy beamed with pride. Pomponia cut in, "Do not put foolish ideas into his head. He is but fourteen."

Fabius could see that this was a touchy subject with the woman, and decided not to push it any further. He noticed something else. "Take care not to let Cato the censor cast his eyes upon you. Your dress might be regarded as violative of the law."

"He wouldn't dare!" she snapped. After the disaster at Cannae, the Senate, as part of the austerity program established to get the city back on its feet, had prohibited women from wearing colorful clothes. Pomponia knew her pale blue *stola*, a long flowing dress gathered in at the waist and fastened at the shoulders with clasps, was of questionable legality, but she regarded the law as utter nonsense and had no intention of observing it.

"I wouldn't count on it," Fabius replied evenly. "Cato has strong opinions. Not even the newfound fame of your son would deter him. I wouldn't want you to test his will."

"Well, I must be on my way," Pomponia said, pulling Lucius behind her. "I shall take care to remain on the lookout for Cato."

"Good day," Fabius called as they hurried away.

"But Mother," Lucius said, reluctantly tagging along behind her, "that is a famous general!"

"That man," Pomponia said hotly when they were out of Fabius' hearing range, "is no friend of our family. Never forget that."

IV

CARTAGENA, SPAIN

207 BC

VIBIANA SAT BY THE edge of a creek, watching the muddy water meander past as she contemplated the incredible things that had happened to her. She kept her thoughts to herself, for only a few feet away stood Maximillian, the relentless bodyguard who had shadowed her every movement since she had become a Roman captive.

Initially, she had hoped that her father would get wind of the fact that she had been captured and make an offer to ransom her from the Romans. When she learned from Scipio that her father had departed with the remnants of his army for Italy, there to join up with her uncle Hannibal, she clung to a bit of hope that the remaining Carthaginian forces in Spain would somehow rescue her. As the days of her captivity passed into weeks, however, it became apparent to her that no ransom offer was likely to be forthcoming—indeed, the Carthaginians had no idea what had become of her! She had worked up the courage to ask Scipio to at least tell them of her fate, but he seemed to be in no hurry to be rid of her. Quite the opposite: he had spent more and more time with her. That first breakfast had turned into a daily routine, and before long he had begun taking his dinners with her. She was careful not to repeat her error of mentioning her uncle, indeed, Scipio had specifically instructed her to tell no one of her family connections, for fear that it would cause animosity in the ranks of the soldiers who shared Scipio's own hatred for Hannibal.

Clearly Scipio was enamored of her, and she found herself fighting her feelings for him. Damn that dazzling smile of his and those ravishing blue eyes!

Nonetheless, she kept telling herself she must not give in to him. She was a Carthaginian—and a noblewoman at that! It was her *duty* to attempt an escape. However, as the weeks had gone by, her hopes had faded in the absence of any opportunity presented by the dour-faced guard and his constant scrutiny. He gave her no privacy, whether at the latrine or in her bath. She had appealed to Scipio to end this intrusion, but he was adamant—she was too valuable a prize to take any chances. And any lingering thoughts of escape had evaporated when she witnessed the fate of Camarissa, one of the harem girls, who had been given over to Titellus, a Roman hero of the battle at Baecula.

Camarissa, weary of servicing her master, had attempted to run away one night. She waited until Titellus had sated himself, then struck him on the head with the handle of his own sword. She managed to slip out of the tent unnoticed and made it nearly to the edge of the stockade before she was caught by an alert sentry.

Having incapacitated her master for days by her rather vicious blow, Camarissa was brought before Scipio, to whom the task of imposing punishment fell. Angered by the assault upon one of his officers, and perhaps with a thought of setting an example for Vibiana, Scipio determined to be harsh.

The woman was hung by her ankles, naked, from a crossbeam suspended between two tall posts. They flogged her mercilessly with heavy straps. She was then cut down and dispatched to the crude men of the baggage train, condemned to a lifetime of slavery in their service as a field whore, available for the taking to any man who desired her.

Even now, Vibiana shuddered, recalling Camarissa's pitiful screaming under the awful beating they had given her. No, she thought, better to stay put and wait for the Roman Army to be defeated.

And, she had to admit with a blush, her time with the Romans had not at all been bad: Scipio had shown her much about himself. He was powerful yet tender, authoritative yet sensitive. Despite her status as a slave, he was kind, almost affectionate toward her. He had even brought in from Rome a full wardrobe of fine clothing for her! If put to torture and forced to the truth, she would admit that she might be falling in love.

It had not taken her long to realize that she had become the property of an extraordinary military man. Soon after his victory at Baecula over her father, Scipio had surprised his commanders and ignored the Carthaginian Army at Ilipa, the last remaining force in Spain of sufficient size to constitute a major threat. Instead, Scipio decided to lay siege to the Carthaginian stronghold at Cartagena. This was a risky proposition since the army at Ilipa was only ten days away. If this force moved down to engage the Romans, Scipio would be caught in pincers between the garrison of Cartagena and the army from Ilipa.

But the army at Ilipa remained in its camp, its commander perhaps afraid of this aggressive Roman, who had so convincingly routed Hasdrubal Barca, and believing that the powerful fortress of Cartagena could not be taken.

Indeed, the siege seemed hopeless. Cartagena's walls were stout and tall, and protected by a wide, deep lagoon. It could not be taken by storm, and it was known that the city housed vast stores of grain and water—it could hold out for years. More than a few of the Romans began to question the logic of Scipio's tactics.

But soon enough, the critics were silenced, and Scipio was elevated from just another promising young general to the ranks of the most honored heroes of Rome, a special favorite of the gods.

Due to some inexplicable tidal phenomenon, the water in the lagoon lowered dramatically for several days. The entire foundation of the citadel's north wall was exposed. If he could not explain his incredible good fortune, Scipio certainly wasted no time exploiting it: siege machines were brought forward, and the wall was quickly undermined by his engineers. The city surrendered, handing Scipio its rich stores of grain and supplies, thousands of Spanish hostages, the local silver mines, and an outstanding harbor. Cartagena at once made Scipio, still only in his twenties, among the richest men in Rome and gave him a powerful base from which he could move against the army at Ilipa.

Equally important, the men of his army now believed that he comported with the gods, that Neptune himself had lowered the waters to bestow victory upon Scipio. One wild tale circulated among the camp followers to the effect that Neptune had appeared in Scipio's mother's bed in the form of a snake to conceive the son who now led the army. Scipio was shrewd enough to let this story go unrefuted. An army's confidence that it could not be beaten was worth a dozen more legions. He even embellished the tale, concocting an elaborate story to the effect that Neptune had appeared to him in a dream the night before the lagoon dropped and promised to help take the city.

Vibiana wisely went along with the ruse. To Vibiana, Cartagena was a gift from the gods: freedom from the rough life of the camp and its guards, and the opportunity to spend more time with Scipio, who decided to delegate all military matters to Laelius and take a holiday.

———

A fire burned in the hearth of a handsome villa Scipio had commandeered for his headquarters. The residence overlooked the lovely bay. The cool, salty sea breeze made it a bit drafty in the evenings, but Vibiana found herself eagerly waiting for chances to dine with him.

"No one has seen me for several days. Perhaps I should go for a ride tomorrow, and let the men know I am still alive," Scipio mentioned one evening to her.

Her eyes twinkled. "Take me with you?"

"I am not sure Bucephalus will appreciate that," he teased.

"I mean, let me ride alongside you. I told you I can ride better than any man."

"Better than any Carthaginian, perhaps," he said, his Roman vanity provoked.

"I challenge you to a race," she said, emboldened.

"Don't be ridiculous," he replied.

"Are you afraid of what the men will say if you lose to a woman? And a Carthaginian at that?"

He glared at her, barely able to suppress a smile. "You may have your pick of the horses," he said a little petulantly.

"After I have won," she said, "perhaps you will regard me as good for something other than mere conversation." She realized this was daringly flirtatious.

He gave her a knowing look, but responded with a shrug. No mere woman could beat him on Bucephalus.

———

Scipio awoke in the morning to find Vibiana waiting in his suite, clad in the leather breeches of a legionnaire and a loose fitting shirt.

"I like you better in a dress," he murmured.

"But I ride better in leggings," she said tartly.

After breakfast, he escorted her through the stables of the Roman cavalry, accompanied by Silanus, who was not at all pleased to be putting his animals on display for the benefit of a Carthaginian prisoner.

Vibiana studied the animals with a trained eye. One by one, she found tiny flaws that might have escaped even Scipio, who felt a growing sense of unease as she worked her way through the mounts.

Finally, she paused before a magnificent black stallion. The huge brown eyes glinted like pieces of gold; ebony skin stretched over the superbly muscled body like silk. The beast was meticulously groomed. "This one will do," she said.

"You can't take him!" Silanus cried, amazed at her judgment. "That is my horse!"

"If you are the horseman you claim to be, then the quality of the mount will not matter," she said to Scipio, taunting him gently. "Unless, of course, you are concerned about the outcome!"

He was infuriated—and bewitched—by the defiant sparkle of her effervescent blue eyes.

"Silanus!" he snapped loudly. "Saddle this animal. And have Bucephalus made ready as well."

Silanus started to splutter in outrage, but Scipio cut him off by turning his back on the cavalryman and stalking out of the stable.

They rode through the city together, and out to a wide, open plain. He cantered slightly behind her, studying her handling of the animal. She knew what she was doing, no question about it. And she made a lovely sight, her graceful body lean and hard in the tight cavalryman's pantaloons, her thick red tresses flowing behind her in the wind.

They reached a low hillock, and Vibiana pointed to two trees, about a quarter mile apart.

"Those two trees," she said. "Two times around."

He studied them for a brief moment, then kicked Bucephalus sharply in the ribs.

"Hey!" she cried, realizing he had started. She kicked her mount, and the race was on.

Bucephalus was enormously powerful, and in a headlong dash could not be beaten. Vibiana had realized this, of course, and so had challenged Scipio to a race involving turns, where the skill of the riders might be decisive.

He was well ahead of her by the time they reached the far tree, but Scipio was forced to slow down considerably to round the marker. Vibiana handled it much more smoothly, and they found themselves neck and neck as they headed back. Again, Bucephalus easily distanced himself from Silanus' stallion, and Scipio determined not to slow down so much on the next turn. This merely had the effect of causing horse and rider to make a wide arc around the tree. Vibiana cut a tighter turn, and Scipio found himself staring at her backside as they headed into the final, decisive lap.

His pride at stake, Scipio pushed his animal to the limit. The powerful warhorse responded like the champion he was, mounting a furious charge to close the distance, nostrils flaring with determination.

Scipio knew he had to make a tight turn this time. He wrenched the reins and leaned into the turn with all his strength. He cut it too close and brushed against the tree. Scipio was thrown violently from his mount, landing on the still-damp grass with a heavy thud that left him dazed and utterly without wind.

Vibiana was nearly at the other tree before she realized she had lost her challenger. She pulled the stallion to a halt and wheeled around.

Scipio had managed to pull himself to his knees, gasping for breath and still seeing stars. He looked at Vibiana in the distance.

They both realized the situation in an instant. Even if he could get to Bucephalus and remount him, her start was such that he could never catch up with her if she chose to escape.

Barely giving it a second thought, she trotted back across the field and dismounted, running over to him.

"Are you all right?" she asked, feeling him for broken bones.

"I think so," he croaked, falling onto his back.

"Well?" she demanded. "Admit it—I beat you flat out."

"I was done in by an accident," he said stubbornly, unable to concede to her. "I demand a rematch!"

She laughed. "I am not sure you would survive a rematch. And next time, I might not come back to you!"

The sun formed a halo about her head as she hovered over him, and he finally accepted what he had been denying for months: he was completely and helplessly in love with the niece of his sworn enemy. And he was happier than he had ever been.

"That," he said, "would be a tragedy I could not bear."

He pulled her close and they kissed.

And within moments, they were pulling each other's clothes off.

———

That night, he gave her a spectacular emerald choker and held her tight in his arms for a long time. He piled thick, luxurious furs upon the floor. There he lay with Vibiana, listening to the crackling of the embers, his head nestled against her bosom. The war seemed as distant now as Rome and Carthage themselves. *If only it could always be like this*, she thought drowsily.

Scipio seemed lost in thought.

"What are you pondering?" she asked softly, propping her head upon her hand.

"I'm just thinking how mischievious are the gods," he said. "For so many years, I have carried this hatred for Hannibal with me, burning in my mind, every waking moment. So the gods bring his very niece into my life, and now we are lovers. How clever they are!"

Vibiana stroked his hair. "Perhaps the gods are sending you a message that you should release yourself from this obsession with vengeance upon my uncle and be at peace in your mind."

She felt him go tense, and realized yet again that this was treacherous territory. "I hope you will not let your hatred of him affect your feelings about me," she said, a little defensively. "After all, I can barely even remember anything about him!"

"No." He kissed her lightly. "My feelings for you are quite separate from him. Let us talk of it no further."

And so they drank sweet Spanish wine into the wee hours, laughing, content and relaxed in each other's arms.

———

The days flew by, and Vibiana was very happy until Scipio announced that they would be returning to the field. Then she whined incessantly, begging to remain in civilization. Scipio would have none of it, so she found herself again subjected to the rigors of camp life.

And now, she could not be sure, but judging from the frenzy of activity in the camp, a major battle seemed imminent. Squadrons of cavalry rode to and fro, scouts and officers came and went from the command tent, and surgeons sharpened their horrible saws. Everywhere around her, soldiers bustled about, readying their weapons, checking their armor, stretching and pushing against each other to loosen their muscles.

She sat with her legs crossed beneath her, watching as old Narcussa prepared the general's battle armor. He carefully polished each piece to a bright sheen before hanging it on a Y-shaped frame. Over the months, she had developed a friendship with the gentle valet. Vibiana had learned much about her lover from the old man, who was prone to gossip.

"What's happening?" she asked.

"The master has finally maneuvered them into a position where they have no choice but to fight," Narcussa said, brushing the white plume that ran down the crest of Scipio's ornate battle helmet. He tested the cheek plates to make sure they were properly fastened and checked the chinstrap. Not that he was concerned that any Carthaginian swordsman would get within range of his master. Narcussa was aware that Scipio observed his battles from a safe distance, where he might have a chance to influence the outcome.

"What do you mean?"

"Well, did you think all this marching we've been doing was just for show?" Narcussa said somewhat smugly. "After we took Cartagena, your army at Ilipa finally began moving toward us. But Scipio's too clever just to line up and slug it out with them. All this marching and countermarching was designed to get us the best ground possible— and I hear it's worked. The enemy is pinned against the mountains, and the master's finally ready to give battle."

"Do you know who commands the Carthaginians?" she asked casually, swirling a pattern with her finger in the dirt floor of the tent. Normally, the commanding general's tent would be pitched over wooden floorboards, but the army had moved so frequently in recent days that the camp had been dashed together hastily.

"It is said that a general named Hasdrubal, son of Gisgo—as distinguished from Hasdrubal Barca—is in command."

Hasdrubal, son of Gisgo! She winced at the name. She considered him a thickheaded oaf, a spoiled son of one of the leading Carthaginian families, who owed his position more to the accident of birth than to proven ability in the field. Now she understood why the Carthaginian Army had dawdled at Ilipa, passing up the opportunity to attack Scipio when he was vulnerable before Cartagena. As a military planner, Hasdrubal, son of Gisgo, was no match for Scipio.

But Vibiana's dislike of the man was more deep-rooted than mere disregard for his generalship. Her father had often spoken of marrying her to him, anxious to merge the two families by their bond. A woman's lot, after all, was to improve the family's standing by serving as barter in a marriage. She had dreaded the thought even before coming under the influence of Scipio.

Clearly, this battle would settle her fate as well as the issue of final dominion over Spain.

"The men are forming up now," Narcussa said, "so that the master can address them."

Vibiana had learned that this was yet another of the peculiar Roman traditions—before every battle, the commanding general harangued his troops, trying to lift their morale for the imminent test of arms. The Carthaginians did so rarely.

Just then, Scipio strode into the tent and hurried over to the frame holding his armor. He reached for the helmet.

"It seems somewhat late in the day for a battle," Vibiana said to him as he strapped on his gear.

"Oh," he replied somewhat distractedly, "there'll be no fighting today. We'll just get into position, then sleep in place. The battle will begin at dawn."

She considered his manner, mentally comparing his calm demeanor to the animated excitement that her father had traditionally displayed on the eve of combat. "Then I'll see you tonight?"

"Of course," he said, holding his arms in the air while Narcussa strapped the cuirass tight about his trunk. Narcussa then affixed a long white cape at the shoulder epaulets and let the garment fall gracefully. Scipio gathered it up casually in his left arm, much as he might a toga.

Vibiana was suddenly angry at the casual way Scipio confronted the frightful risks combat posed. "You seem utterly to disregard the possibility of your own demise."

For the first time since entering the tent, he looked at her. Decked out in his battle gear, he cut an impressive figure. She thought she detected a mischievous twinkle in those sparkling eyes. He decided to have some fun at her expense. "You should fervently hope that does not occur."

"And why do you think I should care if they cut you into a thousand little pieces?" she asked flippantly.

Scipio smiled as Narcussa buckled on his sword. "Because I have left strict orders with the loyal Maximillian: if I am killed in battle, he is to cut your throat before he falls on his own sword."

He hurried out, leaving her standing dumbfounded in the tent with the amused Narcussa.

—◆—

The army was assembled on a hillside, the rolling slopes forming a natural amphitheater for the commander's address. Massed like this, colors unfurled and stanchions raised, the troops were a fearsome symbol of the power and glory of Rome. Scipio could not, of course, speak to over twenty-five thousand men all at once, and so the throngs of men had been divided into groups roughly corresponding to the various positions they would occupy in the line. After each group had been addressed, they would be dismissed to march to the selected battle site.

Scipio, on Bucephalus, rode at a gallop around the far end of the phalanx, the imperial white cape flowing behind him. He held the reins in his right hand, and in his left carried a brown scroll. The high command, comprised of Laelius, Marius, Silanus, and Lucellus, kept station behind him. Each of them wore a red cape. And behind them was the ever-present contingent of messengers, personal bodyguards, and the standard bearer, carrying Scipio's new personal battle flag. The white banner was trimmed in gold and adorned with an eagle, symbolizing Rome herself. In one of its talons it clutched a trident, in tribute to the influence of Neptune; in the other a sword wrapped in ivy, the Cornelius emblem. It was a stirring sight for the men.

He reined in Bucephalus before the first group, the legions under the command of Marius, who would again take the left flank. Under his order of battle, this group would play a critical role, and so he wanted to talk to them first. The men had seen him in this situation before, but even the most distant soldier could detect something different in their commander's manner this time. Scipio waited until his senior officers were in position behind him, then drew in a deep breath.

"Men of Rome," he called out in a crisp, clear voice that carried across the ranks, "tomorrow I will call upon you to vanquish Carthage again. You have done it before—tomorrow will be no different!"

There was a robust cheer.

"But the battle that lies before us now takes on special significance. I have just received word from Rome of new outrages by these Carthaginian dogs."

He held up the scroll.

"Just recently, Hannibal broke out of his camp and attacked the small village of Toriorum. Toriorum was a simple farming village, with innocent peasants trying to scratch out a living. It had no garrison, no walls, no army to defend the people."

Scipio paused, but it was a hard world, and the men sensed what was coming.

"Every person in the town was put to the sword. Every man, woman, and child. It was a vicious, bloody massacre. They were helpless, and he slayed them all." There was genuine emotion in his voice.

"I demand revenge for the innocent people of Toriorum!"

He pulled hard on the reins, and the warhorse reared up as the men shouted another cheer.

"I have offered prayers to the gods for our success tomorrow. Indeed, I promise you that if we are triumphant, I will sacrifice one hundred bulls to the honor of Neptune. Now, our enemy tomorrow is not Hannibal himself. I wish it were. For I do not fear a man who butchers women and children. I pledge to you all, on the sacred bones of my father, that I will bring this Hannibal to battle—and the pursuit begins tomorrow!"

He trotted off as the men cheered and beat their swords on their shields, satisfied that the Toriorum story was an effective way to motivate them for the coming struggle.

———

A camp on the eve of battle always seemed eerie. The stacks of spears were gone, deployed with the infantry. The long rope lines to which the cavalry mounts had been tethered stood bare. The camp was occupied only by a skeleton crew of sentries and the rear echelon personnel. Unlike some commanders, who allowed their armies to travel accompanied by scores of hangers-on, Scipio had taken to the field out of Cartagena with only a thin cadre of noncombatants. He had been determined to remain highly mobile in the face of this enemy, intending to maneuver extensively in the foothills of the Silver Mountains until he found a suitable location to fight. The men left inside the stockade, mostly support personnel associated with the baggage train, were busy preparing bandages and dressings for the anticipated wounded, and filling buckets of water for those awaiting removal from the field. Sometimes these rear-echelon types displayed a fitful nervousness, knowing as they did that if the troops at the front met with disaster, their own lives would be lost when the enemy swept through. Tonight, however, there was a placid calm as Scipio rode past. Apparently, even these people believed that their commander was unbeatable.

Scipio paused at a spit where several men were roasting a pig and exchanged spirited banter with them concerning the upcoming battle. He accepted a thick cut of pork, which he ate hungrily, wiping away the hot grease with the back of his hand. He took a proffered leather wineskin and washed down the meat with a long swig. His face belied the potency of the brew.

His eye caught a young boy who was standing by the fire, admiring Scipio's huge white horse and its gilded armament.

"What are you doing in a soldier's camp?" Scipio asked him. The boy looked at him blankly.

"Begging your pardon, General," said a bystander. "The lad is a Spaniard, doesn't understand a word of Latin."

Scipio looked at the man who had spoken up. "A Spaniard? What's he doing here?"

"He says that the Carthaginians took his family captive, but he was able to escape. He's here to watch you run them out of his country."

Scipio did not smile. "That we will do. But he may find in the years to come that the yoke Rome imposes upon his people is not any lighter." He flicked at the horse and sauntered away, heading for his quarters.

Narcussa was waiting outside the tent and held open the flap for his master. Scipio entered, with Narcussa trailing behind him, and found Vibiana seated on a camp stool. Neither of them spoke as Narcussa casually helped Scipio out of the heavy armor and properly stored it for the next day's use, seemingly oblivious to the sexual desire building between the two.

When the valet was finally gone, Vibiana stood and pirouetted slowly in the candlelight so that he could see how she had prepared herself for him. Even across the width of the tent, Scipio caught the delicate scent of an exotic perfume. Her auburn locks were parted in the middle and swept back, where they emerged from an ivory pin in a burst of curls, accenting her delicate neck and lovely shoulders. She wore the emerald choker, his gift from Cartagena, and a fine pale-green dress of diaphanous silk, cut low to accent her bosom and cinched at the waist with a wide leather belt bearing an ornate golden buckle. The narrowness of her waist only served to further highlight the perfect curvature of her breasts, which Scipio could not resist, as she had learned.

She bent over and flicked the sandals off her feet and then returned her eyes to his, locking in his gaze. Without breaking eye contact, she unfastened the belt and laid it on the table. She then reached down and grasped the hem of her dress, which fell lightly about her calves, and slowly pulled it up and over her head. Naked now except for the glittering choker, she let him gaze upon her beauty for a few moments then hurried to his waiting arms.

Their kiss was long and deep. As she pressed her hard frame against him, Scipio ran his rough hands over her satiny skin, lingering at her breasts, as if exploring for some secret new feature of her body. Breaking the embrace, he lifted her and carried her over to the cot. He set her down and stripped off his tunic as she settled onto the bed.

"I love you," she whispered as he entered her, at once hating herself for admitting her weakness and yet desperately hoping that he might finally break down and confess his own feelings.

But Scipio was lost in his passion, and his only response was to increase the ferocity of his lovemaking until he spent himself, oblivious to her need for him to tell her what she craved to hear.

———

Scipio rolled onto his back, completely relaxed, the concerns of the imminent battle expelled from his mind. Vibiana shifted onto her side and lightly ran her index finger through the thick brown hair of his chest, occasionally flicking at his nipples.

After several long minutes of silence, she finally asked, "Did you mean what you said about Maximillian?"

"Of course," he replied in his most matter-of-fact tone. "I will not allow any other man to possess you."

She considered this remark. Perhaps it was as much of an admission of love as she could hope for from him. But she wanted more.

"What is to become of me?"

He grunted, not wishing to discuss her fate.

She was determined, however, and said, "You cannot bring yourself to admit you love me, even on the eve of what might be our last day alive. Even if you win tomorrow, what am I to do? How long can it be before some tart catches your eye and you decide to warm your bed with her? Or what happens if you return to Rome? What then? Will you banish me to service the men of the baggage train, like you did with Camarissa?" Overcome by such a prospect, she could not keep the tears from streaming down her cheeks.

He wiped away her tears, smiling. "The baggage train? I think not."

He considered the problem. Certainly, he could, under Roman law, free her and, following her manumission, even marry her. This would assure that any offspring would be Roman citizens. But he pondered over such a possibility. He did love her; there was no denying it. But what did love have to do with marriage? It had always been expected that he would take a Roman noblewoman as his wife—a carefully chosen wife could advance his political ambitions, as well as further improve his family's already eminent position in society. Perhaps he might take a Roman as his wife and keep Vibiana as a concubine. But even if he could bring himself to ignore the marital vow—not uncommon in Rome—an honorable Roman woman would likely not tolerate his keeping a mistress. Still, he could not imagine himself finding any woman who could satisfy him the way Vibiana did.

He sighed, weary of the vexing problem. She had no choice but to remain at his side, and so there was no need to tell her of his feelings. He said simply, "You worry too much. Let the future take care of itself."

In a few moments, he was sound asleep.

Frustrated and angry, she turned over, her bony spine pressed against his ribs. She buried her tears in the silk pillow. The uncertainty over her future, she realized, was the harshest part of the captivity Scipio had imposed upon her.

If he would not confess his love for her, she must find some way to escape.

———

Scipio was long gone when Vibiana awoke.

She stirred from the cot, stretched, and noticed she still was wearing the emerald choker. She judged the hour early and wondered if battle had yet been joined. As always, a lavish tray of fruits and breads had been left for her breakfast, but she did not wish to eat. Vibiana went to the large wooden trunk that contained her belongings and placed the choker in the hidden compartment reserved for jewelry. Scipio had been generous—the compartment overflowed with baubles and gems. She crossed back to pick up the elegant garment she had so casually cast aside the previous evening and brought it to the trunk, carefully folding and storing it. Rummaging through, she finally settled on a simple woolen shift with a cord at the waist.

After donning her sandals, she brushed her hair, letting it fall loosely onto her shoulders. She wanted to wash her face but noticed that no one had brought fresh water. She stepped out into the presence of the inescapable Maximillian. Unlike his heavily armored colleagues in the field, Maximillian wore a simple brown tunic and light boots and carried only a small sword belted on his hip. The broad strap was buckled in the last hole to accommodate Maximillian's formidable girth.

"Any news?" she asked the sour guard. His close-cropped head resembled a block of granite, and if he had a neck, she could not see it.

"None yet," he said simply.

She picked up a wooden bucket set outside the tent and said, "I'm going to the river," knowing he would accompany her without comment.

They walked through the camp heading to the upstream side to draw water, since the latrines were dug on the downstream side. The bucket dangled, thumping against her thigh with each step.

Vibiana knew better than to expect the guard to help, for in all her months under his scrutiny, he had not once lifted a finger in her aid.

As she bent over and filled the large bucket with the cool river water, the cord binding her dress fell untied. She stood up, staggering awkwardly under the weight of the water.

"Hold this while I tie my belt," she told Maximillian, handing him the bucket.

He took it, easily holding the weight with both hands. And as she stood before him, retying the cord belt, she was struck by a bold idea, as if slapped in the face. There was no time to debate the merits of her inspiration—there was only time to act.

She stepped toward Maximillian as if to retake the bucket, but instead of seizing the rope handle, she closed her grasp around the short, narrow sword hanging in its scabbard on Maximillian's hip. In a single swift motion, she yanked the weapon from its sheath and plunged it into his unprotected chest.

As she stepped back, Maximillian dropped the bucket and gave her a funny, shocked look. He spluttered and started to reach for her before collapsing in a heap.

The enormity of what she had done swept a wave of panic over Vibiana. Camarissa had been brutally punished, and she had not killed a Roman soldier! Vibiana looked frantically about and saw that she was still alone. What to do now?

She pulled the sword from Maximillian's corpse. She wiped it clean on the grass, then slipped the weapon through her belt and turned to face the river. Taking a deep breath, she plunged into the water, allowing the current to carry her downstream. Vibiana was a good swimmer—another benefit of having kept residency in her father's camp—and had no trouble treading water as the steady current carried her past the latrines and beyond the stockade wall. Perhaps because the bulk of the army was in the field, and the remaining men in camp were preoccupied with preparations for the aftermath of battle, no one spotted her head bobbing in the water as she swept past the last remaining lines of the Roman defensive perimeter. She was free!

Vibiana drifted effortlessly for several miles, reveling in her escape, and wondering how to make her way back to friendly Carthaginian lines. Occasionally, she kicked her legs to stay in the middle of the river. Rounding a bend, she heard the sounds of a battle in the distance. The noise got louder as she drifted along, and with a quick fright, she realized that the river must be carrying her into the heart of the contest.

She swam to the bank with powerful strokes and pulled herself free of the water. She hunched low to the ground, her wet dress clinging to her body, and scurried to the top of a nearby hill. Reaching its crest, cowering in a rush of tall weeds, she lifted her head and gasped in fear at the awesome spectacle before her.

Spread out in a vast mass of confusion across the valley, the two armies were locked in mortal combat. They surged back and forth, neither side able to break through the other's lines. The positions seemed static, making it impossible for her to tell who was winning. Men were falling and dying everywhere, their pitiful screams rending the air.

Scanning the distance, she recognized Scipio's command group, evident by his new battle flag, of which he was so proud. Mounted couriers came and went frantically to and from this group, and it was apparent to her that Scipio's generalship was being stiffly tested.

Slowly, almost imperceptibly, the Carthaginian mass began to fragment and fall back before the Roman onslaught. Up and down the lines, men began to fall out of formation and straggle away from the field. It became apparent that the Romans were winning, and her heart sank as she realized that she would not be able to find refuge with her countrymen.

Not far from her vantage point, she watched as a Roman cavalryman was knocked from his steed and killed in a swirl of activity. The panicked animal broke away from the melee and galloped up the hill, heading straight for her.

This is my chance! The horse, a black stallion with a splash of white on his snout, slowed as it labored up the hill, struggling under the weight of its battle armor. When it was within her reach, she jumped up and grabbed the reins. The animal whinnied in fright and reared, but she was too experienced to let this beast get away. Vibiana skillfully brought the horse under control, soothing it with her voice. Then she stripped away the heaviest parts of the horse's protective armor and swept onto its back. Afforded the superior view from atop the horse, she could see that hundreds of Carthaginians were running for their lives. She rode from the battlefield, heading away from what appeared to be the rear of the Carthaginian lines.

Vibiana's assessment was accurate. Huddled with his most loyal advisers, Scipio knew that the outcome was up for grabs. He dispatched courier after courier, repeatedly bolstering the lines against every threat, seeking to exploit whatever opportunities were presented. He understood that the fight had degenerated past the point where new tactics and maneuvers, or any further order that he could give, might make a difference. Both sides were fully engaged, with all reserves committed. The two grim armies were reduced to slugging it out, with victory swinging upon such fickle intangibles as courage, desire, and conditioning. This would be no Baecula, where Scipio's superior tactics had prevailed and Roman casualties had been slight. Ilipa had turned into a simple bloodbath, brutal and savage.

In the end, superior Roman training and discipline carried the day. The legions, enjoying a slight tactical advantage in close combat with their deadly short swords, relentlessly hacked through the massed Carthaginian lines, suffering monstrous casualties themselves. There was no decisive breakthrough—the enemy simply began to give way as the morning wore on. By noon, Hasdrubal's army was in a full but fairly orderly retreat. Here, finally, Scipio's generalship paid off: with the Silver Mountains at their back, the Carthaginians had no alternative. Faced with annihilation or surrender, many of the surviving combatants gave up and threw down their arms. Those who did not were cut down. By late afternoon, the Romans had won, albeit at heavy cost.

As twilight fell over the exhausted men, Scipio surveyed the carnage with deep regret. Bucephalus slowly picked his way across the battlefield. Scipio was surrounded by a contingent of alert bodyguards. All across the battlefield echoed the pitiful cries of the wounded and dying. The stench was overpowering. Dazed Roman stragglers were reorganized into work parties. Soldiers loaded wounded Romans onto wagons to be carried off the field, while wounded Carthaginians were methodically put to the sword. Everywhere, piles of the dead were stacked for burning. The pyres would burn for days. Given the extent to which the ranks had disintegrated in the chaos, Scipio suspected that it would be some time before he had an accurate accounting of his losses.

Eventually, he reached the far side of the battlefield. There he found hundreds of enemy soldiers huddled on the turf, bound together by long chains, waiting to be marched away. "Well, Laelius," he said, "I think we can quit the field now. This battle is finished."

"As you wish. Please accept my congratulations on another glorious victory." Laelius' tone was flat, as he knew full well that this victory, if indeed it could be called such, had been more grinding than glorious.

Scipio chose not to respond. He turned to head back for the camp.

"Ah, there is one other piece of news," Laelius said, drawing his mount to a halt. "I received the message earlier in the day, but did not wish to trouble you until the outcome of the battle was known." Laelius looked down, wary of having to be the bearer of bad news.

Scipio wheeled his horse about and faced his senior legate, intensity blazing in his eyes. "What is it?"

"The guard Maximillian was found stabbed to death early this morning alongside the river, apparently killed with his own sword. The woman Vibiana has not been found, although search parties are making a valiant effort."

Scipio fell back in the saddle as if struck by a spear. His chin sagged onto his breastplate, his head suddenly unable to support the weight of his war helmet.

But presently, he recovered and drew himself upright in the saddle.

"Recall the search parties, Laelius. She was a common slave, not worth the effort of a search. Perhaps she will fall prey to some marauding band of survivors from this carnage."

Laelius nodded, noting that his general's harsh words were betrayed by the emotion in his voice.

"Come, Laelius, we must make preparations to leave for Rome." Scipio's determination returned. "There's nothing left for me to conquer in Spain."

V

SPAIN

207 BC

B UT THERE WAS CONSIDERABLE work to be done in Spain before
Scipio could return to Rome.

After completing the post-battle rites and formalities, Scipio and
his army marched for Tarraco on the coast, stopping at various towns
and outposts along the way to cement alliances with Rome. For this
reason, his march took the better part of seventy days. Along the
way, he seized dozens of silver mines, claimed ownership of their
product for Rome, and installed his own overseers to operate them.
As the conquering general, Scipio was entitled to participate in the
revenues, and by the time he reached Tarraco, it was clear that his
already significant wealth would swell further. Upon arrival Scipio
dispatched Silanus to Rome, accompanied by many prisoners of
noble rank, to report the liberation of Spain.

At Tarraco he was hailed as a conquering hero, but Scipio found
little satisfaction from this homage. He was anxious to get on with
the business of finally ejecting Hannibal from Italy, and to that end,
began laying groundwork for a grand African Expedition.

He focused his attention upon one Syphax, king of the Masaesulii,
an African tribe bordering the Mauri River, just across the straits
from Sicily. Envoys reported that Syphax might be persuaded to
renounce his treaty with Carthage. Syphax, it seemed, had become
concerned that Carthage might lose the war with Rome, and was

interested in hedging his bets. For anyone considering mounting an invasion of Africa, Syphax represented an important consideration: he was the wealthiest of the African princes, and his territory was strategically critical because it lay between Carthage and what would be the Roman staging areas and base of supply in Sicily. Accordingly, Scipio dispatched Laelius, armed with lavish gifts, on a diplomatic mission to sound out the king concerning a new alliance. This task Laelius carried out with considerable skill, and Syphax, pleased with the tendered booty, offered to reach an accommodation with Rome. However, Syphax insisted on a face-to-face meeting with Scipio to finalize the alliance.

Scipio boarded a trireme, a sailing ship featuring three tiers of oars, for the journey to Syphax's palace in Neapolis, a port on the coast of Africa south and east of Carthage. The long, narrow trireme sat low in the water, built for speed and maneuverability. The bow, which rose nearly twice a man's height above the deck, was festooned with finely carved figures of Tritons blowing shells. Beneath the bow, extending forward from the line of the ship, was the rostrum, a device of solid wood, reinforced with an iron tip, used for ramming other ships in combat. The ship's sides were ornately detailed with gold leaf above the molding; beneath the molding were three narrow slats, each covered with a leather flap, through which the long oars extended, sixty on each side. On the deck was a single mast, set a little forward of midships, supporting a great square sail, held in place by simple tackle anchored to the deck.

Before departing Tarraco, Scipio went to a small altar on the fore-deck and sprinkled salt and barley upon it, offering solemn prayers to Neptune for safe passage and a successful mission. The order to cast off was given, and Scipio went into the cabin to study his companions for the voyage. The cabin was the central compartment of the trireme, running nearly the entire length of the ship below its main deck, and lighted mainly by three broad hatchways. The cabin was the heart of the ship, the home of all aboard. At the aft end of the cabin was a platform, raised by several steps, upon which sat the chief of the rowers. This official, a most stern and unrelenting taskmaster, sat straddled over a drum, used for the beating of time for the oarsmen, and a water clock to measure the reliefs and the watches. Above the chief of the rowers, on a still higher platform, were the captain's quarters, given over to Scipio for this trip. They were furnished with bed, desk, and a large, comfortable chair, into which Scipio deposited himself to observe the ship's routine.

Stretched out casually, rocking in unison with the vessel's motion, Scipio pondered the miserable fate of the naked rowers, each one of them a condemned man, consigned to the galley as the last stop before the grave. Many were captured prisoners of war, chosen to man the galleys because of their strength and durability. Their nationalities might serve as a directory of Rome's conquests: Gauls, Spaniards, huge Celtiberians, and even a few Greeks. He noted with satisfaction that dozens of swarthy Carthaginians heaved and pulled at the oars in a brain-deadening monotony of toil. Along the sides of the cabin, fixed to the ship's timbers, was a succession of benches, situated low and close to the sides of the hull and rising in height as one approached the keel. A walkway ran down the length of the ship, above the keel; it was patrolled by a coarse overseer, maintaining a brutal discipline with a long, coiled bullwhip. On the lower two benches, the rowers were afforded the opportunity to sit, whereas on the third bench, closest to the center keel, the slaves were forced to stand. Leather thongs hung from the ceiling to hold the oars. The cabin was steamy from the heavy perspiration of the rowers' wretched and endlessly repetitive labor, as the only ventilation was provided by the hatches above and the movement of the oars through the leather flaps that shielded the rowers from the waves outside. Each man during his shift was chained to his oar, and not a one of them was unmarked by the whip.

During their breaks, the slaves were herded into a hold beneath the center walkway and locked up, like animals in a cage.

"How long," Scipio asked the captain one evening during the passage, "can a galley slave survive in these conditions?"

The captain, a short but stout native of Corsica, shrugged. "Most of them do not survive more than a year. Malnutrition, disease, exhaustion, the whippings—these things take their toll. The strongest can last up to three years. When they become useless to us, we throw them overboard."

"Would it not be more efficient," he asked, "to improve their conditions and maintain a well-trained crew?"

The captain gave him an odd look. "Why bother? Slaves are plentiful. Besides, if we improved the conditions, it would only worsen their despair. They have nothing to live for; they know nothing but hard labor under the lash. There is not a moment of pleasure in their existence. You notice, we do not even give them the dignity of having a name—the number of their position is all we require to identify them. For them, death is a merciful end to their sentence."

With that, Scipio was silent.

The crossing to Africa was uneventful except for a brief encounter with a Carthaginian navy ship spotted on the horizon, which appeared to be giving chase to the Romans. The captain, understanding the importance of the passenger he was carrying, wisely chose not to chance an engagement on the high seas and kept his distance. Once night fell, he easily lost the pursuing vessel.

Two days later, they put into Neapolis. What a strange and exotic place was the capital of Syphax! Never had Scipio seen so many dark people. As he made his way over a dusty road from the crowded docks to the palace of Syphax, led by a cluster of envoys who greeted his ship when it docked, Scipio marveled at all types of new things— colorful woven cloth, spicy and aromatic foods, unusual carved columns, and towering stone icons. Although there appeared to be a thriving commerce, Scipio noted that the populace lived in abject poverty. The only buildings were crude wooden structures, and there were no sewers or running water. There were privies everywhere, and the stench of these latrines hung in the hot air. The palace of Syphax, therefore, was a startling contrast to the surrounding squalor: constructed of the finest white stone and marble, obviously drawing upon the architectural influence of the Moors, the palace was an enormous, shimmering residence perched on a promontory overlooking the ocean and looming over the surrounding countryside.

Arriving at the palace, Scipio was further shocked to learn that by coincidence, Hasdrubal, son of Gisgo, was calling on Syphax at the same time. Hasdrubal was still reeling from the beating Scipio had given him at Ilipa, and the exasperated courtiers of Syphax were careful to keep the two antagonists apart until Syphax could sort it out.

A more modest man might have been embarrassed by the simultaneous presence of representatives of the two combatants, one of whom was already his ally. Syphax, however, treated the visit as a huge honor: famous generals representing the two greatest powers on earth, each courting his favor. He invited both men to a lavish feast to be held under a flag of truce, which neither general could refuse. For Syphax, the occasion was an opportunity to draw them into talks by which the African might mediate the quarrel between Carthage and Rome, thereby enhancing his own stature.

Scipio was ushered into the king's presence, and found himself in awe. Everything about Syphax was big. He was tall, taller than any man Scipio had ever seen, and puffy, obviously from too much easy living. His wooly cap of brown hair was cut close to his scalp, in the African style, and his huge head sat squat upon a powerful, thick neck. His features were unremarkable, except for his skin, which was of the deepest ebony. His huge hands swallowed up Scipio's in the clasp of greeting. Syphax was a man who was, in many respects, larger than life: garrulous and pompous, clever and daring, mischievous and conniving. His power as king was absolute, and he wielded it with a gusto Scipio found fascinating.

"Ah," said Syphax as Scipio bowed in greeting, "the conqueror of Spain. Never has Rome been so well served."

Scipio bowed at the waist. "It is an honor to meet the great Syphax, whose deeds are legend even far across the water."

Hasdrubal was brought in and introduced to Scipio. Like most of the Carthaginians, Hasdrubal wore a bushy beard that obscured most of his features. He had, Scipio noted, a bulbous red nose, lined with tiny veins, which Scipio knew was a sure sign of overconsumption of wine. More than a few awkward moments passed as the two generals, who just recently had labored so mightily to kill each other, groped for something to say.

Syphax quickly realized that he must be the oil to lubricate their relationship, and he managed to strike up a friendly conversation with them. He took the two opposing generals on a tour of the sprawling maze of rooms that comprised his palace. During the course of the tour, Syphax revealed himself as a collector. He proudly displayed a wondrous wardrobe—closets stuffed with rich silk robes trimmed in glittering jewels—and his harem, populated by more than a dozen females, each swathed in glittering robes and veils. But he was most delighted by his horses. Syphax walked them through his stable, which itself was built of stone as a precaution against fire, and was as spotless as his court. He owned a dozen of the finest Arabian racing stallions and challenged his guests to a race for any stakes they might name.

"Both of you," Syphax said, "could be enjoying pleasures such as these if you could devote yourself to the pursuit of commerce instead of war."

"It was not Rome that commenced the hostilities," Scipio pointed out politely. "It was Hannibal who crossed the Ebro and sacked Saguntum. And it was not Rome that invaded Africa, laying waste to the territory of Carthage and trying to disrupt her allegiances."

"There can never be a peace," Syphax said wisely, "if you continue to kill each other over things that happened in the past. What has happened cannot be undone—we must look to the future, and find a way we can all get along together."

"Rome will never agree to be coequal with any other nation," Hasdrubal said harshly. He clearly was a lout, a poor choice by Carthage for ambassadorial duties.

"Rome has for many years lived in the community of nations and has honored our treaties. May the gods punish us if we cannot live by our word," Scipio replied.

"I agree," said Syphax. "The only thing that sets us apart from the barbarians is our honor, and our ability to conform our behavior to agreements we have previously made."

Hasdrubal chafed at this rebuke but kept his silence.

The tour ended in the huge ceremonial dining room, where dozens of the officials of court waited. Syphax had set out a prodigious feast, with a wide variety of native dishes Scipio had never seen. He ate lightly, wary that the seasonings employed by Syphax's chef might not agree with him.

Syphax, however, gorged himself, and Hasdrubal, as Scipio had predicted, quickly succumbed to the grape. While they ate, a group of athletes performed wondrous feats of acrobatics and tumbling. These performers were followed by a magician, who gave a marvelous show making items vanish and then reappear, to the amazement of all present. Then, to the accompaniment of several musicians, a dancing troupe of muscular women performed a series of energetic and erotic routines, clad in ceremonial African tribal costumes.

Scipio found it no very large challenge to be considerably more personable than Hasdrubal, son of Gisgo, whose tongue quickly grew thick from the wine the bevy of servants kept pouring into his cup. As the evening wore on, Syphax was charmed and won over by Scipio's cleverness.

Toward the end of the feast, Syphax gestured at the dancing girls.

"Any of them is yours for the taking," he said to Scipio. "I can assure you, they will give you more pleasure than you have ever had from a woman."

Scipio considered the opportunity. He had never had a black woman, and he felt a twinge of temptation as he watched the angular bodies moving so fluidly across the huge tiled floor. But the memory of Vibiana haunted him, and he was not yet ready for the company of another woman. Moreover, he was on diplomatic duty, and he did not want Syphax to obtain any advantage over him. He therefore politely declined the offer.

Syphax was surprised. "These women do not meet with your pleasure? I can have others brought before you."

"No, no, they are all quite lovely," Scipio tried to assure him.

A quite different look then passed over Syphax's features. "Perhaps you would prefer the company of a man or a small boy? That, too, can be arranged."

Scipio laughed. "No, my friend, that is not at all the issue. I am here on business of the state, and it would be inappropriate to engage in pleasures of the flesh while such important matters are pending."

Syphax was impressed with Scipio's self-discipline, although both he and Hasdrubal took their pick from the dancing girls and vanished for the evening.

The next day, Hasdrubal, seeing the handwriting on the wall, hastily departed by sea. Two days later, Scipio and Syphax concluded a treaty that provided that the dominions of Syphax would be considered neutral territory in the event of hostilities between Carthage and Rome on the African continent, ensuring free right of passage for armies of both countries. Scipio and Syphax clasped hands at the conclusion of their talks and presented each other with lavish gifts. Scipio gave Syphax an extraordinary golden horse studded with jewels and joked that his gift represented two of Syphax's hobbies.

Syphax gave Scipio a huge golden bowl encrusted about the rim by large rubies. Satisfied that the path to Carthage now was unobstructed, Scipio returned to his camp in Spain.

The weather for the crossing was rough, and Scipio took seasick, lolling about in agony while the trireme pitched and rolled over the waves. The voyage seemed to last forever, and when he finally reached Spain and set foot on terra firma, he offered up prayers of gratitude to be off the water.

———

Vibiana knew that fleeing, panic-stricken soldiers would be desperate for a horse, and so she took care to avoid the hundreds of stragglers streaming away from the battlefield. She confined herself to the woods, avoiding the open fields. The immediate aftermath of the battle would be the most dangerous time, for there were parties of mounted Roman scouts rounding up any survivors they could find.

Hidden by the thick foliage, she watched a squadron of Romans ride down a half dozen enemy infantrymen, who threw down their arms and surrendered. When the Roman commander dismounted and approached the prisoners, he evidently said something offensive—Vibiana was too far away to hear what transpired—and one of the soldiers struck the Roman with his fist. This outraged the other Romans, who, still armed and on horseback, smote the Carthaginians in a bloody slaughter. She shook from the violent encounter that underscored the fate awaiting her if she were to be captured. She called on all the tricks she had learned during her years of growing up with soldiers to put distance between herself and the Romans.

By nightfall, she estimated that she had traveled some twenty miles to the south of Ilipa, and, failing to see any more troops of either nation, she began to relax a little. She was delighted to find in the saddlebags all the equipment required to make a camp, and, even better, the fallen cavalryman's store of gold coins. With money, she realized, she might be able to book passage back to Carthage if only she could make it to a friendly port. Exhausted by the day's events, she decided to stop and rest. She found a suitable spot under a large rock outcropping, and, using the trenching tool, hollowed out a little area beneath the rock to provide shelter in case of rain. Her camp was not far from a brook, and, after letting the horse drink, she tethered the animal to a nearby tree. She attended to his care, removing the saddle and the bridle and carefully rubbing him down with an ointment she found in the saddlebags. She then spread out her blanket and, using flint and steel from the soldier's kit, made a fire. She was hungry, but without a spear or bow, there was no hope of killing any game for her dinner. She foraged about and discovered a thick stand of blackberries. She ate her fill, then stretched out under the advancing darkness and pondered her next move.

She had been trained in astronomy and could identify the constellations. The priests professed to be able to discern omens in the night sky, but she had inherited a healthy skepticism of religious practices from her father, and generally did not believe any of the priests' nonsense. Still, lonely in the vast wilderness of Spain, with no clear ideas where she could safely go, Vibiana offered up a little prayer, hoping for guidance. After some thought, she determined to head for Gades, a small Carthaginian village on the southern coast of Spain. If the Romans had won at Ilipa, there was no major Carthaginian force left in Spain, and it would not take the Romans long to consolidate their grip on the country. It was important to get to Gades as soon as possible, while there were still Carthaginians there.

The next two days were uneventful. Vibiana picked her way through the lush countryside, basking in the warm sun and living off the land. The rolling hills were dotted only with a few easily avoided farmhouses. She covered a considerable amount of ground, generally heading south. By the third day, however, her diet of berries and other plants had become unsatisfying, and she wanted something more substantial. She was now far removed from Ilipa and considered that it might be safe to visit a farmhouse and offer a gold coin for food.

She spotted a likely prospect late in the afternoon: a small log farmhouse flanked by a considerably larger barn and a tiny privy. Behind the house was a smelly pigsty, in which a half dozen hogs lolled. Still wary, and thinking that she might do better by dealing with the mistress of the house, Vibiana concealed herself in a thick stand of trees and waited to scout the occupants.

It soon became apparent that the lord of the manor was nowhere about—perhaps he was off cultivating some distant field. The only person she observed was a barefoot and plump middle-aged woman, clad in plain gray peasant garb, who seemed to be going about the common chores of rural life: slopping the hogs, feeding the chickens, hanging up the wash, and—temptation be damned—baking something delicious. Vibiana's mouth watered at the appetizing aroma and her rumbling stomach got the better of her. Deciding to chance it, Vibiana climbed onto the horse and rode slowly into the farmyard.

A homely yellow dog spotted her and put up a ferocious barking. The woman hurried into the yard to investigate and, seeing that it was not a soldier, told the animal to hush. Vibiana reined the horse to a halt a safe distance from the peasant woman and spoke to her in Spanish.

"I am traveling to Gades," Vibiana called out, "and have run low on provisions. Might I purchase something to eat?"

The older woman looked her over cautiously, and scanned the horizon for others, wary that this might be a trick by thieves. Finally, satisfied that Vibiana was alone, she said, "I have a fresh loaf of bread and some bacon. Would these be of interest?"

Vibiana smiled. "Yes," she said. "I will pay you well for them."

The woman turned and motioned for Vibiana to follow her.

Vibiana cantered into the yard, and at a signal from the woman, slipped off the horse.

"Come inside with me," the woman said in a friendly voice. "It isn't often we get visitors."

Vibiana drew a bucket of water from the well and put it before the horse, tethering the animal to the side of the watering hole. She then followed the woman into the small, windowless house. It was more of a cabin, built of notched logs lined with mortar, with a roof of thatch. The interior was a single room, wherein all the residents dwelt. Vibiana saw a straw mattress in one corner, the only covering on the dirt floor. In the opposite corner was a clay oven, and in the center of the back wall was a stone fireplace. There was a small fire burning, over which hung several pots and kettles. The only furniture in the room was a large oak table, rough-hewn, surrounded by coarse stools.

"What is your name?" the woman asked as she scurried over to the oven and drew out a loaf of thick, round bread, baked to a golden brown finish. Vibiana felt her knees weaken, and she wanted nothing so much as to gorge herself on the loaf.

"Vibiana," she replied with a slight smile. "And yours?"

"I am Kalmina, wife of Octuro, who is at work in the fields." Kalmina spoke with an odd lisp, and Vibiana noticed that the peasant woman was missing both her upper front teeth.

The woman set the loaf of bread on the table and put a mug before it. She brought over a heavy clay urn and poured a thick, yellow milk into the cup. She then fetched a frying pan from the fireplace, still oily with bacon grease, and added it to the presentation.

"Eat," she said. Vibiana gladly set herself onto one of the stools and tore off a thick piece of the coarse, delicious-smelling bread. Whether because of her ravenous hunger or Kalmina's culinary skills, it seemed to Vibiana that she had never had a meal quite so filling.

"Delicious," said Vibiana between bites. Then, she asked, "Do you have any children?"

A look of profound sadness passed over the woman's weathered face. "Three babies," she said. "All dead before their fifth birthdays."

Vibiana paused from devouring her food. "I'm so sorry."

Kalmina shrugged. "It happens. Life is very hard."

Vibiana nodded her agreement and took another bite of the wonderful bread. So intent was Vibiana on eating her meal that she did not notice when Kalmina slipped in behind her, holding a heavy rolling pin. The blow was vicious, catching Vibiana on the side of her head, just behind her left ear.

Everything went black.

———

Her eyes opened slowly, and her first sensation was of a searing pain in her skull. Gradually, the thatched ceiling came into focus, and Vibiana struggled for several moments to remember where she was. And then it all came sweeping back—the escape from Ilipa, the nights alone in the forest, finding this peasant hut, sitting down to eat. . . .

She groaned miserably and tried to rub the spot on the back of her head from which a painful and persistent throb was emanating, but, strangely, she could not. It took several seconds for her to realize that her hands were tied behind her with some type of leather cord.

She was being held captive by the peasant woman!

Two strange-looking men came into her line of vision, and she struggled to see them better. The simple act of focusing her eyes brought another burst of pain, and when she opened her eyes again, she realized there was only one man. His long black hair, clotted thick with dirt, hung low over his face, and what skin she could see was like tanned leather. A tattered garment, of the same gray peasant's wool as Kalmina's robe, hung loosely from his bony shoulders.

"Well," he was saying, "I guess you didn't kill her after all."

Kalmina now entered her line of sight, bending over Vibiana and putting a cool, damp cloth on her forehead. "Well, I had to make sure she didn't get away, and I didn't want to take any chances with her. She's too valuable a catch."

"Please," Vibiana moaned, "Don't. . . ."

The man was now leering at her. He too was missing several teeth, and those that remained were stained and yellow. "Now, milady, what business do you have coming into our little corner of the world, all alone?"

Vibiana groped for a plausible story to tell, but her mind was a muddle.

"That's a Roman horse you're riding, milady," Octuro said, giving her a knowing look. "And you don't look like any Roman I've ever seen. I'd guess that the Romans will pay a handsome bounty for the return of their horse. And since it appears that you stole it, they'll probably pay a bounty for you, too. It's hard to guess what you'll bring on their auction block."

It struck her that neither of her captors had washed for some time. Vibiana felt herself becoming sick and Kalmina, who recognized the symptoms, held a bucket near her head. But she had eaten little before being knocked unconscious, and so she was mostly confined to dry retching.

"I don't think you can travel with her yet, Octuro," Kalmina said. "Better to give her a few days to recover from the wound."

"Yes," said Octuro. "And then we'll see what the Romans have to say about her."

Vibiana felt a cold shiver of terror run down her spine. Back to the Romans!

The next morning, they tried to get her to her feet, but her concussion was too severe. The room spun about her wildly, and in a moment, she crumpled onto the mattress, blacking out again.

This little routine was repeated each morning for three days. On the second day, she was able to take some soup, spooned out by Octuro as if she were an infant, and on the third, solid food. After two more days, Vibiana was strong enough to remain stable on her legs. During this time, she was kept confined to the straw mattress, making use of a nearby bucket to relieve herself. She was vigilant for an opportunity to escape, but Kalmina would not leave her alone in the house. Vibiana became familiar with the woman's routine, comprised of little but backbreaking work from dawn until dusk.

On the fourth day, Kalmina looked her over and said to Octuro, "One more day. You can leave with her tomorrow. But I want her dress and her sandals for myself."

Octuro came around and untied her hands. He gave her a shove into the middle of the room, while Kalmina went over to a trunk wedged up against one of the walls and fished out a coarse brown peasant's shift. She brought it over to Vibiana, and held out her hand, waiting. Vibiana, heart pounding, pulled her woolen dress over her shoulders and, eyes downcast, handed it to Kalmina. She grabbed the garment proffered by Kalmina and slipped it on. It was stiff and scratchy against her tender skin, but better by far than being naked before these two ruffians. She then slipped off the cork sandals she was wearing and gave them over as well.

With that, Octuro retied her hands and pushed her back onto the mattress. Octuro brought over a crust of bread and held it before her to chew on. Kalmina took the lovely dress she had taken from Vibiana out to the well to wash it.

"Yes," he said to her quietly. "We'll have quite a good little journey to the Romans' camp."

His breath was as strong as his body odor. The thought of being violated by this vulgar man, and the punishment that awaited her at the hands of the Romans, pushed her over the edge. Her resolve wilted, and she wept bitterly, twisting her head into the straw mattress in a vain effort to find solace.

The next day, just after dawn, Octuro saddled up the horse and tied a short rope from the pommel to Vibiana's waist, keeping her hands tightly bound behind her. Kalmina brought out a bag of provisions, which she tied onto the saddle.

Octuro was about to climb atop the horse when Kalmina reached out and grabbed him by the scruff of his neck.

"Don't think I don't know what you intend to do with her when you get out my sight," she said to him in a mean tone. "Just make sure you don't damage the goods. She should bring a good price. If you come back with less than a hundred sesterces, I'll be after you with the rolling pin."

Octuro gave her a sheepish look, and scurried to clamber onto the animal. He set off at a light pace, forcing Vibiana to trot just to keep up. She was in reasonably good condition, and managed to stay on her feet, but after climbing a rather steep hill, she had to beg him to slow down. When he thought she had had a sufficient time to catch her wind, he resumed the pace again. So it went throughout the day. He alternated her between a near-run and a merely brisk walk. At midday, he paused only to give her a little water but no food, while Octuro himself munched on bread and some celery that Kalmina had provided.

As night fell, Vibiana was utterly exhausted, her hair a rat's nest of dust and perspiration, her feet filthy and sore from the countless stones and burrs. Her entire body ached, and she collapsed onto the ground, gasping for breath while Octuro made camp. He built a good fire, pitched a lean-to shelter, and then attended the horse.

Soon enough, he came over to stand before her. He pushed her onto her back, and hiked up her dress above her loins.

"Umm," was all he could say, and he pulled up his tunic, showing her his swollen manhood. The fire, directly behind Octuro, cast a hellish glow about the man. Frantic over her impending rape, she pleaded with him.

"No, please, please, no," she wailed, "please don't. . . ."

He took a step closer. His huge penis loomed over her.

"Oh, come on now, don't tell me a wench like you has never had it!" He had a fiendish look, a wild and determined stare that foretold he would be very cruel. "Maybe if you're really good, I'll give you something to eat tonight."

He took another step, his foul smell adding to her revulsion.

Desperate, she kicked at him with all her power, her heels crushing violently into his testicles.

"Aaargh!" he howled, trying to keep his balance and clutching at his groin. He twisted and hobbled where he stood, as Vibiana scrambled onto her feet.

Octuro was doubled over, facing the fire.

Her anger and pain overcame her fear. She closed the space that separated them and drove a knee violently into his buttock.

He pitched forward, trying to keep his feet under him, but stumbled and fell into the fire. Octuro screamed as the flames licked at his dry peasant garment. Frantically he tried to scramble away, but Vibiana was waiting for him. With another determined kick, she sent him tumbling back again into the blaze.

His clothes and hair ignited. Burning now, wailing in panic and agony, he staggered across the little clearing of their campsite until he collapsed in a smoldering heap, his tunic a flaming shroud.

Horrified, Vibiana watched as the flames consumed the corpse, the sickening stench of roasted human flesh filling the night air.

She eventually recovered enough to crawl over to the saddlebags and find a knife. Severing the cords that bound her hands behind her back was no easy feat, and she cut herself repeatedly before she was free.

The inky blackness of a forest night was fast upon her, ruling out any thought of moving the camp to another location. She took the trenching tool and heaped a mound of dirt onto the still-smoldering remains of Octuro. Then, trembling with fear and sickened by all that had befallen her, she wrapped herself in a blanket and tried to sleep. As she lay on a pile of leaves, a thin blanket pulled tight about her, completely alone and buffeted by the gods, she wondered again whether she had been wise to run away from Scipio.

———

Silanus trudged up the steep slope of the Aventine Hill, searched out the modest private residence of Quintus Fabius Maximus, and announced himself to the military guard. While he waited to be admitted, Silanus noted that a number of the clay tiles on the roof were in need of repair. Before he found it necessary to dodge any, he was escorted through the compact house. In the Roman custom, it consisted of a series of rooms built around a central atrium open to the skies above. Silanus was led into a peristyle garden at the rear of the house. The garden was not particularly well maintained; a tangle of grass, vines, and wildflowers encircled a fountain whose sensuous nymph, cradled in the powerful arms of a warrior, eternally poured fresh water from a shell into the basin below. Silanus considered the statue for a moment, and then recognized its symbolism: the Fabii family claimed to be descendants of the illicit union of Hercules and a nymph, which, according to legend, occurred one afternoon by the River Tiber. Despite the relative shabbiness of the surroundings, Silanus was duly impressed as he seated himself on a marble bench. Only the most politically influential men could arrange to have running water brought in lead pipes from the aqueduct directly into their homes.

As he waited for his audience with Fabius, Silanus was filled with more than a bit of envy. Unlike Fabius and all the other elite Romans, Silanus had not inherited a country estate to provide him with an income and a seat in the Senate. He had been forced to make his own way and try to win his fortune through commerce. And he might have succeeded, too, had not things gone against him.

Silanus heard the slap of approaching sandals behind him and turned to greet the commander in chief of all the armies of Rome.

"Do not get up," Fabius said, coming around the seated Silanus and settling himself onto the bench. He carried a thick leather pouch, which he set between them on the marble.

It was remarkable, thought Silanus, that so much power might for so long have been vested in so diminutive a man. Fabius was very short and even in his prime could not have been very imposing physically. The man had gotten to his station in the army by his wiles rather than by his strength. He was completely bald except for a thin fringe of hair just above his ears, and the bony plates of his skull gave his head an angular appearance. His face, covered with tough and leathery skin, was dominated by a large wart on his upper lip, which led some of his critics to nickname him Verrucosus, after the warty chameleon of that name. Silanus felt prickly before the old man's gaze, as the hazel, ferret-like eyes darted back and forth, sizing him up.

"The senators very much appreciated your report concerning the victory at Ilipa," Fabius said in a low, authoritative voice. "Of course, they have not had the privilege of having your earlier reports, which I have valued greatly."

Fabius long ago had learned not to rely on formal dispatches to the Senate from commanding generals in the field: they were too sporadic and prone to exaggeration of their accomplishments and underemphasis of the risks. And so, ever since the catastrophe at Cannae, each Roman general had, unbeknownst to him, an informer on his staff, reporting his superior's every move directly to Fabius in Rome. Careful precautions had been taken to conceal this surreptitious intelligence network: a spy relayed his letters through a relative, for example, to avoid suspicions as to why a junior officer was corresponding regularly with the senior general of the Roman Army.

Scipio's chief of cavalry had been serving Fabius in this manner throughout the Spanish campaign. Months before leaving for Spain, the ambitious Silanus had gotten himself into very deep water financially, through an ill-conceived scheme to speculate in grain prices. He wound up deep in debt and faced the nightmare of being sold into slavery to satisfy his creditors. Upon learning of this sorry state of affairs, Fabius had bought up Silanus' debts. He then put a proposition to the cavalryman: Fabius wanted detailed reports on Scipio's every movement. Silanus had only to perform reliably, and upon his return the debts would be marked paid in full.

"You are pleased," Silanus said with a note of satisfaction, "with my performance?"

"Yes," Fabius replied, lacing his fingers and resting his hands on his lap. "Scipio will be returning to Rome soon. I want you to return to Spain and continue to keep an eye on him. In the meantime, you have kept your end of the bargain. I will keep mine. In this pouch are all your promissory notes. They are yours."

Silanus clutched at the pouch and rifled through its contents. Satisfied that all his markers were accounted for, Silanus heaved a sigh of relief.

Fabius watched the officer with a sense of sympathy, for he too had known his share of financial difficulties, mainly brought on by the mischievous Cato. After the shameful defeat at Cannae, Fabius had arranged an exchange of prisoners of war with Hannibal, agreeing to swap captives on a man-for-man basis, and if either side held more than the other, the surplus prisoners would be redeemed for money. When the exchange was completed, it was discovered that Hannibal still held 240 Romans. But the Senate, whipped into a frenzy by Cato, refused to provide the ransom for these men, blaming Fabius for attempting to rescue men who had fallen into captivity only because of their own cowardice. Fabius, to save face, sold his estates and used the money to recover the prisoners. Some of them had been able to repay him, but many others had not, and so Fabius was reduced to living in this modest house. Even worse, to counter the ever-growing influence of Cato, he had been forced to make an alliance with the wealthy senator Marcinius to have access to money.

Marcinius was a war profiteer, engaging in a dozen different schemes to make money from the upheavals brought on by Hannibal's invasion. Fabius supplied him with information provided by his illicit network of informants, which Marcinius shamelessly used to become even richer. It was, Fabius thought regretfully, an unavoidable necessity, for without the backing of Marcinius, by now Fabius would have lost control of the army to Cato. It was Marcinius who had provided the money to buy up the debts of Silanus.

"Do not be so foolish as to get yourself in such distress again," Fabius lectured the younger man. "Next time, you may not find a benefactor quite so generous."

"Do not be condescending with me," Silanus snapped. "My father was a mere cobbler and did not confer upon me the advantages of wealth and property that propelled you to high rank in the army. I earned my rank with courage and strength!"

Fabius now grew angry. "Some of us," he retorted, "have sacrificed those advantages you recite for the good of the state. I do not live in such humble quarters by my own choosing, I assure you!"

"Well, thanks to Scipio, my winnings in Spain will make me a comfortable man, together with the cancellation of my debts," Silanus retorted, holding up the pouch.

"Ah, Scipio," Fabius said, his face impassive. "Your letters initially were most flattering of him. In some of the later dispatches, however, I detect a note of criticism."

Silanus looked away. "He claimed a prize of war I would have taken for myself. A fine-looking woman."

Fabius' eyes danced with excitement. "What? Scipio keeps a woman in the camp?"

"We captured Hasdrubal Barca's harem at Baecula. Since we didn't get Barca, we made a present of the harem to Scipio. He picked out the best one for himself; the others he gave to the heroes of the battle, myself included. I grew tired of mine and sold her. But Scipio kept his woman throughout the entire campaign. Took her horseback riding once, and let her use my mount."

There was no mistaking the tone of resentment in the cavalryman's voice. Fabius made a mental note to mention it to Marcinius—the officer's apparent resentment of Scipio could prove a valuable resource at some point.

"Scipio's woman—is she with him still?"

Silanus broke into a satisfied grin. "No. On the day of the battle of Ilipa, she somehow managed to kill her guard and escape. We never did find her."

"And what effect did her sudden departure have on Scipio?"

"I wasn't there when he was told. But I understand that he took it hard. I gather he had become rather fond of her."

"Interesting," was all Fabius would say. He did not consider it unusual that Scipio would have a woman in camp—it was a common practice among the younger men.

Changing the subject, he asked a little incredulously, "Do the men really believe he consorts with the gods?"

"That they do," Silanus said. "And after Cartagena, I might too."

Fabius smirked. "There are many deficiencies in the education of our soldiers." He sighed. "One of them, clearly, is a lack of understanding of the operation of tides. I am reasonably sure that Neptune had nothing to do with the lowering of the lagoon."

"Perhaps not," Silanus said. A little grudgingly, he added, "But he is a talented commander. Do not underestimate him."

"No," Fabius said softly, "I never underestimate anyone. I am particularly interested in what you wrote about his wild idea for an expedition to Africa, to attack Carthage. Was he serious, or was he just prompting discussion?"

"Oh, he's serious. Without question. He wants to fight Hannibal."

"I see," Fabius said, deciding not to let this lowly officer in on his private thinking: that the idea was lunacy.

He stood up, the audience at an end. "Good luck, Silanus. Do not confuse the success you have found in combat with the ability to make money. They are very different things, as your experience surely has taught you."

———

As it turned out, Silanus and Scipio arrived at Tarraco within a few days of each other. Scipio turned his attention to an item of unresolved business. Two relatively small cities, Iliturgi and Castulo, located on the River Baetis just south of Baecula, had earned the ill will of Rome when, after the defeat of Scipio the Elder, they had not only refused shelter to the tattered remnants of his army but had betrayed several dozen of these unfortunate men to the Carthaginians, who brutally murdered them. After avenging his father at Baecula, Scipio had considered taking his revenge upon these towns, but with the outcome of the war still up in the air, he had deferred imposition of Roman justice. Now, with the issue unmistakably resolved in favor of the Romans, the timing seemed opportune to settle the books with Iliturgi and Castulo. Scipio and two-thirds of the army marched on Iliturgi. Laelius and the balance of the army were dispatched to Castulo.

Upon arriving at the town, Scipio found the gates closed and careful preparations in place for a lengthy siege. Scipio lined up the men and made an impassioned plea: "The time has come to avenge the brutal slaughter of our comrades and the treachery that would have awaited us, too, if we had happened to seek refuge here. We must make an example of these traitors and fix unalterably in men's minds the knowledge that no one may ever consider a Roman citizen and soldier, however desperate his plight, as fair game for insult and injury!"

With a robust cheer, the Romans swarmed toward the walls. They were met by a veritable blizzard of stones and javelins, as the defenders fought with a passion fueled by the certainty that they must either die fighting or die in chains before their wives and children. The men fell back. Scipio reorganized his force and sent them forward again, only to meet the same reception. Several thrusts by the army that had conquered all of Spain were repulsed.

Scipio walked about the men who had been repelled from the walls as they sat, safely beyond the range of javelins thrown by the town's defenders, gathering their energy for another surge. He felt his anger mount and expressed contempt at the unsuccessful effort. He was met only by the blank stares of men too tired to do anything else.

And then Scipio did a foolish thing. He grabbed an assault ladder from a shocked infantryman and rushed toward the ramparts. He was halfway between the army and the town before the men realized what he was doing. A shout of alarm rose from the troops. In a moment, the men were on their feet, racing to follow their leader. Ladders were raised along a long section of the wall.

But Scipio's rashness left him dangerously exposed. Not even the favor of Neptune could protect him in such circumstances. A well-aimed rock caught him on the side of the head, leaving a huge dent in his helmet and knocking him senseless.

Seeing their leader injured and carried from the field, the Romans were outraged. Silanus saw his opportunity, and with a shout, led a renewed charge against the ramparts. The fight was vicious and bloody, but the walls soon were occupied. And then the soldiers, aroused beyond the ability of Silanus or any other officer to control them, meted out a terrible retribution. Not a prisoner was taken, not one resident was spared from the sword, including women and infants. The slaughter lasted for an hour, as piteous cries filled the air. The town was burned, and what would not burn was demolished.

When he recovered his faculties, Scipio walked through the ruins, surveying the carnage, his face growing heavier with dismay. He paused before the corpse of a woman, still clutching her murdered daughter in a terrible death embrace. Both were caked with congealed blood from gaping stab wounds. It was too much. Scipio wept bitterly, and sought out Silanus.

"You have allowed the men to become a lawless band of murderers!" he shouted, castigating the man in front of the other officers.

"Are we no better than Hannibal?" he demanded, tears flowing down his cheeks. "How can we distinguish what we have done here from what Hannibal did at Toriorum?"

Silanus looked at him blankly. "You said you wanted vengeance," he mumbled halfheartedly.

"I meant to take our vengeance upon those responsible for the crime!" he bellowed, choking back enough tears to sputter his words. "This is a massacre of innocents. Look at this child. What guilt does this child bear? Are we barbarians? Is this slaughter the glory of Rome manifest? May the gods have mercy upon us all!"

Rebuked, Silanus seethed with anger, but could give no answer.

The general cut short his inspection and ordered that the men be assembled. Although his heart was heavy, there was a duty to observe. After a battle, it was the Roman practice to hand out honors to the men for special valor exhibited during the fight. The men could sense that their commander was distraught, for he dully went about the business of issuing commendations, exhibiting none of the enthusiasm that customarily accompanied a victory.

A reward was offered for the first soldier to have scaled the walls of Iliturgi. Two men came forward to claim the honor: a centurion and a common infantryman. A heated dispute at once arose, and many expected Scipio, as a member of the elite class, to back the centurion.

Scipio cut short the debate. He awarded both men a prize, and without another word, left the field.

With the sorry affair of Iliturgi behind him, Scipio marched to join up with Laelius at Castulo. The story of his punishment of Iliturgi preceded him, and by the time he arrived, the Spaniards were ready to surrender. Scipio accepted their capitulation without bloodshed.

There was more mopping up to do, and Scipio and his lieutenants went about it methodically. Most of the territories, having heard of the comparative treatment between Iliturgi and Castulo, quietly made peace, offered tribute, and swore allegiance to Rome. One town, however, called Astapa, refused to give in when approached by a Roman contingent under the command of Marius. And rather than suffer the fate of Iliturgi, the town's elders collected all their most valuable possessions and created a pile of them. All the women and children were made to sit on the pile, and then logs and piles of brushwood were heaped all around it. Fifty armed townsmen were ordered to stand guard there, and a terrible curse was invoked upon any of them who might fail in his duty. These guards stood by so long as the issue of the battle remained in doubt. Upon seeing that the fight was going against them, the guards commenced the brutal slaughter of every single civilian, then torched the whole lot, finally taking their own lives just as the Roman soldiers approached. The sight of this carnage filled even the most battle-hardened veterans with astonishment and horror. Such was the utter destruction of Astapa. The Romans gained nothing from it at all.

At about this time, Scipio's African sojourn developed a most unexpected drawback, as it appeared that he had been exposed while there to some vicious parasite. A virulent illness landed him in a sickbed for days. He was wracked by fever and incontinence, and as the disease grew steadily worse, Scipio began to look like death itself. Laelius and the other commanders feared for his life.

News of Scipio's illness spread rapidly throughout the Spanish territory. The transmission of information being susceptible as it is to exaggeration and elaboration, rumors soon flew that Scipio had already given up the ghost. When this tale reached the Roman garrison at Sucro, charged with guarding the territory south of the Ebro, trouble erupted. The men of this garrison, with no imminently threatening enemy to occupy their attention, had taken to the grumbling that is the natural right of every soldier: if there was no more war to fight in Spain, why should they remain there? Morale deteriorated, orders were not followed, absenteeism increased, officers were harassed, and, outright mutiny followed soon after. The tribune in charge was turned out of the camp, and the rabble appointed two private soldiers, Gaius Albius of Cales and an Umbrian named Gaius Atrius, to command them. These two rascals, believing that Scipio was dead and Spain was up for grabs, began making ambitious plans for a campaign of plunder.

They led an ill-conceived foray against a nearby village, poor enough that there was little booty to be taken other than the human variety. After killing most of the men, the mutineers raped the women and carried them away to occupy the camp at Sucro. Thus emboldened, Atrius and Albius commenced preparations to march against Cartagena, where there were riches beyond belief to be had.

Imagine their dismay, then, when seven tribunes appointed by Scipio himself, now fully recovered, arrived at the camp to uncover the true state of affairs. However, these tribunes seemed more intent on ascertaining the root causes of the unrest than compiling a list of offenders. They received an earful from the men: the payroll had been erratic in arriving, the role of these brave and noble Romans had been undervalued in determining the overall distribution of booty, and so forth. The Tribunes agreed that these complaints were not without merit, and expressed relief that the matter was capable of being set right. They returned to Scipio to report their findings.

Shortly thereafter, the mutineers were pleased to receive an order to report to Cartagena to receive their pay. Convinced that Scipio had forgiven them, the troops formed up and made the march in record time. When the contingent arrived, the seven tribunes rode out to meet the approaching column, and each tribune invited several of the ringleaders to join him for a dinner that evening.

After these traitors had been plied with wine to the point of thick drunkenness, they were seized and bound. During the night, the other mutineers were rounded up, deprived of their weapons, and the next morning were assembled behind the ringleaders—thirty-five men in all, each heavily chained.

Scipio, dressed in full battle gear and looking every bit the picture of health, rode forth on Bucephalus. He gave one of his better orations, expressing shock and outrage at the treason. It was an eloquent display of theatrics. He was careful to let the tension build. The entire contingent of soldiers from Sucro remained unsure of their fate until he concluded his remarks.

"So far as most of you are concerned," Scipio shouted, waving to the unbound mass of men, "I have punished you sufficiently if you are sorry for your mistake. However, Albius of Cales and Atrius the Umbrian and the other leaders of this wicked mutiny shall pay with their blood for what they have done. To the rest of you, if you are sane again, the spectacle of their punishment should bring not pain but joy, for to no one have they been more bitter nor more cruel enemies than to yourselves."

The ringleaders knew they were condemned and manifested their terror with piteous cries of anguish and pious pleas for mercy. But their histrionics were to no avail. One by one the condemned wretches were brought forward, stripped, bound to a stake, and scourged to within an inch of death. Then the heavy sword separated their heads from the rest of their bloody carcasses. This took some hours to complete. Albius and Atrius were held to the end, forced to watch the demise of each of their co-conspirators and wait in terrified anticipation of their own punishment.

When at last the ordeal was completed, the bodies were dragged away and the ground was cleansed. Each soldier was then called forward by name, and in the presence of the tribunes swore allegiance to Rome and to Scipio as their commander, and was given his pay.

Scipio was finally free to turn his attention to Rome.

———

Hannibal had holed up with his army in Bruttium, disgusted by the lack of support from Carthage and railing angrily against the politicians who had left him in the lurch. The Roman navy had proven itself master of the sea, blocking several efforts by Carthage to provide reinforcements to her champion. Frustrated by their inability to break through the Roman blockade and weary of squandering resources in the effort, the Carthaginians had simply given up, leaving Hannibal to fend for himself in the Italian peninsula.

The years of fighting in Italy had taken their toll. Hannibal's original force, the brave men with whom he had crossed the Alps, had been reduced to a skeleton organization. The bulk of his army now was an assortment of Italians who had rebelled against Rome, mercenaries, and conscripts from territories that had sworn allegiance to Carthage. He had little confidence in them, and certainly would not attempt a new offensive against Rome with such a ragtag crew.

Hannibal's principal hope to resume the offensive rested upon the ability of his brother, Hasdrubal, to join up with him. Hasdrubal, defeated by Scipio at Baecula, had managed to reorganize the survivors into a force of some ten thousand men and had sailed for Italy. Much of the fleet had made it through the Roman net, although Hasdrubal had been forced to land in Northern Italy and try to fight his way south to link up with his brother. Together, they could embark upon a new rampage through the Italian countryside.

Hannibal was taking his leisure in his quarters, a fine private residence in Bruttium that had been commandeered for him, when he was advised that he had a visitor, a Roman who had been enlisted to spy for the Carthaginians. Without rising from his couch, he directed that the Roman be admitted.

"Greetings," Hannibal said coldly to the Roman, who held the rank of tribune. "What news do you have for me?"

The tribune, a Roman named Metellus, nervously cleared his throat. "As you know, I am attached to the army of the consul Gaius Claudius Nero, who has been assigned by Fabius the duty of keeping his army between you and Rome."

Hannibal nodded. He knew that the other Roman consul, Marcus Livius Salinator, was charged with the duty of attacking his brother Hasdrubal. Hannibal was not overly concerned. The timid Fabius, more concerned with keeping Hannibal pinned down, had kept most of the Roman Army in Italy with Nero. Hasdrubal had an excellent opportunity to overcome the undermanned force led by Salinator.

"Your brother moved into Umbria, shadowed by the army under Salinator's command. I have come to tell you that Nero a week ago moved north to join Salinator. They plan to attack Hasdrubal with a combined army in the Metaurus River Valley."

Hannibal leapt to his feet. "What? This is completely out of character for Quintus Fabius Maximus!"

"Fabius does not know," Metellus said. "Nero and Salinator have acted on their own initiative."

Hannibal thought for a moment. "Then who is manning the Roman lines just out of sight from the walls of Bruttium?"

"It is a token force. Nero believed that you would not discover his absence until it was too late. He has been proven correct, I daresay."

"Damn you!" Hannibal cursed at the Roman. "Why did you not bring me this news sooner?"

"I was left with only a handful of men in camp. My duties were pressing," Metellus explained. "I slipped away at the first opportunity."

Hannibal began pulling on his leather boots. "Is there anything else of interest?"

"Only that Publius Cornelius Scipio has completed the subjugation of Spain and is on his way to Rome. It is said that he remains distressed by the slaughter at Iliturgi."

Hannibal's head jerked up at the mention of the Spanish town. "What was that about Iliturgi?"

"Iliturgi is a small town in Spain," Metellus explained. "It was loyal to Carthage."

"Yes, yes. I know it well. What about it?"

"Our forces under Scipio attacked the town. Scipio was injured during the battle, and while he was off the field, the men grew out of control. The town was slaughtered. Completely. Every man, woman, and child was put to the sword. Scipio was said to be most upset, although the slaughter was well within the bounds of war."

There was an odd moment of weakness, as Hannibal appeared on the verge of breaking down. He quickly recovered himself.

"Go away," he said to Metellus. "Return to your post, before you are missed. You may pick up your reward before you leave. And next time, do not dawdle for so long before bringing me such important news."

Hannibal hurried out of the villa to rouse his staff. This was an incredible opportunity. Only a token force stood between him and Rome. At long last, he might break through and strike at Rome herself. Nero had taken a great risk, and Hannibal was determined to make him pay. But time was short—they must hurry!

In the midst of giving orders to break camp and take up the march, Hannibal received word that a small contingent of Romans had approached the gates of Bruttium under a white flag, asking for Hannibal. He hurried to the edge of the city and clambered up a rickety ladder to the parapet wall overlooking the gates.

A handsome Roman, wearing the armor Hannibal recognized as a consul's, was mounted on a gleaming white horse, just at the edge of the wall. Behind him, only a short distance back, were a dozen or so escorts, carrying the Roman's personal standards. And then Hannibal's eye caught the other standard, which he instantly recognized as that of his brother, Hasdrubal Barca. Hannibal felt his heart skip a beat.

"You sought Hannibal," he called out to the Roman in a husky voice. "Tell him what you will."

"I am Gaius Claudius Nero, consul of Rome. And I bring you glad portents." The Roman held up a cloth sack, stained with blood. With a sweeping motion, he heaved the bag up and over the ramparts. Hannibal was forced to jump out of the way of the missile. It landed at his feet with a thud, the impact knocking the contents out onto the parapet.

Hannibal looked down at the severed head of his brother. The sightless eyes were wide open, bulging as if Hasdrubal had been still alive when they had hacked it off.

"Take this gift as a symbol of what your effort in Italy is fated to achieve," Nero called out.

And before Hannibal could respond, the Roman wheeled about and stormed away, leaving Hannibal to his grief.

VI

ROME

206 BC

IT SEEMED AS IF all of Rome had turned out to welcome Scipio. The temperamental climate for once obliged. A cloudless blue sky and brilliant sunlight warmed the crowds lining the Vicus Triumphalis, that wide lane running along the western edge of the inner core of the city. The Vicus Triumphalis was a special road, used only for such celebratory events.

The parade formed up in the Villa Publica, a large park just northeast of the Servian Walls, so named for their builder, Servius Tullius. Tullius had erected the barrier out of huge *tufa* blocks nearly 150 years earlier, following a catastrophic raid on the city by an army of Gauls. The route wound its way through the broad Triumphalis gate, made a loop through the Circus Maximus, and then snaked up to the Capitoline, the hill containing a complex of sacred temples ringing the Forum itself. There, Scipio was to accept the accolades of the Senate for his accomplishments.

What a procession it was! Led by three huge floats celebrating the great victories at Baecula, Cartagena, and Ilipa, the contingent then featured a hundred chained Carthaginians, the wealthiest men taken prisoner in the campaign, who would be ransomed for vast sums. These hapless souls suffered merciless jeering at every step by a populace that had been terrorized quite long enough by Hannibal and was delighted to have found a champion who could deliver a success in the field. Behind the prisoners, large draft horses drew dozens of wagons piled high with booty, vast heaps of gold and silver artifacts from the captured territory, more than fourteen thousand pounds in all. Next marched a long train of commanders of the individual legions and their junior officers, each proudly displaying numerous medals and commendations awarded by Scipio for their valor. These men were followed by the dozen men of Scipio's personal escort, bearing his now-famous battle flag and campaign standards. Finally, Scipio himself appeared on Bucephalus, erect in the saddle and bedecked in glittering ceremonial armor. His finest white cape swirled about him with each clop of the horse's prancing hooves on the cobbled street.

Laelius, his black eyes glowing with intensity, had been entrusted with organizing the effort, and he had performed admirably, if irritably. Understanding that far more than mere applause was at stake for his general, Laelius madly scurried through the Villa Publica to make sure that the various elements were properly staged before they cast off. He had arrived at the park at first light to assemble the marchers, and, noting that the crowds had already gathered over the entire route, had waited until the parade was successfully underway before leaving for the Forum to attend to the details of the reception.

In the center of all the fanfare, Scipio was strangely ambivalent to the adulation. Perhaps it was his failure to bag Hasdrubal Barca, or maybe it was the looming struggle over how to deal with Hannibal. It might even, he thought ruefully, be the absence of Vibiana that was bothering him. Whatever it was, he accepted the cheers of the people with casual indifference. He was out to catch a bigger fish and was impatient to get his line in the water.

Still, he was pleased to be home at last. His keen eye noted the scores of new buildings that had been erected during his prolonged absence, including dozens of *insulae*, or apartment buildings, built to house the teeming masses that had deserted the countryside under

Hannibal's scourge. Most of these structures were shoddily built, and hardly likely to endure for many years. Typical of Roman architecture, they displayed the powerful influence of Greek design. It sometimes seemed to Scipio that the Greeks had already developed everything that was refined and elegant about the world. Perhaps, he reflected, the lot of Roman civilization was merely to copy the best that the Greeks had to offer, and extend it to all the corners of the earth.

The road made a sudden bend and he passed by the Macellum, an open-air market of stalls and booths. He smelled fresh baked goods and cooked fruits and vegetables and realized that he had perhaps become too accustomed to the simple fare of camp life. Next to the market was the sparkling Temple of Apollo, whose columns supported a massive roof carved with interpretations of the god's likeness. Scipio paused before the temple as a gesture of respect, and was struck by an idea that he decided to include in his remarks to the Senate.

His entourage entered the huge, oval Circus Maximus, site of the periodic chariot races. The floor of the arena featured a track around a long spine that ran the length of its core. All along the rim of the exterior wall were ornate sculptures of countless heroes who had distinguished themselves racing in the facility. The stadium was packed with more than sixty thousand ecstatic spectators. Scipio clutched the reins in his left hand and raised his right arm in salute to the people as the procession moved around the floor of the arena, Bucephalus kicking up a light dust as he maneuvered to avoid the ruts carved out by scores of chariot wheels. Hearing the throaty roar of the throng, Scipio knew he had their support now, but could he transfer that to the strategy he wanted to take on Hannibal?

It took another hour of acknowledging cheers before the retinue made its way up the winding path toward the Capitoline.

Its route took them past a huge temple, larger and even more ornate than the Temple of Apollo, dedicated to the worship of Jupiter himself. This structure sat at the base of the immense Capitol building, which housed the Forum and all the lesser offices of the Roman government. Behind the Forum stood several other temples. Of these, the Temple of Ops, Goddess of Plenty, was the most impressive, perched on a large podium that housed a huge treasury of silver bullion to be used in a state emergency.

A throng of dignitaries was assembled on the steps of the Capitol, all wearing formal togas, their ranks designated by varied configurations of stripes at the left side. Senators could be identified by the broad purple stripe, and, as the ranking officials, had been given the primary position at the top of the steps. The loyal Laelius had organized a cordon of stanchions and bollards to form a corridor up the steps, and the group lined both sides of this passageway.

The base of the steps was dominated by a bronze statue of the children Romulus and Remus suckling at the wolf's teats. Scipio did not believe the legend associated with the founding of Rome: how could children be reared by a wolf? Nonetheless, the statue was impressive and he drew Bucephalus to a halt before it and dismounted.

The assemblage broke into a sustained applause as he climbed the limestone steps, his armor clanking with each footfall. He paused momentarily and turned slightly, enjoying the high vantage point to look out over the vast sprawling city. The population had swollen dramatically. Scipio realized that these people, having been drawn to the urban life, would probably never leave it. Rome would not be the same, and the thought made him sad. With a sigh, he resumed climbing the broad steps. Finally, he reached the pinnacle, only to find waiting there the one man he least wanted to see.

"Greetings, Publius Cornelius Scipio," said Quintus Fabius Maximus, four times elected consul of Rome, and named dictator to save the city after the disaster at Cannae.

Scipio disliked everything about the scrawny little man, from the darting eyes to the ugly wart on his upper lip, which curled now in a wily smile. Like most old men, his teeth were crooked and discolored.

Judging from his bald pate and creased, leathery skin, Scipio estimated Fabius to be at least fifty. Like himself, Fabius wore full military regalia, sans helmet, as if he had conquered Spain. Scipio noted that Fabius clutched an ebony baton with a golden eagle affixed to the end, the symbol of his office, as if to remind the junior officer of his superior rank.

Scipio was a soldier, and brought himself to attention to salute his superior, striking his breast with his fist.

"You have brought great honor to the arms of Rome," Fabius said in his scratchy voice. "I trust you have had evidence of our appreciation during your triumph."

Scipio stiffened perceptibly at this praise, knowing that a predator often tries to deceive its prey before striking. Off to one side, Laelius also tensed, hoping Scipio would heed his advice to recognize that politics could be as hazardous as combat. Even more so, considering that Scipio could not resort to brute force to save the day in the Forum as he had at Ilipa.

Fabius held out his hand, and an aide slapped a vellum scroll bound in a red ribbon into it. He carefully slipped off the ribbon and unrolled the document to read from it, addressing Scipio and the assemblage:

"As an expression of the gratitude of the people of Rome, the Senate has voted to bestow upon you ten thousand *iugera* of fertile land in Campesium, together with the villa and all livestock located thereon."

Scipio rocked back slightly on his heels at this news as the crowd broke into applause again. Ten thousand acres! As if his booty from Spain had not already made him rich beyond his wildest dreams!

He bowed graciously, acknowledging the applause, and held up his hand for silence, quickly granted.

"I thank the Senate for this honor. I have been blessed by the gods with the opportunity to conquer for Rome a new territory," he said solemnly in a voice loud enough for all to hear. "For myself, I recognize that the victory was won by the men of the legions under my command, aided by the kind fortune bestowed upon us by the great god Neptune."

Laelius noted the murmurs of approval from the crowd. *That was good*, he thought. *They like humility in a young officer.*

"I shall not overlook the generosity of the god Neptune," Scipio said. "I hereby pledge to the people of Rome that I will raise a temple to his honor, a temple worthy of the triumph he has granted us."

Laelius arched his eyebrows as the crowd burst out with a roar of approval. Apparently, Scipio had taken his advice to heart and was proving quite adept at politicking.

The portly senator Flavius Marcinius Calvus, rumored to be profiteering from Hannibal's periodic raids throughout the countryside, stepped forward.

"All Rome shall take note of your noble gesture," said Marcinius in a deep, sonorous tone. "Let us now retire to the feast we have planned in your honor."

With that, the throng swept Scipio away, heading for the Palatine district. Most of Rome's elite kept homes there, including Marcinius, who would be hosting the reception for Scipio. Laelius watched them go, hoping that his young general would not make any gaffes. He turned his thoughts to the line of floats, prisoners, and trophy wagons still assembled at the base of the Capitoline, awaiting his attention. The immensity of his task soured his demeanor, and he decided to get about the job.

The principal street that encircled the fashionable Palatine district was the Clivus Victoriae, and the most modest of the houses, generally occupied by the mercantile class, fronted this boulevard. A number of side streets trailed off from it, leading up the steep hillside, the idea generally being that the higher one went to build a home into the spongy earth, the better the view back to the north where the bulk of the city's grandest buildings were located. One of these lanes, the Vicus Trabonius, wound upward all the way to the peak, where the newly built home of Flavius Marcinius Calvus had been carefully sited to provide a brilliant facade to counterpoint the large public buildings.

Marcinius had retained the architect Xaerxes to build his home. It was a controversial choice. Xaerxes was a noted artisan who had traveled extensively throughout Greece and Macedonia and brought back many of the classical refinements so evident in the architecture of those countries. Quite a number of his innovations had become the rage among the elite circles of Roman society. Xaerxes was also known to prefer the companionship of male lovers, a practice universally condemned in public if somewhat tolerated in private. In Marcinius, Xaerxes had found an ideal patron who gave him unfettered discretion in the choice of materials and the implementation of his designs. The result was a spectacular palace, extraordinarily lavish, that only fueled the rumors about the source of his client's seemingly newfound wealth.

Marcinius had acquired several smaller houses ringing the top of the hill and had them demolished to make way for his immense structure. Then, he had consented to a controversial design that was either a disaster or a stroke of brilliance, depending on one's choice of critic. Rather than follow custom and orient the front of the house to the north, facing the Capitol, Xaerxes had built a lane to follow the crest of the hill back around to the south, and there provided a grand portico entrance framed by pilastered columns on either side of shallow stairs that rose to an elegant veranda. And for the all-important north facade, the architect had created a monument in the form of a broad expanse of granite with likenesses of the gods carved in relief, giving context for the temples in clear view from its regal balcony. The balcony itself opened onto a huge study, in which it was said the senator concocted his money-making schemes.

The house itself was an expansive rectangle of open and airy rooms built around a lush garden, where a pool stocked with fish reflected a sculpture garden of voluptuous nymphs, mermaids, and goddesses. The brick-and-mortar structure had been completely sheathed in the finest marbles, painstakingly chosen for their complementary hues. Innovative shutters with louvered panels could be opened and closed to admit or block light and air through the windows without the necessity of removing the entire shutter. A select group of muralists had been commissioned to depict the events of Roman history on the plastered walls, so that the house itself might even be considered a museum.

Having erected so magnificent a structure, Marcinius could hardly be expected to be penurious when it came to furnishing the dwelling. Here again, no expense had been spared to satisfy the exacting tastes of Xaerxes. Enormous jade vases replete with profusions of flowers flanked polished ebony statues. Doors of cast bronze inlaid with silver beckoned entry to rooms furnished with extraordinary works of carpentry and upholstery from all corners of the known world. Intricate tapestries, delicate porcelain figurines, gleaming golden urns, and an abundance of decorative embellishments adorned every corner of the palatial estate.

"It's fantastic," Scipio was forced to admit as his host guided him on a tour of the grounds. The rest of the invited guests were assembling in the atrium garden, where a lavish feast had been laid on. Scipio had changed out of the formal military garb and now was clad in a simple white toga, unadorned with any insignia of his station, and plain leather sandals.

"Well," Marcinius said with a slightly weary tone, "I gave Xaerxes an unlimited budget, and I'm afraid he exceeded it."

Scipio smiled, trying to comprehend what this splendor must have cost. "I shall endeavor to avoid retaining him to renovate my new villa," he said.

Marcinius arched a heavy eyebrow and glanced at Scipio with a sidelong look. "Do you expect to retire to the countryside?" he asked, careful not to sound too anxious.

Scipio considered the question for a moment, and was struck by a startling realization: they wanted him to take up residence in the Campesium, distant from the seat of power. That was why they had granted him the estate! Oh, they were crafty, his adversaries. He began to understand what he would be up against if they would gamble a huge estate just to try to get him out of their hair.

He decided on evasion. "I have not seen it yet. How can I say?"

Marcinius, far too skilled a politician to push the direct approach, countered with circumspection. "You have had enough triumph for an entire career, and you haven't even settled down yet. A young man like you needs to find a wife, establish a household, and start a family."

An image of Vibiana flashed through Scipio's mind. He quickly dismissed the thought. "I cannot think of such domestic matters while our most hated enemy continues to breathe Italian air," Scipio said, his pride getting the better of his discretion.

"I understand you have sworn an oath before your troops to bring Hannibal to battle," Marcinius said.

Scipio did not shirk. "It is true."

"I cannot approve," Marcinius said without reproach. "After Cannae—with fifty thousand of the flower of our youth lost on a single afternoon—I cannot see lining up against Hannibal again. Fabius is correct: no boastful movements to confront Hannibal. There is considerable dissatisfaction with our dear consul Nero, who took a frightful risk by leaving his post to join in the attack on Hasdrubal. He will not be trusted with another command."

Scipio took in this intelligence without showing any trace of emotion. He had regarded Nero as his most serious rival. If Marcinius was right, Scipio's path to the consulship was unobstructed.

"All we must do is hold our breath and wait for Hannibal to wear himself out," Marcinius was saying. "Already we see Hannibal unable to hold his conquests, being constantly forced to forage for food and money. You have won the war in Spain for us, and Fabius is winning the war here in Italy. There is no reason to go charging off after Hannibal and invite some new disaster."

Marcinius paused before an enormous mural, depicting the legend of the Iliad. The detailing was intricately balanced, and various scenes were intermeshed in a burst of bright colors—the painter must have labored for months at his project. Marcinius pointed to a corner where two superbly muscled nude men were locked in mortal combat. "Hector and Achilles," he said. After a pause, he added quietly, "That is the essence of the tragedy. It was hopeless for Hector. Achilles could not be beaten in a head-to-head combat. I fear that Hannibal may be Carthage's Achilles. I was a friend of your father's. I would not want you to share Hector's fate."

Scipio hardened his gaze. "Even Achilles was vulnerable—and so is Hannibal."

"Achilles was defeated only through the intervention of the gods," Marcinius pointed out.

Scipio nodded, acknowledging the point. "Just as Neptune intervened to help me at Cartagena," he said in rebuttal, and quickly moved away to let the point sink in.

The course of their tour brought them back to the atrium, where a small group of musicians filled the night air with light background music. The atrium was illuminated by a half dozen special lamps, each featuring fourteen flaxen wicks burning olive oil. Scipio glimpsed at the buffet spread out in the sculpture garden. Large tables for the guests were arranged around the long, elegant reflecting pool fed by three working fountains, a feat of modern plumbing.

As with everything in this house, the spread had been carried to wretched excess. An immense table was laden with all manner of poultry, from broiled squab to baked wild turkey, stuffed with a mouthwatering blend of breading and rice. At either end of this menagerie lay two enormous roasted pigs, each with a carver to cut a slice to the guest's preference. Another table towered with huge platters of roast mutton, veal, and thick country sausages, and massive portions of prime rib of beef. Those with a preference for fish would not be disappointed by the wide variety of smoked tunnyfish, fresh tuna, broiled scallops, and boiled calamari. A smaller table bore salads and bowls filled with all manner of greens mixed with tomatoes, shallots, celery, and carrots and glazed with three different combinations of dressings utilizing varying quantities of olive oil and garlic. And there was an astounding offering of vegetables, ranging from braised broccoli to steamed cauliflower to a tantalizing mixture of exotic marinated peppers, eggplant, and squash. It seemed to go on forever—olives, artichokes, cheeses, breads, dumplings, fruits, pastries, cakes dipped in honey, jellies, figs. . . .

Dozens of servants scurried about, keeping the tables well stocked and topping off the guests' cups with wine. Marcinius had spared no expense. The wine was not watered, and a handful of hired guards ringed the atrium to intervene quickly if anyone got out of hand. No drunken sot would do any harm to the extraordinary furnishings!

"I trust that our modest feast meets with your approval," Marcinius said, seeing that Scipio was rendered speechless at the breadth of the offerings. "Come, there is someone you should meet."

Marcinius took Scipio by the arm and led him to the center of the atrium, where he caught the attention of a somewhat young, lanky man with a thick head of blazing red hair and piercing gray eyes, who was engaged in an animated conversation with several men Scipio recognized as senators.

"Our women cheapen themselves with all these cosmetics," the man was saying to the senators, speaking with a passion borne of sincerity, a rare thing in Roman politics. His relatively common clothes and lack of jewelry, as well as his dialect and gestures, betrayed him as a man of the countryside, clearly a plebeian. "We should pass a law making it illegal for a Roman noblewoman to appear in public wearing cosmetics."

"Now, Cato," said a handsome senator, thoroughly patrician in his bearing and manner, "we get enough complaints about the law concerning colorful clothing. I cannot imagine the trouble we'd have if we outlawed cosmetics!"

"Gentlemen," Marcinius cut in amiably, "let's not have any politicking concerning the public morals at a gathering dedicated to the honor of our famous general, Publius Cornelius Scipio. Scipio, this is Marcus Portius Cato, of Tusculum, our censor."

Scipio bowed respectfully to the wiry redhead, acknowledging the immense power of the man's office. The public censor was responsible for counting the citizen population and organizing it, according to wealth, into the voting blocs called *centuries* for meetings of the Assembly. But the censor also controlled the public treasury, leased public property, settled water rights, constructed and maintained public buildings, and arranged for the construction of roads and sewers. This young man certainly was a force to be reckoned with.

"And this gentleman I believe you already know," Marcinius said, indicating the carefully manicured and coiffed senator who had been arguing with Cato.

"Indeed," Scipio agreed, shaking hands with the senator. "Greetings, Quintus Valerius Caldus."

Caldus nodded in Scipio's direction. "I was a longtime admirer of his father's," Caldus explained to Cato, who of course as a plebeian was regarded an outsider among the circle of Roman elite.

"Cato here is living proof of the opportunity for advancement that our Roman society provides," Marcinius said in his most placating voice. "After you left for Spain, he came to live in the city, and very efficiently went about the business of making himself a patron of so many clients that he was not even challenged in the last election."

Cato gave his much older colleague a cynical look. "All that I know about the business of being a patron," he said, "I learned from you, Marcinius."

Marcinius bowed slightly at this backhanded compliment. The client-patron relationship was the bedrock upon which the Roman Republic was built. Less fortunate Roman citizens could obtain a measure of political and legal protection and a source of money in an emergency by agreeing to become the client of a wealthy and powerful patron. In return, the client was obligated to be present in his toga to accompany the patron daily on his way to the Forum, so as to enhance his patron's prestige through the exhibition of an entourage. And, of course, the client owed the patron support at election time. No senator stood as patron to more clients than did Marcinius.

Cato changed the subject. "It is indeed an honor to finally meet the great general," he said, speaking more to the bystanders than to Scipio. "All of Rome is singing your praises."

Scipio noticed that Cato was squinting hard at him, and he realized that Cato must be plagued with poor eyesight, which perhaps explained his lack of military service.

"Rome," said Scipio in reply, "merely is pleased finally to have something to celebrate."

He was surprised at Cato's response.

"I believe that the distress Hannibal has inflicted upon us is only the punishment of the gods for our own wicked ways," Cato said earnestly. "Our morals have declined, and so it is only natural that our enemies seek to exploit our weakness."

Scipio had not heard this theory before, and Cato plunged ahead.

"There is no better evidence of the sad state of Roman cultural development than this very house," Cato said, evidently unperturbed about insulting Marcinius in his presence. "Everywhere about us, we see the Greek influence. Greek is the universal language—even we Latins use it to communicate with our allies. Are we unable to develop a Roman architecture or Roman art? Are we condemned to blindly follow the Greek pattern in all of our culture?"

Before Scipio could reply, Cato drew closer.

"Speaking of Greeks, I understand that some of your own senior officers indulge in the Greek habit. Given this, it is not difficult to understand how you could have been confronted by a mutiny while you were in Spain."

The ferocity of this assault, in so pleasant a setting, caught Scipio completely off guard, and he began to splutter a response, but Marcinius cut in, gracefully extracting Scipio from the awkward confrontation.

"Excuse us," he said smoothly to Cato, "but you must not monopolize the general's time since there are so many other noble Romans who wish to make his acquaintance. You will have an opportunity to continue your discussion later, I am sure."

With that, he hustled Scipio away and led him to the proscenium opening to the atrium, where each guest was being greeted by a young woman.

"Who does he think he is?" Scipio muttered, angered at Cato's slur against his officers.

"Cato has appointed himself the guardian of Roman morals," Marcinius said. "That makes him a threat to the liberty of us all. Ah, here is the apple of my eye."

They were now in the presence of the woman.

"Father, where have you been?" she asked lightly. Then, realizing that the guest of honor stood with her father, she blushed and bowed in his direction. "Excuse me," she said to Scipio, "but I have been struggling to recognize all of these people. You are better suited for this job, Father, since you seem to know everyone in Rome."

Marcinius laughed agreeably, and his massive belly quivered. "Scipio, meet my daughter, Marcia. She has been the keeper of my household since her mother died years ago."

Scipio bowed in return and took this young lady under consideration. In the Roman custom, she had no personal name, but rather took a feminized version of her father's family name. A classic Roman beauty, she had been granted smooth skin, lightly olive in color, a large, voluptuous mouth, straight nose, and lustrous brown eyes beneath thick lashes. Her straight black hair was pulled back behind her ears and formed into a complex braid that extended well down her back. A cream-colored sleeveless dress flattered her figure, which appeared to be full with just a whisper of thickness through the hips. Scipio thought it odd that so striking a beauty would still be unmarried, since Roman girls as young as thirteen were frequently the subject of arranged marriages. He decided to wait for the answer to this puzzle.

Marcia recognized his scrutiny and blushed again. Awkwardly, she excused herself and hurried off.

A keen observer, Marcinius too had taken note of Scipio's appraisal of his daughter. "I can't come to grips with the fact that she's a woman now," Marcinius said, watching her scurry into the crowd. "She was only a child when her mother died, and I'll always think of her as a six-year-old. I can't bear to arrange a marriage for her, although there have been plenty of suitors, believe me. Cato included!"

Seeing Scipio's shocked reaction, Marcinius laughed. "Yes! Can you imagine my Marcia married to that windbag? Well, turning down suitors is a tricky business. To avoid ill will by the family of any rejected suitor, I have made it known that I have allowed Marcia to pick her own husband."

For the second time in a short interval, Scipio was startled.

"I know it's highly unusual. I'm sure our friend Cato disapproves of my break with Roman tradition. But it is an expedient way to avoid the dilemma of picking her husband. Come, Scipio, let us receive your admirers."

Scipio and Marcinius took up a position at the entrance to the atrium and began greeting the long line of well-wishers. All of the elite members of Roman society had been invited. Although Scipio knew most of them only on a casual basis, nearly all of them were eager now to claim his friendship. He was particularly dismayed at how many of these near-strangers professed to have been close friends of his father or grandfather. It seemed to him that the most complimentary individuals were the ones who had been most critical of his appointment to lead the expedition. Still, he found himself warming to the task, feeling the political juices beginning to flow.

A servant approached Marcinius and whispered something in his ear. The senator nodded and then sent the messenger along.

"Scipio," he said, "we have a special visitor asking for you. Come with me." Marcinius led him back into the foyer and through a long hall, making his way toward the front entrance.

As they rounded a corner, Scipio looked up and saw two familiar faces. He broke into a broad grin.

"Mother! And Lucius! But what are you doing in Rome?"

Before anyone could answer, Pomponia rushed to her eldest son and clutched him tight against her for long moments, fighting back tears. She had never fully recovered from the brutal circumstances of her husband's death and had lived in constant fear while Scipio was in the field, nearly going into a panic whenever a message from Rome arrived, terrified that it would bring dreadful news. Now, reunited with him, she could not contain her emotions, and she wept freely.

"Let me look at you," she said, pulling back slightly, and dabbing at her tears with a silk scarf. She ran her hands over his face and neck. "Oh, you're so tan. And your skin is so dry—you promised me to rub yourself with oils every day!"

They all laughed, and Scipio noticed that his mother had aged in his absence, undoubtedly from worry. Her hair had gone completely gray and telltale dark circles sat under her eyes—the same sparkling blue eyes she had passed to him—and at their corners were clearly discernable lines. Reminded of the toll his ambitions had exacted from her, Scipio wondered whether he should defer his plans for a new campaign.

He looked up at his brother, Lucius, only sixteen, who was taking it all in quietly and patiently awaiting his hero brother's attention. Lucius was the image of his older brother, similar in looks and bearing, a Cornelius, no question about it. Scipio released himself from his mother's arms and clasped his brother's arm in the formal military greeting.

"I see that you intend to keep up the family tradition," Scipio said, taking note of the thin purple stripe running down the left side of his brother's toga.

"May the gods bless my career as they have blessed yours," Lucius said, clearly proud of his brother's accomplishments.

Scipio started to suggest that he intended to take Lucius into the field as a junior officer in his next campaign, but conscious of the sad look in his mother's eyes, he decided not to bring it up now. Instead, he said, "There'll be plenty of time and no shortage of opportunity for you, Lucius. Come, now, why didn't you tell me you were coming to Rome? Did you see the parade?"

"We wanted to surprise you," Pomponia said, putting her arm around her son's muscular abdomen. "And of course we saw the parade. You looked magnificent on that horse."

Marcinius stepped forward. "May I suggest that we rejoin the feast? I'm afraid that mob will leave nothing for us to eat if we don't."

They laughed again and moved toward the atrium. Marcinius let the family members get ahead of him, then slipped away to mingle with the crowd. Politics was his vocation, and an occasion like this was a gold mine of opportunities to spread his influence.

He moved fluently through the guests, who had by now begun a ferocious assault on the delicacies in the sculpture garden, carrying their hauls to the seating area adjacent to the reflecting pool, there to gorge themselves relentlessly at Marcinius' expense. Marcinius possessed the most important attribute of any good politician: a prodigious memory for the details of people's lives. He remembered their names, their ancestry, their occupations, what their children did, to whom their children were married, the sexes of their grand-children, and all the other minutiae of their existence. This of course had the effect of making whomever he was speaking to feel they were important too, if so important a man as Flavius Marcinius Calvus, senator of Rome, was so knowledgeable about their affairs.

He came upon Quintus Fabius Maximus, holding court with a half-dozen or so minor officials, favor-seekers, and assorted syco-phants. Unlike Scipio, Fabius had not changed out of his ceremonial armor, as if he needed constantly to remind himself of his own rank.

"Ah, our host," Fabius said in that squeaky voice of his. "You've outdone yourself this time, my dear Marcinius."

The group surrounding the general murmured its approval, which it would have done even if he had suggested that the sky was brown rather than blue.

"It pleases me that our modest celebration meets with your approval," Marcinius said in reply. "I wonder if I might take a word with you privately."

With a nod of his head, Fabius dismissed his entourage, and the hangers-on scattered, heading for the food.

"I see," Marcinius said to his colleague when they were gone, "that your treatments have failed to produce the desired outcome." Marcinius knew that Fabius, always self-conscious about his nearly hairless pate, saw a barber who had prescribed a mixture of deer marrow, bear fat, hellebore, and pepper to stimulate hair growth.

Fabius frowned. "Yes," he sighed. "The barber assured me that smelly concoction would produce results. Well, I smeared it on my head every night for a fortnight, without any benefit, as you can see. If I were still dictator, I'd have the rascal hung upside down in the Macellum."

Marcinius chuckled.

"How fares our distinguished honoree?" Fabius asked, a note of contempt in his voice.

"He is content," Marcinius said, looking across the atrium to a throng of people who flocked about Scipio. "His mother and brother are here, all the way from the Cornelius estate at Florentia. I suspect they'll keep him occupied for a while."

"Were you able to discern his intentions?" Fabius asked cautiously.

"Not with certainty. But I think your effort to retire him to the Campesium will not work. He's got his sights set on Hannibal. And he's a very determined young man."

Fabius spat into a nearby golden urn, exquisitely detailed with likenesses of tigers and eagles. "Hannibal? He thinks just because he had success against the rear echelon of the Carthaginian Army in a backwater like Spain that he can go head to head with Hannibal? I could have taken Spain myself with half the men we gave Scipio, if I hadn't been so preoccupied with keeping Hannibal bottled up in southern Italy."

Marcinius could not help but look askance at his companion. The senator harbored no illusions about the relative merits of Fabius' military skills versus Scipio's. He also had a clear-eyed view of how he would have to coach his colleague to manage the problem presented by Scipio's return to Rome.

"I have always admired your willingness to face the facts and analyze them for what they are," he said amiably. "You did so after Cannae, refusing to let our wounded 'Roman honor' drag us into any more foolhardy contests with Hannibal. And so it surprises me that you let yourself feel threatened by so young and easily distracted a man as our dear accomplished Scipio."

Fabius prickled at the suggestion that he was letting his ego get the better of him. "The young man has a talent for the military life, there's no denying that," he said in reply. "But Hannibal is another matter indeed. I have been in the field against him, face to face. He moves his cavalry like lightning and has a gift for concealing infantry in the natural features of the terrain. Just when you think you've finally got him beaten, he springs some trick, and the next thing you know, all the men are running for their lives."

"I do not think we are in disagreement concerning the need to prevent our gallant young comrade from rashly exposing us to another catastrophe," Marcinius said evenly. "The question is, how can we stop him?"

Fabius stroked his chin, thinking. He truly was sickened by the carnage the war had wrought, not only in terms of lost lives and damage to property, but in the upheaval of Roman society. Tremendous changes in trade, agriculture, and finance were brought about by the war. Furthermore, he was aware that Marcinius was motivated by far different considerations. The senator had done very well by Fabius' containment strategy. Every time Hannibal went on a rampage, property values in the assaulted region would plummet, and Marcinius' agents would swoop in to pick up the bargains. He'd bought up half of Italy at dirt-cheap prices. And then, when Fabius got around to winning back the conquered and devastated territory, Marcinius would sell at huge profits.

"The people are, of course, appreciative of your selfless efforts to contest every inch of Roman soil in Hannibal's hands," Marcinius said carefully, "but there will also be considerable agitation to send Scipio to do battle with Hannibal. Clearly, the young man holds definite promise, and in due time I myself may come to favor entrusting him with a large enough army to do the job."

Fabius cocked his head toward Marcinius, listening carefully. He noted that the senator had said *in due time*. That meant he had something else up his sleeve for now.

"We must not lose sight of the fact that Hannibal is one of the great generals of history, like it or not. Perhaps on a plane with Alexander himself. Why, he has completely routed our most experienced generals, including Scipio's father at the Ticinus. And how can we ever forget the disaster at Cannae? Our fine consul, Terentius Varro, commanded an army three times the size of any Scipio has ever commanded—and he met with catastrophe. No, Scipio's day may come, but that day still lies in the far-off future."

Fabius nodded, imagining how well that argument would ring in the halls of the Forum. However, a problem presented itself. "Your position is well-phrased, Marcinius," he said. "But what are we to do with him in the meantime?"

Marcinius smiled. "That is a solution, my dear General, that I hope Scipio himself will present."

Fabius looked at Marcinius. Now that the senator had made it clear that he would join with Fabius in keeping Young Scipio from doing anything foolish, he decided to disclose what he knew about Scipio's plans. "I suspect I know what he has in mind."

Marcinius was a little surprised. Why had Fabius been withholding information? These military types were all the same, always distrustful of the very civilian government they were sworn to serve. He sighed, weary of intrigue. "And what might that be?"

"Perhaps you did not take sufficient notice of Scipio's communication to the Senate regarding his negotiations with Syphax, king of the Masaesulii."

Marcinius was genuinely confused. "I thought it a little odd that he would leave his command in Spain to conduct personal negotiations with an African potentate for a treaty of neutrality. This has no benefit to Rome that I can see, and so, yes, I gave it little attention."

"I have reason to believe that the treaty of neutrality is extremely important to Scipio," Fabius said, pausing for effect. "Scipio is planning an invasion of Africa and intends to march through the territory of Syphax en route to Carthage."

Even for Marcinius, who was a veteran at not showing reaction when he heard startling propositions, this was too much. "An invasion of Africa? To attack Carthage? That's preposterous!"

"Actually, it wouldn't be a bad idea, but for the fact that Hannibal is here, posted on our very doorstep. We cannot give Scipio the resources necessary to prevail in a campaign in Africa, and still maintain a sufficient force to protect us from Hannibal."

"But I thought Scipio wanted to bring Hannibal to battle," Marcinius said, still trying to think through the implications of what he was hearing.

"He does," Fabius said. "But he wants to fight Hannibal in Africa, not here."

"Well," Marcinius said, "we certainly will have our hands full with this matter."

"Yes," Fabius agreed. "I hope we are up to the challenge."

———

Pomponia and Lucius preceded Scipio through the buffet, piling their silver platters with an assortment of delicacies, and took places at the head table, on a dais constructed at the center of the reflecting pool. Scipio found himself contented, as if his mother's presence had somehow muted the fires of ambition burning in him. The family sat, laughing gaily and exchanging catty observations about other members of Roman high society who were plowing their way through the food.

"There's the freedman, Quintio Petrarcus Vindicus," Pomponia said in a whisper, indicating a rotund individual helping himself to a huge portion of roast mutton. "He was a slave in the house of Vellucius, and then, after he managed to save up enough to buy his freedom, bought out his former master's grain business. They say he made a fortune by speculating in grain when Syracuse went over to Carthage. But he got out just before word arrived that Marcellus had recaptured the city. And now Marcellus and Quintio are partners in a number of ventures."

Scipio frowned, unwilling to believe that a Roman general would tip a money-grubbing merchant about the outcome of a battle before the news was announced to the public. He was also surprised to learn that his mother was such a gossip. He turned to Lucius and asked, "What do you think of Marcia?"

Lucius gave him a curious look. "Why, Scipio, I thought some camp girl had stolen your heart," he said mischievously.

Scipio lifted his index finger to his lips, indicating for Lucius to hush, but it was useless. Both members of his family apparently knew all about his assignations with Vibiana.

"Oh, don't act the prude with me," his mother said with a twinkle in her eyes. "Do you think I don't know what goes on in a military camp?"

Scipio blushed hotly. He would not discuss this with his mother, and turned the subject back to Marcia. "I only asked because I understand that her father has allowed her to pick her own husband. How strange!"

"Well, here she comes now. You can pursue whatever course you choose," Pomponia replied.

Marcia, as the official hostess of the event, was entitled to a place on the dais. She stepped lightly onto the platform, bearing a small plate with only a few vegetables. She took a place directly across from Scipio.

He introduced her to his mother and brother, then said to her casually, "You've barely sampled your own feast."

"Oh, food doesn't interest me," she said lightly, picking at a marinated artichoke. "And preparing for this feast has taken all my energy. I can never enjoy anything that I've been so involved in putting together."

"Well, I certainly am grateful for all your trouble on my behalf," Scipio said.

She looked up at him with a peculiar expression. "Oh, *please*," she said. "Sitting here makes me the envy of every unmarried woman in Rome—and more than a few married ones as well."

Scipio shifted uncomfortably, still unaccustomed to his newfound fame. "I should think that living in this house would have made you the envy of every girl in Rome, long before I came upon the scene."

"This house," she said emphatically, "is a millstone about my neck. Do you have any idea what it takes just to keep it clean and organized, and to keep the servants from robbing us blind?"

"Certainly more effort than organizing an army for battle," Scipio laughed. A servant filled his goblet with wine, while another poured a sweet nectar from pressed fruits into Marcia's cup. No Roman noblewoman would be seen taking wine in public.

Marcia sipped the beverage and wrinkled her nose. "You men have all the luck," she said.

Scipio found her charming, intelligent, and certainly attractive. She would make someone a good wife. But as he had indicated to her father, he had no desire to consider marriage—not while Hannibal awaited him. He decided to restrict the conversation to meaningless small talk.

"I notice that your father has many likenesses of Apollo throughout the house," he said, pointing to one particularly imposing statue nearby.

"Yes," she agreed, obviously disappointed that he had changed the topic. "Father makes a sacrifice once a week, to pray for our success in the war."

"I should think that he'd be more inclined to worship Janus," Lucius said under his breath. By his tone, Lucius no doubt intended a disparaging comparison to the two-faced god, whose one face looked to the future and the other to the past.

Scipio shot his younger brother a hostile look at this rude remark, but Marcia, well-versed in brushing aside the insults her father received, did not take offense. "Father has his critics and his supporters," she said sweetly. "But I understand that you yourself enjoy a special relationship with the gods, Neptune in particular."

Scipio looked at her in alarm. He did not know whether his mother had heard the tale about how his conception came about, and did not want her to find out now.

But Marcia was well mannered and did not push it. Instead, she said, "Father's respect for the gods is genuine. He is very religious. You may find that a useful bridge by which to win his support for any new glorious adventures you may have in mind."

Pomponia spoke up. "I've always believed that the gods had great things in store for Scipio," she said to Marcia, "but I fear even the gods can be frustrated by Senate politics."

"I was given the Spanish command by the people of Rome," Scipio pointed out.

"Ah, but times have changed," Marcia said perceptively. "The Senate had no better ideas when they allowed the common assembly to pick a leader. That will never happen again, now that things are going better."

It occurred to Scipio that his own success might now become his greatest obstacle. Clearly, the fear of Hannibal seemed to have receded, and there was a seeming indifference to his continued presence in the country.

"The righteousness of our cause," he said somewhat pompously, "will overcome any opposition."

Marcia gave him an odd look: was it an expression of latent affection, or a warning as to her father's intentions?

"Righteousness," she observed, "is the last thing that will influence the Senate."

Later, as the celebration was in full swing with the guests taking in a scandalous performance by barely clothed Assyrian dancers, Marcia approached Scipio.

"Come with me," she said. "I want to show you something."

Intrigued, he followed her out of the airy atrium and through the house to a grand stairway, elegantly cut from fine mahogany.

"Half the forests of Gaul must have been taken down to make these stairs," Scipio joked as they ascended to the second floor.

Marcia opened a bronze door, expertly balanced on its hinges so that, despite its massive weight, it swung with only a light touch from her hand—another marvel.

She led him into Marcinius' private study. The room was dark, and she lit several lamps, enabling him to see the walls lined with finely finished teak shelves, which bore row upon row of vellum scrolls and papyrus sheafs. In the center of the room stood a long desk of polished marble, delicately balanced upon a richly detailed bronze tripod base.

"Father says this is the finest private library in Rome, and that means in the entire world. He has collected an impressive variety of writings, including an original manuscript of Aristotle himself, purporting to give lessons to Alexander."

Scipio walked around the room, lightly touching some of the volumes. He was surprised that Marcinius, who pursued his wealth through the coarsest of methods, would devote his winnings to such refinement.

He found himself facing Marcia for an awkward moment, then stepped back.

"There's something else," she said, taking him by the hand to lead him over to a large wall panel installed in a track built into the tiled floor so that it could be rolled back easily. Scipio gasped at the panoramic view of the city, dominated by the Capitol, as it came before his eyes. Thousands upon thousands of torches and lamps blazed across the skyline, giving the city a shimmering effect. It was a fantastic image—he had never before seen the city from such a pinnacle.

"It must be the destiny of such a city to rule the world," Scipio murmured, awestruck by the sight.

"Perhaps," said Marcia, also looking out. She turned to face him. "Do not make the mistake of thinking that all of Rome shares your ambitions for her."

Scipio nodded. "For many, the lining of their pockets is all that matters." There was bitterness in his voice.

"You were born into money, and so have always taken it for granted," she said. "You do not appreciate that life is hard. There are so many troubles: famine, disease, war, taxes. All these things take their toll. Money helps to ease the burdens of life. That is why so many of our citizens make the pursuit of it their true religion."

Scipio was surprised at such frankness from so obvious a beneficiary of the privileged life.

"It is not clear that the war has been bad for Rome," she said carefully, as if laying out some elaborate design. "Hannibal has made as many fortunes as he has ruined. There are powerful interests who may not want to see Hannibal defeated."

Scipio felt the hairs on the back of his neck rising at this treasonous remark. The very idea that any Roman would seek to prolong the suffering of the countryside under Hannibal's scourge for mere profit was a disgrace. And yet he held his temper in order to hear her out.

"Just consider, for example, what has become of the real estate situation in the city. So long as Hannibal is laying waste to the agricultural regions, the masses huddle in fear behind Rome's walls, driving up rents and encouraging speculation of all sorts. Do you think that the speculators are ready for peace?"

He shifted uneasily.

"And do you recall how, in Rome's darkest hours after our defeat at Cannae, all those noble Romans holding public contracts came before the Senate and offered to defer receipt of payment until the end of the war?"

Scipio nodded. He considered the gesture, which enabled the Roman treasury to be dedicated to the rebuilding of the army, a prime example of the kind of sacrifice required to win the war. "They were patriots," he said.

Marcia sighed as if she were teaching a slow-witted pupil. "Those contracts are to be paid eventually, with interest. There is a very active trade in them, representing, as they do, lucrative investments. Those who arrange such trades earn handsome commissions. Ending the war will put an end to the trade."

Scipio felt overcome by an awkward discomfort. He was a man to whom propositions made sense only if presented in black and white. This mere wisp of a girl was telling him that all things came in shades of gray. Clearly, the world was more complex than he had imagined. Scipio was a man of action: give him an objective and he would meet it with all the vigor and energy at his disposal. But Marcia had brought him to this pinnacle to show him that the higher one goes, the less clear the objectives become.

"I shall overlook your outrageous suggestion that any Roman citizen wishes anything other than prompt and total victory over our enemies," he said stubbornly, his vanity preventing him from admitting she was right. "Even if there are some who would put their own profits before the interest of the state, they represent only a handful of elite personages. The people are tired of the war, and they hunger for victory."

"How strange it is," she said, reverting to her sweet tone, "that a Cornelius should find himself relying on the masses."

"Others have drawn the same observation. I only want what Rome's destiny demands, and if I must have recourse to the people to accomplish it, that is what I will do."

She smiled, as if amused at his naïveté. "Even among the masses, from whom you would draw your strength, you are not without critics."

This alarmed him, for he had thought, judging from the parade today, that he held the people in his sway.

She saw that she had piqued his curiosity. "Cato, for example, is someone of whom you should be wary."

Scipio remembered what Marcia's father had said about rejecting Cato's offer of marriage and smiled. "From what I hear," he retorted, "it is *you* who should be wary of Cato's designs!"

She rolled her eyes, laughing. "Cato posed an extraordinary threat, requiring an extraordinary precaution. Hence, I am to pick my own husband. But do not think that Cato is in the running! They say he is so cheap he drinks the same wine as his slaves, and none of the walls in his home are plastered! And he is very harsh with his slaves: when they become too old to work, he sells them for whatever he can get. And then, of course, I could never respect him, not after what he has said about you."

Scipio's brow knitted in concern. "And what is that?"

"He has suggested that you want only to return to the old ways, in which the patricians ruled and the plebeians served under their heels."

"That's absurd," he snorted hotly. "The patricians and the plebeians have shared power in the Senate for over one hundred years. I have only met this man Cato this very night. How could he say such a thing about me?"

Her eyes met his. They were lovely, liquid and full of emotion. "Cato may have bad eyesight, but he sees well enough to recognize you as a dangerous rival. He is no military man, but he is well aware of the popularity a victorious general may achieve. To someone like Cato, the man who beats Hannibal may be more dangerous to his career than Hannibal himself."

"But he has supported sending other generals to face Hannibal. Any one of them might have prevailed."

She shook her head as if hesitating to reveal a final truth. "We have sent fools to do battle with Hannibal—and none bigger than Varro, who was himself a champion of the plebeian classes. Fabius is no fool, which is why he keeps avoiding a confrontation with Hannibal. But you . . . you are something else again. You are too intense, too dedicated, too determined. You men tend to see things in terms of your own worst habits. Men like Cato are ambitious for themselves, and so they cannot believe your ambitions are merely for Rome. And then there is this nonsense about your special relationship with the gods, which you clearly choose to perpetuate because you think it somehow gives you an edge. Thus, you have rivals you do not even know about. They will not want to let you take the field against Hannibal because they think you might win."

Scipio was reeling. He felt as if he had been neatly cut open and filleted by the incisive scalpel of her political acumen.

"Come," she said, "let us return to the feast before people start talking about our prolonged absence."

As she turned to go, he reached out and grasped her arm.

"These rivals of mine—surely your father is among them."

She did not respond.

"Why, then, do you tell me these things, that I may overcome all of them?"

A knowing look passed over her features. "That," she said simply, "is a mystery you'll have to figure out for yourself."

VII

Rome

205 BC

Scipio was not so strong-headed as to ignore good advice, so he spent the late fall months carefully currying favor among influential Romans at all levels of society. In this effort, he put his new wealth to considerable advantage, relentlessly acquiring clients and cementing several advantageous relationships by agreeing to invest in mercantile ventures to exploit the Spanish territories. Several prominent men approached him seeking to arrange marriages with their daughters. By declining, Scipio might have caused considerable resentment among the rejected suitors, but he was able with his sincerity and intensity to convince the disappointed fathers that he meant soon to return to the field to bring about an end to the war, and that he could not allow himself to think of anything else until his work was finished. He carefully omitted the specifics of just how he intended to accomplish his goal.

Scipio took up residence in a respectable rented home on the Aventine. The large and airy brick-and-mortar house was of typical design yet gracefully appointed, with a delightful peristyle garden that nicely suited Scipio's love of the outdoors. He purchased a bevy of slaves to assist Narcussa in the day-to-day administration of the household, including a Macedonian taken prisoner years earlier during the unsuccessful raid on the Italian coast by King Philip shortly after Cannae. This raid had caused quite a stir in Rome:

Philip, thinking to add to his dominion while the Romans were pre-occupied with Hannibal, had landed a sizeable force in Italy, only to be sent packing back to Macedonia by a coalition of Italian states. Philip's opportunism, coming as it had when the Romans were at their low ebb, had left a bad taste in many a Roman mouth. There was certain to be retribution when the war with Carthage finally was over. At any rate, Scipio's Macedonian was highly skilled at culinary matters, and, thus equipped, Scipio entertained often.

During this time, Scipio took care to keep in top physical con-dition, each day subjecting himself to a rigorous physical regimen, including practice at the martial arts, working with a sword twice as heavy as normal so as to strengthen his arm and quicken his reflexes. And he dutifully made the social rounds, enduring a seemingly unending string of weddings, feasts of religious celebration, and din-ners. At all of these events, he was lavishly praised and toasted as the conqueror of Spain. These gatherings would have been unbearably tedious but for the frequent appearance of Marcia, always accom-panied by her father. She continued to feed Scipio valuable political information, and gradually the painful memory of Vibiana came to be superseded by his fondness for Marcinius' daughter.

Also during these functions, Scipio developed a profound dislike for Cato the censor. The man was always performing for the bene-fit of anyone who might listen, constantly exercising his formidable powers of speech. He had become a successful lawyer, providing his services in lawsuits without demanding a fee of any kind, and was making a name for himself as a vigorous and effective orator. But, oh, how he inveighed against the luxurious refinements of life that Scipio and other wealthy Romans held dear! Cato was perfectly content with a cold breakfast, a frugal dinner, the simplest clothing, and the most modest of cottages in which to live. Bad enough that he might choose such deprivations for himself, but he seemed utterly intoler-ant of any diversity from his particular views.

Even worse, he was pompous, constantly handing down all nature of pithy sayings and pronouncements on the moral decline of the Roman people. At one party, Scipio summoned up all his resolve to hold his tongue as Cato held forth.

"This proposal," said Cato, regarding a bill pending in the Senate to make a free distribution of corn to the public, "is quite unjustified. But it is difficult to argue with the belly, since it has no ears!"

After the laughter had died down, he said, "The Roman people are like sheep: you cannot budge one of them on its own, but when they are in a flock, they all follow their leaders in a single body. In the Assembly, they allow themselves to be led by men whose advice they would never think of following in their private affairs."

Quintus Valerius Caldus, his slightly graying locks combed back on his leonine head, had heard enough. "How unusual for a champion of the plebeians to suddenly be so critical of his chosen favorites," he said, his rich, dignified voice tinged with sarcasm.

"Do not confuse my criticism of the corn bill with any conversion to the patrician outlook," Cato snapped in reply. "There are hundreds of plebeians for each and every patrician. They sooner or later will have their way."

"You are an advocate of rule by the mob, then?" Caldus asked sharply.

"I believe in the power of the people," Cato retorted. "But they are prone to temptation and laziness. It is our role as leaders to rein in their worst tendencies."

Scipio had heard enough and drifted away to seek the pleasure of Marcia's company.

Perhaps as a subconscious affront to Cato, Scipio began devoting considerable time to developing plans for a spectacular temple honoring Neptune, relying heavily on the influence of Greek architecture. Having heard Marcinius' lamentations about the cost of his home, Scipio decided to pass on Xaerxes and instead selected an architect named Nodemas to design the temple. Land was procured on the Via Apulia, between the temples of Cybele and Apollo, after considerable wrangling over the price. The centerpiece of the temple was to be an enormous likeness of the god himself, sixty feet high, holding a trident poised for action, reigning over scores of denizens of the deep. Oddly enough, there seemed to be no Roman talented enough to undertake the complex commission, and so Scipio was forced to resort to a Greek sculptor. As contracts were awarded for the construction of the massive edifice, Scipio took care in the selection of builders to lay a political foundation as well as one of stone.

In the year-end elections, Scipio's efforts bore fruit. The Assembly, already dazzled with the conquest of Spain, was eager to embrace a winning general after years of lackluster candidates. Scipio was elected consul with no dissenting votes; the other consul elected was Publius Licinius Crassus, the handpicked candidate of the Marcinius-Fabius faction. And, regrettably, Cato was re-elected censor.

The new year was duly celebrated with the customary ceremony to install the new consuls. Scipio and Crassus marched in a parade, preceded by scores of priests and officials bearing bundles of rods wrapped around an ax, symbolic of the consuls' authority to have a man beaten or his head cut off. The highlight of the event was the sacrifice of one hundred white oxen, fulfilling Scipio's pledge made on the eve of the battle of Ilipa. The entrails were read by the priests, to whom Laelius had paid a visit the night before, bearing a hefty bag of sesterces. The auspices were therefore pronounced favorable, to everyone's relief. Having satisfied the requirements of custom and religious law, the procession of officials walked to the Capitol, where the Senate was convened to greet the new consuls and formally review the state of the nation.

By custom, at this meeting of the Senate, the new consuls would draw lots in order to determine their respective spheres of authority, traditionally in Italy, Sicily, or Gaul, depending on what was the particular trouble spot of the hour. However, since Scipio had other plans in mind, he made a motion to dispense with the drawing of lots so that he might present a plan for ending the war. Everyone was eager to hear his plan, of course, and Marcinius and Cato went along, deciding to save their thunder for the right moment. Their supporters immediately fell into line, and the motion carried.

Scipio, looking trim, relaxed, and very handsome in a brand-new toga, moved solemnly to the Rostrum, at the center of the Forum. He paused to take in the setting, wishing his father could be present for this moment. The chamber was immense, ringed with tall and slender Ionic columns supporting a massive vaulted ceiling of terrazzo tile. Each of the columns featured elaborate ornamentation at the base and gilding at the top, forming a glittering ring about the entire hall. Between the columns were finely carved statues of various deities: imperious Jupiter with his lightning bolt, impish Apollo with his flute, old Neptune with his trident, stern Mars with his spear, the sensuous Venus, and on and on. The senators, over three hundred in all, sat in concentric semicircles on white marble benches stacked to form an amphitheater. The marble made for uncomfortable seating, and one could tell whether a particular day's debate was likely to be lengthy by the number of senators who carried pillows to cushion their noble rumps from the unforgiving surface. Lighting was provided by rows of candles set in golden candelabra. At the center of the wide semicircle were two curules, ivory backless chairs reserved for the consuls.

Finally, Scipio spoke, in a loud, clear voice that betrayed not a whit of nervousness but carried the timbre of his conviction and intensity.

"My friends, for fourteen long years our native land has lived under the shadow of the intruder, Hannibal. Far better men than I have taken the field against him and fallen victim to his wily tricks—my own father included. Our people have fled the countryside to cower in fear behind the walls of Rome, and Hannibal has marched through Italy, making his mischief, plundering and persuading our allies to abandon a Rome that cannot protect them. Our armies, under the leadership of our noble and distinguished colleague Quintus Fabius Maximus, have had all they can do to keep themselves in position between Hannibal and Rome, to protect our mother city from his scourge."

He paused for effect.

"If so great a man as Quintus Fabius Maximus could not drive Hannibal from our soil, I do not pretend to suggest that I could do any better. Therefore, I do not propose to take the field against Hannibal himself."

It was as if he had thrown a bucket of cold water on them. In a few moments, they began to recover, and a loud murmur rumbled through the hall: had their young champion lost his nerve?

Marcinius, however, leaned forward and kept his eyes on Scipio. Thanks to Fabius, he knew what was coming.

Scipio held up his hand for silence.

"My friends, the key to winning the war does not lie on Italian soil, but rather in Africa. It is there I propose to go. If you will but give me the men, the ships, and the resources, I propose to strike at Carthage herself. I will do to Carthage what Hannibal has done to us. I will inflict so deep a pain on the territory and people of Africa that Carthage will cry out for Hannibal to return to save them. That is the way to rid ourselves of Hannibal's shadow!"

The Senate erupted in a roar of animated conversation as little debates erupted here and there over the merits of Scipio's bold idea.

Scipio again obtained silence to continue making his case.

"The path to Carthage is open before us. Our treaty with Syphax assures us safe passage through his territory. I propose to depart with a consular army from Sicily and establish a camp in his territory, from which we will impose a terrible retribution upon the territory of Carthage."

He paused to look over the assemblage, which was entranced by the sweeping strategy he had put before them.

"Italy has suffered long; let her for a while have rest. It is Africa's turn to be devastated by fire and sword. It is time a Roman army threatens the gates of Carthage, rather than the reverse. Let Africa be the theater of war henceforward. For fourteen years, all the horrors of war have fallen thick upon *us*—terror and defeat, the devastation of our farms, the desertion of our friends. It is *her* turn now to suffer the same."

Scipio returned to the consul's curule at the head of the semicircle and waited patiently as Fabius got to his feet and shuffled to the spot Scipio had just vacated. Fabius was showing his age, but the man was still a potent force, and the chamber grew quiet without any signal from him.

"I know very well," he began with a sigh, "that in opposing this proposal to invade Africa, I shall have to face hostile criticism on two counts. First, I shall be blamed for my natural tendency to avoid precipitate action, which the young sometimes call fear or indolence, although my strategies have proven sound in practice. Secondly, I shall incur the charge of ill will and envy of the daily increasing fame of our brave young consul. From this latter suspicion surely I am defended by my past life and character, and by the distinctions I have won during my dictatorship and consulships: I have had so much honor as both a soldier and a statesman that I should think I have had too much of it, not too little."

This drew a laugh from the senators, who felt as comfortable with Fabius at the podium as they might be in a pair of old boots.

"Is it likely that now, at the end of my career, I should enter into jealous rivalry with one in the very flower of his manhood for the prize of this African campaign? Do you think that I would suggest that the task should be assigned to an old man worn out not only by work but by the sheer burden of many years? My duty is to live and die with such glory as I have already won. I prevented Hannibal from defeating us, and thus enabled you who are young and strong to bring him finally to his knees.

"Our enemy is Hannibal. With his army intact, he has been entrenched in Italy for nearly fourteen years. Hannibal is formidable still: to prefer to fight elsewhere may well look more like fear than contempt. Why then, Scipio, do you not gird yourself for the campaign that lies before you? Tell us no more that when you have crossed to Africa, Hannibal will surely follow you. Cut short those devious ways and march directly to where Hannibal is at this moment, and fight him there. You want the victor's palm for ending the war with Carthage? Remember that it is only natural to defend your own before attacking what is another's. Let there be peace in Italy before there is war in Africa. Let us feel safe ourselves before we proceed to threaten others."

This brought a murmur of approval from the Marcinius faction.

"You claim that your object is to draw Hannibal after you. So whether you fight here or there, it is with Hannibal that you will have to deal. Will you be stronger alone in Africa or here in Italy, supported by your colleague Crassus? Is not the recent victory achieved by Nero and Livius against Hasdrubal—the very same Hasdrubal you allowed to slip between your fingers in Spain—sufficient proof of what can be accomplished by two consular armies operating jointly?"

There was another rumble of agreement, and Scipio felt the tide shifting against him.

Also sensing the momentum was in his favor, Fabius tried a different tack. "Do not forget, Scipio, that when you set your eyes upon Africa, all your adventures in Spain will seem as child's play. What comparison between the two is there? With no threat from hostile fleets, you sailed from Italy to Spain and marched along a route already made safe by Roman outposts. On the Ebro you found an army hungry for battle to avenge your father. You captured Cartagena at your leisure, for the army commanded by Hasdrubal, son of Gisgo, made no effort to defend their allies. And even after you had conquered Spain, your own troops rose up in revolt, which you were forced to put down by the most brutal of means. These accomplishments are in no way comparable to a campaign in Africa, where there is no harbor open to our fleet, no conquered territory, nowhere to stand, nowhere to go, surrounded everywhere by hostile enemies."

Satisfied with his oratory, Fabius returned to his seat escorted by a round of applause.

Keep your wits, Scipio said to himself as he rose to reply.

"I do not pretend, Fabius," he said, bowing in the direction of the old general, "that I do not wish to rival your fame. Indeed, if you will pardon my saying so, my ambition is to surpass it if I can. Upon such ambition between the generations, Rome has become great, and ever should it be so.

"I am gratified by this solicitude for my well-being, yet I must say I am most puzzled by it. When my father was killed and no one else stood up to take the Spanish command, why is it that not one word was said about my youth, or the enemy's strength, or the difficulties the campaign would encounter? Are there more armies now in Africa, led by better generals, than I faced in Spain? Was I an older or more experienced general than I am now? Does it seem more natural to fight the Carthaginians in Spain than in Africa? Fabius seems to belittle my accomplishments: three Carthaginian armies beaten decisively, innumerable towns taken by force or terrified into submission, no trace left of our enemies, and the wealth of Spain poured into our coffers. Should I return, by the grace of the gods, victorious from Africa, no doubt he will again belittle my triumph!"

This brought a round of vigorous applause from Scipio's backers.

"Can there be any clearer illustration of the value of taking the offensive than Hannibal himself? There is a big difference between devastating your enemy's country and seeing your own ravaged by fire and sword. And it is fear of the unknown that always gives the darkest dread. Once in the enemy's country, you can have a clear view of his circumstances. In Africa, the Carthaginians are treacherous friends and harsh masters: her allies are fickle, ready to change sides at a whim, as we have seen in our friendship with Syphax."

He had saved his best thunder for the last, and he let them have it now.

"Fabius, I do not fear Hannibal—indeed I shall have him. But I shall draw him after me, and force him to fight on his native ground. The prize of victory will be Carthage herself, and even if I lose, Italy will be rid of Hannibal. But I pledge to all of you, upon the blessing of the gods, that we shall have victory!"

He resumed his seat to a chorus of cheers. It was clear that the Senate would be closely divided, and it was with Cato and his allies that the balance of power lay.

Cato now drew to his feet and decided to address the Senate from his seat, located to the right of the center rostrum. "I consider myself privileged to be sitting in judgment at such a notable debate, upon which the very future of our country may depend. In noble Fabius we have the voice of a most judicious reason, an approach that has more than once saved us from the folly of hot-blooded soldiers whose bold words far exceeded their modest abilities. And in our famous new consul, we may perhaps finally have the champion we have for so long awaited, who can rid us once and for all of this terrible enemy. The choice is not an easy one, my friends."

He stroked his chin, as if in deep thought, then spoke again.

"Our public funds have been exhausted by the maintenance of a war on two fronts, Spain and Italy. Now, with the necessity of maintaining garrisons in Spain, can we afford to open a third front in Africa? And even if the funds can be found, there is another danger that troubles me. Suppose that Hannibal, seeing the departure of our new consul with the military resources necessary for his campaign, chooses not to follow but rather marches on Rome? Are we to place the fate of our country in the hands of the few men left behind to shield us from Hannibal? No, my colleagues, the plan strikes me as too risky. Better to continue to hound Hannibal and wear him down until we finally get the better of him."

The members of his faction dutifully murmured their approval.

"There are other reasons to question this campaign," Cato said, warming to his theme. "All around us, we see every day the striking changes this war is visiting upon our society. No one wants more than I do a prompt end to this tragedy. But is a campaign in Africa the way to go about it? A campaign that will, even if successful, result in thousands of new foreigners in Rome, and introduction of all manner of unsavory new influences? I say that we should preserve ourselves and our country for the traditional values of our fathers, and that means expelling Hannibal and his murderous supporters without further delay."

Scipio resolved not to show disappointment at his apparent defeat and held his face impassive, waiting.

One of his supporters, Gaius Tullius Nosa, could also see that they would not have the votes to prevail, and rose to speak. "Fellow senators," he said, "this is a most serious matter, as our distinguished colleague Cato has indicated, which would affect the fate of our nation. I suggest that we defer action today and reconvene the Senate tomorrow, after we have all had a night's rest to ponder the issue."

Marcinius glanced at his ally, the senator Quintus Valerius Caldus. A crafty Senate veteran, Marcinius did not wish to delay the vote, knowing that even loyal backbenchers could sometimes be swayed by last minute enticements. Clearly, Scipio did not have the votes today, and now was the time to bury his proposal. Caldus was looking at Marcinius, waiting for directions. Marcinius shook his head.

"I call the question for a vote," Caldus said.

Unfortunately, Cato was an idealist as much as a practical

politician and did not want to be seen as becoming a puppet of Marcinius. Confident that he could hold his supporters in line, he called out, "There is merit in the suggestion of our colleague Tullius. I join his motion for a recess until tomorrow, at which time we shall decide the question of an African campaign."

That settled it, and within minutes, the senators were filing out of the chamber, abuzz with conversation.

——

Later that evening, Scipio huddled in his dining room with several of his closest advisors, including his brother Lucius, Laelius, and several other men from the army. His retainers had spent the afternoon seeking to crack the Marcinius-Cato alliance by buying off enough defectors to prevail. However, Scipio's adversaries were equally skilled at such tactics, and so the result was merely a bidding war, with the price of a senator's vote escalating throughout the day. In this game, Scipio, even with his substantial resources, could not hope to prevail against the far wealthier Marcinius.

"Well," said a dejected Scipio after hearing the reports, "at least we've made Marcinius considerably poorer today."

"He'll never notice," replied an equally despondent Laelius.

"Take courage," said Gaius Tullius Nosa. "We'll just have to take the case to the People's Assembly."

The thought of that struggle gave Scipio little cheer. "Votes in the Assembly can be bought just as easily as in the Senate," he said.

A heavy silence hung in the room as they sat there, racking their brains for a solution.

A knock by a servant interrupted their thoughts. "The lady Marcia has come calling, and wishes to speak with Master Scipio. She is waiting in the *tablinum*," he said.

The men exchanged puzzled glances as Scipio rose and, gathering his toga about him, left the room.

The tablinum, a reception parlor where guests were commonly greeted, was comfortably furnished, like the rest of the house. He found her, still wearing a thick wool shawl against the damp winter, seated on a chaise lounge located between a large porcelain vase on one side and heavy brass candelabra on the other. Two burly bodyguards who had accompanied her to the house stood nearby. Their short daggers were clearly visible. One of the changes wrought by the war was that the streets of Rome were now populated with all nature of scalawags and desperate beggars, and no self-respecting young woman would think of going out on an errand unaccompanied. When Scipio entered the room, Marcia waved for the two men to leave them alone, and they dutifully retreated out of sight.

"To what do I owe the pleasure of this visit?" Scipio asked amiably after the men were out of earshot. He was pleased that she had come, regardless of the reason.

She stood up and removed the shawl, revealing a fine purple linen dress, tucked elegantly about her shoulders to display her smooth brown skin and graceful neck. She draped the shawl over a nearby bench, moving fluidly, the lines of her body unmistakable beneath the delicate fabric.

"You've made my father very unhappy today," she said lightly. "All afternoon his political associates have been coming and going from his study with bags of money. At dinner this evening, he was complaining that you've cost him quite a bundle."

They laughed. He took her by the arm, and together they sat down on the chaise.

"Well," he said, "I've done my best, but your father is a master of the game. It looks like he's going to win."

"Father is accustomed to winning," she pointed out. "What do you expect to do next?"

Scipio stood and began pacing back and forth. "I suppose there is no choice but to take up Fabius' challenge and march directly against Hannibal."

"What makes you think they'll let you do that?" she asked incisively.

"Well, why not? Fabius as much as dared me to do it on the floor of the Senate today."

"From what I hear, they have no intention of allowing you to lead an army against Hannibal. They plan to argue that your proposal today shows you are still too immature to be trusted with a life-and-death struggle against him. That's why they elected Crassus consul. They want to give him command of the forces in Italy, knowing that he will follow Fabius' wishes—no risky or decisive confrontations."

This news wounded Scipio, and he slumped back onto the couch beside her, frustrated and angry.

"So the mighty Scipio, conqueror of Spain," she said with a sly smile, "is thwarted by a portly old man who can't even lift a sword?"

He tensed, stung. "Over the last months, I have grown very fond of you," he said slowly, looking away as if it were hard for him to express his feelings. "I had begun to hope that perhaps there was more than mere politics between us. And I had let myself come to believe that perhaps you felt the same."

She took him by the hand and pulled him closer, forcing him to turn back to face her.

"You were not deluding yourself," Marcia said quietly. "I have longed to be with you every moment that we're apart."

"Then why do you mock me now," he said bitterly, "on the eve of my failure? Thanks to your father, the Senate will not approve the African Expedition, and I suspect we will not prevail in the Assembly, either, given what I know of your father's ability to buy votes."

Marcia stroked his cheek gently with the back of her hand. Her skin was like velvet compared to his own, turned nearly into leather from so many months of exposure to the elements during the rigors of campaigning.

"I do not mean to mock you," she whispered. "I only wish to know why it is that you choose not to take up the key with which you can break my father's lock on the Senate."

Puzzled, he looked at her blankly, not following her meaning. Seeing that he did not understand, she drew back.

"I am sorry if I strike you as naïve in these matters," Scipio said earnestly. "I am a direct and simple person, but this business of politics is complicated. It requires the ability to see what is not shown, to hear what is not said. I'm afraid my skills lie in other areas."

"This isn't about politics," she snapped, a tear running down her lovely cheek.

At once her meaning became plain to him, and he took her in his arms. She fell into them, and he kissed her passionately.

"I love you," he whispered, and she responded eagerly.

He pulled away and let her regain her composure. "What will your father say," he asked mischievously, "when we tell him we're getting married?"

She felt overcome with joy that he finally had spoken the words. Her tears flowed freely now, and he wiped them with the soft cloth of his tunic.

She composed herself enough to say, "My father has never been able to deny me anything I asked for. And he has given me the right to choose my husband. I think he believes I'm too particular ever to find anyone who suits me."

Scipio laughed.

"Just promise me one thing," she said quickly.

"Anything."

"Tell me that you truly love me, and that you're not just using me to get your way with my father."

Scipio again shook his head. "You must not have been listening earlier. I do not play such political games. I love you, Marcia, and that is that. We will be married, regardless of what happens in the Senate, or anywhere else."

She kissed him again, and he felt a stirring passion he had not known since his last night with Vibiana. Sensing his desire, she broke away and said, "I think we had best go and break the news to my father. He'll have a lot of work to do tonight, undoing what he's been putting in place all afternoon."

They laughed together, and he took her arm and led her to the dining room to share his new circumstance with his friends.

———

A hammer blow could not have struck Marcinius with stronger force. He slumped into his chair, his craggy jowls sagging onto his stout chest, and his eyes, which normally skipped about like a fly on the surface of a lake, turned dull and downcast.

The young couple standing before him had just announced their intentions, though of course he had become suspicious the moment they had entered his library, hand in hand.

After a few moments, the shock began to subside, and Marcinius felt his brain beginning to work again.

His first reaction was anger. "Do you expect me to believe," he said hotly to Scipio, "that your intentions toward my daughter are sincere? If so, why did you wait to declare them until after it became clear that you lacked the votes to prevail in the Senate? This is the most crass effort to manipulate a young girl's heart that I have ever seen!" He practically spluttered with rage.

Before Scipio could answer, Marcia leaped to his defense. "If you must know, Father, it was I who called on Scipio tonight to declare my feelings."

This was a fresh shock. Such lascivious behavior by a noblewoman was unheard of! Marcinius reeled. True, he had granted her the right to pick her own husband, but he had certainly expected her to select a suitor who already had obtained his blessing.

He shook his head ponderously, as if it were a massive weight. "I never thought I'd say this, but thank the gods that your mother is not here to see this. Clearly, I have failed badly in your upbringing."

Scipio spoke up. "Marcinius, your attitude surprises me, our political differences notwithstanding. I am a Cornelius, the third generation to serve as a consul of Rome. I am wealthy in my own right, and, if I may say so modestly, have already compiled a distinguished record in the service of Rome though I am still comparatively young. I do believe many fathers would be proud to have me as a son-in-law."

Marcinius scratched his head, forced to admit that the union had possibilities he had not considered. Scipio did seem to have the aura of greatness all about him, and the man who defeated Hannibal would have all of Rome as his apple. That could provide a whole host of new opportunities. But there was his alliance with Fabius to consider—how could he simply switch allegiances?

Too, he was a devoted father. The thought of his beloved daughter leaving from under his protective wing was more than he could bear.

"No," he said stubbornly, "I cannot allow it."

Marcia had been expecting this, and now brought to bear her most potent weapon. Waves of tears began to roll down her cheeks, quickly puffing her lovely brown eyes into a swollen red mass.

Marcinius felt himself wavering and tried to be resolute. "Now, Marcia, you know I cannot bear to see you in tears. But this cannot be. I am pledged to support Fabius in his conduct of the war, and he has spoken against Scipio's plan."

"So you would put your crass political considerations before the happiness of your own daughter? How strange it is that you care more for Fabius than for me! You are right—I am glad Mother is not here to witness how you break my heart on what should be the happiest day of my life." She spat these words with venom, and they cut him to the quick.

"Sir, I am in love with your daughter," said Scipio, seeing the old man's anguish. "I ask your blessing to take her as my wife."

Marcinius was a veteran of politics. There was perhaps no man alive more skilled at discerning whether a man was sincere simply by judging the inflection of his voice. Scipio's words, he had to admit, had the force of truth.

Finally, he looked at Marcia and asked simply, "Do you love this man?"

"Yes, Father, absolutely and totally."

Her voice, too, had the ring of sincerity. He threw up his hands in despair, seeking a way out of this dilemma. A new idea took hold in his crafty mind.

"Scipio, you propose to go back into the field, and you may end up in combat with Hannibal himself. I will not have you make a widow of my daughter, in the prime of her life. I will give this wedding my blessing, but only if it is deferred until after you return from Africa."

This stratagem was received in quite different ways by the two lovers. Scipio felt overjoyed, for Marcinius had said *after Africa*, clearly implying that he would provide the votes to pass the expedition. He did in fact love Marcia, but his ambition still burned intensely. Marcia, on the other hand, in her eagerness for the marriage, wanted no part of a delay.

She started to protest, but Scipio beat her to the punch. "Your proposal strikes me as fair and eminently reasonable, Marcinius, knowing as I do the hazards soldiering life entails. I agree."

That sealed it, for with her father and her fiancé in agreement, there was little else for Marcia to do but to go along. Still, she was hurt by the quickness with which Scipio had agreed, without consulting her. She realized, with more than a bit of regret, that he was like all the rest of the Roman men, and, ultimately, her wishes would receive short shrift.

Marcinius brought himself to his feet and embraced his daughter, then shook hands with his future son-in-law. "Well, this is going to cause quite an uproar," he said ruefully. But, seeing that his daughter had a happy glow about her, he smiled. "Do not be troubled, little bird," he said, using the name he had called her as a child. "I shall see to it that the votes are there tomorrow."

With that, he sent them on their way and summoned servants to begin taking messages to his various allies. A long night of work lay before him.

———

Content with his day's effort, Fabius lay stretched out on his back, naked, on a padded wooden bench in his bedroom when the message from Marcinius arrived summoning him to an urgent parley. Above him, a formidable and equally naked Germanic masseuse—he marveled at the thick patch of yellow hair between her stout thighs—was patiently administering to his needs. At his advanced age, Fabius required a long period of foreplay before he could manage to penetrate a woman, and he had observed that, for some inexplicable reason, heavy women were more likely to arouse him. The session was considerably advanced when the message arrived, and so the timing was most inopportune. Having believed that the legislative threat posed by Scipio's proposal was well under control, Fabius was exceedingly irritated by the summons and spent a number of long minutes waiting impatiently while several slaves wiped the rubbing oil from his body and prepared him for the short walk up the Palatine. He slipped into a simple red tunic and common sandals, then donned a military-style marching cloak as protection against the wintry night.

He made the trip accompanied by three guards, permanently detailed from the Garrison of Rome to guard his residence. The guards too had been roused from a quiet night of duty, and they were most anxious to keep their superior from detecting any effects of the sour wine with which they had been wiling away the dull hours of the watch. Drinking while on duty was a serious offense, and things would go badly for these fellows if the senior general of the Roman armies should detect their transgression. They had naught to fear, however, for Fabius paid them little attention as he stomped resolutely up the winding path leading to Marcinius' palatial residence.

Fabius was escorted into the magnificent library, where he found his longtime colleague on the far side of the room, leaning against the balcony rail, gazing out at the skyline. Beside him was Marcinius' Senate ally, Quintus Valerius Caldus, who also had been hastily summoned from his night's rest.

Feeling that no greetings were required under the circumstances, Fabius snapped, "What business of the Republic could possibly require my attention at this hour?"

Marcinius turned and regarded his longtime ally with a sad look. He walked over to an ornate table and, taking two richly detailed golden cups, poured his guests a drink.

Fabius barked, "I cannot imagine what possibly could be so calamitous that you think I must be braced with the spirits before I can hear the news."

This stopped Marcinius in his tracks, and so he slugged down some of the liquor himself in a single gulp, then belched. He wobbled over to his desk, which was laden with a number of bags that presumably held varying amounts of money, and plopped into his chair.

"Well?" said Fabius impatiently.

Marcinius looked up at Caldus, then turned to the old general with a wry expression. "My daughter has come to me tonight to ask my blessing for a marriage."

Fabius began to think Marcinius had lost his mind. "You have my congratulations. But why does that particular news require that Caldus and I be summoned to hear it in the middle of the night?"

"Her fiancé is Publius Cornelius Scipio."

It took several long seconds for these words to sink in, and when they finally registered, Fabius slumped onto a stool set before Marcinius' desk. He reached out and took the cup of wine from Marcinius and drained it.

Caldus remained stoic at the news. He asked simply, "What did you tell them?"

Marcinius set his elbow on the desk and then rested his head on his hand. "I could not deny her," he said flatly.

Fabius' reaction surprised him. "I too have daughters," he said with a sigh. "I understand what you have been through."

They sat quietly for several long moments, each man pondering his next move.

"I suppose we have made a serious error in underestimating Young Scipio's ambition," Fabius said finally, and could not help from breaking into a wide grin. "At least he selected *your* daughter as the target of his strike."

Marcinius shook his head. "They are in love."

Fabius made a dismissing gesture with his hand. "Nonsense. He wants to lead the African Expedition, and will stop at nothing to obtain the consent of the Senate. I expected him to try something, but this is truly extraordinary."

Marcinius felt his temper rising. "Do you take me for a doddering old fool? I have interviewed them myself, this very night. I have made a career out of knowing a lie when I hear it, and I have heard plenty in this job, believe me. They are in love, let there be no doubt."

Caldus understood that there was nothing to be gained with Marcinius by further questioning Scipio's motives, and moved on to another topic.

"I do not suppose," he said, "that you can continue to lead the opposition to your future son-in-law's proposal."

Marcinius shook his head.

"And I further reason that in the absence of your active opposition, Scipio will prevail upon the Senate to approve the African Expedition."

The old senator nodded.

"If he takes your daughter as his wife and then goes to Africa, she may be a widow before a child can even be born."

Marcinius' eyes narrowed to mere slits. "I have taken a precaution against that eventuality," he said. "I have imposed a condition on my blessing of the match. The ceremony is to be postponed until after Scipio returns from Africa."

Fabius turned this over in his mind. A plan was beginning to take shape. "We have been partners for many years, you and I. Our alliance has saved Rome from many precipitous schemes, and brought us to where we are today," he said wistfully. "Hannibal is cut off, Carthage is nearly exhausted after the loss of Spain, and victory is in sight without placing the Republic at no small risk."

With this, Marcinius rocked back in his chair. "Yes," he said. "You have withstood harsh criticism, but your grand strategy has worked. Scipio now seems intent on upsetting the cart."

"Perhaps," Fabius said slowly, "there is more than one way to skin this cat."

"What do you have in mind?" Caldus asked.

"Scipio envisions a general invasion of Africa, with a full consular army," Fabius said, thinking out loud. "But our friend Cato made a very telling point today. We cannot afford to strip the country of the cream of its defenders, leaving only a skeleton force in place between Hannibal and Rome."

A veteran negotiator, Marcinius sat impassively, waiting for the proposition.

"Suppose we give him his expedition, but limit his force to, say, ten thousand men. That should be enough to give him a grand adventure on the coast of Africa, and protect him from any real harm. We don't want your daughter to be broken-hearted, after all! But the main elements of the army will remain in Italy, to continue to defend against Hannibal."

Caldus brought his hands together, pressing his fingertips against each other as if in prayer. "Only ten thousand men? That's rather transparent."

Fabius shrugged. "Make it fifteen thousand, then. Three full legions." Then he had an idea. "Let him take the legions in Sicily. Those men will see it as an excellent opportunity to salvage themselves."

"The legions in Sicily?" Marcinius asked uneasily. A slight smile began to form around the corners of his mouth. The survivors and stragglers of the horrific defeat at Cannae had been reconstituted into three legions, then more or less banished to service in Sicily for the duration of the war. Most Romans regarded these humiliated men as unfit for any other duty, having so disgraced themselves on the field before Hannibal. "You yourself sent them there after Cannae, saying they were unqualified to defend Rome any longer. Now you would give them to my future son-in-law for an offensive?"

"As great a general as he claims to be, he should not require any better men. The point is, even if Hannibal is recalled, not even Scipio would be so foolhardy to face him on Carthaginian territory with so limited an army."

"You will, of course, take your usual precautions to assure an accurate flow of reports?"

Fabius tilted his head a bit and laughed. "That will not be difficult. Our friend Silanus has gotten himself into trouble again. This time, he had some clever scheme involving imported goods. Unfortunately, the ship carrying his cargo was captured by pirates, and he was forced to cover the delivery by buying substitute goods at a much higher price. His creditors are threatening him with slavery again."

The corners of Marcinius' smile now spread over his entire face.

"From what you have told me, I believe our friend Silanus would spy on Scipio just for the pleasure of making trouble for him."

He reached across the broad marble desk and clasped hands with Fabius. "I am pleased," he said, "that our alliance still has some time left to run."

He turned to Caldus. "Tomorrow, here is what we will do."

———

Their plan unfolded neatly the next day in the Senate. Fabius rose to address his colleagues. No man, he admitted, should ever place his own pride before the welfare of the State, and, therefore, he had to confess that, upon reflection, he had spoken hastily in opposing Scipio's proposal. Indeed, he had come to see the considerable merit in it. But, lest they think the cautious old leopard had changed his spots, he could also appreciate the very sound reservations cited by Cato. Accordingly, he felt a compromise might be achieved, and put before the Senate a suggestion that Scipio be given the three legions in Sicily for his campaign in Africa, while the remainder of the Roman Army be placed under the safekeeping of Crassus to keep Hannibal at bay.

This sudden change of the political winds might have blown the senators over, but when Caldus rose to second the motion, it was immediately apparent that Marcinius had blessed the arrangement, and their loyal backers were ready to go along.

Scipio, for his part, was shocked by the proposal to constitute his force with the Sicilian legions. He had expected to take with him into Africa a full consular army, a minimum contingent of thirty-five thousand men. But he was sufficiently self-possessed to avoid a confrontation with what appeared to be a coalition he himself had assembled. Moreover, his pride prevented him from complaining that three legions would not be enough, notwithstanding his grave reservations about the inadequacy of the force. He got to his feet and stated that he found Fabius' proposal entirely acceptable.

Cato, watching this little farce play itself out, was incensed that his own complicity in agreeing to the overnight postponement of the vote had brought about the very opportunity for the compromise now about to be approved. He also recognized that he was cleverly boxed in: Fabius had acknowledged his reservations and addressed them. To continue to object would make him appear unwilling to accept a solution devised by the two best military minds available to the Senate. This was an untenable position for a nonsoldier, however influential he might be on civilian matters. Scipio would go to Africa—enjoying an astounding opportunity to gain fame and fortune.

The motion passed without a dissenting vote.

Cato was seized by a sudden inspiration, and he rose to his feet.

"My friends," he said, "so historic an undertaking as we have just approved stirs me to action. Our noble consul and his able staff of officers certainly can use some help in organizing the effort, and I offer to join the campaign and serve as quaestor. As my military colleagues know, the quaestor is responsible for keeping the records of a campaign. He must oversee the finances and keep the official account of the operation for the military archives. I wish to oversee the finances and ensure that the effort is carried off with minimal cost to our already overburdened treasury."

Scipio looked as if someone had thrown cold water in his face. The last thing he wanted in his camp for the duration of the campaign was the contentious Cato, haggling over every sesterce and glorifying his own role for the archives.

Before Scipio could respond, however, Caldus was on his feet. He did not even need to glance at Marcinius for approval. The senator was able to see in a heartbeat that Cato's gambit was a gift from the gods—getting Cato out of their hair in Rome was too good an opportunity to pass up. But instinctively, he knew how to pursue the matter. He must not seem too eager to let Cato go. And so he said to the Senate: "The learned censor shows deep patriotism by offering to serve in the grand expedition. But the office of censor is far too important to our people to have Cato dashing off to faraway lands on a military mission. He is needed right here, to continue the important programs he has commenced. We cannot spare him, and I urge him to reconsider his generous offer."

Cato recognized Caldus' maneuver for what it was, but also knew that the stakes were such that he had to choose. If the expedition succeeded, the participants would rule Rome for the rest of his life. He had to be a part of it, or else cede the future to Scipio.

"Quintus Valerius Caldus is wise, as always, and his support of our program is a welcome change from his previous positions," Cato replied. "The people of Rome managed for quite long enough without me as censor, and they can do so again. Nothing is more important to our future than the success of the African Expedition, and as a patriot, I welcome the opportunity to participate. Accordingly, I offer to resign the office of censor if the Senate will approve my offer to serve as quaestor to the campaign."

With a nod to Marcinius, Caldus sat down, satisfied that he had gotten more than he had hoped out of this exchange. He caught a glimpse of Fabius on the other side of the chamber. The old man was grinning broadly, also reveling in the unexpected windfall.

Scipio knew there was no point in challenging the combined strength of the Marcinius and Cato factions, and threw up his hands in resignation. "I accept the gentleman's generous offer," he said simply, and the Senate ratified the appointment.

There being no further business, the senators adjourned and began filing out of the chamber. A few minutes later, on the steps of the Capitol, Marcinius clasped his arm about Scipio and announced to a surrounding throng of well-wishers that, upon the general's successful return from the upcoming campaign in Africa, he would offer

Scipio his own beloved daughter to be the young man's bride. This brought a round of cheers and applause, for the wide-awake retinues of both men could instantly grasp the political implications of the combination by marriage of the two factions.

Not everyone, however, received this news favorably. Trailing behind Marcinius and his future son-in-law, and still smarting at the beating he had taken only moments earlier, Cato felt a new resentment burning in his breast. He had long had his eye on the daughter of Marcinius, and merely had been waiting for an opportune moment to present himself again as a suitor. Those hopes were now crushed, and he resolved to himself that a day of reckoning lay ahead for these connivers.

———

The day following the Senate's action, Scipio was taking his leisure in the lovely garden of his rented home when Narcussa appeared and announced that Scipio's mother was waiting in the tablinum. He jumped to his feet and hurried to greet her.

Expecting her to be robustly congratulatory after his victory in the Senate and the announcement of his impending marriage, he was taken aback when he saw her stern countenance, her forehead wrinkled in concern.

"Mother, how nice to see you," he said, a bit uneasily, giving her a little hug. He paused to take note that she wore a bland gray *stola*. Pomponia's son was consul now, and she did not wish to embarrass him by flaunting the law concerning colorful dresses. "I assume you've heard the news?"

"Yes," she said, a little bitterness in her voice. "As always, I learn about your exploits from others."

This hurt him. "I was just preparing to send you a note," he said awkwardly. He took her by the hand and led her to the divan, where they sat, facing each other.

The harshness of her look softened, and she said, "Oh, do not feel guilty on my account. I know how busy you are. I care only for your happiness. This girl, Marcia. Do you love her, truly?"

He was surprised at her question, having expected her to be pleased with the social implications of the bonding of the Cornelius and Marcinius families.

"Well, yes, of course. I proposed marriage to her," he replied.

"In Rome, proposals of marriage have nothing to do with love," Pomponia said, her mother's intuition at work. "I have known too many people who have entered into marriages for reasons of business or politics, and wound up miserable all of their days. Scipio, do not marry her unless you love her. A loveless marriage is a curse from the gods. Nothing will make you more unhappy."

He smiled at this bit of parental advice. "Do not trouble yourself, Mother. Yes, I love her."

"You do not sound convinced," she said. "I think you are still infatuated with that girl you had in Spain."

He blushed and looked away.

"Don't be embarrassed," she said, taking his hand. She could see the pain the mere mention of the girl brought over him. "You *were* in love with her, weren't you?"

"She was nothing, a mere prize of war," he said testily. "And how did you ever find out about her?"

Pomponia gave him a critical look. "Do not make the mistake of thinking that what you soldiers do in camp is not known to those of us who remain at home," she said. "Even after men are married, they may have dalliances while on campaign. But you are too famous now. You must comport yourself upon the assumption that everything you do—*everything*—will become known to the public, the same as if it were announced on the steps of the Forum."

He did not respond, perhaps because he did not want to acknowledge the truth she spoke.

"Well, you can say she was a 'mere prize of war,' but the look on your face betrays your true feelings. Heed my advice, Scipio. Do not marry this innocent child of Marcinius until you are certain you have expunged your feelings for this Spanish girl of yours."

"I am over her," he said flatly. "And besides, she is gone. Escaped into the forests of Spain. I will never see her again. Marcia will be my wife, and I will be a good husband to her."

Pomponia could see that further discussion was pointless, and decided to change the subject. "Does she share my dismay over the fact that you are going away again?"

He could plainly see the tears glistening in her eyes, and he took her into his arms. "Now, now, Mother. I must go, for the good of the country. I can bring about an end to this war, and then I'll be home for good."

"But Africa?" she sniffed. Pomponia pulled a small cloth from some hidden place inside her stola and held it to her tired eyes. "It is so far away, and so hostile!"

"It's actually closer than Spain," he said, trying to get her to smile. "And we have arranged to be welcomed by an ally, Syphax. So do not trouble yourself—I will be fine."

"Yes," she said, "I know the gods have a special design for you. But I didn't come here expecting to talk you out of it. I came for a different reason."

He was intrigued. "And what might that be?"

"Since the news arrived last night, Lucius has been able to talk of nothing but joining you on the expedition. Please do not let him go with you. He's just a boy!"

Scipio had been dreading this conversation. Lucius had been pleading with him to take him along on the expedition. And at seventeen, he was entitled under the law to volunteer for service in the army.

"Lucius is a man now, Mother. You must let him choose his own path."

"What a terrible life this is!" Pomponia cried. "First your father, then you, now my baby! All of you Cornelius men cannot wait to leave me all alone and go off in search of your glory, to be gained at the expense of killing people."

Her tears flowed freely.

"I could not bear to lose you both," she said. "I beg you, do not let him go."

Scipio's heart ached at seeing his mother so distressed. A thought occurred to him. "If he does not go with me, he certainly will volunteer to serve under Crassus. Neither of us can stop him from doing that. Would you rather have him under my protection, albeit in Africa, or subject to the vagaries of fortune under the command of Crassus?"

Pomponia gave him a terrified look.

"Yes," Scipio said. "You cannot deny him his military service. And I fear what might happen to him in the camp of Crassus, face-to-face with Hannibal."

These words hit the mark, and she resigned herself to her destiny. "Promise me," she said, clutching his arm, "that you will not send him in harm's way."

Scipio shook his head. "He must live the life of a Roman soldier, and do his duty, wherever it may take him. But I can promise you, I will not let him be foolish."

Pomponia wiped at the tears with her cloth. "I am afraid that is the best I can hope for," she said, trying to smile.

"That, and the complete success of the Expedition," he added.

"Very well," she said, a note of resolve in her voice. "I shall resume my regular rounds at the temples."

Scipio laughed and got to his feet.

"Come, Mother, let us have something to eat, and then I will join you in your first trip to the temples, to pray for our success in Africa."

———

Bruttium

Sometimes it seemed to Hannibal the rains would never stop. All of Bruttium seemed to be one giant swamp, and the entire camp looked like it had been mired in the muck forever. Men, animals, and weapons alike were coated in mud. The banners, which in bright sunlight seemed so colorful, hung soggy on their poles, and the pen where the elephants were kept was a hopeless morass of mud and manure.

He was weary of this miserable country and frustrated that the victory he had longed for had escaped him. Fabius would not repeat Varro's error and bring on a pitched battle. For the last five years, Hannibal had been forced to keep moving, trying unsuccessfully to lure the Romans into a general engagement. It seemed as if he had been in Italy forever—fourteen years of his life were invested in the campaign. He could not even remember anymore what his homeland was like. And, as had everyone else, he had suffered losses.

Hannibal's demeanor, already soured by the brutal circumstances of his brother Hasdrubal's death, was only exacerbated by the foul weather. The entire camp was abuzz with talk of his latest cruelty. To break the boredom of winter camp, and intending to take a measure of revenge for the death of his brother, he had ventured forth two weeks earlier, intending to raid the district of Casinum. His guide, however, an unfortunate Italian peasant pressed into service by the Carthaginians, had mistakenly thought Hannibal wanted to go to Casilinum, and so led them in that direction. The region, however, was surrounded by mountains, through which only a narrow defile led down to the sea. While Hannibal was marching down into this valley, the Romans, acting on orders from Fabius himself, took advantage of their knowledge of the roads to send a contingent of four thousand troops around to block the pass, while the rest of the army occupied the heights above. The Romans attacked the Carthaginian rear guard, killing about eight hundred men. Hannibal, having discovered the error, had the guide crucified on the spot.

But taking vengeance on a hapless peasant would not rescue his army. Hannibal gave orders to take some two thousand oxen they had captured, and to fasten to their horns bundles of twigs. After nightfall, his men lit these torches and drove the cattle toward the passes where the Romans were posted. When the torches began to burn into the raw flesh of the cattle, they stampeded into the Roman lines, terrifying the sentries and putting the troops into confusion and panic. The Romans fell back from the defile, enabling Hannibal's troops to march through to safety.

He came into his tent and found there waiting for him two of his officers, Mago and Hamilcar, and a man who was wearing a common wool cloak over his Roman army uniform. It was the spy, Metellus, come to give him news again. Hannibal utterly despised spies, but found them a necessary evil, and considered himself lucky that so many of the Romans were willing to betray their country for mere silver.

"Speak," he grunted to the man, who was shivering nervously, and not just from the cold. "What news do you have?"

"A new consul will arrive soon to take command of the army facing you," the man stammered.

"Scipio?" Hannibal asked, affecting a casual air. He took a small dagger from his belt and began cleaning the dirt from under his fingernails.

"No," Metellus replied. "Publius Licinius Crassus."

Hannibal put the knife down and approached the man. "Who?"

"Publius Licinius Crassus. He served as second in command to Nero at the battle when your brother—"

Hannibal shoved the Roman angrily, knocking him backward over a chest.

Mago gave Hannibal a disapproving look while Hamilcar picked up the now terrified Roman. "My lord," he said gently, "your treatment of our spies does not enhance our ability to recruit them."

Hannibal waited for the Roman to gather his wits. "What are Crassus' plans?"

"Crassus is handpicked by Fabius. He will continue to follow Fabius' edicts. You will not have a confrontation with the army facing you, and if you try to provoke a battle, we will withdraw."

Hannibal sighed. He had long ago realized that to rail about Fabius' tactics was only to waste his own energy.

"What about Scipio?" he snarled.

The spy studied his feet. "Scipio is charged with the invasion of Africa. He has taken leave for Sicily, where he is to organize the three legions that survived Cannae to accomplish the task."

Hannibal looked at his officers, and all three men broke out laughing. Metellus shifted nervously from one foot to the other.

"He intends to strike at Carthage, with only three legions?" Hannibal could not believe the audacity of the Romans. No matter how many times he had beaten them, they kept coming back for more. "Too bad. I was looking forward to getting a firsthand look at this young Roman general."

"You very may well get that chance," Metellus said meekly. "Scipio believes you will be recalled to counter the threat he will pose to your home city."

This too brought a round of derisive laughter.

"Does Scipio truly believe that Carthage cannot contend with a mere three legions on our home territory?" Hannibal asked, incredulous.

"Not only that," the man replied, "but he also believes that he will make his fame by defeating you, with Carthage as the prize of victory."

"Take this man away and pay him," Hannibal said abruptly. "I do not wish to hear any more of this nonsense."

Metellus now screwed up his courage. "On the subject of pay," he said, "the danger grows ever greater. Once Crassus joins the army, I will be at considerable risk."

Hannibal tilted his head and looked at the man with his good eye. His officers, familiar with this expression, got out of the way.

"Name your price," he barked.

"You don't understand," the man said. "I cannot do this anymore. This is my last report."

"Tie this man backward onto his horse, and wrap one of our battle flags around him. Brand his cheek with my insignia and send him into the Roman lines."

Metellus' bones turned into jelly. "They'll know I've been here," he pleaded. "Do you know what they'll do to me?"

"I believe the punishment is beheading, but only after they have stripped most of the flesh from your body with their scourges," Hannibal said, his tone pleasant for the first time.

"No," the man pleaded as the two officers began to remove him. "Don't do this to me. I'll keep reporting."

"And why," Hannibal said as they dragged the struggling Roman out of his presence, "do you think I would trust a man who betrays his own people?"

◧ BOOK TWO ◧

THE ALPS

LAKE
TRASIMENE

ITALY

ROMA

CANNAE

BRUNDISIUM

MEDITERRANEAN SEA

LILYBAEUM

SICILY

UTICA

CARTHAGE

TUNIS

NEAPOLIS

NUMIDIA

ZAMA

VIII

LILYBAEUM, SICILY

205 BC

PERCHED IN A TALL log watchtower, Scipio and Laelius watched intently as the infantry assembled below them went through the drill. A hot sun beat mercilessly down upon the heavily perspiring men, but Scipio was unrelenting: he insisted that they carry out their training in full battle gear so that he could understand how they might react in actual combat situations. And the sun in Africa would only be worse. It was critical that the men be acclimated to fighting in oppressive heat.

The legions were formed up in a standard line, with cavalry deployed on both flanks. The alignment presented absolutely no unusual features in the organization of the maniples and cohorts, the tactical divisions of the legions. Seeing the formation, an observer would think himself facing an unimaginative general intent on bringing on a battle "by the book."

Upon the signal of a trumpet, however, the columns of velites—light infantry and skirmishers—that ran vertically through each of the three ranks fell out of line and dropped back. This had the effect of forming long, narrow lanes running perpendicular to the lines themselves. These lanes were evenly spaced, and the soldiers on either side of each lane sheathed their swords and took up long spears. The legionnaires who had fallen out of the formation double-timed to the rear and gathered to form a phalanx in reserve.

"I think they've got it," Laelius said.

"It's about time," Scipio grunted.

Laelius was relieved to see the army finally responding properly to Scipio's commands. There was considerable concern about many of these men, the survivors of the disaster at Cannae. These legions suffered mightily from the ignominious disgrace of their performance in that battle, and no Roman commander had since dared trust them. They had been assigned to guard duty in the relative backwater of Sicily where they'd sat, largely inactive and growing resentful of their ill treatment, for most of the war. Scipio's arrival and enthusiasm for the coming campaign had energized them. He had personally met every man, scrutinizing with his critical eye their fitness for duty. Hundreds had been cashiered out of the army, and he had then spent two months recruiting replacements from the Italian mainland, offering bonuses and other inducements, much to the protest of the new quaestor, Cato. Tension had mounted steadily between the two men, and finally, Scipio had banished him from the field command group, relegating Cato to a desk at the headquarters. This brought the expected howl of protest, but they were in the field now, far from the Senate, and Scipio's command was absolute.

"If you had had these men in Spain, we would have been home a lot sooner," Laelius observed to his commander.

"In Spain, we faced second-rate generals. These men must be ready for anything." Scipio leaned over the ledge of the observation post and called out to a young man on a horse below, "Tribune, have the men return to their positions and repeat the exercise."

Lucius Cornelius Scipio winced at his brother's order. Like every man on the field, he was drenched in sweat, and based on the fine performance just executed, had been expecting an order to take a break, not another run-through. More than three dozen men already had fainted in the humidity. But he had begged his brother to bring him along on the African Expedition, and he was not about to start complaining. Lucius spurred his horse forward and issued the command.

There was a loud groan as the order spread. The men were clearly tired and thirsty. They lumbered back into the original formation and waited again for the sound of the trumpet.

"Your critics might suggest," Laelius said in a circumspect manner, "that by the nature of your preparations, you intend to engage Hannibal if confronted by him."

"The Senate's decree directs me to attack Carthage. I intend to do just that, regardless of who stands in the way," Scipio answered.

"I believe the language used by Fabius in the decree was, 'attack Carthage if prudence and circumstances allow.' I note that you have spent little time in these exercises drilling the men in the techniques of orderly retreat."

"You insult these men," Scipio snapped, "if you suggest that they intend to show their backsides to the enemy."

"What will Hannibal do when he sees what you're up to?" Laelius asked as the horns sounded and the men scurried to repeat the creation of lanes in the assemblage.

"I do not intend to show him this trick until *after* he's committed the elephants," Scipio said. "Every man down there is a veteran. They won't break and run at the mere sight of the beasts when the charge begins. Just as the elephants approach the front line, I'll give the signal. By then, it'll be too late for Hannibal to do anything."

"With any luck, the animals will panic, and their handlers will do our work for us," Laelius suggested. The Romans had observed that occasionally the war elephants would get out of control and could even turn on the Carthaginian infantry attacking behind them. This had, on occasion, foiled an otherwise effective attack. For this reason, each handler was equipped with a mallet and a long metal spike; if his animal panicked, he would drive the spike into the elephant's brain from the back of its neck, killing the beast before it could jeopardize the effort.

"I don't intend to count on luck," Scipio replied.

"Is that why you continue to make sacrifices to Neptune?" Laelius asked, coyly.

Scipio grinned. "You are skeptical of my daily offerings?"

"The support of Neptune no doubt will be invaluable," Laelius rejoined, "but I should be just as grateful for a few more legions in the field when Hannibal finally shows his ugly face."

The reserve phalanx was now in place. Scipio was pleased: the entire maneuver had been executed in less than two minutes.

"Tribune, return the men to camp, then tell them they are dismissed for the day," he called out.

The men were marched in formation back to their encampment under Scipio's watchful eye, then discharged. Most of them trudged to their tents to doff their armor, then hurried down to the white, sandy beach to seek relief in the cool ocean. Scipio, followed closely by Laelius, climbed down a rickety ladder nailed to the side of the watchtower, occasionally pausing to swat at the ubiquitous mosquitoes. Once on the ground, he motioned to a coterie of nearby staff officers to mount their horses while Scipio himself climbed onto Bucephalus. An aide handed him an ivory baton with a golden eagle on one end, the symbolic emblem of his imperium as consul of Rome. He held the baton on display in his right hand and dug his heels into the horse. The contingent of officers then rode into the town of Lilybaeum, where the senior staff officers had taken up residence in several comfortably furnished villas.

Scipio had chosen to make the town his headquarters because it offered the largest harbor in which to assemble his invasion fleet. His villa, rented from a local wealthy grain merchant, was a relatively modest masonry structure chosen solely because of its position on a high bluff, providing a commanding view of the harbor and the wharfs. Scipio's offices were in the rooms with windows facing out to sea. Each time a ship was rowed into the port and added to the armada, a staff officer made a notation of its size and capabilities on a long roster, which Scipio reviewed daily.

From the bluff, the blue harbor made a beautiful sight, ringed by steep cliffs of reddish-brown granite, dotted here and there with small houses, bleached white by the relentless sun. Normally bustling with all nature of mercantile activity, the port had been radically transformed by the massive military effort that had taken shape under Scipio's command. The harbor had been closed to all private shipping, much to the dismay of the local citizens, who loudly protested at the sacrifice they were being asked to make for the war effort. Their complaints fell on deaf ears.

Nearly every seaworthy craft along the coasts of Italy and Sicily had been commandeered for the invasion effort and brought to Lilybaeum, where over four hundred ships now lay at anchor. Over three dozen huge quinqueremes, featuring five decks of oars, were reserved for use as troop transports; these would be the last ships loaded. Scores of smaller triremes, fast and maneuverable, were detailed to provide protection against attack should any Carthaginian fleet appear to contest the landing. Several of these were out in the Mediterranean on patrol, their distant bright sails adding a dash of color to the seascape. Scipio intended to make one of these sleek boats his flagship, having decided that in a pinch, his ability to flit about the massive formation could be important. The other ships, a motley collection of designs, were earmarked as transports for the huge mass of matériel the army would require during the expedition.

A vast array of gear, weapons, siege implements, foodstuffs for both man and beast, and clothing was stacked in seemingly endless rows across the wharves of Lilybaeum. Scipio had given orders that the army should bring food and water sufficient to last forty-five days, including cooked rations for fifteen days. Within this time, he was determined to have put the army in a position to live off the land. This enormous pile of supplies jammed the piers as the ships were loaded with their cargoes. Here, too, the army engineers had transformed the waterfront, adding several new piers in an effort to speed the work of the stevedores. The transfer of the large and heavy baggage wagons to the boats was a particularly grueling task, requiring the construction of large cranes to lift the bulky wooden carts from the piers to the waiting boats.

The cost of all of this activity had brought an unending stream of complaints from Cato. But his protests, like those of the residents of Lilybaeum, went unheeded by the consul, who would not be deterred from his mission.

All about the frenzied scene, armed guards patrolled to prevent sabotage and hold pilfering to a minimum. One misguided individual caught stealing from the army's provisions had his hands tied behind him and was then hauled up and hung by the wrists from a lanyard. The man's shoulders were instantly separated by the abrupt strain upon the joints; his piteous groans continued for several days before he expired. The decomposing body still hung in plain view, a grim reminder that Scipio intended to let nothing impede his invasion plans.

It seemed to Scipio that the loading of the ships had taken forever, and it was by the sheer force of his personality that he had pushed the dockhands and sailors to nearly superhuman efforts in order to speed the process. He had put the idle time to good use, continually drilling the soldiers until they responded like a finely tuned instrument. Now, he knew, the men were getting restless, wanting to get on with the business of the invasion. If they dallied much longer, they would lose their edge, and further training exercises would be counterproductive. Fortunately, preparations were nearly complete, and the ship commanders were advised of their departure dates.

The general plan of the invasion was to set sail for Thapsus, a small and unfortified city on the coast of Africa, far to the south and east of Carthage, lying just outside the territory governed by Syphax.

Reports indicated that the land there was very fertile, capable of supporting the army indefinitely, and that the local population could be quickly overpowered before any forces from Carthage could arrive to intervene. Once established in a secure base on the African continent, Scipio intended to march straight through Syphax's kingdom to carry out raids on the territory of Carthage itself.

Arriving at his villa, Scipio dismissed the rest of the officers for the afternoon and went inside accompanied only by a bodyguard. To his considerable regret, he found Cato waiting for him. The quaestor, all arms and legs, looked a little uncomfortable in his ill-fitting standard-issue army tunic. As a further concession to the military life, he had cut his thick red mane close to his head, in the common military style.

"Greetings, Cato," Scipio said, making little effort to conceal his contempt. "I commend you on the continuing progress we are making in loading the ships."

Cato did not mistake the sarcasm in the consul's voice. But he had come on a mission, and would not allow himself to be distracted.

"Scipio, I must protest again the frightful expenditures you are incurring. The Senate authorized an invasion—they did not authorize you to drain the treasury to pay for it!"

"I am taking the steps I deem reasonably necessary to discharge my duty, as established by the decree of the Senate," Scipio replied, his tone even.

"You are spending money at a frightful rate," Cato cried, his voice shrill.

"Your protest is duly noted," Scipio said. "Is there anything else?"

Cato fought to contain his fiery temper. "Now, see here, Scipio, I too am a senator, and a former censor. You cannot simply ignore my protests! I insist that you take action at once to restrain your spending habits."

"I will be called to account to the Roman people not for the money

I have spent, but for the battles I have won," Scipio snapped in reply.

"Very well, then, I must resign my office in protest, and will return to the Senate to report on your practices."

Two pairs of eyes locked in a frigid exchange of ambition.

"The struggle to conquer Africa will be infinitely more difficult without you," Scipio said after a moment, "but somehow, we will persevere."

"Your pride will be your undoing," Cato hissed.

"You will forgive me if I wish you ill winds for your voyage back to Italy, for I shall be praying for favorable winds to push the fleet in the opposite direction."

Cato turned sharply on his heel and stalked out of Scipio's presence.

Scipio, agitated and angry, summoned Narcussa. The slave helped him out of the heavy armor, including the new gold-encrusted cuirass that his elevation to consul now entitled him to wear. It was a beautiful work of art, festooned with the trident of Neptune above the Cornelius standard, flanked by a banner labeled *Hispania* for his conquest of that nation. Narcussa then directed two other slaves to draw a hot bath in the expansive brass tub for his master, and, while the water was being heated in large pots over a fire in the kitchen, attempted to massage the tension from Scipio's neck and shoulders. Finally, the bath was ready, and Scipio gratefully eased himself into the hot water. Narcussa brought forth a coarse brush and scrubbed him from head to toe, washing away the dust of the day's drill.

As Scipio relaxed, soaking out his aggravation with Cato, word arrived that one of the patrolling triremes had intercepted a ship purporting to carry envoys with a message from Syphax. Because tensions were high over concerns about an effort by Carthage to attack the invasion fleet, these visitors had been detained on the wharves while they were questioned to ensure that they were not Carthaginian spies.

Scipio climbed out of the bath and, while being toweled dry by

Narcussa, ordered that the envoys be brought to him at once. He also dispatched messengers to summon Laelius and Lucius to hear what these men had to say.

———

Feeling that he should meet the delegation with proper formalities, Scipio changed into a white toga of expensive linen, draped with the regal purple-and-gold cloak evidencing his consulship. Laelius and Lucius arrived, both in scarlet-and-gold formal military dress. Laelius looked particularly heroic, his chest emblazoned with a lifetime of medals of valor.

"Rumor has it," said Laelius upon greeting his consul, "that the quaestor has resigned."

Scipio cocked his head slightly in Laelius' direction. He was in no mood for flippancy. "If you feel that we cannot prevail against Carthage without a record keeper in camp, I shall permit you to join him."

Laelius winced at this rebuke. "No, I do not think his absence will impair our chances on the battlefield. But what he can do to you in Rome—that is a different matter!"

"Very well," Scipio replied. "You are hereby appointed as the new quaestor. I would rather have you keeping the official account of the campaign anyway."

Before Laelius could splutter out a protest at this addition to his duties, servants entered carrying platters of food. Scipio had ordered that a meal be set out so that he might offer gracious Roman hospitality to the representatives of Syphax.

The envoys, four men in all, were ushered into the large dining room in the company of two centurions, who, at a nod from Scipio, removed themselves. All four of the diplomats were older men, heavily bearded in the African fashion. Their skin was dark and dry from years of exposure to the African sun. Although each was swathed in colorful ceremonial silk robes, one man, apparently their leader, wore a turban held together just above the center of his forehead by a fabulous amethyst stone, mounted in a glittering golden brooch.

"Greetings, gentlemen," Scipio said amiably. "I am Publius Cornelius Scipio, consul of Rome. My officers, Garibus Paullus Laelius and Lucius Cornelius Scipio, join me in saying that we are honored to play host to emissaries of the glorious and mighty Syphax. All that we have shall be at your disposal. We shall be humbled to make you comfortable during your visit."

The ambassador in the turban bowed from the waist. "The kindness and hospitality of the great Roman general Publius Cornelius Scipio is legend," he said, flashing perfectly white teeth as he spoke. "I am Hogaba, praetor of the people of the Masaesulii. You may recall that we met when you visited Syphax in Neapolis." He motioned for his colleagues to step forward and introduced each as they did so. "This is Bomilcar, chief magistrate of the people; Culchas, nephew of the king; and Helorus, high priest of the temple. We bring you greetings from our most imperial and deified potentate, Syphax, king of the Masaesulii."

Scipio nodded his head at each introduction, determined not to show the growing sense of anxiety he was feeling. These envoys were not mere messengers: they represented a delegation of the highest level of government officials at the disposal of Syphax. What could be so serious?

"We are honored," he said, "that so wise a king as Syphax would send visitors of such noble rank. You have had a long journey. Perhaps I might offer you food or drink."

Hogaba shook his head. "Normally," he said smoothly, "I would sacrifice one of my own limbs for the opportunity to take a meal with so grand a personage as the conqueror of Spain. Regrettably, however, the business that brings us into your presence is best conducted outside the pleasures of food and drink."

Scipio glanced at Laelius, who too had realized something very important was in the wind. Lucius, rather young for the subtleties of international politics, seemed unfazed by the proceedings. Scipio walked over to the consul's ivory curule chair in the center of the room. He set himself down onto it and folded his hands in his lap. He said coldly, "In this chair, I represent Rome herself. Let her hear what you have to say."

If Hogaba was offended by the sudden chill in Scipio's tone, he did not show it.

"My lord Syphax has instructed me to inform you that circumstances affecting his kingdom have changed considerably since your visit. There has been bloody fighting between our people and forces of the kingdom of Numidia. This fighting has taken place primarily because Syphax, by treaty, feels he must recognize Tychaeus, the son by adoption of Gala, now deceased, as rightful heir to the throne of Numidia."

Scipio stroked his chin slowly. "I thought that Massinissa, nephew of Gala, was successor to the throne."

"Gala never produced a male heir, only daughters," Hogaba explained, his eyes shining brightly. "Therefore, Massinissa was the successor. Shortly before Gala's death, however, one of his daughters prevailed upon him to formally to adopt her son, Tychaeus, as his own son. Extraordinary, don't you think? Adopting one's own grandson?"

Scipio shifted uneasily. He was beginning strongly to dislike the oily African standing before him.

The envoy continued his story. "Massinissa and his followers refuse to recognize Tychaeus as king; he claims the throne for himself. He insists that a man cannot adopt his own grandson, although there is no precedent in tribal law specifically addressing the question. The result of Massinissa's challenge is that a brutal civil war now rages throughout Numidia. Carthage has chosen to recognize Tychaeus as the rightful king and has persuaded Syphax to do the same. Massinissa has declared war on both Carthage and Syphax, as well as Tychaeus."

Scipio was confused. "What does this trouble with Massinissa have to do with relations between Syphax and Rome?"

"Syphax has been sorely troubled by Massinissa," Hogaba said wearily. "He has repeatedly raided our territory, inflicting terrible damage and many casualties. As you are unfortunately aware, Massinissa is a formidable opponent."

He paused, diplomatically skirting what he presumed was Scipio's painful memory of his father's defeat at the hands of the Numidian cavalry. "Carthage has offered her assistance in the fight against Massinissa, and Syphax has accepted."

Scipio held his face impassive, although his head was beginning to reel at the implications of this new alliance.

"Having accepted the aid of Carthage, Syphax feels honor-bound to come to her defense if she is attacked. And I have been directed specifically to inform you that most certainly any visitors to our soil who would make war against Carthage must also be regarded as our enemies."

Scipio sat rigid, determined now that he would not let these heathens detect his distress. As a strategic thinker, he at once realized that their message was a catastrophic blow to the plan of the invasion: the path to Carthage now lay blocked by the armies of Syphax. The Romans had been counting on arriving at the gates of Carthage with their small army substantially intact. This new betrayal meant that the Romans would have to expend precious manpower fighting their way past Syphax before Carthaginian territory was ever reached.

"I have heard with my own ears the pledge of Syphax to remain neutral in the contest between ourselves and Carthage. Indeed, I have shaken hands with Syphax concerning our treaty, and sealed our pact with gifts," Scipio said through clenched teeth. He got up and crossed over to a table, which held the ornate golden bowl Syphax had presented him when their deal had been concluded. "Would he now renege on his sacred word of honor?"

Hogaba studied the tile pattern in the floor, obviously distressed by having to communicate such distasteful behavior. Finally, he said, "Syphax regrets that events have brought him to this, but the threat of Massinissa is too great. Rome cannot defend her own territory from Hannibal—how can she possibly help Syphax deal with Massinissa?"

These words put Scipio into a hot fury. He struggled to maintain a modicum of diplomatic protocol, and finally muttered, "Get out of my sight."

Hogaba bowed again and turned to leave.

Laelius, in a flash of inspiration, stepped forward and put his hand on Scipio's shoulder. "Hogaba," he said, "I myself helped to arrange the treaty between Rome and Syphax, and so you can understand my distress at hearing that your king chooses to abrogate the arrangement. If he chooses to take Rome as an enemy rather than as a friend, so be it. Many others have made the same mistake, and cried bitter tears for their folly. Before we embark on so fateful a course, I should be remiss if I did not at least inquire whether we might offer some inducement to persuade Syphax to change his mind."

A sudden surge of hope swept over Scipio, as he realized Laelius was right. They had bought Syphax once, but had evidently been outbid by Carthage. Perhaps it was only a matter of price.

But a sad look came over the African's features. "I was sent to pass a message, not to negotiate. I am afraid there is no basis for repairing the relations between our two countries. The arrangement between Carthage and Syphax has been sealed by marriage. A beautiful noblewoman of Carthage has been given as a bride to Syphax. He is quite taken by her. I am certain nothing can turn his head now."

Both Scipio and Laelius were deflated. The passions of African kings were legendary. If Syphax had been bought with female flesh, with which he was now entranced, there was nothing to be done.

Hogaba and the others were nearly out of the room when Laelius asked a final question.

"Who is this woman," he asked, "that Syphax would choose to fight Rome because of her?"

Hogaba stopped but did not turn to face them.

"Her name is Vibiana, daughter of Hasdrubal Barca, whose head was taken by the consul Nero. She is the niece of Hannibal himself."

———

W hen the envoys were gone, Scipio walked over to a large window that looked out over the harbor. He stood silently, his hands clasped behind him, gazing out to sea. A gentle evening breeze had kicked up, rustling the folds of his imperial cloak.

Laelius, after several long moments, recovered sufficiently from his shock to speak. He did not know whether Scipio had been aware of Vibiana's parentage. Even if he had, the general certainly had never spoken of it to him. He knew there was nothing he could say that could possibly console his general, and so he simply asked, "What are your orders, Scipio?"

Scipio leaned his right hand on the windowsill and shifted his weight to one foot. The other hand he put on his hip. He seemed completely at ease.

"Lucius," he said, "what do you recommend?"

"I fear this is a major setback," the youngster said, stating the obvious. From his tone, he evidently did not understand the blow his brother had just received. It occurred to Laelius that no one had ever mentioned Vibiana's name to Lucius, and so the youth could not appreciate the pain that now was eating at the consul.

"I don't see how," Lucius was saying, "we can fight our way through Syphax and still have any hope left if Hannibal shows up. You'll have to postpone the invasion while we form a new plan of action."

"Laelius?"

"The decree of the Senate certainly contemplated that we would have an unobstructed passage to Carthage through the territory of Syphax," Laelius said, hoping a resort to legalism might influence Scipio since, as consul, he was sworn to uphold the law as established by the Senate.

"Nothing in the text conditions the invasion upon the continuing validity of our treaty with Syphax," Scipio noted.

"Well, no, there was nothing explicitly stated. But they only gave you fifteen thousand men. We cannot hope to be successful with such a modest force if you must also fight Syphax."

"Perhaps," Scipio said, "old Neptune will grant your wish for a few more legions."

Laelius was not sure whether his general was serious. He said nothing in response, sensing with a terrible dread that Scipio had already made up his mind.

Scipio turned and faced his officers. When he spoke, his voice conveyed such intensity and determination that they knew to challenge him would be futile.

"The fleet," he said, "sails tomorrow."

———

Thousands of civilians lined the cliffs to watch the departure. It was a thrilling spectacle—men scurrying aboard transports, ships raising their sails, formations gathering with countless oars splashing into the white-capped waves. Other Roman fleets had departed from Lilybaeum, but never before so massively or with such determination.

Scipio was the last to board, and with all eyes upon him, he paused to offer a sacrifice to the gods. Before the animal was slain, he offered a prayer, calling out in his booming voice, "O Gods and Goddesses of the seas and the lands, I pray and beseech you graciously to assist all our enterprises. I pray that you will bless these soldiers, and bring them home as victors, enriched with spoils and plunder. Grant us the power of vengeance on Rome's enemies, and give to us the means to inflict upon the Carthaginians the sufferings they have labored to inflict upon us."

The victim was then knifed, and Scipio, according to the custom, flung the entrails into the sea. Then, with a broad wave, he bounded down the gangplank to the boat, accompanied by cheers from thousands of throats. Morale was outstanding: the men believed that at the end of their voyage lay certain victory rather than a hard campaign. At a word from the master of the rowers, the first oars bit into the waves, and Scipio's flagship moved out of the harbor.

Many of the civilians lining the cliffs waved white cloths to wish good luck to the departing warriors. But among the spectators was a single Roman who did not share their enthusiasm.

Cato stood fuming, furious that he had taken himself out of the invasion, and that Scipio had accelerated the departure in an effort to thwart any effort Cato might mount in the Senate to have him recalled. As he watched the flagship recede into the distance, he vowed again to have his vengeance upon the career of Publius Cornelius Scipio.

———

Laelius, aboard a trireme, formed up twenty such ships and moved to the left of the fleet. Scipio and Lucius, at the head of twenty more triremes, took up a position on the right. By prior agreement, for ease of recognition during the night, battleships would carry a single light and transports two. Scipio's flagship was distinguished by three lanterns.

The wind was good and quickly carried them out of sight of the island of Sicily. Shortly thereafter, however, they ran into a dense fog, which made navigation difficult. The thick weather continued through the night and well into the next day. Fortunately, the sea remained relatively calm, and so sickness among the troops was minimal. Late in the afternoon, the breeze picked up and the fog lifted. They then made good time, and before long, the pilot told Scipio he could make out the coast of Africa. Hearing this, Scipio offered another prayer for the success of his mission, and then gave the order to seek a harbor. The hour of the day was late, however, and upon consideration, the fleet cast anchor for the night.

The next morning, the weather was crisp and clear, obviously a good omen, and Scipio's flagship scouted the coast for a favorable spot to go ashore. He noticed a nearby headland and was told it was the Cape of Apollo, south of the eastern arm of the bay of Tunis. He gave orders to sail for the cape. The first men ashore were the engineers, who immediately set to work erecting temporary piers so that the supply ships could be efficiently unloaded. By the end of the day, the entire infantry and most of the cavalry, including horses, had been landed without any resistance, and a substantial amount of gear and supplies had been unloaded onto the beaches.

Scouts were dispatched, quickly locating a fine position on high ground not far from the beached ships. An intense effort was made to fortify the site, and by nightfall a formidable defensive embankment guarded a space where the formal camp could be erected.

The scouts reported that the fleet had in fact been seen from the coast and that the nearby towns were in a panic. The roads were clogged with hordes of fugitives taking to the inland hills, seeking to carry with them their livestock and belongings. Another report declared that Syphax had dispatched a contingent of cavalry to interfere with the landing, although no one had actually seen these horsemen. Scipio nonetheless established pickets well outside the defensive perimeter and spent most of his first night in Africa making plans for the next day.

He wanted to make his presence felt quickly, and so at dawn he left the infantry to continue work on establishment of the camp and the harbor, riding out with a full complement of cavalry. His target was the nearby town of Capussa, a wealthy farming community located in a valley, flanked by a dense forest. The cavalry devastated a number of farms on the ride to Capussa, taking hundreds of refugees into custody in the process. The Romans then fell on the lightly defended village with a fury. In a matter of minutes, over eight thousand occupants were rounded up and, while their homes were torched in their plain view, pronounced to be slaves of Rome. Afterward, the enslaved Africans began making their way under guard back to the Roman camp, from there to be taken directly to Sicily as the first installment of booty from the campaign.

While this activity was underway, Scipio received a report that Syphax's cavalry had been spotted nearby, over a thousand strong, riding toward the pillar of smoke hanging over the town. Several of the officers argued for a prompt withdrawal, but Scipio, seeing an opportunity to send a message to Syphax, quickly moved his force into the forested hills surrounding the only lane leading into Capussa.

The enemy horsemen, who turned out to be Carthaginian riders under the command of a Masaesulii officer, galloped right into the trap. At the trumpet signal given on Scipio's word, the Romans sprang from their concealment and fell upon the enemy in a murderous rampage that lasted only a few bloody minutes.

One prize of this encounter was the Masaesulii commander, who, upon realizing he had blundered into a hopeless situation, gave himself up without even striking a blow. When the hapless officer was brought into Scipio's presence, Scipio was struck by an idea. He ordered that the Council of Elders from the town of Capussa be identified and brought forward. This was done: a dozen of the town's leading citizens found themselves facing the Roman invader.

Upon Scipio's order, the right hand of each man was amputated with an ax. The severed hands were tossed into the fine golden bowl Syphax had given Scipio, smearing the rich metal finish with congealed blood.

Scipio saw with delight the dread in the African officer's eyes. "No," he said to the trembling man, "this fate is not for you. You will need both your hands to carry the bowl. Take it to Syphax. He gave it me as a gift to symbolize the value of his word. Tell your king of my actions today. Tell him that this is how Rome deals with kings who would fail to honor an agreement sealed with a handshake."

As he watched the chained officer being led away, Scipio was joined by Laelius.

"Do you really expect," Laelius said quietly, "that Syphax can be intimidated out of his alliance with Carthage?"

"I expect," Scipio said as he climbed onto Bucephalus, "precisely the opposite. I wish to draw Syphax himself into the field against us so that we might crush him."

IX

Neapolis, Africa

204 BC

THE NORMALLY JOVIAL SYPHAX sat morosely on a huge tufted purple cushion ringed with scarlet fringe, holding court before a phalanx of ministers, advisors, courtiers, and assorted dignitaries. The throne rested on a raised platform at the back of a large chamber of massive limestone blocks, beneath an ornately detailed vaulted ceiling. Syphax prided himself on being a fine builder, and his glittering palace had been the crown jewel of his bold program of public works. Here he listened glumly as the scribe before him recited the latest outrages wreaked upon his countryside by the Roman invaders.

Scipio and his army had been in Africa for three months, during which they had burned or leveled every structure they had come into contact with, and captured or killed tens of thousands of civilians. During this time, his one-year tenure as consul expired. The Senate, delighted with the steady flow of trophies and plunder, happily extended his command, appointing him pro-consul for the duration of the campaign. This was done over the objections of Cato, whose arguments concerning the cost of the campaign again fell on deaf ears.

Scipio had appropriated vast quantities of crops and livestock for his invasion force, to the extent that the urban populations were feeling the impact of sharply reduced food supplies. Syphax had dispatched numerous military missions to intercept the invader and protect his kingdom, but each of these efforts had ended in disaster. The steady stream of severed hands arriving at his palace had thrown the whole government into a panic.

Scipio's program of total devastation had finally begun to run out of steam simply because there was nothing left standing in the vicinity of his camp upon which to work his will. Thereupon he had moved his camp down the coast to the heavily fortified coastal city of Utica. The Roman fleet blockaded the city by sea, and Scipio had laid on a brutal siege, determined to reduce the city and her defenders either by the operation of his siege equipment or by starvation. Syphax had pleaded with Carthage to dispatch her fleet and break the Roman stranglehold on the harbor of Utica, but the Carthaginians, fearful for their own safety, had refused. As a result, commerce throughout Syphax's kingdom was at a standstill, the populace was terrified, and the reserves of his treasury were being depleted at a frightening rate. His ministers clamored that something had to be done.

But Syphax sat, obstinate and unmoving. Spurning Rome now appeared to be a monumental mistake. His thoughts drifted back to the intrigue that had resulted in his renouncing the treaty with Scipio. Syphax had long coveted the territory of Numidia, and indeed had been secretly plotting an invasion for some time. With the imbecile Tychaeus on the throne, there could be no doubt about the success of his invasion, whereas if Massinissa were in charge, the invasion would be too risky.

Carthage recognized that the strategic importance of Syphax outweighed their duty to Massinissa, who had served them loyally in Spain. They meant to make Syphax's territory their battleground, rather than fight Scipio on their home soil. Accordingly, they had secretly promised Syphax that, in return for renouncing his arrangement with Rome, they would not intervene in his invasion of Numidia. It was Carthage that proposed to Tychaeus that he accept a force of Masaesulii warriors as his bodyguards. These warriors, when the invasion was launched, would kill Tychaeus, paralyzing the government at the critical moment and laying open the entire country to a lightning sweep by the Masaesulii. The invasion planning was well advanced when Scipio landed, but it had been indefinitely postponed thanks to the Roman rampage.

Syphax realized now he should have never made the bargain with Carthage. What had possessed him to believe Carthage's assurances that Scipio would abandon his plans simply because the route was obstructed? Unhappily, he admitted the answer: once he had gotten a look at Vibiana, he had lost his head.

He mulled over his alternatives. Hogaba had dutifully reported that the Romans were willing to deal, and, after absorbing the vicious retribution being dealt out by Scipio, he had considered renouncing the treaty with Carthage. But the treaty was sealed by marriage, so he would be forced to divorce Vibiana. This would not be difficult, since as king he could merely proclaim himself divorced. Such action, however, would no doubt make him a laughingstock, and the ever-present intrigue swirling about the court might lead some daring courtier to attempt a coup. He looked warily out over the faces in the crowd—plenty of ambitious eyes gauging carefully his response to the crisis. Already there might be a plotter in his court, ready to rise up against him. Moreover, if the Carthaginians got word he was considering renouncing the treaty, they surely would launch a preemptive strike against the Romans, and he would find himself crushed between the two combatants.

"Well, your highness?" Hogaba stood before him, evidently having proposed something.

"I shall consider it," Syphax said noncommittally, figuring he could find out later what the praetor had suggested. "Is there anything else?"

The minister of the treasury stepped forward. "My lord, there is a long line of individuals seeking compensation for the damage inflicted to their property by the Romans. Will you hear their pleas?"

Syphax shook his head, regretting another mistake. At the outset of the invasion, he had sought to quell the panic by announcing that his treasury would make good any losses inflicted by the invaders.

"Not today," he said miserably, dismissing the bureaucrat with a wave of his hand.

A murmur of disapproval rumbled through the chamber, and he snapped up his head with a look that silenced the throng. He was still the king, and could have any of their heads on a post with a mere gesture.

"I am weary," Syphax said, and struggled to his feet. "I shall be in the royal chambers."

Her eyes closed, Vibiana floated in a huge porcelain bath, her body soaped by a dark and silent female servant who was, like herself, immersed in the hot water. Exotic oils and perfumes had been stirred into the bath to soften her skin and prepare her for the razor, for Syphax insisted that his women be shaved smooth when they were brought to his bed. It did not bother her that Syphax was not monogamous—indeed, his appetites were so voracious that she was grateful to be spelled regularly by the women of his harem.

She certainly had not expected to end up as the wife of an African potentate, when once she had been so roughly scrubbed in the icy water of a horse trough by a Roman sentry. As they so often had over the years, her thoughts swept her back to Scipio's tent, to the pleasures they had shared in Cartagena—and then to his stubborn refusal to secure her future, and the day when she had stabbed Maximillian and made her escape. After the horrid encounter with Octuro, Vibiana had made her way to Gades, a small town on the coast of Spain just across the Straits of Gibraltar from Africa. At Gades, there was a significant Carthaginian community, and she was able to break the news of the disastrous defeat suffered by Hasdrubal, son of Gisgo. The Carthaginians, realizing there was no longer any army left in Spain to defend them, made preparations to quit the country, and Vibiana, revealing her family identity, had no difficulty securing passage.

She returned to her home city, where initially she was greeted as something of a celebrity for having escaped the Romans. She made a serious error, however, when in a careless moment she related to a group of women the details of her captivity. Before then, she had intimated that the Romans had respected her noble birth, and she had escaped with her virtue intact. But a woman in the custody of a Roman was a subject of sympathy only if she resisted to the point of death. The fact she had survived, even flourished, in Scipio's custody must mean that she had enjoyed the experience, and hence was damaged goods. Thereafter, she was ostracized for not having sufficiently resisted her Roman captor, and no self-respecting Carthaginian male would have anything to do with her. The pain and humiliation of her treatment at the hands of her own people was exceedingly difficult to bear, and when the news arrived that her father had been brutally murdered by the Romans, she was despondent, feeling all alone and cut off from the world.

It was Hasdrubal, son of Gisgo, who approached her with the suggestion that she offer herself as a bride to Syphax as a way to cement Carthage's effort to thwart Scipio's invasion plans. She saw an opportunity to escape what had become an unbearable situation in her homeland, and to strike a blow at the man who not only had spurned her love but also had brought about her miserable condition. She accepted.

In retrospect, it seemed laughable that she had been concerned that Syphax would not find her desirable. She had meticulously prepared herself to be introduced to him, selecting a shimmering translucent yellow gown that displayed just a hint more of her bosom than the limits of propriety would permit. Syphax was no stronger than Scipio—one glance at those marvelous breasts and he was hooked. He had to have her, and if the treaty with Rome was an obstacle, it could be annulled with the stroke of a stylus. This, of course, was done before the marital vows were exchanged.

Now, after months of living at the African's court, she realized that she merely had traded one master for another. True, she was the wife of a rich and powerful king, with all the luxuries and privileges that his wealth and station could bestow, but he regarded her as just one more item for his collections, a vessel into which he could expend himself when the mood suited his fancy. She had known true love with Scipio, and there was no love in this king's caress, no delight in her company, no smile at the sound of her voice. She was trapped, as much a prisoner now as when Maximillian had shadowed her every move.

The water was growing cool as the slave girl finished rinsing her. Vibiana rose from the bath and stepped onto the intricately mosaicked floor. Two servants were ready with large, absorbent towels, and they patted her dry. She went to a nearby couch, where a highly skilled eunuch barber waited to attend her so that she might be found pleasing by her husband.

The unpleasantness lasted only a few moments, and when he was finished, he rubbed her mons with a scented oil. She got to her feet and stood patiently as another attendant dabbed a bit of rouge on her cheeks and lined her lovely eyes with pale blue eyeshade, enhancing their color by the contrast. Her hair was brushed to a luxuriant glow, and she stepped into a sheer nightgown the color of cinnamon before proceeding to the bedchamber to await the arrival of Syphax.

———

Vibiana lay stretched out upon a plush divan as Syphax shuffled into the massive bedchamber, looking forlorn and downcast.

"This is the first time," Vibiana said coyly, "that Syphax has not smiled when casting his eyes upon me."

Syphax grunted and went to a stand holding a large bowl of water. He splashed some onto his weary face and turned to look at her. Even now, with his country in shambles and his very kingdom at stake, he was struck again by her stunning beauty. Propped up by large pillows, her thick hair formed a halo about her head. She was by far the most desirable woman he had ever had. But there were plenty of women, and no mere female could possibly be worth the misery the Romans had inflicted upon his kingdom.

"You are the cause of all my woes," he said dully, knowing that what was done could not be undone.

"Do not blame me for your troubles," Vibiana rejoined. "You are your own worst enemy. You mistakenly thought you could not only have me but also have Carthage as your friend, and you would have nothing to fear from the Romans. Now Scipio is laying waste to your country, but you lack the courage to do anything about it."

This impudence angered Syphax, and he stormed across the room, taking her by the shoulders in his iron grip. "For such impertinence I should have you beaten," he raged.

But Vibiana met his gaze, unafraid. "You are brave when dealing with a woman, but you sit here behind your walls, afraid to give battle to Scipio."

With catlike reflexes, he struck her viciously with the back of his hand, snapping her head back.

"I have been betrayed by Carthage," he snorted. "They will not dispatch their fleet to the aid of Utica, and they insist on keeping their army intact between our territory and their city, in case Scipio gets by me," he said bitterly.

Tears flowed freely down Vibiana's lovely cheeks, streaking the rouge, and, as quickly as he had felt anger at her brash words, Syphax began to feel desire.

She recognized that look on his face and drew back. "Would you think of love when you are on the verge of losing your kingdom to the Romans?"

This hurt him, and he slumped onto the divan, overcome by anguish. "Carthage will not come to my aid. What am I to do?"

"You can be a man," Vibiana taunted him. "Why do you need Carthage to take on Scipio? He has come into Africa with only three legions. You have here at Neapolis over sixty thousand troops. Not even Scipio can overcome such odds. The palace is rife with rumors that you are afraid of Scipio."

He glared at her. "What traitor would dare question my courage?"

"Your nephew, Culchas, for one. He's been suggesting that he could rid the country of this Roman nuisance. Even Hogaba is said to be sympathetic."

Syphax's bearded chin sagged onto his stout chest. "Scipio has never been beaten," Syphax said miserably. "He defeated your father at Baecula, and Hasdrubal, son of Gisgo, at Ilipa. It is said that the gods hold him in special favor. Some even say that he himself is a god."

Vibiana laughed scornfully. "I can assure you," she said in a caustic voice, "that he is a mere man, just like you."

Syphax jerked his head up and looked at her through eyes that had become narrow slits. She realized she had made a serious blunder, and an icy fear swept over her. Syphax got up and went to the table that contained his personal toilet items. When he returned, he was holding a straight razor, which he brandished before her face.

"Hasdrubal, son of Gisgo, told me that you were Scipio's captive, but that he respected your noble birth," Syphax said, a wild look in his eyes. "Something tells me that I have been lied to."

He pressed the razor against her throat. "On our wedding night, when I questioned the absence of your virginity, you told me you had been injured on horseback."

She knew instinctively that if she showed a hint of fear, he would kill her.

"I satisfied Scipio just as I have satisfied you," she said quietly, amazed at how calm she was. "I ran away from him, but I married you."

This was quite a revelation. Syphax turned over in his mind how he might use it to his advantage. He had been lied to about his bride, and certainly this would be regarded as sufficient justification for renouncing the treaty, given the failure of the consideration. He realized, however, that he would become the butt of endless ribald jokes concerning his having married a woman who had already been taught the secrets of the marital bed by the very Roman who even now was raping the countryside. This pricked his vanity, and he knew he must seek some other option. As he pondered the matter, he began to feel a powerful measure of satisfaction. He himself had been smitten by this woman—could Scipio have felt any differently? Now, merely by possessing her, it was as if he already had won a victory over his nemesis. Suddenly, he saw clearly why Scipio had assaulted his kingdom with such vengeance: Scipio was in love with Vibiana and wanted her back.

"Cutting my throat," she said, "will not give you revenge against the man we both hate."

Syphax lowered the razor and stepped back. Vibiana felt herself beginning to breathe again.

"Perhaps you are right," Syphax said, a sly grin spreading across his features. "It is time for me to take to the field against the Romans."

Vibiana smiled.

"And you are going with me."

Her satisfaction changed to terror. "But—but why?" she stammered.

"It is said that Scipio never attacks an army formed up against him, but rather absorbs the first strike and then counterattacks. This is especially important when he is badly outnumbered, as he will be against us."

An evil gleam radiated from Syphax's face. "I will let it be known that you are in my camp. If necessary, I will put you on display before his lines."

His eyes glowed with delight as his imagination worked. "Naked, perhaps. That ought to draw him out."

Rome

There was nothing like being free, Quintio reflected as he studied a scroll containing figures from his latest series of grain trades. The profits were substantial, as was his satisfaction at again having successfully parlayed the Romans' ever-growing hunger for grain into more wealth for himself.

They think themselves so high and mighty, Quintio observed, *and yet they are so easily manipulated by their own greed.* Hadn't he, after all, outsmarted them all? From the day he was captured in the forests of Gaul and driven, naked, under the lash to the slave markets in Rome, he had angled to win his freedom. Luck, of course, had proven as important as wile. It was pure, dumb luck that had caused the granary owner Vellucius to pluck him from the auction block and put him to work shoveling grain from the barges into silos from dawn to dusk. In no time, Quintio had worked his way up, until he was actually in charge of his master's stores of wheat and corn. It turned out that Vellucius was not a careful bookkeeper, a deadly failing for a grain merchant, whereas Quintio was blessed with an innate ability to work with figures. Once he recognized his master's weakness,

Quintio began squirrelling away a few sesterces here and there—
money Vellucius never missed—and then cleverly turned his modest
stake into a small fortune by shrewd bets upon grain prices. It was
risky, for the flow of grain was prone to wild fluctuation: the weather
was fickle, slave revolts interrupted the harvests, pirates often stole
the grain while it was in transport, and on and on. Quintio soon
enough discovered that he had been favored by the gods with an
impeccable sense of timing. He was able to divine in advance movements in the price of grain, and consistently put himself on the right
side of the market. In only a few months, he had accumulated more
than enough to buy his freedom.

Once free, Quintio went into partnership with his former master,
and soon thereafter, bought him out. Quintio rapidly established
himself as one of the leading grain merchants in Rome. His sense of
timing remained flawless, and in no time he had ensconced himself
in a lovely home on the Aventine, waited upon hand and foot by
the most lovely female slaves. He took his pleasure with them, too,
a delight that had been denied when he was another man's property.
The fact that he had once been a slave himself made him a stern
master. He knew all the tricks, and he could be quite cruel in dealing
with a wayward slave who might be so foolish as to try to cheat or
steal from Quintio.

Still, for all his success, Quintio realized that he was, at best, a
minor player upon the stage of Roman society. To climb further, he
needed capital, and lots of it. For this reason, he had been intrigued
when he heard that Marcus Portius Cato had resigned from the
African Expedition and returned to Rome. Many Romans thought
that Cato had made a mistake by resigning the powerful office of
censor to seek glory in the campaign, and then withdrawing from it
even before the invasion was underway. Quintio, however, sensed an
opportunity, and for this reason, had invited the rustic senator to a
meeting at his granary weighing house, located on the banks of the

Tiber, just east of the Capitol.

A servant announced that his guest had arrived, and admitted the tall, wiry outlander into Quintio's tiny office on the second floor. Cato's manners were unrefined, but Quintio recognized in his visitor's eyes a piercing cunning and an intense ambition that could be turned to his own advantage.

"Greetings, Marcus Portius Cato," Quintio said, getting to his feet and shaking hands with the much taller and thinner Roman. "Welcome to my humble offices."

"I see that you do not allow yourself to display the trappings of your newfound wealth," Cato said with a note of approval in his scratchy voice, referring to the bare walls and simple furnishings of Quintio's offices. "In this, you are a man after my own sentiments."

"Indeed," Quintio said, a slight smile crossing his fleshy face, "given my background, it is better if I do not make myself conspicuous."

"You do not wish to be conspicuous," Cato said slyly, coming to the point of this visit, "but you wish to associate with powerful Romans, I gather."

"Cato is perceptive," Quintio said, lacing his fingers together and then resting his joined hands on the swelling mound of belly separating him from the edge of the desk. "I see many opportunities for making money, but they require capital. Capital that you and your wealthy friends in the Senate can easily provide."

"The patricians believe it is beneath the dignity of a noble senator to participate in mercantile activities," Cato pointed out.

"You are not a patrician," Quintio rejoined, "and nothing in the tradition suggests that a wealthy Roman, senator or not, should not be a silent partner in any undertaking. I know quite a few, in fact, who have done so."

Cato's eyebrows, a much fainter shade of red than the hair atop his head, jerked up. "Marcellus, for example?"

Quintio's face was placid. "You are referring to the unfortunate rumor that Marcellus passed information to me about the situation in Sicily, enabling me to recognize a substantial profit on the grain harvest? Such rumors demean the reputation of an outstanding Roman patriot, and I will not dignify them with a response."

Cato knew a lie when he heard one. But Quintio was suggesting far more. He wanted Cato to know that he could be trusted to keep his mouth shut about their dealings, no matter how spectacular the undertaking.

"Why me?" Cato asked the freedman. "Why do you choose to bestow upon me, an ex-censor, somewhat in disfavor for his recent resignation from the African Expedition, the benefits of these 'opportunities'?"

A smile returned to Quintio's face. "I have followed your career with some interest. I think your misfortunes in Sicily are a temporary setback, and that you will earn your way back into a position of considerable influence and power. I would like to be of assistance. And you, of course, with all your wealthy friends, can help me assemble the money I require to carry out some of these interesting *opportunities* I mentioned."

Cato scratched the back of his neck while he thought it over. Quintio seemed to be a man who would do anything for money, and he could always make use of such an operative in the comeback he was already plotting. Certainly, the rebuilding of his coalition would require substantial funds, and if what he had heard about Marcellus was true, he could use a man of Quintio's wiles and skills.

"Very well," Cato said at last. "How do we begin?"

"Excellent!" Quintio said, clapping his hands together. He opened a drawer in the desk and took out a map of Sicily. "Let's try something simple first so that you can gain some confidence in my judgment."

Cato listened excitedly as Quintio laid out a clever scheme involving farmland on the island. The freedman might be base and disgusting in many respects, but he clearly had a knack for business. Cato felt suddenly pleased: there was a way out of the abyss into which he had plunged himself. With Quintio's help, he would climb back to the pinnacle of the Roman government. And once there, he would have a thing or two to settle with Publius Cornelius Scipio.

X

Utica, Africa

203 BC

Scipio sat stolidly on his ivory curule chair, listening impatiently as his commanders explained the difficulties they had encountered in breaking the defenses of Utica.

The city was located on a steep bluff overlooking the harbor. Although the Roman fleet had effectively blocked any resupply from the sea, the ground assault had gone very slowly. The steep approach made it extremely difficult to haul up siege engines and artillery. Moreover, the Utican fortifications were exceptionally well designed. A wide trench had been dug, and the excavated dirt heaped in the center of the trench to form a core for the wall. Stout stone walls were erected on either side of the core, with the inner wall much higher than the outer wall, so that even if the outer wall were scaled, the attackers would not be able to fire their javelins into the town. The walls were three meters thick, and the stones themselves were locked together with ingenious metal clamps so that it was very difficult to break the wall down. The Romans, at incalculable loss to the slaves employed in the effort, had managed to erect a long shelter against the edge of the structure. Beneath this shelter, workers could maintain their efforts to breach the wall while protected against the flood of stones, burning faggots, and boiling oil the Utican defenders rained down upon them.

Laelius and Lucius had just returned from an inspection of the siege works and were not enthusiastic.

"I've never seen anything like it," Laelius said. "Cartagena was child's play compared to this."

Scipio tugged on his ear, unwilling to admit they were bogged down. "Can't we tunnel underneath it?"

"We have excavated six meters, and still have not reached the bottom of the foundation," Lucius replied. "And we have captured prisoners who tell us that the foundations of the inner wall are even deeper."

"Is their information reliable?" Scipio asked his brother, thinking that the prisoners might be lying to mislead the Romans.

"The captives have been put to every torture. If they are lying, they have forfeited their lives doing it."

Scipio turned to an officer named Gracchus, who was in charge of the day-to-day siege operations. "What is your estimate of the time required to break through?"

"It's impossible to say," Gracchus replied. "Perhaps four months, maybe even longer. And even after we break through, we'll have a stiff fight on the other side of the wall."

Scipio jumped up from his chair and began pacing back and forth. "We cannot delay here for that long! We must come up with something else."

The clatter of approaching horses interrupted the conversation. Scipio stepped out of the tent to investigate, followed by Laelius and the other officers. He saw a squadron of cavalry reining in before them. In their company was a familiar black youth, clad in a richly colored native robe.

"Massiva!" Scipio cried out. "Don't tell me we've captured you again!"

"He approached us under a white flag," the cavalry commander said. "He claims to have a message for you. We have searched him thoroughly."

"Well, then, come down off that horse, and let us make you comfortable."

Massiva dismounted and clasped hands with Scipio and Laelius, who introduced him to the other officers present. The party then went back into Scipio's tent. Servants were set scurrying to fetch wine and food.

"How have you been?" Scipio asked as they settled onto a bench, feeling almost a paternal fondness for the African. He realized that Massiva had matured since that day at Baecula: he had grown into a handsome, dignified young man.

"I am well," Massiva responded, "and eternally in your debt for your kindness when I fell into your hands." He held up his right hand, showing off the elegant gold ring Scipio had given him.

"You see," he said, "I have it with me still."

Scipio made a dismissive gesture. "There is no debt between us. I acted out of respect for your uncle, for I found him to be a worthy opponent. Now, what brings you to my camp?"

A hot anger burned in the youth's brown eyes. "You are aware of the treachery of Carthage and Syphax in plotting to support Tychaeus' claim to the throne of Numidia over that of my uncle Massinissa? Never has such an outrage been attempted upon the people of Numidia. Gala was a tottering old fool, duped by his greedy daughter into adopting his own grandson."

Scipio gave him a sympathetic look. "We too have suffered from the treachery of Syphax. Our campaign against Carthage was forced to take a different tack because of his conniving."

Massiva nodded. "He is a dog, that Syphax. The desire for revenge burns deep in the breast of my uncle."

"So?"

"Massinissa is encamped only five days' ride from here, with six thousand of the finest Numidian cavalry. He has instructed me to come to you and offer an alliance against Syphax and Carthage."

Scipio felt his heart skip a beat. "An alliance between Rome and the claimant to the throne of Numidia would be of interest to the Senate. What terms does Massinissa offer?" he asked warily.

"Massinissa and his cavalry will join you to march first against Syphax," said the youth quickly, his face aglow with excitement. "After you defeat him, Massinissa will join you in the assault on Carthage herself. In return, Rome will recognize Massinissa as the rightful king of Numidia, and dispatch your legions to aid him in forcing Tychaeus from the throne."

Scipio looked up at Laelius. Both understood full well the potential boost such an alliance could give their campaign.

"It surprises me," said Scipio evenly, "that Massinissa would agree to attack Syphax first, rather than deal with Tychaeus."

Massiva said earnestly, "Massinissa believes we must take advantage of the opportunity Syphax is presenting for a decisive engagement."

Scipio looked confused. "What do you mean?"

Massiva gave Scipio an odd look in response. "Surely you know that Syphax and his entire army are on the march against you?"

A murmur rustled through the coterie of Roman officers. Their scouts had picked up no such indications.

"What are their numbers?" Scipio asked, embarrassed at the failure of his intelligence sources to detect this movement.

"It is said that he has brought fifty thousand infantry and ten thousand horse with him."

Several of the Romans paled at these numbers, which they could not hope to overcome.

"That is not all," Massiva said. "Carthage, seeing the force that Syphax has committed to the field, has ordered Hasdrubal, son of Gisgo, into the field to support Syphax in his march against you. Hasdrubal brings along an additional thirty thousand men."

Laelius swallowed hard. Fortunately, the fleet was nearby. There certainly was time to evacuate the army to Sicily before the approaching host of enemy soldiers could engage them.

Scipio, however, remained calm. It occurred to Laelius that the greater the danger, the less concerned Scipio became. The general asked simply, "Has Syphax announced his intentions?"

"Before departing from Neapolis," Massiva said, "Syphax addressed his people from the steps of his palace. He promised to return to them the living body of Scipio for such punishment as they may see fit. That, or your head."

"Clearly then," Scipio said with a laugh, "an alliance with Massinissa may be the only thing that saves it."

"We have had promises from other Africans," Lucius said cautiously, "which we have come to find wanting. Why should we give any more credence to the word of Massinissa?"

Scipio shot his brother a cross look for asking such an impolitic question. One ill-advised remark like this might break down the potential alliance.

"Do not insult my uncle by comparing him to Syphax. Massinissa is a man of his word," Massiva said hotly. "If he is lying, may your god Jupiter strike me dead, here and now, with a bolt of lightning."

This was a powerful oath, and the soldiers were impressed. Scipio stroked his chin in deep thought for a few moments, then said, "Return to your uncle. Tell him that I wish to parley with him. Take Laelius with you to make the arrangements."

———

One week later, the two leaders met at a tent that had been established roughly equidistant between their respective camps. By prior agreement, both generals were allowed only one attendant, and all men were to be unarmed. Massinissa brought along Massiva, and Scipio was escorted, of course, by Laelius.

The two men sat down across a simple wooden camp table placed in the middle of the tent. Their respective aides took up positions behind them.

Scipio tried to size up the Numidian. He was older than Scipio, perhaps thirty-five, taller and far more powerfully built. When Massinissa moved, his muscles rippled beneath his velvet black skin, which appeared taut over his frame. He looked as if he had been chiseled from a block of ebony. His hairline had receded considerably, exposing a broad expanse of forehead above rich brown eyes that seemed to blaze with a keen intensity. His nose and mouth were classically African, broad and flat. The rest of his face was covered by a thick, wooly beard laced with flecks of gray.

"There are many," Massinissa began amiably, "who believe that you are a god. Perhaps that would explain your success against my men at Baecula."

Scipio smiled, but his eyes held little warmth. "It would be a blasphemy for me to claim to be anything other than the grateful recipient of the blessings of the gods," he said a little stiffly. "As for Baecula, you served under a poor commanding general."

A grin spread across the Numidian's features, revealing flawless, gleaming teeth. "I tried to tell Hasdrubal you were up to something with that peculiar formation, but he was too proud to listen to anyone."

"I regret only that it was my fellow consul Nero who had the pleasure of taking Hasdrubal Barca's head," Scipio replied, a note of bitterness in his voice. "I had hoped to claim that honor for myself."

"The desire for revenge is powerful, is it not? You will understand, then, why I have sought you out for alliance. I am the rightful heir to the throne of Numidia. Carthage and Syphax, for selfish reasons, have conspired to deprive me of my inheritance. I will work my vengeance upon them both."

"It is strange how politics can change things," Scipio observed. "We have been enemies, trying to kill each other, because you found it expedient to aid Carthage. Now you would have us as allies because you believe it expedient to aid the enemy of Carthage."

Massinissa ran his tongue across his upper lip, considering his response. "I do not come before you as a mere supplicant. I offer the support of my men and my skills as a fighting commander, which, you will have to admit, you may be able to put to good use in the coming battles, especially given the numbers Syphax and Hasdrubal intend to bring to bear against you."

"I do not question that the strength of your army would be a valuable resource in the challenge that lies before us," Scipio responded. "But our experience in Africa has not been pleasant. Carthage breached the treaty that ended our first war by capturing Saguntum, thus touching off this war that has brought so much misery upon our heads. And Syphax breached a treaty by which we had thought to make a rapid transit through the land of the Masaesulii."

"That is why I propose that I help you conquer Syphax and Carthage *before* you help me overthrow Tychaeus. I will be the one at risk of a broken promise."

Scipio nodded. This was indeed a persuasive argument.

"This alone should be adequate evidence of my good faith, especially since you would appear to be at a severe disadvantage in numbers. If I were being duplicitous, I would not be casting my lot with someone so badly outnumbered."

Scipio glanced at Laelius. The Numidian's words had the ring of truth.

"And should you require further evidence that my intentions are honorable, I offer you something else." He tilted his head back to address Massiva. "Bring it in."

Massiva scurried out of the tent and returned moments later, carrying a large leather pouch, which he set on the table before Massinissa. The Numidian stood and, grasping the pouch, dumped its contents onto the table.

Laelius gasped. There, on the table before him, lay the armor of Scipio's father, brutally taken from his corpse after he fell in the battle with Hasdrubal Barca. Massinissa had taken a large risk by showing it to Scipio, for if the negotiations failed, surely Scipio would challenge the African to a duel to regain the prize. Although, looking at the African, Laelius had his doubts about whether Scipio could survive such a contest.

Scipio fought to retain his composure as he reached out and ran his fingers over the heavy helmet, its red plume faded and mangled, and the gold inlaid cuirass that had been custom-fitted to his father's chest. There was a deep gash just below the left breast, where the spear that claimed his father's life had entered his body. After several long moments, Scipio picked up the belt and scabbard and drew out the sword.

"This is an omen from the gods," Scipio said reverently. He clutched the grip. "With this sword, the sword of my father, I will conquer Carthage, and slay anyone who stands in my way, even Hannibal himself."

No one spoke as he turned his wrist slowly, making an arc in the air with the blade, getting the feel of the weapon.

Scipio looked at Massinissa. "And then, my friend, we shall turn our attention to ridding your country of Tychaeus, and installing you as the rightful king of Numidia."

After working out arrangements for Massinissa to move his camp to join the Romans, Scipio returned to his own camp, a journey of some two days. When he arrived, he was pleased to find a letter from Marcia. Befitting her wealth, the letter was not written on a common wax tablet, but rather was inscribed in ink, made from a mixture of fine soot and water, and recorded on vellum, a sheet of wafer-thin animal skin.

While Narcussa set about the bittersweet task of polishing and repairing his father's armor, Scipio sat down to read the note.

My Dearest Scipio,

The steady flow of slaves and booty from your campaign certainly has Rome all agog with heady anticipation of your ultimate success. Every time another dispatch arrives with news of some new triumph, Cato seems to sink a little lower. He's absolutely green with envy and full of remorse over abandoning the campaign because of a dispute over money. Believe me, the people aren't worried about money now, at least not while the flow of plunder continues unabated. And Fabius, that rascal, is going about the city claiming that the idea to invade Africa was his all along! Little else is spoken of, and the people seem to believe that any day now word will arrive that you are knocking at the gates of Carthage itself.

Your exploits are even more appreciated in light of the latest dispatches from your co-consul, Crassus. It seems that he managed, in spite of Fabius' instructions, to get himself into a fight with Hannibal in the neighborhood of Croton. Evidently, neither side managed to get adequately formed up, and the engagement was something more of a skirmish than a pitched battle. We rather got the worst of it, I am afraid. The report is that we lost over twelve hundred men.

Since Cato is unable to disparage your reputation, he has instead been buying votes with the public treasury. He persuaded the Senate to approve a new road from the Cattle Market to the Temple of Venus. He has financed this improvement with a new tax on the sale of salt, which has produced plenty of grumbling, believe me!

The only other news of any interest is the outstanding performance of the athlete Gemininus at the recent Roman Games. He swept every event, including the wrestling, which is my favorite. If my saying so is not too scandalous, the sight of all those nude young men exerting themselves is quite arousing—all the more reason I wish we were already married.

Every hour that we are apart seems like a day. I never should have gone along with Father's demand! Please be prompt about your business, so that we might quickly become husband and wife.

I long for that day. I promise that I will be a good wife to you. And I know that you will be a true and loyal husband.

There is not much more to say. Please hurry home and make me your bride.

Marcia

Scipio put the vellum down and watched as Narcussa cleaned and buffed his father's armor.

"Was there any news during my absence?" he asked the servant.

"Not really," Narcussa said. "Oh, there was a little excitement when one of the men knocked over a candle and set fire to his tent. You know, in this dry climate, the flames can spread like wildfire. Before anybody could do much, over a dozen tents were burning. The only thing that stopped it was the spacing between the rows. It can be very dangerous in these camps, you know."

"Indeed," Scipio replied, the germ of an idea forming in his mind. "Well, we'll just have to be more careful."

Syphax and Hasdrubal, son of Gisgo, had been moving their huge force toward the Roman encampment slowly and deliberately. With their vast superiority in numbers, the leaders felt that they only needed to be methodical in going about their campaign, and success was bound to result. They were troubled, however, by the fact that winter was rapidly advancing upon them, and there was some sentiment among the senior officers that the army should go into winter camp and postpone any major engagement with the Romans until spring.

Syphax's attitude toward the question of a winter camp changed radically when an envoy from Scipio arrived, suggesting that negotiations be undertaken for a peaceful conclusion to the hostilities. Hasdrubal, son of Gisgo, was reluctant to negotiate, feeling that with so superior an armed force, they should get on with the offensive.

Syphax, however, once again was enticed by the prospect of earning a reputation as the arbiter of peace between the two combatants. It also occurred to him that with the Romans out of the way, he could turn his attention to eliminating Massinissa so as to cement his control over the territory of Numidia. He therefore decided that it would be worthwhile to explore the negotiations. Word of Scipio's offer was communicated to Carthage, and a response came that, given the immediacy of unfavorable inclement weather, further offensive operations should be suspended and conversations regarding a peace treaty undertaken while the armies were holed up.

The Carthaginians were concerned about the reliability of their ally, and so set up their camp only a stone's throw from Syphax and his army, the better to keep a close watch on his activities. Row upon row of wooden huts were erected in a sprawling expanse to house the men. Syphax's Masaesulii, perhaps reflecting their nomadic origins, were poorly organized and pitched their huts, constructed of reed and thatch, here and there, wherever their fancy struck them, and with little formal organization. Hasdrubal protested over this chaos to Syphax, but the king, preoccupied by the hope of avoiding any clash with the Romans, paid little attention to these complaints.

As the winter set in, group after group of Roman envoys visited the camp, bearing various proposals for peace. The central theme in all these messages was that the Romans would withdraw their challenge to Africa if Carthage would withdraw Hannibal and his army from the territory of Italy. This bargain seemed eminently fair to Syphax, but the king felt compelled to relay each proposal to Carthage for reaction. This process, which took nearly two weeks, utilized a system of outposts established across the frontier, between which riders hurried with the messages. During each exchange, the Roman envoys and their servants were housed in a hut not far from Syphax's lavish quarters, so that they could be made comfortable by his hospitality.

Unbeknownst to Syphax or Hasdrubal, son of Gisgo, each party of envoys included a handpicked group of centurions, chosen for their proven intelligence and ability. These men were humbly dressed as servants, and while the envoys were in consultation, they wandered freely about the camp gathering information about the entrances and exits, habits of the sentries, the locations of the arsenals, and the shape and layout of the camp, both as a whole and in the respective portions occupied by the Carthaginians and the Masaesulii. Included in the information they obtained was the fact that Syphax had brought along his bride to keep him company throughout the frigid nights.

The two camps seemed convinced that the mere existence of their threat had brought the Romans to sue for peace. Indeed, judging from the progress of the negotiations, in which Carthage gradually added oppressive terms and the Romans seemed to be capitulating, it seemed clear that Scipio had no stomach for giving battle to a superior force. All this talk of peace led, as it inevitably does, to a neglect of proper precautions against the possibility of hostilities. The centurions reported that the sentries were disorganized and frequently derelict in their duty, and that many of the soldiers in the camp passed their nights by drinking themselves into a stupor.

Armed with this intelligence, Scipio summoned his officers and Massinissa's commanders into council and laid out his plan for the following night.

Throughout the next day, preparations for an assault on the enemy camps unfolded at a feverish pace and under strictest security. No one was allowed to leave either the Roman or Numidian camp, lest Scipio's plans be betrayed. By late afternoon, the infantry columns were formed up, and just before sunset, the trumpets sounded and the march began. Moving at rapid speed, Scipio's forces by midnight had reached the outskirts of the joint camps of Syphax and Hasdrubal, son of Gisgo. By prior arrangement, Laelius and Massinissa split off silently and moved with a large contingent of men into position outside the Carthaginian encampment.

Scipio himself headed for Syphax's camp. A squadron of Romans, dressed again as the same servants whose presence in the camp had by now become commonplace, entered the stockade through an unguarded gate and filtered out to preordained locations.

Torches were set against the huts ringing the entire perimeter so as to form a hellish ring of fire to entrap the residents. The reed huts were like tinder, and the flames immediately began to spread, first to the immediate surroundings, then inward throughout the entire camp. The terror and confusion were abject. Most soldiers stumbled from the huts without even realizing their quarters were under attack, leaving behind their weapons. Sentries abandoned their posts at the gates in order to fight the blaze. At this point, the Romans poured through the unmanned gates and set upon the Masaesulii warriors as they staggered about, barely comprehending the ruthless slaughter underway.

At the Carthaginian camp, better precautions were in place, and all the gates were duly fortified with alert guards. These men, however, upon seeing the conflagration in their ally's camp, supposed the fire to be caused by some accident, and mistook the cries of the wounded and dying men to be the result of a disastrous emergency. Many of them, anxious to assist their ally, threw open the gates and rushed out, taking with them buckets to fight the blaze rather than their weapons. Laelius and Massinissa were waiting for them, of course, and within moments, the Roman column had thrust its way through the gates and hastily set ablaze the wooden huts of the Carthaginian camp as well.

It was a hideous and fearsome sight, the orange flames licking relentlessly through row after row of neatly ordered huts. The night sky glowed from the angry inferno. Men dashed about here and there, thinking to give battle to the fire, only to find the drawn swords of the enemy waiting to end their lives. Countless men and animals perished from the flames and smoke alone—scores of them never even got out of their burning huts. The surprise was total, the devastation complete.

Meanwhile, over in the Masaesulii camp, Scipio and a carefully selected complement of his most ferocious fighters cut their way through the chaos toward Syphax's quarters. A rather formidable structure had been erected to house the king and his entourage. Syphax stood on the porch of this makeshift palace, barely able to comprehend the catastrophe that had befallen him. Then he saw Scipio and his escort making their way toward him and realized with a sickening dread that this was no mere careless disaster, but rather the result of a well-planned and executed strike. Syphax realized that it would be futile to attempt an escape, and the thought of being paraded in chains through the streets of Rome as Scipio's miserable captive was intolerable. He summoned his bodyguards about him, and with a roar of defiance, charged at the oncoming Romans. Syphax made directly for Scipio, meaning to personally engage his adversary in combat.

The two leaders locked up with each other in a mortal struggle, furious hatred blazing on each man's features. Neither held a shield. Scipio, wielding his father's sword, felt intense pain in his arm each time he parried a blow from Syphax, whose strength, fearsome enough in normal times, seemed enhanced by the desperate nature of his situation. Both men gasped for breath, their lungs aching from the acrid smoke that hung in the air. Back and forth they raged, Scipio relying on quickness, Syphax on his superior strength. As in many such contests, speed won out: Syphax aimed a sweeping blow at Scipio's head and missed, leaving himself exposed for only a second. In that moment, Scipio jammed his blade up through the African's noble breast, lifting him off his feet. Instantly, Scipio saw the light of life go out of Syphax's eyes, and knew he had won.

The phalanx of bodyguards, seeing their king slain, scattered in a wild effort to save their own skins, but to no avail. Scipio pulled his sword from Syphax's corpse with a mighty heave, and, with flesh and gore dripping from the blade, reached down to rip off the golden royal amulet from Syphax's neck. With a cry of triumph, Scipio bounded up the steps and into the palace.

He stormed through the structure, frantically searching room after room until, finally, he rounded a corner and found Vibiana huddled on a divan with a robe clutched about her. Her eyes focused on the amulet Scipio carried, and she cried out, knowing her last hope was gone. Scipio swept across the room and put the tip of his sword at the base of her throat.

And hesitated.

He was startled by her lunge, and the small dagger in her hand that grazed the side of his neck, drawing blood though he nimbly avoided her thrust. He caught her arm with his free hand, and, twisting her wrist, easily disarmed her.

"Did you think me as easy to slay as Maximillian?" he asked her, his voice hoarse.

"Go ahead, kill me," she wept. "Better to die here and now than to be your slave again."

Scipio moved back and lowered his sword, feeling the pain from the wound in his neck beginning to throb. "I did not come to Africa, and fight these battles, for the mere privilege of killing you with a sword," he said angrily. "I have other things in store for you."

XI

Utica, Africa

203 BC

T HE NEXT MORNING, THE officers gathered in council at Syphax's captured residence to review the details of their victory. Scipio's commanders were stunned by the totality of their success. Even Massinissa was awed at the terrible carnage Scipio's daring night raid had inflicted upon his mortal enemy. It was estimated that fewer than two thousand Carthaginians had escaped, although apparently Hasdrubal Gisgo was among the lucky few to get away. The dead were too numerous to count, and the mere task of stacking the bodies into huge pyres was expected to require several days of work. Over fifteen thousand men had been taken prisoner, including several Carthaginians of noble blood, and more were being rounded up hourly by the search parties Scipio had dispatched. The attackers had captured over 175 military standards, 2,700 horses, and six live elephants—eight others had been killed. These animals were a major prize, for Scipio would make use of them to advance the training of his men in the new formation he planned to employ against Hannibal, should a showdown ever come about. Scipio announced that the vast quantity of weapons taken from the enemy would be thrown into the sea as a tribute to Neptune.

The officers were pleasantly engaged in the task of dividing the spoils when the issue of Vibiana arose. Word had spread through the camp that Syphax's wife was one and the same woman as the wench

Scipio had been bedding in Spain. This presented a major problem.

Silanus could not resist the opportunity to make his general uncomfortable. "She is guilty of taking the life of a Roman soldier, and very nearly killed you as well," he said, pointing to a large bandage on the side of his commander's neck, over which Scipio had taken considerable ribbing. "I demand that she be punished for her crime. The penalty is well known. Her life is forfeit: you may crucify her or burn her at the stake. It is highly unusual to crucify a woman of noble birth, and so the torch is more likely the instrument of her punishment."

Scipio said nothing.

Laelius saw Scipio's discomfort and had an idea. "On the other hand," he said, "she is the wife of the deceased king of the Masaesulii, himself a declared enemy of Rome. In such circumstances, the custom is to transmit the widow to Rome for the judgment of the Senate as to her fate. Sometimes, the widow can be ransomed by her father's family, but I am unaware of any case involving a captive who took the life of a Roman soldier. Under the circumstances, I cannot believe she will be shown leniency."

"In Africa," Massinissa spoke up, "a woman is the property of the man who captures her, regardless of her station."

Silanus was indignant. "A Roman army is bound by Roman law, not by the custom of the country in which it happens to be operating. This woman killed a good and loyal Roman soldier who had many friends among our ranks."

Laelius turned to Scipio. "I know that you may have feelings for her, but the men will be resentful if she is spared her rightful punishment."

Scipio glared at Silanus. "What do you estimate my share of the prizes taken last night to be?"

Silanus scratched his stubbly face, not having had an opportunity to attend to his personal toilet due to the night's events. "It is difficult to predict with certainty. The market for slaves is depressed, with the supply you've been sending to Rome. The nobles will of course be ransomed and will bring a hefty sum. In all, you should clear certainly not less than a million sesterces."

Silanus could not restrain his envy. Scipio was richer than ever.

Scipio rose. "Tell the men that the entire proceeds of the sale of the captives will be divided among them as a gift from their grateful commander."

The men gasped as they considered the impact of Scipio's extraordinary generosity, each trying to calculate what his share of the wealth might be.

He looked at Laelius. "I know of nothing in the custom that requires a captive to be transmitted to the Senate while the campaign is still underway," he said. "Since I cannot have Syphax to put on display when I return to Rome, and since you failed to capture Hasdrubal Gisgo, I appear to have no trophies to exhibit upon my return. The wife of Syphax will have to suffice. I shall turn her over to the Senate. Until then, I wish to keep her with us. Surely the men will not object to such a simple plan."

The Roman officers, even Silanus, shrugged. With the fabulous gift Scipio had just bestowed on them, they were not about to challenge him: justice, after all, was a relative thing.

Laelius, however, would have none of it. "Scipio, you are engaged to be married to the daughter of the most powerful man in Rome. Are you so naive as to believe that word of your carrying on with this wench will not reach her ears?"

Scipio's temper exploded, and he grabbed Laelius by the tunic. "Do not suppose that your friendship with my family entitles you to challenge my will," he stormed. "I will not have someone who prefers the company of boys question my dealings with women!"

The faces of the men in the room were ashen, and Scipio knew at once he had gone too far. Shocked at the words that had issued from his own mouth, he released Laelius and stepped back. Before he could say anything further, Laelius stalked out, looking like a wounded animal.

None of Scipio's officers would look him in the eye as he settled heavily back into the curule chair.

Finally, Lucius spoke up. "All of you, leave us alone." He waited until the last soldier had departed, then said, "He has been a loyal officer and retainer to our family. You must apologize."

This strained Scipio's pride. "I am the commanding general," he said stubbornly.

"Laelius was only speaking for your own best interest," Lucius pointed out. "You cannot keep this woman. It will cause a scandal in Rome."

Scipio rubbed his eyes, still smarting from the smoke the previous night, as if he were weary. "If my victory in Africa is great enough, it will not matter."

Lucius, realizing the truth, looked down at his brother. "You are in love with her, aren't you?"

Scipio remained silent.

"Your silence betrays you," Lucius said, grinning. "Very well, then. I know you well enough by now. You will have your way, and the rest of them will just have to adjust."

Scipio looked up and smiled. "Yes," he said, "even Laelius. To whom I owe an apology."

———

Scipio found Laelius in his tent, accompanied by a manservant, looking for all intents and purposes as if he were packing to leave.

Seeing Scipio enter, Laelius drew himself to attention.

"Take your ease," Scipio said uncomfortably, unaccustomed to such formality with his longtime confidant. He gestured toward the trunks in varying stages of being packed. "What are you doing?"

"I am preparing to quit the camp, and your service," Laelius replied, his tone neutral. He resumed folding a scarlet tunic.

"You cannot do that," Scipio said, a little petulant. "You are enlisted for the duration of the campaign, or until I release you, which I do not intend to do."

"You are mistaken," Laelius rejoined. "I came along on this expedition as a volunteer. You never administered the oath of loyalty to me. If you try to remember doing so, you labor in vain. I am therefore here of my own free will, and as a free citizen of Rome am at liberty to leave when I see fit."

Scipio realized Laelius was correct. It had been assumed, without any discussion, that Laelius would join the African Expedition, and so no formal swearing-in ceremony had ever been held for Laelius, or for any other members of the high command, for that matter. Angry with himself for this oversight, Scipio glanced at the manservant and said in a harsh tone, "Leave us. I wish to speak alone with your master."

The slave, a slender lad not older than twenty, looked at Laelius.

Laelius nodded his head. Watching him depart, Scipio was struck by the young man's good looks. Apparently a Spaniard, he had a rich, olive complexion and a well-muscled build. Scipio realized that the boy probably was Laelius' current lover. He was not revolted by this: any number of prominent Romans, following the custom of aristocratic Greeks, were openly known to enjoy the delights of both male and female love. His own father had tolerated Laelius' preferences, and so Scipio had always regarded it as something of an oddity, or a mere bad habit.

"We have been together for far too long, and have been through too much together, for you to just up and leave," Scipio said plaintively when the youngster was out of earshot.

Laelius said nothing, his attention focused on folding the tunic.

"And what of your pledge to my father, to serve me loyally and protect me wherever I go?"

"A pledge of loyalty is deemed discharged by the disloyal act of one to whom the pledge is given," Laelius said, resorting to legal niceties, as he was prone to do. "You have humiliated me in front of my peers. My ability to function as your second-in-command is irreparably compromised. I cannot continue in that role."

"But you must! We are on the cusp of our greatest triumph. The road to Carthage lies open before us. We have only to march to her gates and demand that she yield. The campaign is at its most critical stage. I must have your assistance."

Laelius walked over to a large, open trunk and began stowing tunics. He shifted several pieces of armor, using a tunic as a wrap to keep them from rubbing against each other. After a few moments, it became apparent to Scipio that Laelius did not intend to respond.

"I know you were only speaking for what you believe is my own best interest," Scipio said, trying a different tack. "I lost my temper. It was a stupid thing to say. I did not mean to hurt you."

"You most certainly did," Laelius snapped. "You have worn the mantle of command long enough to know that a harsh word from a general is as deadly as a sentence of exile."

Scipio, miserable, slumped onto a cot. Was there nothing he could do to reverse his error? He decided on a final attempt.

"Throughout my career," Scipio said softly, "you have protected me against my own worst instincts. You have been the voice of caution to rein in my lofty ambitions, which I admit occasionally have exposed me and the men to danger. You are like a part of me. I cannot defeat Carthage without you any more than I could lift a sword without my arm."

This gave Laelius pause. It was an extraordinary admission from one who had garnered so much fame so early in life. It revealed that Scipio retained a basic humility, that his impulsive ego had not yet overcome his good judgment. If Scipio had matured enough to realize that he owed his success to the continuing efforts of many, many others, perhaps there was hope for him after all.

"And what of your relationship with this slave girl?" Laelius asked sharply. "Would you put it before your friendship with me?"

Scipio looked more miserable than ever. "Please," he said, "do not put me to such a dilemma."

Laelius stroked his chin with his thumb and his forefinger. "You are in love with her, aren't you?" he sighed. "Well, I was in love once myself. There is no point appealing to your head in such matters; you must follow your own heart. To do otherwise is to commit yourself to a lifetime of misery."

"I cannot truly follow my heart unless you are at my side," Scipio said cleverly.

Laelius felt himself giving in. He felt very much like a father who, having reprimanded his son, feels almost guilty himself. "Very well, my friend," he said at last. "Let's set our sights on Carthage."

Overjoyed, Scipio jumped up from the cot and clutched Laelius in a long, heartfelt embrace. Upon separating, he said mischievously, "You never told me you were in love. What happened?"

A grieved look passed over Laelius' features. He hesitated for a few moments, and then said simply, "He died."

"Oh," Scipio said a little awkwardly, again wrestling with the discomfort of realizing that Laelius had been in love with a man. "I'm sorry. Was he killed in the war?"

Laelius looked down, reluctant to answer.

"I pledge to you that your secret will be safe with me," Scipio said earnestly. "Sometimes, speaking of such matters helps to lift a burden from the soul."

"I have no doubt that you will keep this particular secret," Laelius said, looking fondly up at the taller Scipio. "My lover was your father."

It took several minutes for Scipio to recover from the shock of Laelius' revelation. The whole gamut of human emotions swept over him during this interval: disbelief, anger, disbelief again, then finally, a wistful sadness for the loss they both so keenly felt.

"Why did you wait," Scipio asked, when he had finally recovered enough to speak, "all these years without telling me?"

"He did not want you to know until you were ready to handle it," Laelius replied. "He was so very proud of you, but somehow never was able to let it show. Roman discipline, I suppose. Or perhaps he wanted you to keep striving for his approval. You are very much like him, you know. Afraid of nothing, willing to stop at nothing, determined to have your way, totally dedicated to the Roman cause. Of course, you have already accomplished more in your brief career than he did in all of his. Unlike you, however, he had the opportunity of a boyhood uncluttered by the specter of war, and so he was more worldly than you. And by this, I do not merely refer to his sexual habits."

At this Scipio blushed.

"He was a keen student of politics and the arts, two pursuits in which your education has been a bit lacking, I am afraid. They are related, after all. He would have approved of your engagement to Marcia, and most certainly would not approve of the comedy you seem determined to play out with this Carthaginian girl. At least, I hope it is only a comedy and does not become a tragedy. In a tragedy, after all, the hero is undone by his good intentions."

"It hardly seems appropriate to cite my father as a source of moral authority," Scipio retorted, "given his behavior with you, in light of his marital vows!"

"Better in many respects to skirt the marital vows with a man rather than a woman," Laelius laughed. "It's much less risky. There is little chance of discovery, and, after all, how can a woman be envious of another man? She would, even if she learned of the relationship, dismiss it as a mere aberration. But another woman! That's a different kettle of fish indeed. Better to face a hundred Hannibals, or a thousand of his damned elephants, than to confront the hellcat Marcia will become when she learns of your interest in Vibiana."

Scipio shifted uneasily. "When I asked for her hand, I genuinely felt affection for her. And I thought I would never see Vibiana again," he said defensively. "I shall, at the appropriate time, explain to Marcia the circumstances and ask to be released from our promise to marry."

"That explanation will never hold water."

"But it's the truth!" Scipio protested.

"Surely," Laelius said sharply, "you obtained enough schooling in Roman politics during the recent campaign to learn that truth is the least relevant concern of any public official."

Scipio threw up his hands. "I must be true to myself. To do otherwise, as you say, is to be sentenced to a lifetime of misery."

Laelius sighed, saddened at the heavy burden the young man carried. Scipio was in love, and there was nothing to be done about it. They would simply have to play out the string, and see what the gods had in store for him. He drew himself up. "What are your orders?"

Scipio eyed his officer warily, suspicious of this sudden change in direction. "What do you recommend?"

"We have a week or two of work here before we can commence a general movement of the army against Carthage," Laelius observed. "The weather is likely not to be favorable, and so there is considerable risk that we could yet fail in our mission."

"How so?"

"The vagaries of the weather make marching at this time of year very hazardous. The men might arrive at Carthage decimated by the climate or by disease, and so make easy pickings for the garrison of Carthage. And what's more, we have yet to draw Hannibal out of Italy."

Scipio had been contemplating a lightning march against Carthage. But Laelius' advice, he had to admit, was sound.

"I suggest," Laelius continued, "that we dispatch only a token force on a march against Carthage, to clear the way for us and give plenty of advance notice of our threat. Our main force, however, can remain in place before Utica, maintaining the siege there. The Carthaginian scouts will no doubt exaggerate the size of the army marching on them, and I suspect the city will be in a panic."

"So you would give them the chance to recall Hannibal?"

Laelius put his hand on Scipio's shoulder. "You have made a believer of me," he said. "Rome will not be safe while Hannibal heads an army. We must defeat him, and you are the only Roman capable of doing so."

"Clearly," Scipio said after several thoughtful moments, "having pleaded with you to rejoin me, I can hardly ignore your advice!"

———

Scipio returned to his command tent, his arm about Laelius' shoulders, and, upon arriving, ordered Lucius to summon every officer who had been present at his unfortunate outburst. Lucius, relieved to see the old comrades reunited, scurried to carry out his brother's order. Within a few minutes, the entire cadre of commanders was reassembled.

"A brief while ago," Scipio addressed them, "all of you bore witness to my insult of a man who has been more loyal to me than my own right arm." He pulled Laelius forward and put his arm around him. "I was a fool to say these things, and I renounce them. Further, I apologize to Laelius, here and now, with all of you as witnesses."

The soldiers mostly studied their feet. This was an extraordinary performance, for each had been around his share of generals, and very few of these exalted commanders—and certainly not a consul of Rome—would even admit an error, let alone apologize to a sub-ordinate for it.

"Now I know," Scipio said, gazing placidly at Silanus, "that some of you are old-fashioned, and will think the less of me for giving an apology, or may think Laelius undeserving of it. Let there be no grouching behind my back. I mean to clear the air of this matter once and for all. If any of you has anything to say, say it now, to my face."

Oddly enough, it was Massinissa who spoke up after a few uncomfortable moments of silence. "Any fool can get himself appointed a general. All of us are witness to the fact that there have been more fools than wise men in that position!"

This drew a round of laughter, which relaxed the tension in the room.

Massinissa continued, "However, to admit the error of one's ways, and to beg forgiveness for a slip of the tongue committed in the heat of anger is a sign of strength, not of weakness. I for one consider myself fortunate to serve such a man, and I salute you both."

A murmur of approval rumbled through the group.

Scipio, sensing a golden opportunity to cement the restoration of Laelius' status, announced, "Laelius has made a sound proposal regarding our conduct of the campaign henceforward, with which I completely concur. He will tell you all about it."

Scipio turned to leave the tent.

"Where are you going?" Lucius asked.

"I am weary," Scipio replied with a grin. "I trust all of you will understand if I wish to obtain some rest. I will be in my quarters."

They all exchanged knowing glances as he swept out, for it was common knowledge that the woman Vibiana had been held there since being taken captive the night before.

———

Over and again, Vibiana cursed herself for having lunged at Scipio with the precious dagger, rather than using the weapon on herself. Suicide was out of the question now. She had been thoroughly searched—there had been considerable guffawing at her shaved pubis—heavily chained, dressed in coarse sackcloth, and deposited into the custody of two stone-faced Roman guards. These legionnaires evidently had been given strict orders concerning their scrutiny of her, for they had kept their eyes locked on her for the duration of their surveillance. Their expression had not changed in the hours she had been restrained in Scipio's tent, not even during her periodic fits of weeping over her miserable fate.

Twice taken prisoner by the Romans! *What god did I offend*, she asked herself repeatedly, *to merit this cruel destiny?* Her mood alternated between pitiful despair and paralyzing fear.

First, despair: she knew her situation was utterly hopeless. The Masaesulii were shattered and their king, Syphax, was dead. Culchas was successor to the throne, but she expected he would immediately sue for peace with the Romans, hoping to preserve some scrap of autonomy for his country in return for clearing the path to Carthage. Certainly, Culchas would not make her freedom a condition of any peace treaty!

Then fear: Vibiana was well aware of the retribution Romans imposed for the murder of one of their soldiers. The stories concerning the atrocities at Iliturgi and Astapa were chilling, and kept forcing their way to the forefront of her consciousness. And, of course, she had been made to watch the terrible whipping administered to Camarissa. Could Scipio be as harsh with her?

But where was Scipio? Why had he kept her waiting all these hours before handing down sentence? And why had he made her wait here, in the very tent where they had made love so many times?

Her reveries were abruptly interrupted when Scipio strode into the tent, clad in the regal tunic of a consul. Vibiana, unfamiliar with Roman custom, did not grasp the import of his garb. With a gesture, Scipio dismissed the guards and poured wine from a golden decanter into a goblet. He sat down on the curule chair.

"Are you aware of the significance of this chair?" he asked. Vibiana remained silent, her eyes fixed on the floor.

"I am a pro-consul of Rome, having been freely chosen as such by the People's Assembly. You are not familiar with the consular office? All the power and authority of Rome is vested in me," he said, picking up the imperial rod and rolling it delicately in his hands. Its slender ivory shaft was cool to the touch, and he ran his fingers over the intricately cast golden eagle. He snapped in his most authoritative tone, "You must answer for Maximillian!"

At the sound of the murdered guard's name, she quivered, summoning up reserves of strength she did not know she had in order to retain her composure.

"Your fate is the subject of considerable controversy."

Crying now, she looked away, not wanting to let him see her weakness.

"The preferred disposition of your case among my officers is to burn you alive. At least, that seems to be favored over crucifixion, which is another of my options."

Vibiana blanched. Death by fire—the most horrible of punishments! Her mind raced back to the death of Octuro, and his last piteous howl as the flames devoured him. Even now, it echoed in her ears.

"There are others," Scipio continued, "who insist that I should have you transported back to Rome so that the Senate may pass judgment on you. They are politicians, of course, and there is some chance that they might be less harsh. They would probably vote to bury you alive, in the manner reserved for punishment of a vestal virgin who has betrayed her vows. Are you familiar with the technique?"

She could no longer tolerate this exposition. "Why must you torment me so? Are you such a beast that you savor my anguish? If ever you felt anything for me, I beg you now, pronounce your judgment, whatever it may be! Surely the carrying out of the sentence cannot be so hard to bear as the cruelty by which your delay tortures me!"

He considered her for a moment, then said quietly, "The pain you feel now is nothing compared to the anguish I endured after your sudden departure."

She was stopped short by this revelation. "What do you mean?" she whispered, barely comprehending.

"I mean that every night I have passed alone since you left me has seemed like an eternity. And when I heard that you had been made the bribe by which Syphax was lured away from his alliance with Rome, I nearly went mad with envy."

"Nevertheless," she said sharply, "the gods have blessed your cause, and delivered me into your hands. Here I am, for you to take your revenge."

"Revenge," he said, "is not what I seek."

"Then what do you seek?"

He paused, for what seemed an eternity. Finally, he breathed, "Your love."

She looked up at him, incredulous. "How can you speak to me of love? You do not love me. I am nothing more to you than an object for your pleasure. You cannot relate to me unless I am in chains, helpless before you. You do not want to be my lover. You want to be my master!"

Scipio pondered this point for several moments, then called for the guard.

"Remove the irons from this woman," he commanded. "She is free to go."

The guard, who only minutes earlier had been under the strictest command to prevent her escape, was astonished.

"Obey my order," Scipio barked, "or you will bear her chains."

This snapped the man out of his shock, and he rushed to unshackle her, then scurried from the tent, the heavy links clanking as he moved.

"This freedom you offer me is a farce," Vibiana said testily, massaging her wrists, rubbed raw from the bonds. "I have nowhere to go, no means of sustenance. I cannot survive in the desert. I am just as much your prisoner, chained or not."

Scipio got up and went over to his trunk. He returned carrying a heavy, brown canvas sack, which he set down with a thud on the table. From the sound alone, Vibiana surmised that the bag contained a large sum of money.

"One hundred thousand sesterces," Scipio said. "More than enough to enable your comfort wherever you may choose to go."

This incredibly swift change of fortune left her bewildered. Only moments earlier, she had been steeling herself for a hideous death; now, she was free, and rich. She was conflicted.

"But why do you do this?" was all she could manage.

"Because I desire you to stay. But if you do, I wish your love to be freely given. As is mine."

Could this be? These were the words she had longed to hear; his failure to say them four years before had led her to run from him, toward nothing but misery. She reeled at this revelation, skeptical of its dizzying implications.

"Oh, yes, I'm sure you want nothing more than to love me *here*, on the battlefields of Africa. But when it is time for you to return to Rome, what will happen to me then? I refuse to be cast aside when you are finished using me as you will! Surely the conquering hero will be expected to take a noble Roman wife, while his murderous Carthaginian whore is thrown to the Roman wolves?"

Scipio met Vibiana's scathing gaze and spoke with calm, steady power. "When I have defeated your uncle, the people of Rome will deny me nothing. I want you, Vibiana, and I shall have you, here and everywhere I go, for the rest of my life."

She felt a quaking at her core and bit her lip to keep from crying out. She believed him—both his words and the depth of love beneath them. She reached out for him, collapsing with relief into his arms.

"Never leave me again," Scipio whispered, kissing her fervently.

"No," she said, moments later, tears flowing. "I will never leave you freely. But my fate seems always to take me where I do not wish to be."

Scipio kissed her again, longer and deeper.

"I will not allow it," he said. "There is no power on earth that can take you away from me. We are together now, and I will let nothing tear us apart again."

XII

ROME

203 BC

AFTER REREADING EACH DISPATCH for the third time, Quintus Fabius Maximus set the two rolls of vellum on a beveled wooden table situated in his sparsely furnished study. He picked up several carved stones and used them to anchor each respective communication at the corners while he considered their import. He drew his woolen cloak tight about him, for the February air was damp and chilly. Fabius did not want to expose himself to any illness, which at his age could prove fatal. Certainly, he did not want to take sick now, when the end of the war might finally be in sight.

He had often fretted as to whether he would live long enough to see Rome triumphant over Carthage. Fabius picked up a cloth and pressed it against his gum, trying to stem the bleeding from yet another lost tooth—his mouth, like the rest of him, bore the ravages of old age. Nothing but soup and soft foods for him, according to the doctors. Now, he was relieved to realize that, with any luck at all, he would still be around when the war finally was won.

Oddly enough, the two letters had arrived within an hour of each other, each borne by special military courier. How unusual, Fabius thought, that such monumental correspondence, originating so far apart, would reach him almost simultaneously.

In strictly military terms, of course, the second package to arrive was by far the more significant, even momentous. It was a message from the new consul, Sempronius, who had been elected in the fall and installed in January. Sempronius had assumed command of the Roman Army in the field facing Hannibal, succeeding the unfortunate Crassus, who had been given the simple instruction "do nothing" and proved himself utterly unable to execute it, with disastrous consequences. The other man elected consul, Tiberius, had been dispatched to Gaul to keep an eye on the ever-restless hostile tribes there. Scipio, on the strength of his smashing success against Syphax and Hasdrubal Gisgo, had had his command of the African Expedition extended for another year.

Sempronius' missive was straightforward and to the point: his scouts had picked up incontrovertible indications that Hannibal was preparing to depart Italy with his army. A Carthaginian transport fleet had put in at Brundisium, having evaded the Roman naval patrols. Sempronius' spies were reporting that the Carthaginian government had recalled their greatest living general to save them from the marauding Scipio.

Fabius turned the import of this news over in his mind, struggling to grasp all the ramifications. If Sempronius' intelligence was correct, Scipio's strategy had been vindicated by events. Even equipped with a laughably inadequate force, he had in fact drawn Hannibal home to defend his fatherland. It was an extraordinary accomplishment.

But what to do next? Fabius wondered. Certainly, the navy ought to make an all-out effort to intercept Hannibal and destroy him on the high seas, where he would be most vulnerable. Elephants, after all, could not swim. Carthage was probably sufficiently terrified that they would make huge concessions to obtain a negotiated settlement of the war, although it would have to be up to them to make the first move—the tides of war, after all, were clearly surging for Rome. And of course, Scipio and his army must be summoned home before Hannibal could arrive on the scene to reverse his country's fortunes and inflict yet another humiliating defeat upon the Romans.

Ah, but the recall of Scipio was made extremely problematic by the news contained in the other letter, which had been the first to arrive.

Fabius had easily reinstated the arrangement with Silanus, again buying up his debts as security for the cavalryman's faithful performance of his reporting duties. Silanus, desperate to keep himself off the slaver's auction block, had proven eager to bargain.

It was by this means that Fabius had learned of the treachery of Syphax, in advance of Scipio's formal notification to the Senate, which arrived well after the army had already been invested in Africa. Fabius had been angered at Scipio's seeming recklessness in proceeding with the invasion in the face of the obstacle thrown up by Syphax, without even consulting the Senate. Why, he had wondered at the time, was Scipio in such a hurry to take on Syphax? Now, the answer to the riddle was sitting on the desk before him.

Scipio's Spanish harem girl was, in fact, the daughter of Hasdrubal Barca—Hannibal's own niece! And Scipio, having recaptured her during the burning of Syphax's camp, had restored her to his bed rather than turn her over to the Senate. Indeed, Silanus reported that Scipio was in love with the girl. Incredible!

Fabius allowed himself a wry smile. Marcinius was going to have an absolute fit when he heard the news. Well, it served the old fool justly: had he not warned Marcinius, after all, that Scipio was merely exploiting his daughter to win command of the expedition?

Thinking of Marcia saddened Fabius. By all indications, she was truly in love with that scoundrel Scipio. Despite her naïveté, she was a lovely and charming girl. This would break her heart.

He sighed. There was no point in delaying the inevitable. It was time to convey the news to Marcinius.

———

Fabius had steeled himself for an angry outburst when Marcinius was informed of the sordid details of Scipio's behavior, and so he was not cowed by the senator's raving upon hearing them. He was caught totally off guard, however, by what Marcinius, after calming down, proposed to do about it.

"We must order him to engage Hannibal and fight him to the death," Marcinius said, his cunning eyes darting back and forth like a viper's.

"Engage Hannibal? Are you mad? We have not given him nearly enough men: the entire army will be wiped out."

An evil look passed over Marcinius' features. "Yes?"

Fabius could not believe what he was hearing. "Now see here, Marcinius, we cannot condemn three legions to death just so that you can settle a score, however justified your grievance with Scipio may be."

"And why not? They are survivors of Cannae. They should have died there anyway. You yourself have said as much."

"That was before their exemplary service in Africa," Fabius retorted. "And besides, that was just idle talk. What you are proposing is outrageous. I cannot be a part of it."

Marcinius folded his hands on his lap and glared at Fabius with a deadly earnestness. "Marcia must never learn of Scipio's unfaithfulness. It will shatter her. She is truly in love with him. She may never recover, and might live out her days as a spinster, shriveled up and full of hate. I will not have it."

"Why is it any better to have her grieving over a fallen Scipio?"

"Because, my friend, that is a pain from which she can recover," Marcinius responded. "She will still be in love with an ideal, and have a sense of what a proper relationship between a man and wife can be. If she learns of Scipio's callous treatment of her, she will never trust anyone, and perhaps never again fall in love. She is in the flower of her womanhood. This will crush her. I cannot permit it to happen."

Fabius shook his head stubbornly. "The war is all but won. If Scipio is recalled, Carthage will negotiate for peace. We know that from their behavior even before Syphax and Hasdrubal Gisgo were eliminated. But Hannibal presents an entirely different proposition. If Scipio remains in Africa, and is wiped out, the fortunes of war shift back to Carthage. Aside from the issue of jeopardizing so many Roman soldiers, your idea could snatch defeat from the jaws of victory. The gods finally have brought us to the cusp of success—let us not fumble it away!"

"Ah, but if Scipio wins, Carthage will have to beg for peace. The terms will be much more favorable for us."

"But you do not expect Scipio to win! Indeed, you do not even expect him to survive the battle!" Fabius sputtered.

"I have the power," Marcinius snapped, "to work my will."

"Not if I oppose you. The Senate would be divided, and in such circumstances, the military outlook would prevail."

"I am not so sure. Scipio has his enemies, with the displaced Cato at the top of the list. He has been hungering for revenge ever since he got back from Sicily."

"I do not doubt that you can sway votes in the Senate," Fabius responded. "But I would oppose you with all my influence."

"That would be a very foolish thing to do, Fabius." The two men glared at each other.

"What is that supposed to mean?" Fabius demanded.

"I rather suspect," Marcinius said in a vile tone, "that the revelation of the existence of your little reporting system would not sit well with all the distinguished generals who have been victimized by it."

Fabius felt his blood run cold. "You would not . . ."

"I most certainly would. Are you prepared to end your career as an outcast, scorned by the top officers of the army, the very organization to which you have dedicated your life?"

Fabius sat quietly, trying to calculate what might happen if Marcinius carried through on his threat. Some of the men he had spied upon, Scipio among them, were known to be hot-tempered. There was no telling what they might do.

"We sent Scipio on a mission," Marcinius said, sensing that his colleague was wavering. "There is no reason to change that mission now, not when we are so close to the decisive victory for which we have all longed. Indeed, Scipio himself has sworn an oath to bring Hannibal to battle. Judging from his success, it must be the will of the gods that he honor the vow. Why should we interfere? Indeed, I am not sure Scipio's faction in the Senate would go along with your effort to recall him. They think they have a winner, after all."

Fabius arched his eyebrows in agreement with the latter remark. Certainly, Rome was already basking in the glow of victory. The news from Sempronius—Hannibal out of Italy at long last—was going to make everyone delirious, as if the war were over. If he tried to withdraw the army from Africa, he certainly would come under the usual vitriolic criticism. Fabius the Delayer, Fabius the Timid, Fabius the Do-Nothing: he was weary of these insults.

Marcinius bore in. "Come now, you must admit that Scipio's boldness had accomplished far more than you ever dreamed possible. I hardly see how we can deprive him of his opportunity for the ultimate honor. The man who vanquishes Hannibal will be the toast of the city. Indeed, I believe I shall propose a resolution to the Senate, bestowing a new name on our dear young commander. We shall call him 'Africanus,' for the territory he has conquered. And the Senate shall bid him proceed with all due haste to Carthage, there to claim for Rome all the riches that he might rightfully demand."

"You would risk the very fate of Rome over the emotions of your daughter?" Fabius said faintly.

"Direct your observation to Scipio," Marcinius said, his mood ugly again. "It is he who has set the stakes."

Fabius turned on his heel and stalked out. Marcinius watched him go. Then, still furious at Scipio, he decided on a wild gambit. This was too sensitive to entrust to a scribe: he took up a clean patch of vellum and his pen and began to write.

Brundisium

A cold rain pelted Hannibal as he watched the remnants of his proud army being loaded onto the heavy transports at the port of Brundisium, the last stronghold in Italy still under Carthaginian control. A heavy bank of fog rolled toward the shore from the distant waves. The fog was a gift from the gods: it would shroud the army's departure from the Roman galleys known to be patrolling in the vicinity. The gray skies reflected his mood, as well as the outlook of his senior officers, who stood at his side. Carthage had been hard-pressed to assemble a fleet for the crossing and indeed there were not enough boats to transport the entire army and its animals. Since ships were at a premium, a decision had been taken to kill the elephants and the horses rather than let them fall into Roman hands. Hannibal had been assured that an all-out effort was being mounted at Carthage to assemble an adequate force with which he could confront the Romans under Scipio. Or Africanus, as the Roman Senate had voted to entitle him.

Only a few thousand of the men who had crossed the Alps with Hannibal remained; survivors of so many battles he could not even remember them all. His losses had been replenished so often that he knew only a handful of the replacements by name. His own body was ravaged by the experience in Italy, scarred and worn from the constant burden of command.

How different things might have been, he thought wistfully, *if only I had marched straight to Rome after Cannae. That is what Scipio would have done!*

He set his jaw at the thought of Scipio. Hannibal was observant enough to know that his men were worried about facing this Roman, who seemed to be protected by the gods themselves. Indeed, many were saying that he was himself a god! Certainly, the man had been blessed with good fortune. Hannibal was looking forward to the challenge. After all these years of small, unfulfilling hit-and-run skirmishes with the Romans, he craved a decisive battle. Regrettably, the fight would have to take place on Carthaginian territory, but such were the fickle fortunes of war.

No matter, Hannibal thought. *After I have eliminated Scipio, I shall return to this country and conquer it once and for all.*

The last of the men were aboard their ships, and the harbormaster indicated for Hannibal to come aboard the flagship. There was undisguised anxiety on the faces of the sailors, for it was known that their imminent departure had been announced to the Roman Senate, which had ordered the Roman navy to do everything in its power to intercept them on the high seas.

Hannibal hated sailing. Aside from the inevitable seasickness, the stench of the ships themselves was intolerable: the miserable galley slaves were chained to their oars, naked, standing in their own waste because the cramped ships had no latrine facilities for them. He had ordered that the flagship be rinsed of their feces before he boarded, but knew that in only a few hours, the smell would be back.

And so Hannibal dawdled. So much of his life he'd invested in this country, and now for naught. His own country was reeling from the effects of the war, her fortune depleted, and the flower of her youth decimated. The thought of Rome ascendant in the world was more than he could bear.

"My lord," the harbormaster pressed, "we must be underway quickly if we are to have any chance of evading the Roman galleys."

Hannibal stepped onto a gangplank leading out to the ship. He turned and looked back at Italy a final time.

"A curse on you," he uttered, and spit on the soil. "Take me below," Hannibal growled at the ship's captain. "I do not wish to watch the shore recede behind me, for my eye is fixed now on the enemy who awaits us."

XIII

UTICA, AFRICA

202 BC

THE FORMAL DECREE OF the Roman Senate arrived at the camp outside Utica, where the grim siege operation was making slow but methodical progress. A considerable portion of the wall was now under excavation by hundreds of slaves pressed into the effort by the Romans, and the siegemaster was hopeful of a breakthrough soon. In an effort to induce the Uticans to give up, Scipio had issued a proclamation to the effect that he would make of Utica whatever the Uticans selected: like Iliturgi, they could all suffer the penalty of the sword, or like Castulo, they could surrender gracefully and accept the yoke of Roman rule. Thus far, there had been no response from the town fathers.

Scipio was enormously proud of his new status. He assembled the entire army and had the decree read aloud to the men, bowing to their cheers when they heard the part conferring on him the title of *Africanus*. No Roman soldier in the field had ever been so honored. For several days, he insisted that everyone around him refer to him by his new title, even Vibiana, who was completely unimpressed.

"Is it not premature," she suggested one warm evening as they were taking their meal in the company of Lucius, Laelius, and Massinissa, "to be named conqueror of Africa while Hannibal is on his way to save Carthage, which has not surrendered?"

"I shall bring that state of affairs about shortly enough," Scipio replied, slightly piqued at her display of disrespect before his confidants. "Perhaps then you shall see fit to confer upon me the honor the Senate of Rome has already seen fit to bestow."

Vibiana smiled sweetly at Scipio, and he at once forgot his displeasure with her catty remark. As always, she looked ravishing. Her thick locks were piled high on her head and swept into an elegant coiffure that accented her lovely neck, set off by a glittering ruby. The stone had been selected to complement her wine-colored gown, cut from the finest silk to be found in Africa. Her earrings were clusters of pearls set in gold. The gown and the jewelry were new: not surprisingly, Scipio had ordered her entire wardrobe and chest of jewelry burned, as if the flames might expunge any trace of the touch of Syphax.

The first night they were reunited, Scipio had grilled her for details about her love life with Syphax, being particularly interested in techniques employed by the African to give her pleasure. Wisely, she had refrained from explaining that Syphax's principal lovemaking advantage was his enormous size, an attribute Scipio could never match. Instead, she told him about Syphax's delight in giving her pleasure orally, a practice the more straightlaced Scipio found disgusting.

"Is that why he had you shaved?" Scipio demanded.

"Probably," she said demurely. "Perhaps you should explore that territory, and learn for yourself."

He was revolted. "To a Roman, to be called a *cunnum lingere*, or licker of the female genitals, is the worst insult one can receive," he explained.

"Very well," she responded, a mischievous look twinkling in her eyes. "I certainly would never want you to fall into disrepute over something that gives me pleasure."

Since that conversation, their lovemaking had been passionate, intense, and completely ordinary. Scipio had made a determined effort to make up with energy and frequency what he was unwilling to supply in diversity. She was delighted, of course, to be back in his arms, but, still, she missed some of the exotic practices to which Syphax had gleefully subscribed.

Scipio motioned for a servant to carry away the silver platter from which he had been eating. It still bore the remnants of his meal, a tasty concoction of broiled quail, served in a spicy asparagus sauce. As Scipio rinsed his hands in the nearby finger bowl, the servant replaced the platter with a large tray of assorted fruits. Scipio seized a handful of sweet purple grapes. He popped several into his mouth and offered some to Massinissa, who was also finished with his main course. The stout African held up his hand to decline, and instead plucked several dates from the tray.

None of his dinner companions seemed to pay much attention to Vibiana's challenge to Scipio's new status. Laelius, always more politically astute than his commanding general, had other things on his mind. "The language in the decree is most peculiar in one respect," he observed. "The command is direct: 'Engage Hannibal as soon as possible and fight him to the death.' Something is brewing there." He picked up the embossed vellum scroll and again pored over the text of the decree. "Such a direct command is completely out of character for Fabius."

Scipio shrugged off such concerns. "Rome is merely determined never again to suffer before the scourge of Hannibal," he explained. "After all, in the first war with Carthage, we allowed his father to remain in power, and Hamilcar devoted all his energies to rebuilding Carthage's fortune with an eye toward resuming the hostilities. We were foolish to offer peace on such generous terms. Hamilcar clearly regarded the peace as merely a truce, or a breathing spell. Small wonder, then, that Rome should encourage us to finish off his son."

He offered Vibiana the tray of fruit, but she declined. The dress seemed slightly tighter about her waist than it had when it was fitted, and she decided she had had too much to eat already.

Laelius stroked his chin thoughtfully. "This seems more than mere encouragement," he said, clearly worried. "They are quite explicit in their order, and there is nothing said about what we should do in the event there is an opportunity to negotiate a peace treaty."

"It seems unlikely that Carthage would recall Hannibal merely to serve as a diplomat," Scipio said, drawing a laugh from the others. "Since all of you are so concerned about the dreaded Hannibal, let us hope that the Roman navy for once does its job, and deprives us of the opportunity to engage our great rival."

"Indeed," said Massinissa, joining the conversation for the first time. "That would free us at last to resolve our business with Tychaeus."

Scipio turned and put his hand on Massinissa's shoulder. "I know, my friend, that the desire for retaliation burns hot. After all, I waited for years to have my revenge upon Hasdrubal for what he did to my father."

He glanced at Vibiana. She had never given a hint of any sense of grief over the death of her own father. Perhaps she had reconciled herself to the loss while married to Syphax.

"I pledge to you that when we have concluded our business with Carthage, we will not waste a day in settling your score with Tychaeus."

"At the rate things are going," Lucius commented, "Tychaeus himself may do us the favor."

Scipio nodded. Tychaeus had proven himself an utter despot on the throne, and daily hundreds of Numidians, horsemen mostly, showed up at the Roman camp, seeking to pledge loyalty to Massinissa and join his cause. These converts had swollen the ranks of Scipio's army to well over thirty-five thousand men, and he drilled them relentlessly to form them into a cohesive fighting unit. The army, which now was equally balanced between infantry and cavalry, was quite unlike any Roman force ever fielded. Scipio reveled in putting them through their paces, honing the system of command and practicing over and over again the peculiar tactic of forming lanes in the ranks. Unlike the others, he had absolute confidence in the maneuver, and so did not shirk from the possibility of an encounter with Hannibal.

"Still," he said to Massinissa, "you will not have peace of mind until you have what is rightfully yours, indeed, what you have earned in your service to Rome."

"That, at least, is clear in the decree," Laelius agreed. The Senate had formally acknowledged the valuable service rendered in the African campaign by Massinissa, and had recognized him as the legitimate king of Numidia. Scipio was authorized to render assistance to Massinissa in restoring him to the throne.

Vibiana casually ran her finger along Scipio's bare thigh, exposed by the simple white tunic he was wearing. Understanding her signal, he stood up and stretched.

"The hour grows late," he said, feigning a yawn, "and we have a long day of drilling awaiting us. Thank you for being my guests this evening."

The guests exchanged knowing glances at this abrupt dismissal and left the lovers to themselves.

Elsewhere in the camp, Silanus, in the privacy of his tent, put down the scroll of vellum after having reread it for the fifth time. He rubbed his hand over his chin, pondering the implications of the communication from Marcinius. The senator had explained that Fabius had told him of Scipio's dalliance with the Carthaginian girl. He made it clear that he was outraged over what he regarded as Scipio's breach of his promise to marry his daughter, and he intended to do something about it. But Silanus simply could not believe the proposition, and he grasped the scroll and read the key paragraph again.

I am determined that Scipio must not return from Africa alive. Therefore, I have caused the Senate to order him to engage Hannibal and fight him to the death. Should any circumstances come about that make this impossible, or should Scipio survive the battle, I look to you to perform a service for me. Upon whatever pretext you can devise, engage Scipio in a contest and kill him. Do not concern yourself over the consequences—Fabius and I control the Senate and will see that you are exonerated. And for your trouble, I am prepared to pay the sum of ten million sesterces.

Ten million sesterces! It was a mind-bending sum, more wealth than he could even imagine. That Marcinius was able to pay, he had no doubts. The senator was widely recognized as the richest man in Rome—just look at his house!

As he had since the first time he had read those words, Silanus groped for a basis upon which to challenge Scipio to a duel. It occurred to him: why wait until *after* a battle with Hannibal, which none of them might survive? Better to do the deed and earn the fee before testing the fates on the field against Hannibal and his elephants. The bare outlines of a plan began to form in his mind. But it would be risky, bordering on mutiny.

Still, he had been offered so vast a sum that he felt compelled to make his challenge to Scipio. He resolved to bide his time and pray to the gods that Scipio would present him with an opportunity.

Silanus located writing materials and composed a response to Marcinius:

Marcinius,

I have received your proposal. Scipio has indeed taken the widow of Syphax into his bed as his concubine—she who was the bait by which Syphax was lured by Carthage to break his treaty with Rome. I will eliminate the man who has insulted your daughter.

Silanus

A few days later, less propitious news arrived: Hannibal had evaded the Roman patrols and landed his army in Africa. At first, there was concern that Hannibal would march directly against the Romans, but it soon became apparent that Hannibal had no such strategy in mind. The elephants that had been promised him upon his return were late in arriving and turned out to be completely untrained. Even worse, the Numidians, who had always formed the most effective elements of the Carthaginian cavalry, were defecting to the Romans in droves. Hannibal insisted that replacements be found for the cavalry and that the elephants be carefully integrated into the army before he would take to the field against Scipio. Therefore, Hannibal remained in camp a day's march away from Carthage, in position to block any sudden thrust Scipio might make toward the capital, but showing no signs of making any move to engage the Romans.

Scipio was desirous of drawing Hannibal away from his base. Leaving behind a token force to maintain the siege of Utica, he ventured with the bulk of his army into the fertile plain between the Mediterranean coast and the River Bagradas. This rich soil formed the breadbasket of Carthage, providing most of the city's food supply. With a ruthlessness that put even his efforts against Syphax to pale, Scipio resumed his brutal campaign of destruction and enslavement, utterly ravaging the countryside, leaving no field of crops untouched. Scipio's movement southward, away from the coast and toward the territory of Numidia, had the further benefit of sending a shock wave of fear through the palace of Tychaeus, who was terrified that Scipio and Massinissa were marching against him. Massinissa, of course, encouraged this speculation by putting out considerable misinformation concerning their intentions. The flood of defectors from Tychaeus continued to swell.

Among the Numidians streaming into the Roman camp were scores of spies planted by Hannibal, and he soon was receiving daily reports concerning the rate at which Scipio's forces grew. Still, he procrastinated. The elephants were obstinate beasts, and their training could not be rushed. Even more important, the infantry and cavalry—badly depleted and in need of shoring up anyway—had to be carefully coordinated with the charge of the massive animals, or their employment in battle could easily result in disaster. His wary preparations were not at all what the war faction of the Carthaginian Council had in mind when they recalled their champion, and they issued a series of demands that Hannibal proceed immediately to evict the Roman intruder. Their pleas became more strident as the effect of Scipio's raids began to be felt in dwindling food supplies and concomitant runaway inflation in the prices of food that was available. Not surprisingly, as things got worse and all classes of Carthaginian society shared in the suffering, the war faction's influence waned, and pressure mounted to seek a negotiated settlement with the Romans.

Since even before the outbreak of the war, so many years ago, a small but vocal faction of the Carthaginian Council had been agitating for peace. Their principal spokesman was a nobleman named Hanno, who had for years been predicting that the war with Rome inevitably would lead to the ruin of Carthage. He had fallen into considerable disrepute during the heady early days of the war, when Hannibal racked up victory after victory. But Hanno had remained resolute. Rome, he argued, had superior resources and far more manpower; this combination eventually would prove irresistible, and untold suffering lay ahead. He even had been so bold as to propose a peace treaty after the victory at Cannae, when the fortunes of Rome were at their absolute nadir. Hanno had been hooted down then, but with the Romans now raping their homeland and Hannibal seemingly unwilling or unable to do anything to stop them, his daily entreaties for an armistice were finding receptive ears.

Before long, the clamor was irresistible. Alarmist reports poured in that the Romans had occupied the entire River Bagradas valley and that the city was facing starvation in the coming winter. Hanno's allies nearly carried a motion in the Council ordering Hannibal to sue for peace. This finally decided it for Hannibal; he could delay no longer. He hurriedly completed his preparations, formed up his baggage trains, and marched southwesterly from Carthage, generally following the line of the River Bagradas so as to maintain resupply by that artery.

The Carthaginian fortunes seemed to improve when word arrived that Tychaeus, determined to eliminate Massinissa, was riding to join Hannibal with some two thousand cavalry. Hannibal was concerned about the reliability of these horsemen, given the apparent popularity of Massinissa among the Numidians, but he was assured that Tychaeus' force was comprised of individuals he had favored during his rule, and so they could be counted upon to stand fast in a fight. Nonetheless, ever wary, Hannibal began to formulate a battle plan that would rely on his infantry and the eighty young elephants that would form the point of his attack.

His army was preceded by scouts, of course. Several of these were captured by the Romans and brought before Scipio, who decided on a bold ploy. Rather than execute the captives or torture information out of them, he held a feast in their honor, hosted by Vibiana and himself, and then casually escorted the scouts on a thorough tour of the entire Roman and Numidian camps, welcoming them to see whatever they wanted. He then sent them back to Hannibal with an escort.

Scipio's gamble paid off handsomely. What the spies reported threw the Carthaginian camp into a black mood. The confidence of the Romans was growing daily with the additions to their ranks. Moreover, they were utterly convinced that their Scipio Africanus was a man of destiny, decreed by the gods to be the conqueror of Carthage. They were well organized, highly trained, completely equipped, and ready for a decisive battle.

Word of this incident reached Hanno in Carthage, and he laid the news before the Council. It proved to be the last straw. Within days, Hannibal received an extraordinary order: he was to make contact with the Romans and inquire whether the peace terms that had been under discussion before the attack on the camps of Syphax and Hasdrubal might still be available.

This communication reached Hannibal when he was barely five days' march away from where the Roman camp was thought to be. Hannibal flew into a blind rage, hurling the wax tablet containing the order into a fire. He swore vile oaths against the entire leadership of his country. Even his officers, accustomed to his moody temperament and having witnessed dozens of outbursts, stood silently by, frozen in terror at the intensity of his anger.

"I swore an oath when I was only a boy," he raged, "never to be a friend to the Romans. My entire family has fallen victim to their swords. Under no circumstances will I sue for peace!"

Hasdrubal, son of Gisgo, summoned up the courage to speak. "You must at least ask for a parley," he said.

This set Hannibal off in a new paroxysm, and several of the commanders present began to fear he would be overcome by apoplexy. He grabbed the golden pole of his personal battle standard, which had seen him through so many encounters with the Roman Army, and bent it over his knee, a prodigious feat of strength.

But Hasdrubal was nothing if not stubborn. "Orders are orders," he said.

"Bah, the orders are given by those not fit to lead. I will resign my commission before I will humble myself before the Romans, and their general they dare to call 'Africanus.'"

"Things have gone badly for Carthage," Hasdrubal pointed out. "I can understand how Scipio could have managed to surprise the camp of Syphax. His camp was poorly guarded, and there was a lack of discipline. But my own camp was maintained under the strictest military order."

Hannibal squinted at Hasdrubal Gisgo with his only good eye. "Are you suggesting that you agree with those who believe Scipio is a god?"

"Do not forget that I have met him, face to face," Hasdrubal replied. "He is no more a god than you or I, but he certainly is blessed with good fortune. Consider the fact that the tides shifted for him at Cartagena! And he is a competent commander, as we saw at Baecula and Ilipa." Hasdrubal sighed. "Yes, I fear he may be a favorite of the gods. And if he is, there is nothing to be gained by bringing him to battle."

"I, too, have been blessed with great victories," Hannibal scowled. "Why am I not accorded equal status?"

"No one questions your status," Hasdrubal said, trying now to soothe his general's ego. "After all, you are the man Carthage has turned to in this hour of crisis. And no one else could possibly win from the Romans the kind of concessions they will make to avoid facing you in battle. This is why you cannot resign your commission."

"But if I bring him to battle, I will beat him! No concessions will be necessary!"

Hasdrubal was patient. "It is time to do what your own father before you did: negotiate a truce in order to allow the city to rebuild her strength for a subsequent effort against the Romans. Certainly, Carthage was down to its last hope in recalling you from Italy. It is imperative to obtain some breathing time."

This argument seemed to sink in, and, after a full day of fretful meandering, Hannibal summoned forth a clerk and dictated a message to Scipio, requesting a parley.

Tychaeus, having now linked up his force with Hannibal's, got wind that a message was on its way to Scipio, and in light of the Roman Senate's decision to recognize Massinissa as king of Numidia, was extremely upset about any word of peace talks. He appeared shortly thereafter at Hannibal's tent to lodge his protest, interrupting a staff meeting held to arrange details for the peace conference.

Tychaeus was a man of average height and build, but he spoke with a whine in his voice that indicated a constant petulance with everything he found about him. This tone invariably exhausted the good will of everyone he came in contact with.

"The Roman Senate has already recognized Massinissa as the legitimate ruler of Numidia," he complained to Hannibal. "The Romans surely will make an issue of it during the negotiations."

Hannibal, no stranger to duplicity, and wanting to keep the African available in the event the negotiations failed, was quick to assure Tychaeus that Carthage would never betray their ally. "Do you think that I am anxious to make peace with the Romans? Do you think that I will agree to harsh Roman terms?"

Tychaeus did not answer.

"I assure you," Hannibal said, striving to make his face seem as solemn as possible, "this alone might be the issue upon which the chance for peace might be shattered."

Tychaeus, smelling a rat, was unconvinced. "Let me then accompany you to the parley, so that I can be assured that I am not betrayed."

Hannibal glanced around at his commanders, who were shifting about uneasily at this demand. "Do you dare to challenge my word?" he asked the African, his tone harsh.

Tychaeus realized he might have gone too far, but he also knew that his own kingdom was at stake. "No," he replied, "I do not mean to impugn you personally, but I must have assurance that my interests will not be cast to the wind in the negotiations between the two great powers in the world."

Hannibal assumed a friendly smile. "You have my personal assurance. And besides, our conversation will be conducted in the Greek tongue, which I do not believe you know."

Tychaeus shook his head. This was true. Reluctantly, he realized he must put his fate in the hands of the Carthaginian.

And so it was that two of the most honored generals in the history of the world scheduled a conference to be held at the humble little village of Zama.

———

It was not much of a place, really, certainly not big enough to be regarded as a town. A few dozen respectable houses built of wood and brick were occupied by tradesmen. Mostly, however, scores of mud and thatch huts housed the poor peasants who scratched their living from the land. The peasants would regularly bring their produce into the public marketplace at Zama, the village's only notable feature, where agents for the merchants of Carthage would gather to conduct business. Zama was just another village in the countryside of North Africa, a completely unremarkable spot.

The Romans established their camp about four miles away, at an even smaller hamlet called Naraggara. The camp was well fortified against attack, as Scipio did not want to suffer the same trickery he had utilized against Syphax and Hasdrubal.

The scouts reported that Hannibal had set himself in place on the other side of Zama, about eight miles away, atop a steep hill ideally suited for defense.

On the evening before the the momentous meeting, Scipio gathered in council all his officers, both Roman and Numidian, from senior commanders like Laelius and Massinissa to the most junior tribunes. It was a clear night, muggy and hot, made even more uncomfortable by the dozens of torches that had been posted on stakes to provide light. Seated around a long table open to the night sky, Scipio laid out the case. They could take their chances and bring on a battle, or they could entertain a proposal for peace. He explained that, in his view, the tidings for a decisive combat were favorable, and, as he did not fear a confrontation with Hannibal, they should be strict in demanding terms. The officers were in consensus: the terms offered were to be extremely harsh, so as to assure that Carthage never again would be capable of posing a threat to Rome's mastery. Carthage would be made to burn her entire navy, and to pay a huge indemnity of reparations for all the damage inflicted upon Italy. And Hannibal would have to swear an oath never again to take up arms against Rome.

Silanus saw the opportunity he had been looking for to instigate an argument with Scipio. He rose to speak against the idea of negotiations.

"What of our orders from the Senate?" he asked. "We are to engage Hannibal, and fight him to the death. There is nothing said about a peace treaty! If we talk rather than fight, we'll return home in disgrace."

Scipio was surprised at this outburst and tried to mollify his colleague. "The terms we have been discussing certainly are the equivalent of a victory won with blood. I am sure all of Rome will rejoice if we can deliver peace without killing any more of her soldiers."

But Silanus was stubborn. "You're starting to talk like Fabius," he sneered.

Scipio chafed at this comparison. "A Roman general in the field always has had the authority to negotiate terms of a truce, and submit them to Rome for ratification. Nothing in the Senate's order changes this practice."

Silanus shook his head. "Your argument is not persuasive. If the Senate had intended you to exercise the customary prerogatives of a field commander, they would not have given so unmistakable a directive regarding our adversary." He paused, then said, "I believe you are willing to entertain peace terms because you know that it will take us months, if not years, to work out all the details. During this time, we will have to remain in Africa, removed from our homes and families."

Scipio knew something serious was afoot. He glared at his commander. "Why do you accuse me of wanting to remain in Africa any longer than is absolutely necessary? I too have a mother in Italy, whom I have little seen since I entered into the service of Rome at the age of thirteen!"

Silanus met his general's gaze, then hurled his accusation. "The longer you dally in Africa, the longer you postpone the punishment your concubine must inevitably receive in Rome."

A shocked silence hung over the group.

Scipio glanced at Laelius, who could only shake his head in dismay. Had he not warned Scipio that this woman would be nothing but trouble? Silanus' words verged on mutiny. Was Silanus speaking only for himself, or were other officers in on this confrontation? Coming on the eve of what could be Scipio's grandest triumph, having forced Hannibal and Carthage to ask for terms, the results could be tragic.

"You have served me loyally," Scipio said in a low voice between clenched teeth, "and so out of loyalty to you, I offer you the opportunity, here and now, to renounce your ill-considered statement."

Silanus looked around the cordon of commanders, seeking support. All he found were impassive faces. "I renounce nothing," Silanus snapped.

Scipio rose and stepped back from the table. He was the only officer at the gathering who was unarmed, and so he motioned to Lucius for a sword. Lucius, his heart pounding at this stunning turn of events, unsheathed his weapon and handed it to his brother.

Silanus, too, bared his sword. The officers formed a large ring around the two men, knowing that such a challenge could only be settled by a test of arms.

The two adversaries slowly circled each other, crouched with knees bent, feet apart, holding their swords chest high before them, the other arm extended for balance. Silanus did not hesitate and charged forward with a vicious jab at Scipio's exposed breast. The swords clanged as Scipio neatly parried the blow. Silanus' momentum carried him past Scipio, who deftly stepped aside and, as the cavalry commander went by him, put his boot on Silanus' backside and gave a stout push. Silanus stumbled and fell from the kick, flat onto his belly.

There was a general appreciation among the spectators that Scipio, had he chosen to be quick, could have pounced on the sprawled cavalryman and cut his throat, which certainly would have been acceptable behavior under the circumstances.

But Scipio did not seize his advantage. Instead, he waited for Silanus to get to his feet and gather himself for another thrust. Again Scipio met the challenge with his blade. This time, the two men exchanged a series of blows, the steel shafts gleaming in the moonlight. They locked up momentarily, hilt to hilt, and while in this close proximity, Scipio smashed his fist into Silanus' ear.

Dazed by the force of the blow, the horseman staggered and dropped his weapon.

The spectators now expected Scipio to finish it quickly. Scipio put the tip of his blade at the level of Silanus' navel. There was a no more painful killing blow than to be gutted with a sword. Silanus trembled and clenched his teeth, trying to brace himself for the lethal strike.

"I could kill you now," Scipio said, "but if I do so, I may go into battle without knowing whether there are others who share your views."

He stepped back slightly. "If there are any others of you here who would support this man, come forward now." His voice quavered with emotion. "If there is anyone who would believe that after all these years of toil and sacrifice that I want anything other than a victory over Carthage and Hannibal, let him now speak. If there is anyone who believes I am not the messenger appointed by the gods to carry us to victory, step forward now! I shall give you the same opportunity here in the ring as Silanus has had to prove your claim with the strength of your arm. I will kill every last one of you if necessary, and face Hannibal alone."

There were no takers.

"Pity Silanus," Scipio said, running the man through with his sword. Silanus cried out in agony as the cold blade ripped him apart. Scipio pulled out his shank and struck the dying man in the face with the hilt. Silanus crumpled onto the ground, writhing in excruciating pain. "It is tragic that you should have chosen to die by the hand of a Roman, on the eve of our triumph."

In a few moments, the man was dead. Scipio looked about him to ensure there were no other challengers, then threw the sword into the dust.

"Take him away," Scipio muttered. "And remove yourselves to your quarters. I wish to be alone."

He pushed his way through the cordon of men, who began slowly to shuffle away, and went inside his tent.

Vibiana had heard the commotion, and watched the confrontation from inside the tent, her head stuck out through the flap. When she saw Scipio coming toward her, she withdrew to a bench and sat, anxiously awaiting his arrival.

Agitated and tense, Scipio strode into the tent. He glanced at her and realized from her demeanor that she had witnessed the combat. He began pacing back and forth.

When it became obvious that Scipio was not going to explain what had happened, she finally asked in a whisper, "Why did he challenge you?"

Still fretful over the ominous event, he related the nature of Silanus' complaint.

"Do you believe any of the others feel as he did?" Vibiana asked quietly, suddenly aware of the complications her presence in the camp had created for him.

"No," Scipio replied. "You saw for yourself that no one stepped forward to join him. I believe they are still loyal to me."

"Then do not trouble yourself further by it," Vibiana said. She got up and went over to Scipio, and they embraced. He held her tightly, and she put her head on his strong shoulder. She ran her fingers through his dark, curly hair.

"I do not understand it," Scipio grumbled. "Silanus was a good and loyal officer. He grew wealthy by my victories. Why should he challenge me before the others about our relationship, to the point where it cost him his own life?"

She pondered it for a few moments, and realized, "I am still in danger, am I not? I may yet end up at the stake."

He shook his head vehemently. "If we overcome Hannibal, I will be the hero of Rome. The people will give me my wish, even if the Senate tries to make trouble," he replied gently, brushing his lips across the soft skin of her neck. "Put your fears behind you. I will not let them harm you."

He stroked her hair, then her cheek, and slowly she began to feel soothed. She brushed back a tear, as if hesitating to tell him something. Finally, she moved her head back so she could look him in the eye, and said impishly, "At the least, you must protect me for several more months."

He arched an eyebrow and looked at her oddly. "What do you mean?"

She ran her fingertips lightly across his well-muscled back, wet with perspiration from the struggle with Silanus. "I mean that I am going to have a baby."

He was shocked at first, unable to respond. "A baby?" was all he could manage.

"Yes," she said. Then, seeing the befuddled look on his face, she added a little tartly, "You can rest assured, the child is yours."

Finally comprehending, he broke into a broad smile as a flood of emotion swept over him. "Are you sure?"

She laughed. "About being with child, or the identity of the father? Yes, I am sure about both."

He swept her off her feet, and while he held her in his arms, he kissed her again, longer this time. Finally, coming up for air, he grinned and said, "A baby! And on the eve of our meeting with Hannibal. This must be a favorable sign from the gods!"

"I had begun to believe that I was incapable of having a child," she said. "After all, both you and Syphax had plenty of opportunities, and I never conceived. But it has been three months since I last passed blood, and all the signs are there. I have been waiting for an opportune moment to tell you, but under the circumstances, I thought you could use some cheering up."

He set her down without releasing her hand and led her to their bed.

Scipio kissed her again, nibbling her lips with his own. She felt his hand slip underneath her dress and make its way slowly up her thighs. She shuddered with pleasure and began to move her hips in rhythm to his touch. She pressed herself against him, craving the feel of his body.

Scipio caressed her swelling breasts under the fine silk of her gown. He pushed it off her shoulders and down over the small mound of her belly as they lowered themselves onto the bed.

"This won't hurt the child, will it?" he asked.

"No," she whispered breathlessly, guiding him into her.

When it was over, she held him tightly, never wanting to let him go.

"I love you, Vibiana. I love you so much."

"And I love you," she said. "Enough to have your child, and enough to remain at your side, wherever that may be."

He closed his eyes. Soon, lost in the luxurious drift of fulfilled contentment, he fell off to sleep, the thoughts of Hannibal, Rome, and war banished from his mind.

———

As several officers carried away the bloody corpse of Silanus, Laelius took a torch and decided to go to the cavalryman's tent, there to assemble the traitor's belongings for shipment back to Rome. Like all

Roman soldiers, Silanus had a will on file with the army's clerks to dictate the distribution of his property.

In the tent, Laelius found a candle and lit it. He began arranging the dead man's possessions. There really was little to do, for most of Silanus' things were already neatly packed in his trunk, and only a few pieces of clothing and personal effects were set on a small camp table. Laelius picked up these items and carried them over to the trunk, which was unlocked.

He opened the trunk, a large wooden box decorated with an ornate pattern of tortoise shells, and began putting the things away. This required some reorganization, and as Laelius was moving Silanus' possessions about, his eye fell upon a rolled-up piece of vellum tucked underneath a neatly folded tunic. He would not have given it a second thought, but there was something odd about this roll of vellum. The wax seal was still intact, as if Silanus for some reason had wanted to preserve the identity of the sender. Laelius held it up to the candle and was startled to recognize the formal seal of Marcinius. Why was so powerful a senator as Marcinius corresponding with a cavalryman?

Laelius unfurled the scroll and sat down on the cot to read the letter, squinting to make out the words in the flickering candlelight. Minutes later, his hands shaking, he put the scroll down.

He had known that Marcinius would be upset with Scipio, but this was extraordinary. The powerful senator had actually put a bounty—and a phenomenal sum, at that—on Scipio's head, and all because of Scipio's dalliance with the Carthaginian woman. His mind raced as he considered the implications. Marcinius was a powerful and wealthy man. He could make untold difficulties for Scipio, even if he had failed in his effort to kill him. But, of course, this scroll was damning evidence of a plot to kill a pro-consul. For this, Marcinius himself could be sentenced to death. The scandal would be colossal. Yet many Romans would probably sympathize with Marcinius, given

Scipio's cavorting with the Carthaginian girl, a known murderer of a Roman soldier. And with his vast wealth, Marcinius could almost certainly bribe himself out of trouble. But poor Marcia—her own father plotting the assassination of her fiancé!

Laelius' mind went numb as he considered the consequences should the contents of this letter become known. Two of Rome's most prominent families, Cornelius and Marcinius, would become sworn bitter enemies, rather than merged in marriage. The scandal that would ensue if this information ever saw the light of day would rock the very foundations of Roman society.

He did not know what to do with his discovery, but he did fully understand the implications if it were to be revealed. He folded the vellum into a small square and stuffed it into his tunic just as Massinissa came into the tent.

"Can I be of assistance?" the African asked.

"No," said Laelius, struggling to appear calm. "There is nothing unusual here."

If Massinissa thought anything was out of the ordinary, he gave no indication of it.

"Are there any signs of a disturbance among the men?" Laelius asked.

"No," Massinissa responded. "Apparently, Silanus acted alone. How peculiar! He was the last officer I would have guessed would try to start an uprising. What could have possessed him?"

Laelius now knew, of course, but dared not reveal the truth to Massinissa. Instead, he said simply, "Who knows? Come, Massinissa, I have packed his belongings. Let us retire for the night, for we have a momentous day before us tomorrow."

XIV

ZAMA, AFRICA

202 BC

SCIPIO AROSE EARLY THE next morning and prepared himself carefully. Narcussa gave him a delicate shave with a razor he had honed as sharp as possible, not wanting his master to meet the terrible Hannibal with a face full of nicks and cuts.

By prior agreement, the two generals were to confer just outside Zama under a white flag of truce, each accompanied by only one aide. Scipio had chosen Laelius, of course, and Narcussa was just affixing Scipio's white consular cape to his shoulder epaulets when Laelius rode up.

"Greetings, Scipio," Laelius called out, trying to sound as cheerful as possible. "Have you recovered from the challenge of last evening?"

The general nodded as Narcussa reverently fitted the ornate helmet of Scipio's father onto his head. The crest was new, composed of an imposing tuft of crimson bristles running down the center. Narcussa had polished its gold and brass fittings to a gleaming sheen, and it reflected the bright sunlight as Scipio moved his head. The golden cheek plates hung down over his jaws, and Narcussa pulled the strap tight to secure the heavy gear on his head.

"Did you patrol the camp last night?" Scipio asked.

"Of course," Laelius said uneasily. "After an incident like that, I wasn't about to just simply go to bed."

"And?"

Laelius had been agonizing over whether to tell Scipio of his discovery in Silanus' tent. Now, realizing that his general needed to be intent upon the imminent meeting with Hannibal, he decided to withhold the information. "You need not fear. Silanus apparently had no supporters in the camp. To a man, the legionnaires are still with you."

Scipio grunted with satisfaction as the steadfast Bucephalus was brought forward, also bedecked in the finest ceremonial raiment, and Scipio mounted the beast. Vibiana came out of the tent now, a robe wrapped about her, and he waved at her as he moved off.

She watched him ride away, filled with a strange premonition that something odd, something totally unexpected, was going to happen. For a brief moment, she thought of running to him to tell him of her fears, but quickly ruled out the idea: it would not serve him well to receive her advice in front of the other men.

Massinissa and Lucius waited with a mounted escort of several hundred riders, both Roman and Numidian, each carefully chosen for his fighting ability in case some treachery should unfold at the parley. Each struck his breast with his right fist in the customary Roman salute as Scipio rode up, and he returned the gesture. The contingent then rode through the camp, along a route lined with legionnaires and Numidian soldiers, cheering and waving their standards. They set off at a brisk pace for Zama. The landscape was unremarkable, consisting mostly of cultivated fields, and they covered the distance in a short time. The group trotted over a low rise and saw a small white flag affixed in a field, the spot chosen for the meeting by the envoys. The Carthaginians had not yet arrived. Scipio left his escort at the top of the ridge, some several hundred yards from the flag, and rode down to the marker with only Laelius at his side. Laelius was carrying Scipio's now-famous personal battle flag, its white crest billowing in a stiff breeze.

Despite the breeze and the early hour, the harsh African sun climbed swiftly in the cloudless sky, and in the humidity, Laelius felt perspiration drenching his tunic beneath the heavy armor. They reached the flag and waited patiently for many long minutes.

The anxiety began to weigh on Laelius. He turned to Scipio, who seemed remarkably passive, despite the historic confrontation awaiting them. "Well, Scipio, here we are," he said, his voice shaking with excitement. "What favor the gods have shown us, bringing us here to listen as Hannibal himself asks for peace. Whoever would have thought such a thing possible?"

"Certainly not our critics in Rome," the general replied. Scipio himself was surprised at how calm he was. Somehow, despite all the years of anticipation for this confrontation, he was strangely complacent. He knew he held the upper hand, and, unlike so many other Romans, he had never feared Hannibal. If Hannibal wanted to make peace, it would be on Rome's terms. If not, they would finally see who was the better general.

"Over there," Laelius said, pointing at an approaching mass of men on horseback. "It seems that Hannibal is intent on intimidating us."

Hannibal's entourage approached, led by literally dozens of men bearing the accumulated trophies of Hannibal's career. Row upon row of standards captured from defeated legions, battle flags taken from fallen generals, and stacks of fasces stripped from the consuls who had fallen to Hannibal's generalship preceded his entrance to the field.

It occurred to Scipio that there were more symbols of Roman authority in the approaching procession than could be assembled from all the armies and officials of Rome presently in office. He could not help but shudder before the frightful display of Hannibal's prowess.

The procession formed a long line facing the Romans and then parted slightly so that two men could pass through on horseback. Scipio immediately recognized Hasdrubal, son of Gisgo, having made his acquaintance at the palace of Syphax, and so gave over his attention to the other man, who must be Hannibal.

"Hannibal is on the left," he said quietly to Laelius, who had never met either man.

He was surprised at Hannibal's diminutive stature, and as they got closer, Scipio could see that Hannibal's left eye was missing, an ugly scar running along the ridge of his eye socket. He seemed old—he was, after all, over forty-five—and almost frail. But his features radiated a keen intensity, and Scipio knew better than to regard his adversary lightly.

Within seconds, the two Carthaginians pulled up to the flag, and both generals dismounted. There was an awkward moment as they regarded each other, unsure whether to exchange a hand greeting or not. Perhaps it was mutual admiration that struck them silent.

It was Hannibal who recovered sufficiently to speak first. Everything he had heard about the Roman seemed true: he was handsome and noble of bearing, impressive in his consular armor. It was not difficult to see how this Roman could inspire his men to daring feats. When Hannibal spoke, he did so in Greek, which puzzled Scipio, for certainly after so many years in Italy, Hannibal had become conversant in Latin.

"Africanus," he said, almost smirking at the title, "if fate has decreed that I, who was so nearly victorious over Rome, should have to be the one Carthaginian to ask for peace, I am pleased that destiny has at least given me the pleasure of asking it from you, and no other. Is it not also an irony of fate that your father was the first Roman against whom I took up arms, and now, so many years and so much bloodshed later, I must come to his son to sue for peace?" Hannibal paused and gestured toward the vast display of captured Roman insignia. "We both have had our share of favor from the gods. Just as you have seen your fortunes shift from a series of defeats to a series of triumphs, never lose sight of the fact that just as swiftly, the tides may shift back again. Do not forget that what I was at Trasimene and Cannae, you are today. Fortune has smiled upon you—conqueror of Spain, victor over Syphax in only an hour—two huge camps left in ashes."

At this, Hasdrubal winced, not wanting to be reminded of his own role in the disaster.

"Your army is behind that hill, and mine behind me. Who can say what the outcome will be if we put our luck to the test of arms? I should be sufficient warning of what fate may bring. Not long ago, I was but a stone's throw away from the gates of Rome herself. And now, today, I stand before you, my brothers slaughtered, my allies defeated, my native city almost under siege, begging that I deliver her from the terrors I inflicted upon yours.

"Certain peace, Africanus, is better and safer than the uncertain hope of victory. The one is in your hands, the other in the hands of the gods. Remember not only your own strength but also the chances of war. Nowhere do our results less match our hopes than in battle. In making peace, everything is yours; refuse to make it, and you must take what the gods choose to give you."

Laelius was impressed with these opening remarks. Hannibal had managed to present himself with a semblance of dignity despite his distressed situation, and had deftly reminded Scipio that in combat, anything could happen. The stakes were high. How would Scipio respond?

But Hannibal did not intend to let Scipio set the tone of the negotiations, for he continued. "To set terms is the privilege of one who grants peace, not one who asks for it. But perhaps we at Carthage are not so unworthy as to suggest our own penalty. We do not object to leaving you in possession of all that you have conquered in the war: Spain, Sicily, Sardinia, and all the islands of the Mediterranean. Let us be confined upon our own continent, never to venture forth again to acquire territories. And, of course, it is altogether fitting that some amount of treasure should change hands, to ease the burden of the pain we have inflicted. The amount you may set yourself."

Laelius struggled to keep his face impassive. This was an attractive offer: Carthage would forever renounce any interest outside of Africa, and pay money to boot.

"I am fully aware," Scipio said carefully, "of the infirmity of our human endeavors, and I do not ignore the role Fortune will play in determining our fate. Neither, however, can I ignore the facts. We were not the aggressors in the war for Spain—it was your destruction of Saguntum that induced us to take up arms. The gods are our witnesses to your aggression, for it is they who have brought about your present unfortunate circumstance."

Hannibal remained silent at this indictment.

"I know full well that in battle we face a thousand chances, any one of which may turn the day against us. But as things are, on the brink of battle you have come before me in spite of your most bitter reluctance, and I do not feel compelled to respect your feelings."

At this, Hannibal was surprised. How did Scipio know of his tirade before agreeing to seek the peace negotiations? Perhaps he too made use of spies. If so, was he aware of the tenuous condition of the Carthaginian Army, and his inability to adequately prepare his elephants?

Scipio continued, "A sum of money certainly will help salve the wounds your treacherous aggression has imposed over these long years. Perhaps ten thousand talents of silver will be adequate."

The three other men gasped. It was a staggering sum, oppressive to the point of being outrageous. Not even Laelius had imagined such a preposterous number might pass from Scipio's lips. It was enough money to fund the entire Roman army for twenty years!

Hannibal struggled to retain his self-control. "I must put it before the Council of Carthage," he muttered, certain that the cowards in control there inevitably would agree.

"I recognize that such a sum cannot be raised at once," Scipio said. "It will be sufficient if the indemnity is paid over the next fifty years."

Hannibal paled at the idea. The annual installment would be a tremendous drain on the Carthaginian economy. If the Roman's intention was to prevent Carthage from further adventures abroad, this enormous burden would have its desired effect.

"That is not all," Scipio said quickly. "Our experience with Carthage, indeed, with all of our dealings with Africans, leads us to be distrustful of their veracity. Under no circumstances will we allow ourselves to be brought into conflict with you again. You say that you will confine yourself to Africa. We can only be assured of this if you deprive yourselves of the ability to conduct war beyond your borders. Carthage must burn her entire war fleet."

Hannibal's jaw was set to twitching by the impudence with which Scipio was dictating his terms. Still, ships could be rebuilt. . . .

"Our concern is particularly acute as it applies to your own personage," Scipio said sharply, "for you alone have made yourself infamous in our eyes. You must swear a holy oath, in our presence, never again to take up arms against Rome."

Laelius thought that this would break the deal. Hannibal, having vowed as a boy never to be a friend to the Romans, could not swear an oath such as Scipio had proposed.

But to his surprise, Hannibal nodded readily. "As you can see for yourself, Africanus," he smiled, "I am an old man. It is not for me to take up the sword again once this war is settled."

Scipio felt a deep unease at the ready willingness of Hannibal to forsake his legendary hatred of Rome. Did he hold a sacred oath so lightly as to think that he could break it?

"There is another matter," Scipio said frankly. "Your betrayal of Massinissa, who served you so ably, is a most foul perfidy that must be corrected. Rome has recognized him as the rightful ruler of Numidia. Carthage must do the same, and bring about the removal of Tychaeus from the throne, using force if necessary."

Hannibal held up his hands in a dismissive gesture. "Tychaeus is an imbecile, hardly worthy of mention at so momentous a meeting as this. Massinissa will be installed upon the throne immediately upon the conclusion of our armistice."

"Then I have nothing further to demand of you," Scipio said. "These are the terms upon which I will make the peace."

"Ah," said Hannibal, "then there is but one other small favor I must ask of you."

Scipio regarded the scrappy little man warily. What could he possibly want?

"Your kindness in hosting a feast for my captured scouts is now the subject of legend," Hannibal said, a little obsequiously. "They informed me that you are holding as a prisoner my own niece, the widow of the unfortunate Syphax. She is the only remaining member of my family. As a personal matter, I request that you to return her to me."

Scipio's heart was racing. Did Hannibal understand the true nature of his relationship with Vibiana, or was this merely a casual request? Would Hannibal make the return of Vibiana a condition of the settlement? And if he did, could Scipio dare defy him?

"That is out of the question," he snapped.

Laelius shifted uneasily in the saddle. Surely Scipio would not throw away an entirely desirable settlement—and fight a frightful battle with Hannibal—over a mere woman! The men would not stand for it.

Hannibal, of course, knew full well of the intimate nature of Scipio's relationship with the girl when she was his captive in Spain, for her experiences were well known in Carthage. And from his Numidian spies, he had learned that Scipio had resumed his carnal affair with her. Hannibal couldn't have cared less about the girl herself—he had only the faintest memory of her as a child, and hadn't seen her since the sack of Saguntum, all those years ago. This was merely a ploy to strike at Scipio individually, to deprive him of his personal trophy in the victory he was about to claim over Carthage.

"Perhaps you do not understand," Hannibal said mischievously. "She is the only daughter of my brother, the circumstances of whose death you are well aware. I intend to restore her to her family estate outside Carthage. And Hasdrubal, here, will be her husband."

This was more than Scipio could bear. "The negotiations are closed," he said coldly. "You may have your peace, or you may have your battle, but you may not have Vibiana."

At this, Hannibal was genuinely shocked. Clearly, his spies had not accurately perceived the depths of the Roman's feelings for the girl. But it was unthinkable that this haughty young Roman would throw away a highly favorable peace settlement over a Carthaginian woman.

"My demand is well within the bounds of propriety," Hannibal insisted, his pride beginning to get the better of him. He could stand before this Roman and bargain away Carthage's fortune and her fleet, but he had made a simple, personal request. He had meant to wound Scipio personally, but by making his demand, he had placed his own honor at stake. Would Scipio provoke a confrontation over this? Hannibal groped for a way out of the embarrassing situation in which he had placed himself. He was struck by an inspiration. Never had he met a Roman who could not be swayed by money. "Certainly, the family of a prisoner is entitled under your Roman custom to propose a ransom. Perhaps you could name your price."

"She is not available for ransom," Scipio insisted.

Hannibal now was at a loss. "You would wager the fate of your entire campaign, indeed, the fate of the Roman people, upon a mere girl, who is my own niece?" he asked, incredulous.

"Do you withdraw your request?" Scipio demanded.

Hannibal's pride now got the better of him. "My request was

personal. If you choose to deny it, you do me an insult I cannot abide."

Scipio turned and grabbed the pommel of his saddle.

Using all of his strength, he managed to haul his armored body onto Bucephalus. He noted that the Carthaginians, like the Numidians, used stirrups, whereas the Romans did not.

"Prepare to fight," Scipio said, looking down at the Carthaginian. "I shall report to my men that you have found the burden of peace intolerable."

He wheeled the big horse about, kicked him in the ribs, and set off at a gallop.

Laelius, dumbfounded, recovered sufficiently to do the same, and managed to catch up with Scipio about halfway back to the waiting escorts.

"Have you taken leave of your senses?" Laelius shouted.

Scipio reined in his horse and drew to a halt. Laelius pulled up alongside him.

"Are you mad?" Laelius cried. "You have obtained the agreement of Carthage to the most harsh peace terms ever imposed. With the reparations you have demanded, we would all be wealthy beyond our wildest dreams, and without risking our lives in combat! That was no simple African potentate you were talking to—it was Hannibal, the same Hannibal who took all those trophies you saw. If you make this peace, you will be worshipped in Rome as a god—forget about Marcinius and his daughter! You have even insulted Hannibal by making him renounce the oath he took in his father's presence. Is that not enough? Send me back to them, and let me tell them you have reconsidered."

Scipio's eyes glowed like hot irons. "I will not give up Vibiana."

Laelius tried to reason with him. "Scipio, I know how you feel about her, but this is a matter of life and death."

"She is carrying my child," Scipio said simply.

Laelius nearly fell out of his saddle. Bad enough Scipio was in love with this wench—now she was pregnant? Finally, he recovered enough to splutter, "She is only a woman, pregnant or not. Thousands of good Romans will die if we fight. The fate of Rome hangs in the balance! You cannot do it. The men will not stand for it."

"The men will never know," Scipio retorted. His eyes narrowed, and he pointed at Laelius. "Unless you tell them. And if you do, I will kill you."

An image of Scipio's fight with Silanus flashed through Laelius' mind. The absolute conviction in Scipio's voice convinced Laelius that further protest was futile.

He watched as Scipio kicked his horse again and took off for the Roman lines. He turned around, his heart heavy, to look for the Carthaginians. Hannibal too was on his way back to his escort. There would be a battle, and only the gods could say who might prevail. A flock of birds passed overhead, flying from the direction of the Romans toward the Carthaginians. Laelius said a quiet prayer, hoping that the birds were not an omen that the gods had granted Hannibal's wishes and shifted the fortunes of the war.

And the thought struck him: *What will I say about this in the official archive?*

He laughed out loud at the insanity of it all.

XV

Zama, Africa

202 BC

THE MEN WAITING ON the ridge could sense from the grim demeanor of Scipio and Laelius as they approached that something had gone badly wrong in the negotiations. Scipio told them simply that Hannibal had refused a most generous offer, and had personally insulted both him and the Romans by an obstinate refusal to negotiate seriously.

"Hannibal wishes to give battle," Scipio shouted angrily to his troops, "for he believes that we will be found wanting. It is now up to you, and the gods, to prove him wrong!"

These words had their intended effect, as a shout of outrage arose from the men of the escort. Laelius, the only other person who knew what had really transpired, kept dutifully silent, managing to maintain a stone-faced look as Scipio explained his version of what had happened.

The rest of the day was a blur of activity. The elation that had been evident in the camp when Scipio and his escort had left quickly gave way to determined concentration upon their return, as the soldiers scurried to attend to the myriad of details that must be addressed to ready for a fight. Preparations were undertaken at a frantic pace, for few had expected the negotiations to fail. To boost morale, word was passed by the high command that Hannibal had insulted not only the Romans, but Scipio personally.

Scipio returned to his tent briefly, to be assisted out of his ceremonial garb. Vibiana realized at once that the talks had broken down and that a fight was imminent. Scipio was clearly distracted, his mind focused on the substantial task of preparing the army for battle, and he barely paid attention to her as he changed.

"What happened?" she finally asked.

He looked up, as if noticing her for the first time. "We were unsuccessful in the negotiations. There is going to be a fight, tomorrow."

He seemed strangely distant, and his tone was maddeningly dismissive. She knew he was holding something back.

"There is something you are not telling me," she complained.

He was finished now, having slipped into a formal consular tunic and military sandals. He tried to give her a smile.

"Later," he said, "when there is more time."

And then he was gone.

She did not see him again until much later, when he returned exhausted from a hectic day and evening of issuing orders and addressing the troops. Every position had been clearly laid out, every tribune and centurion informed pointedly of what was expected of him. The weapons had been made ready, and the first elements of the infantry were lining up in columns, to begin the march to Zama, so as to be in place at daybreak.

Vibiana was quite upset with Scipio by the time he entered the tent, her mind having churned throughout the day with fear and anxiety, as well as wild speculations about what might have caused the talks to break down, bringing them to the brink of confrontation.

"I must know!" she demanded as he slumped into the curule chair and poured himself some wine.

He looked at her vacantly.

"Are you going to tell me what happened?" she asked, her voice a little shrill.

Scipio sipped some of the wine and shook his head. "We met

at Zama," he said simply. "Hannibal would not agree to my terms. There is going to be a battle. That is all."

She was not about to be put off so lightly. "There is something you are not telling me," she said. "Hannibal is in no position to refuse your terms. If the talks broke down, it had to be something other than the details of a peace treaty. Like some ridiculous dispute over 'honor' or 'pride', the kind of thing for which you men routinely kill each other."

She thought she detected a look of irony on his features. "What else is worth dying for?" he asked.

Vibiana grabbed his hand and put it on her stomach. "You should be thinking about what is worth living for!" she cried, tears flowing freely. "What of our child? What of our life together? Would you go into battle with no thought for the baby? Or for me?"

Scipio rubbed his weary brow with the tips of his fingers. "I have had thoughts of nothing but the child," he said flatly. "Until last night, I frankly wanted to fight Hannibal, to settle once and for all who is the better man. But when you told me you are with child, I decided to try to make the peace, to avoid any further bloodshed. I want to be with you always." He stood up and took her in his arms. "Oh, Vibiana, I want to see my child born, and grow old in a world safe under Roman rule, free of the horrors of war, as you and I have witnessed them. But Hannibal was stubborn—he would not make the peace."

She looked into his eyes. "But what could have been so momentous as to make a battle inevitable? Could you not have compromised?"

He looked away. "That," he said simply, "I cannot say."

Angry again at his obstinacy and his obvious refusal to level with her, she pushed away from him and went to the other side of the tent, where she collapsed onto the bed, sulking.

Seeing that there was nothing he could do, Scipio said, "I am joining the priests in their prayer vigil. If you can find it in your heart to offer a prayer against the interest of your own countrymen, please do so."

Vibiana did not watch him leave the tent. After a few minutes of feeling sorry for herself, she had an idea. She rose from the divan and found a robe to wrap about herself. She brushed her hair a bit, then stepped out of the tent.

She knew the guard posted outside, an Etruscan named Polybius.

"Polybius," she said politely, "I wish to see Laelius. Would you be so kind as to take me to his quarters?"

Polybius thought this a little odd, but he was not about to get on the wrong side of this fiery redhead, having heard about what she had done to Maximillian. "Certainly, my lady," he replied in his most respectful voice.

She found Laelius seated at a table, writing on one of a stack of wax tablets.

"Writing your farewells, Laelius?" she asked upon coming into the tent, which was considerably smaller than Scipio's appointments.

Laelius looked up at her and managed a wan smile. "An old habit of mine," he said. "Before every battle, I write to my supposed friends, telling them what I really think of them. That way, I must survive the struggle, to prevent my letters from being delivered."

She smiled and sat down across from him.

He looked at her critically. "I understand that congratulations are in order."

She was pleased that Scipio had broken the news about the baby. "Perhaps," she said affectionately, "I can persuade him to name the child after you."

Laelius was horrified. "Oh, no," he said quickly, "the child, if it is male, must be named for Scipio's father, who was a very fine man indeed."

"I was only teasing," she said, laughing. Vibiana reached across the narrow table and took his hand. "Dear Laelius," she said wistfully, "I fear that my child may never see his father. How could you let him walk away from a peace treaty?"

"That seems a strange question, coming from the principal beneficiary of his stubbornness," Laelius said, a note of bitterness evident in his voice.

He saw at once from her quizzical expression that she did not know what he was talking about, and a bolt of panic swept over him as he realized that Scipio must not have told her the truth about what had happened that morning at Zama.

"What do you mean by that?"

He remained silent.

"Please, Laelius," she pleaded. "Please! You're not like the rest of them—you can understand how I feel! I love him! And he is hell-bent on bringing about a frightful battle with the most dangerous man in the world."

Laelius' eyes were downcast, and he chewed on his lower lip, reluctant to tell her the truth.

Vibiana squeezed his hand with all her might. "Please . . . ," she whispered, tears streaming down her cheeks.

He looked up into her captivating eyes and realized how Scipio had managed to fall so completely under her spell.

"The deal was done, the terms were settled," he said dully. "And then Hannibal made a demand Scipio would not grant."

She looked at him blankly. "What could it have been, that he would jeopardize everything to fight Hannibal over it?"

Laelius looked down.

"What?" she demanded.

"Hannibal's demand," Laelius said, "was that you be returned to Carthage, to be wed to Hasdrubal Gisgo."

She gasped in shock.

"Yes," said Laelius, seeing her disbelief. "Hannibal said he wanted you back because you are his only living relative, but I do not believe him. His demand was surely designed for a single purpose: to hurt Scipio."

She turned her head and looked away.

Laelius got up and fetched a small cup of wine, which he brought over to her. He looked down at her.

"It is a pity that I prefer the company of males, for if I did not, I might have a better understanding of how it is that men seem so ready to fight to the death over you," Laelius said with a sad smile.

She looked up at him and tried to return his smile.

"I must go to him now, and put a stop to this madness," she said, her voice determined. "I cannot allow thousands of men to die because of me."

Laelius' eyes widened in disbelief. "You do not understand," he said sorrowfully. "If you tell Scipio what I have said, I am a dead man."

Vibiana's head sagged, and she sat quietly for several long minutes. Finally, she got up and kissed Laelius lightly on the cheek. "Very well," she said, leaving the tent, "let us pray that Scipio, for once, is right about being a favorite of the gods."

"Indeed," he said to himself, picking up the folded letter from Marcinius. "Only the gods can resolve this folly."

Scipio lay prostrate on a blanket spread on the flat, grassy plain before an altar that held a fine marble sculpture in the likeness of Neptune. The god's image was flanked on either side by brass urns in which an aromatic spice burned. Behind Scipio, also flat on their bellies, were half a dozen barefoot priests, clad only in hooded white robes. At Scipio's behest, the priests had kept a vigil throughout the night, offering up prayers to all the gods as wave after wave of soldiers marched past on their way to Zama, urging that the Roman cause this day be favored with victory.

He prayed with an intensity borne of the stakes to which he had committed the army. Before nightfall, they would know whether Rome or Carthage was destined to allocate laws to nations, for the prize was not Italy or Africa, but eventually the whole world. And for the losers, the peril was as great: the Romans, alone in a foreign land, had no route of escape; and Carthage, her last reserves committed to the hands of her finest general, bore the threat of total destruction. Not once, however, had Scipio wavered during the night. It was Hannibal's demand, not his, that had brought them to the brink. And he understood it for what it was: a personal affront, intended by Hannibal to injure him in a way the Semite could not threaten with weapons. Anger, not fear, filled his breast.

On the far horizon, the sun was beginning to show, streaks of orange lacing a dawn sky already full of gray clouds. The air hung thick and moist, a harbinger of another day of oppressive heat.

Mingled with the incense, the scent of burnt flesh hung above the worshippers, from dozens of sacred birds that had been sacrificed in offerings to the gods throughout the night's vigil. After their entrails had been read, the remains had been tossed into a golden brazier and burned. Uniformly, the auspices had been good: Scipio was confident that his favor in the eyes of the gods would continue.

Laelius, looking very grim and clad in his battle armor, came upon the scene and shook his head. It was all so unnecessary.

"Come, Scipio," he said coldly. "It is time."

Scipio finished his prayer and got to his feet. Narcussa and other servants hurried forward with his father's armor, and in a few moments they had Scipio ready for action.

He paused and placed his hand on Narcussa's shoulder. "Do not fear, my loyal Narcussa," he said, fighting back emotion. "The gods will bless us today."

The old man gave him a hearty grin and slapped him on the back.

"You will make your father's spirit very proud today," the valet said bravely. "From wherever he is watching, I am sure that he is glad you are wearing his armor. His strength will be with you."

Scipio clasped the loyal old servant by the arm for a long moment, then looked for Bucephalus, waiting nearby. He was surprised and delighted to see the horse being held in place by Vibiana. He walked over to the animal and took the reins from her. She managed to give him a little smile, and ran her fingertips lightly over his face, trying to burn his features into her memory in case these might be their last moments together.

He clutched her in his arms, and they clung to each other for a few brief moments. But duty beckoned, and all too quickly, he released her. He climbed onto the horse and wheeled the stallion about, his immaculate white cape swirling.

"Destiny awaits us," he shouted, and rode away, followed by Laelius, Massinissa, Lucius, and dozens of other officers.

With Narcussa at her side, she watched, breathless and tearful, until they were out of sight. She then went to their tent and took out one of Scipio's ceremonial swords and set it on the table. Her eyes on the blade, she resolved to use it on herself if Scipio did not return, and said a prayer, asking for the strength to carry out her resolution if it became necessary. Her prayer completed, she sat down to begin the interminable wait for news of the outcome.

XVI

Zama, Africa

202 BC

THE GROUND UPON WHICH the two armies had aligned themselves was completely unremarkable, with only a few trees and
bushes as identifying landmarks. The field generally was flat except for
small rises at its opposite ends, upon which the respective commanders
established themselves. The Romans, having arrived at Zama first, had
maneuvered so as to gain possession of the northerly hill, preferring it
because it featured a fresh spring. Hannibal on the other promontory
would have to go a considerable distance to get water from a tributary
of the River Bagradas, flooded by the autumn rains. Given the heat, this
disadvantage might have a bearing if the battle wore long.

Hannibal, however, had no such intentions. He understood
perfectly well that for the first time in his career, he was facing the
Romans with his circumstances reversed. He had numerical superiority in infantry, but was considerably inferior in cavalry, thanks to
voluminous Numidian defections. Therefore, he had devised a clever
and unorthodox plan to take the Roman and Numidian horse out of
the action early on. Upon seeing that the Numidian cavalrymen under
Massinissa were deployed on the Romans' right flank, Hannibal, under
the guise of giving Tychaeus a chance to confront his challenger face-
to-face, dispatched his own Numidians to his left flank, directly across
from Massinissa. On the Romans' left flank, or Hannibal's right, the
Roman cavalry was in place, now under the direct personal command

of Laelius. Hannibal placed his own Carthaginian horsemen in front of them, commanded by Hasdrubal, son of Gisgo. However, he gave unusual orders to both his wings of cavalry. They were to engage the enemy briefly and vigorously, and then break off the fighting and run. But regarding the retreat, he was explicit: rather than run south, toward the Carthaginian rear and the protection of the infantry, Hannibal wanted his horses to flee both easterly and westerly, sideways and away from the main body of troops. He had been around cavalrymen for years and was certain that mounted warriors, seeing their adversaries turn and run, could not resist taking up the chase, with all thoughts of their role in the ongoing battle thrown to the wind. Hannibal was particularly confident that the trick would work with Massinissa, whom he was sure would be hot to bag Tychaeus.

With the Roman and Numidian cavalry thus removed from the field, Hannibal then intended to launch his main attack. Here, the main element would be his eighty elephants, more than he had ever utilized in a battle. He hoped they would stampede through the Roman lines so that a follow-up surge of his infantry could finish them off.

The Carthaginian infantry itself was a motley assemblage of nationalities, and Hannibal elected to deploy them in the reverse order of his affection. Accordingly, his first line consisted of Ligurian and Gallic mercenaries and a large contingent of Moors, all of whom were lightly armed so that they could move quickly to follow up the breakthrough that the elephants would achieve. Behind the first line were native Libyans and Carthaginians, more heavily armored, who were to be prepared to finish off the legionnaires should things go well. And in reserve, some 200 yards behind the second line, were Hannibal's trusted veterans of Italy, battle hardened and utterly reliable. By keeping his best troops in reserve, Hannibal felt ready for anything the Romans might attempt.

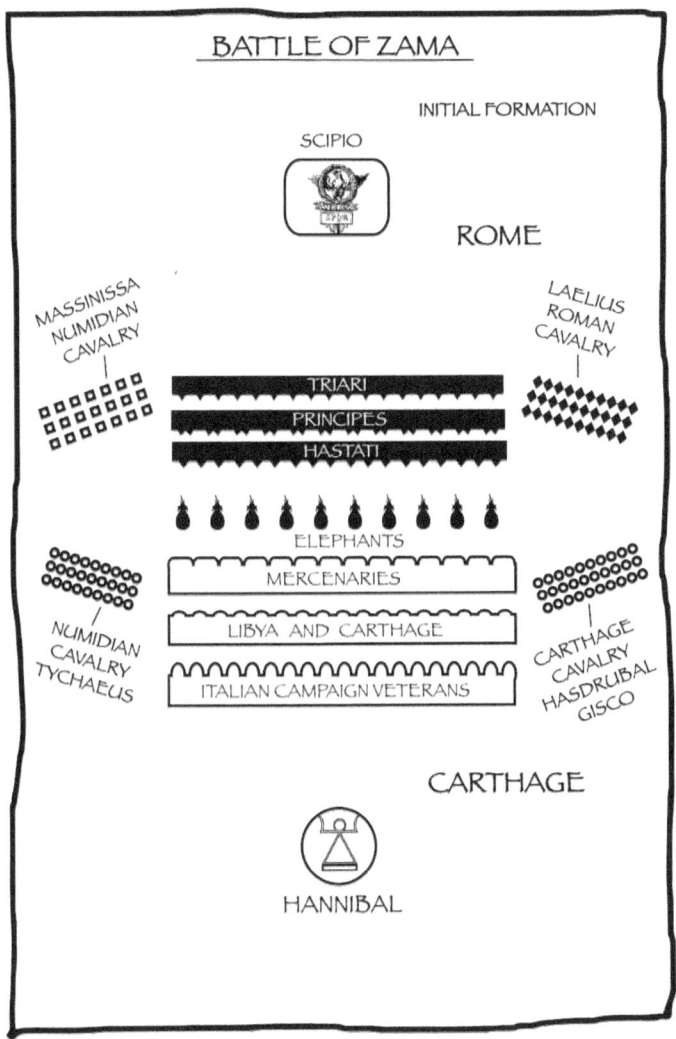

The night before, he had assembled his most loyal troops and addressed them, laboring mightily to lift their morale. As Scipio had done with Laelius, he had cowered Hasdrubal, son of Gisgo, into silence regarding the real reason the battle would take place. Instead, he told them that the negotiations had broken down over his refusal to betray their alliance with Tychaeus. The men were somber, fully appreciating the price of defeat: their homeland would stand naked before the invading Romans, completely vulnerable to their fury. Sensing their anxiety, Hannibal chose not to remind them that they were the last line of defense. Instead, he admonished them to remember their triumphs in Italy and all the generals they had beaten—Scipio was no different! He emphasized that the Romans they were facing were the disgraced Sicilian legions, the very same men who had humiliated themselves by surviving the battle at Cannae. And he assured them he had worked out a foolproof strategy that would rout the Romans. "It will put Cannae to shame!" he insisted.

But even his most resolute retainers looked worried. They had heard the stories told by the captured scouts, and they were well aware of the flaws in the force they would present to the Romans at dawn. Hannibal saw their fear, and knew the danger. He was not stirring them, and uncertainty in the minds of the men was far more dangerous than the Roman short sword! Finally, he resorted to strolling through the ranks, stopping here and there to reminisce with a veteran about some particular exploit or heroic deed.

Coming upon one man, whose mouth was downturned in concern, Hannibal asked him his name.

"Pammaro," said the soldier.

"Pammaro," replied Hannibal, "you seem distressed. Why should that be so?"

Figuring he had nothing to lose, Pammaro was honest. "They have the better cavalry, and I regret the disparity."

Hannibal grinned, magnificent in the moment of his greatest challenge. "But there is one thing, Pammaro, which you have not noticed."

"What is that?" the man asked.

"In all the numbers of men opposite us, there is not one named Pammaro!"

At this, they all broke into laughter, and the mood lightened. He sent them away, feeling better about their chances and hopeful that their leader's wiles once again would get them through the day.

And, indeed, Hannibal was delighted when he saw the Roman infantry take up their positions, for it appeared that Scipio had come forward with absolutely nothing out of the ordinary. The formation was completely routine: the hastati, principes, and triari were in their normal alignment, separated by columns of the lightly armored velites, which ran back through all three ranks.

"Always the same," Hannibal said excitedly to nearby Mago, a note of contempt in his voice. He had seen this formation dozens of times—it would not withstand the elephants. "This is the best the famous Scipio Africanus can give us? Not even the innovation he used against my brother at Baecula?"

Mago smirked. "He knows what is at stake, and so he does not wish to take chances. After all, it is you he is facing this time."

Slowly and cautiously, the two armies advanced toward each other, closing until they could make out each other's faces. At this point they paused, mixed feelings stirring in all hearts, confidence alternating with fear. Each man tried to size up his enemy, to estimate his strength with his eyes. Soon enough, they would test that strength with their arms.

———

On the far side of the field, atop his vantage point, Scipio and his officers were tense. They had never seen so many elephants! Someone had counted them: they were twenty across and four deep. Each of the huge beasts had sheets of chain mail hung over its sides, and a large brass plate covering its forehead for protection. On the back of each elephant was a large, castle-shaped basket, called a howdah, in which the handler and two spearmen huddled. Not even at Cannae had Hannibal enjoyed such an advantage. Would Scipio's strategy work against such a formidable number of beasts?

It was Lucius who pointed out to Scipio that the regal crest of Tychaeus had taken up a position directly across from Massinissa.

"Apparently, Massinissa will get his chance to settle his score today," Lucius said.

"Hmm," Scipio mused. "I only hope Massinissa doesn't get carried away and forget about what we expect of him."

Down on the battlefield, Massinissa was well aware of the identity of his antagonist. He sent Massiva riding up and down the ranks to shout that it was Tychaeus facing them, and that the battle had become a fight to determine who would be their king. This set the men to cheering, and Scipio fretted for several moments that they would break out of their ranks and begin the battle prematurely.

His concern was misplaced, for it was Hannibal who raised his arm and then brought it down swiftly, the signal for his cavalry to begin their attack.

The trumpeters for Tychaeus and Hasdrubal spotted the signal and sounded the charge. With a deafening roar the Numidians and Carthaginians galloped forward.

This surprised Scipio. He had expected the elephants to begin the contest, and indeed, his own order of battle called for his cavalry to attack the enemy flanks after the infantry was engaged.

Massinissa and Laelius, not wishing to absorb a cavalry charge in a static position, did not wait for Scipio to react to the unexpected opening gambit by Hannibal. They ordered their own forces forward to meet the challenge. The masses of men on horseback thundered toward each other, closing the distance separating them in seconds, and struck each other with a terrible fury.

In an instant, the orderly ranks collapsed into a mad scramble of rearing horses, slashing swords, and dying men. The sheer force of the impact knocked many of the combatants off their mounts; most of these unfortunates were trampled beneath the waves of oncoming riders. The swordplay was furious, the fighting intense.

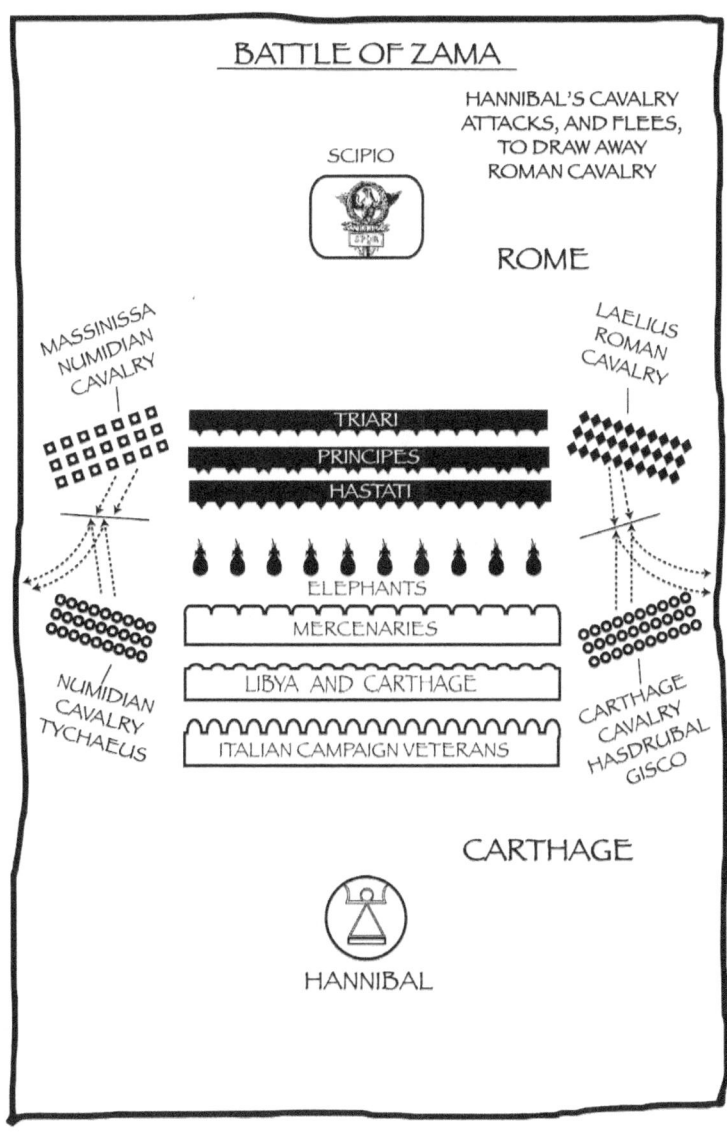

Massinissa fought like a man possessed, hacking his way through the enemy, his eyes fixed on Tychaeus' standard, which, not surprisingly, was at the rear of the swarming chaos. Beside him, young Massiva fought just as hard, determined finally to prove himself to his uncle.

The fighting raged for a few minutes until the Romans' advantage of greater numbers began to make itself felt. The Carthaginians and their allies began to falter, and in the space of a few heartbeats, they commenced to fall back.

"Look," cried Lucius, "They're running for their lives!"

Scipio felt a pulse of excitement as he realized that the enemy cavalry were breaking away from the fight and turning their backs to his forces. But just as quickly, he realized that there was something peculiar afoot. Typically, when an attack collapsed, it did so in a random fashion, as the engaged soldiers gradually realized that their colleagues were falling back. This rout, however, was too simultaneous. In a flash, Scipio recognized the trick: it was a planned retreat, just like at Cannae! Then, too, he realized it was different: at Cannae, Hannibal had pulled back to draw the Romans into a trap. Here, the fleeing men were running away from the field, off to the east and west, abandoning their infantry colleagues to fend for themselves.

The officers in Scipio's command group were cheering the success of their cavalry, slapping each other on the back and commenting that the battle was as good as won.

An instant later, Scipio understood the object of Hannibal's plan. Both Massinissa and Laelius had lost control of their soldiers in the wild melee of pursuit. His biggest advantage—the cavalry—was being drawn away from the field. What he had left was the infantry, and here, thanks to the conniving of Fabius and Marcinius, he had inferior numbers facing the frightful herd of elephants. Everything was going to turn on his untested maneuver. This was not at all how he'd thought things would go. Damn Hannibal!

Scipio grabbed Lucius and shouted frantically, "Quickly, ride after

Massinissa, and get him turned around."

Lucius gave him a peculiar look.

"Don't you see?" Scipio said. "It's a ruse. Hannibal knows we have the advantage of cavalry—and we have just forfeited it! You must catch up with Massinissa and get him back into the fight. The real battle has not yet begun!"

Lucius looked out over the field and realized Scipio was right: their cavalry was rapidly dispersing to the east and west in a mad scramble to catch their opponents, thereby completely taking themselves out of the action about to get under way in the center. And even the inexperienced Lucius could see, from the mere numbers of men facing each other, that the Carthaginians had a clear advantage.

Lucius kicked his horse in the ribs and galloped off to follow his orders. Scipio grabbed a nearby messenger and repeated the instructions, then dispatched the man to get the word to Laelius.

The two Romans had not even reached the bottom of the hill when Hannibal, extremely pleased with his success in neutralizing his opponent's advantage, unleashed the second phase of his attack. To a blare of trumpetry, the wall of elephants began their charge toward the Roman lines.

Scipio saw the elephants commence their attack, and took a deep breath. This was it: all the months of planning and training now were on the line. He motioned for his signalman to wave a large red flag.

Reacting to the signal, the Roman trumpeters, buglers, and cornet men put up such a barrage of martial music that some of the elephants—those not properly trained—took fright and stampeded off to the flanks, impeding the progress of the other elephants, and generally creating chaos before their drivers could plunge the metal spike into their brains.

While the handlers struggled to get their charges back into formation to resume the attack, the Romans executed their maneuver: the velites quickly withdrew to the rear, leaving wide lanes between the other legionnaires.

Hannibal leaned forward in the saddle and pulled on his beard, fretful at this bizarre turn of events. Now this was something different! And ominous. "What are they up to?" he asked. No one had an answer.

As the elephants approached the front line, the hastati launched a withering barrage of their pilum at the oncoming animals. Dozens of these javelins hit their targets, penetrating their armor and wounding the beasts. Many of the wounded animals went berserk with pain and fear, and again the orderliness of the assault briefly disintegrated.

Still, there were simply so many of the elephants that dozens now reached the Roman lines and began to wreak havoc. For several agonizing minutes, Scipio began to despair that the plan had failed—the hastati were being trampled, and the Roman ranks began to scatter into a disorderly rabble.

Hannibal had been worried when he saw the Romans execute their peculiar maneuver, wondering what Scipio was up to, but now he was pleased by the carnage the elephants were causing in the Roman ranks. He decided it was time to release the first line to charge at the frayed Roman lines. With any luck, the added weight of the Ligurians and Gauls would push the elephants through the entire Roman front. He gave the signal, and with a shout, his thousands of mercenaries took off on the run for the enemy.

Fortunately for the Romans, courage and discipline generally prevailed: most of the men resolutely stood their ground, sacrificing themselves, and kept jabbing at the elephants with their lances, trying to get their spear points up and under the protective chain mail. The animals, faltering before these blows, began to back off despite the prodding of their handlers, and suddenly found the open paths the Romans had formed for them through their lines. The beasts quite enjoyed this unexpected respite, and rumbled forward through the lanes, beyond the control of their handlers. And the handlers now were reluctant to use their spikes, for they realized that if they killed their mounts so far into the Roman lines, there was no hope for their own escape.

Within a few minutes, most of the surviving elephants were well behind the Romans, where the reserve force of velites was able to attack them individually.

Scipio sat back in the saddle, overjoyed that his tactic had worked: the elephants had been shunted off harmlessly through the lanes, and into the rear, where they could be disposed of in routine order. Most importantly, the main body of his force remained intact, and the stalwart tribunes and centurions were quickly getting the hastati re-formed and ready to meet the hordes of enemies that now were nearly within sword's length of the front lines.

Across the way, Hannibal felt the first inklings of dread as he realized the elephant charge had been cleverly dissipated, failing to shatter the Roman front. He knew that the lightly armed Ligurians and Gauls, without the battle elephants preceding them, were going to be cut to pieces. Indeed, the Gauls fought characteristically bare-chested and therefore would be easy pickings for another barrage of pilum. Hannibal briefly considered committing his second line to the charge but decided merely to move them forward a few hundred yards and await the Roman counterattack. He still had the advantage of numbers, and this advantage would dictate the outcome if he could just draw the Romans into an all-out struggle before the enemy cavalry regrouped.

Hannibal's hopes rose momentarily as his mercenaries clashed with the hastati. At first, the Romans were driven back by their more mobile opponents, and for several minutes there was confused fighting up and down the line as the air was rent by the wild battle cries of the fanatical Gauls. The Roman line was strained but never broke. Quickly enough, the sheer weight of the Roman armor began to prevail as the hastati, encouraged by the cheers of their colleagues in the rear, literally pressed the enemy back with their shields.

As the mercenaries fell back, Scipio gave the signal for the Romans to advance. Soon the mercenaries were being pressed back against the very spears of their own second line, which not only failed to give them encouragement, but upon Hannibal's express orders, refused to make openings to admit them. Thus trapped between the Romans and their own allies, the Gauls and Ligurians took the full brunt of the Roman counterattack. The ground soon grew slippery with their blood.

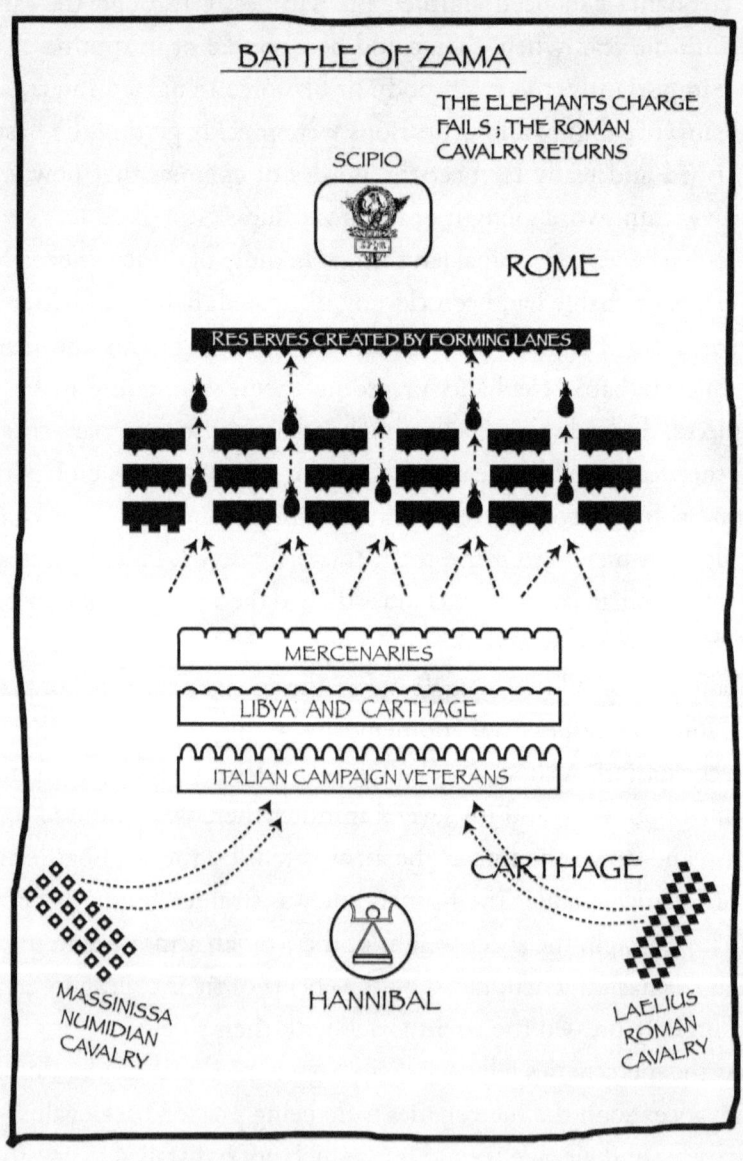

Now the Romans came upon the fresh second line, consisting of Libyans and native Carthaginians. These men were fighting for their homeland, and the resulting combat was without quarter. The sound of clashing metal mixed with the cries of the maimed and the dying. It was almost every man for himself, and like so many battles, the fighting degenerated into an endless series of individual contests. At this point, there was only survival. Yet, over and over again, the Romans—four or five, ten or twelve—would reform and line up shield to shield, exhibiting the famous discipline of the Roman soldier!

"Come on, damn you," Hannibal muttered. "Make the mistake. Commit your reserve."

From his distant perspective, Scipio could see that his men were caving in the Carthaginian second line, and he pondered whether to order an all-out push to break through. But the Carthaginians were throwing up a fierce resistance, and his own troops had taken considerable losses. Even worse, they were losing all semblance of formation. He looked warily at the Carthaginian third line, waiting patiently to counter any breakthrough. From their colors and standards, it was apparent that these men were Hannibal's veterans from Italy, and Scipio reasoned that Hannibal had saved his best for last, hoping that the Romans would be disorganized and bloodied when they came up against the finest men in his army.

That decided it for him. He ordered that a recall be sounded.

Many of the Romans, caught up in the thick of the fray, and mistakenly perceiving that they were gaining the upper hand, were angered by the recall, but obeyed their orders and dropped back. The Romans carefully withdrew about a quarter of a mile to begin their reorganization. Not surprisingly, the weary and battered Carthaginians did not give pursuit, for their unit commanders also sensed the need to dress their lines.

Hannibal was briefly angry with the second-line commanders for failing to press the advantage, but as the forces disengaged, it became apparent to him that his losses had been heavy and that the survivors were in no condition to resume the offensive. Those men still standing were exhausted from the heat and the exertion of their struggle. Clearly, a pause was in order.

Taking stock, Scipio was able to see that the hastati were badly decimated and that some different formation was called for. He decided to elongate his line, with the hope of enveloping the entire Carthaginian line in a frontal assault. Accordingly, he ordered the second-line troops, the principes, to move out from behind the hastati and take up a position to the right of the center. The third rank, the triari, were ordered to the left. And the velites, who had finished mopping up the few remaining elephants, were ordered forward into the center to replenish the depleted ranks of the hastati. The entire Roman army now formed one long, thin line, running across a front of nearly two miles.

The issuance of these orders and the execution thereof took some time, and Hannibal put the respite to good use himself, managing to get his completely unraveled first and second lines back into some semblance of order. Of course, the survivors of the first wave were very sore about the rude treatment they had received from their allies, but they realized they could hardly hope to quit the field and save their skins, so they dutifully took up their assigned positions and waited for the action to resume.

As Hannibal watched the Roman strategy taking shape, he considered concentrating his force to break through the long but narrow ribbon of enemy foot soldiers. However, as the Romans continued to spread their width to the east and west, it became clear that if he narrowed his front, the Romans would come crashing down upon the Carthaginians to strike them on the flanks, their most vulnerable spot. *No*, he thought, *the only choice is to spread our own line and fight the Romans face to face across the broad front they are presenting.* He did not wish to separate his Italian veterans, however, and so orders were issued for the front line to divide in two and move off to the right and left, while the trusted reserve was brought forward to fill the gap thus created in the center.

Scipio recognized Hannibal's responses to his own movements. All the resources of both sides were now committed, and unless his cavalry was recovered to rejoin the battle, the outcome was going to be a test of resolve as much as anything else.

"Where is Massinissa? Where is Laelius?" he pleaded to a nearby tribune. But the man had no answers, and Scipio reluctantly decided that further delay was pointless. He gave the signal to advance.

In fact, Laelius already was struggling to get his troops back under control—quite difficult given the broad range over which the hot pursuit of the enemy had taken them. Fortunately, Laelius had kept his standard bearer at his side, and so Scipio's messenger was finally able to identify his command group and catch up with them. Laelius listened intently as the man relayed Scipio's instructions. Understanding that the outcome of the battle hung in the balance, he energetically redoubled his efforts to recall his forces and get them into some semblance of formation.

Massinissa, meanwhile, had completely given himself over to the chase of Tychaeus, with Massiva and a hundred or so men following hard on his heels. Tychaeus and his escort, a handpicked contingent of bodyguards whose loyalty had been bought with considerable sums of money, had a significant head start and in all likelihood could have easily outdistanced their pursuers, but for one unfortunate fact. The autumn rains had swollen the River Bagradas and its tributaries well beyond their normal banks, and Tychaeus, unfamiliar as he was with the terrain around Zama, found himself trapped. He came over a ridge and yanked hard on the reins. A flooded waterway stretched out before him, in either direction, as far as his eye could see. There was no hope of fording the swirling brown waters. He drew his sword and turned, prepared to make a stand.

Massinissa was a little ahead of his colleagues when he came upon the awaiting Tychaeus. Finding his hated adversary ready to fight, Massinissa pulled to a halt and waited for the others. When they had gotten themselves arranged, Massinissa, with Massiva at his side, gave a shout and thundered up the ridge toward his enemy.

The fight was short and lethal. Dozens fell on both sides, and the whining Tychaeus acquitted himself surprisingly well, cutting a swath through the mingled antagonists until he came upon Massinissa.

The two rivals for the throne of Numidia squared off. Massinissa, of course, was considerably larger, and he struck his first blow with such a fury that Tychaeus, in meeting it with his own sword, was knocked from his mount. Tychaeus hit the ground hard, but picked himself up in an instant. He proved quite nimble on his feet, ducking around and about Massinissa's blows, easily staying out of the mounted man's reach. Frustrated, Massinissa swung his left leg over the saddle and slid off his own mount.

The two men circled each other, hatred blazing in their eyes. Massinissa stepped forward and jabbed at Tychaeus, who parried the blow, grunting with the effort. Massinissa swung his sword in a long arc, a mean blow aimed at Tychaeus' helmet. Tychaeus met the swipe with his own blade, but he was not nearly as strong as Massinissa. The force of Massinissa's strike knocked Tychaeus' blade back into his own helmet, which split under the blow and left a nasty wound across Tychaeus' forehead and into the top of his head. Tychaeus staggered backward and managed to rip away the damaged helmet, keeping his sword level in front of him. Blood streamed down his face from the gash, obscuring his vision. Tychaeus struggled to retain his equilibrium as a wave of shock from the injury swept over him.

Massinissa, now consumed by fury, lashed out again at Tychaeus, who was wobbly on his feet. This strike managed to slash through Tychaeus' abdomen, the tip of Massinissa's blade carving a deep gash. Tychaeus suddenly appeared very tired, and his legs seemed incapable of holding his weight. The sword seemed too heavy to keep uplifted in a protective position.

Massinissa knew that revenge was his, and he struck home a final blow, running his blade through Tychaeus' breast with such force that the tip emerged clean through the other side.

Massinissa brought up his foot and kicked Tychaeus, releasing the hilt of his weapon. Tychaeus staggered backward, sucking for air, then fell dead into the dust.

Realizing the fight still raged about him, Massinissa took up the sword Tychaeus had dropped and bent down over his dead enemy. With one determined stroke, he separated the head from the corpse and lifted it aloft, bellowing in rage.

All eyes turned to see Massinissa standing there, blood and gore from the severed head gushing down the Numidian's strong arm. In an instant, those followers of Tychaeus still alive threw down their arms and surrendered.

Massinissa transferred the head onto the point of a spear and gave it to Massiva. "Let this be my standard now," he cried, still consumed with the blood fever of his fury.

Just then Lucius came upon the scene, his horse panting wildly from the hard ride he had made to overtake the Numidians.

With a glance, Lucius took in the scene, and, seeing Massinissa drenched with blood and his gruesome trophy aloft, realized that the huge African had had his revenge.

"Congratulations," Lucius said, unable to think of anything else to say. "I bring you an urgent message from Scipio. Your pursuit of Tychaeus has taken your men from the field, where they are sorely needed. You must gather your forces and return to the fight. We may already be too late."

Massinissa, his heart still pounding, nodded. He staggered over to his mount and was helped up by one of his men. Reaching into some hidden reservoir of energy, he summoned up the strength to turn the horse about and face Massiva.

"Come, Massiva," he croaked. "Our work today is not yet finished."

With that, he galloped off in search of his army, which by now was scattered to the winds.

———

The sun was high in the sky when the Romans began their final attack. Scipio's hopes for enveloping the enemy rapidly dissolved as the Romans came upon the very core of Hannibal's army. The Romans soon enough discovered how these veterans had managed to win so many battles—the Carthaginians fought with a savage fury, with the utmost disregard for their own safety and a view only to disposing of the Romans.

For their own part, the Romans themselves showed Hannibal a resolve he was unaccustomed to facing. The shame of Cannae was pent up in them, and this was their chance for vindication. They fought for their lives, and for their honor. They met the enemy's violence with a burning fury of their own, stoked by years of ignominious service in Sicily. Hannibal soon enough realized that the outcome was beyond the ability of either general to affect. Posted on his hilltop, he resigned himself to utter irrelevancy, and consigned his fate, and the fate of his country, to the hands of the gods.

Back and forth they raged, neither side able to gain an advantage. Bodies piled up and the ground was soaked with flesh and blood. Some of the wounded managed to crawl away, picking their way to the modest safety of an occasional tree or shrub, clambering over the vast clutter of fallen weapons and armament.

Still, the Carthaginians had better numbers, and slowly, bit by bit, they began to push the Romans back. Scipio was contemplating another recall when his adjutant grabbed him by the arm and pointed to the east.

Scipio's heart skipped a beat. He recognized Laelius' standard, at the head of hundreds of cavalry, bearing down on the Carthaginians. Laelius had done it! He had recovered enough men and gotten them organized to mount a strike that he apparently intended to direct at the rear of the Carthaginian line. But would this be enough to turn the tide of the battle?

Hannibal at the same moment saw the Roman cavalry making its way to the backside of his badly distended line. There was much consternation in the officers around him, but he hastened to reassure them: there could not be more than a thousand of the cavalrymen, certainly not enough to rout the stalwart veterans anchoring his center. He waved wildly for the trumpeters to sound a warning.

Even amid the melee on the field, several Carthaginian officers heard the alert and turned to see the oncoming Romans. They managed to get a substantial number of infantry turned around to meet the charge.

Scipio marveled at the scene of absolute confusion playing out on the field below him. It was now impossible to tell who was winning, or even what the original formations had been. The entire battle had degenerated into a mass of individual struggles, with the din barely overcoming the cries of the wounded and dying.

"It is too terrible," Scipio murmured to the adjutant beside him. "May the gods help them."

The Roman cavalry stabilized the situation on the field but failed to break the Carthaginian resolve. The awful hacking continued, and Scipio wondered whether either side would emerge victorious. *Where*, his mind screamed, *is Massinissa?*

A few seconds later, he had his answer. Off to the west there appeared a dark mass, almost resembling a monstrous horde of ants, which seemed slowly to be crawling toward the tangle of men below him.

The Roman officers gave another cheer as it became apparent that Massinissa had managed to recover most of his force and bring them back to the battle.

"Hurry, damn you, hurry!" Scipio cried, not sure whether the Romans could hold out long enough for Massinissa to make his impact felt upon the battlefield.

His fears proved unfounded. The Numidians hurtled across the plain, spurring their animals to a final exertion. They slammed into the unprotected Carthaginian left rear, and in a few minutes, the tide of combat had irretrievably shifted against Carthage.

Hannibal had seen them coming and made frantic efforts to send a warning. But the confusion on the field was so widespread by now that no one noticed the trumpet signals. The general was no dreamer. Seeing the onrushing Numidians, he realized that his grand strategy had failed, mainly because he had been unable to rout the Roman infantry before the cavalry got back into the fight. Sick at heart, he drew his sword and began to ride toward the battle, determined to go down fighting with his men.

He was restrained, however, by the other officers, who prevailed upon him to withdraw from the field. Carthage may have spent her last resources, but while Hannibal remained alive, there was hope for negotiations with the victorious Romans. With Hannibal dead, she would be devoid of any assets with which to bargain. Reluctantly, Hannibal allowed himself to be persuaded, and he left the field with his entire officer corps.

Their Roman counterparts saw their opponents' command flags and standards withdraw behind the hilltop, and a crescendo cheering arose: Hannibal had quit the field. They were victorious!

The soldiers engaged in the actual fighting gradually became aware of Hannibal's departure. It was as if the absence of his spirit somehow drained the Carthaginians of their will to resist, and the proud veterans slowly succumbed to the methodical slaughter inflicted by the Romans and Numidians.

By nightfall, not a single Carthaginian soldier on the field was left alive.

XVII

TUNIS, AFRICA

202 BC

I MMEDIATELY AFTER THE BATTLE, Scipio stormed and plundered the Carthaginian camp, killing the handful of soldiers left on guard and seizing vast stores of supplies and treasure, including all the trophies Hannibal had so brazenly displayed to the Romans only the day before. The spoils seized from the quarters of Tychaeus were rightfully bestowed upon Massinissa; the remainder Scipio dispatched to Rome, together with an account of the glorious victory. To transmit this message, he chose none other than the loyal Laelius. Laelius, thinking he might be able to do Scipio some good in Rome, readily agreed to make the journey. There was no sign of Hannibal, and rumor had it that he had headed for the coastal town of Hasdrumentum, rather than flee for Carthage itself. Upon returning to camp, Scipio hurried to the altar and offered up prayers of thanks for his success, then ordered that an extravagant feast be held on the day following the completion of funeral rites for the fallen soldiers.

The cleanup of the battlefield took the better part of a week, with the autumn rains slowing the progress considerably, and so when the victory festival was held under yet another day of gray skies, there had been time to make spectacular preparations. There were all nature of entertainments and revelry, the ranks of the captured slaves having been scoured for talented dancers, musicians, jugglers, and magicians. Various athletic games inspired considerable wagering on their outcomes. A vast quantity of food was set out for the victors, as well as huge jugs of wine, which were enthusiastically drained. Scipio presided over a formal ceremony at which he handed out dozens of trophies and ribbons, honoring scores of men for acts of valor. As a special honor, he bestowed a captured standard from the vanquished Carthaginians upon Laelius, in absentia, for his timely reappearance upon the battlefield.

But for the Numidians, the highlight of the event was the ceremonial crowning of Massinissa by Scipio as the undisputed king of Numidia. The symbolism of this act was not lost upon the crowd: it was Rome who now was arbiter of the world's affairs. Massinissa then pronounced his first decree, an order extending an amnesty to all former followers of Tychaeus, provided they would swear an oath of loyalty to Massinissa and pay him a tribute of silver. This was certainly preferred to the awful punishment he might have chosen to inflict upon his former enemies, and hundreds of the lean, wiry Africans lined up to make their peace with their undisputed new king.

Watching it all, Vibiana was torn. She was relieved that Scipio and Laelius had come through the terrible battle unscathed. But she also was overcome by a wistful sadness, for she knew that her native country had lost the war. Even worse, Carthage now lay helpless before the harsh terms the Romans might choose to impose. And she expected events would move swiftly, making it unlikely that she would remain in Africa until the birth of her child.

The day after the feast, while many of the soldiers lay about, groaning from the effects of overindulgent celebration, Scipio met with his senior officers and decided to split the army. Massinissa and his Numidians were to make a slow and highly noticeable path for Carthage, raising as much ruckus as possible, while he and the Romans made for Tunis, where he intended to establish a new base for the final movement against Carthage. He also sent orders for the Roman fleet at Utica to break off its participation in the siege and join him at Tunis.

Scipio was anxious to get to Tunis. Leaving Vibiana with the main vanguard of his army, he hurried on horseback toward that strategically important coastal city, accompanied only by Lucius and his retinue of bodyguards.

Tunis was not much of a city, comprised mainly of short, squat buildings dotting the steeply sloping hills that surrounded the harbor. The streets were not paved nor even covered with gravel, and as a result of the autumn rains had been turned into a foul-smelling quagmire of mud mingled with garbage and manure.

Word of the victory at Zama preceded Scipio's arrival. The city fathers, quite clearly wishing to align themselves with the victor, met the Romans at the city limits, handing over the keys to the city and begging Scipio to state the terms by which Tunis might align herself with the new masters of the world. In a matter of minutes, Tunis became a new Roman ally. Scipio was escorted to the finest home in the city, the residence of a rich silk merchant, commandeered for the use of the victor over Hannibal. After pronouncing himself satisfied with his quarters, Scipio requested a sailing ship, from which he desired to reconnoiter Carthage by sea.

But the advancing winter weather delayed his departure for several days, and somehow, word of his plans reached Carthage. And so Scipio was surprised when his ship was met by a Carthaginian vessel sailing under a white flag of truce, hung with wooden fillets and olive branches of supplication. The boat carried ten envoys, leading citizens of Carthage, sent by Hannibal's order to sue for peace. As the two vessels drew alongside each other, the Carthaginians held out symbols of supplication and begged for mercy from their Roman conqueror. Scipio brusquely directed them to remove themselves to Tunis, where he would hear their entreaties.

Scipio then sailed on to the harbor of Carthage, now not so interested in reconnaissance as in humiliating his enemy. His battle flag was hauled atop the mast of the ship, and he was rowed up and down the harbor, studying the city that had challenged Rome for mastery of the world. The harbor was lined with ships of the Carthaginian navy, the force that had so badly failed her nation during the war. The Carthaginians were advocates of speed and maneuverability, and so their ships were much smaller than either the Roman triremes or quinqueremes. They featured only seventeen oars on a side and were fitted with a long, tusk-shaped battering ram made of wood sheathed in copper. As an innovation, the ram was detachable so that after ramming an enemy ship, the Carthaginian could withdraw to watch the adversary slowly sink. Tremendous bales of a green leafy plant were stacked along the wharves, and Scipio asked his guide, a swarthy Tunisian merchant, what these might be.

"Cannabis," replied the merchant, who was very nervous about Scipio's brazen display. He was terrified that the Carthaginians might take up Scipio's challenge and come out into the harbor for an engagement. "They brew it into a tea that they use to relieve the tedium and lift the spirits of the rowers."

Seen from the harbor, Carthage was a sprawling metropolis covering more than seven square miles. The city was encased on the north, east, and south by a massive stone wall, every bit the equal of the Servian Wall of Rome. It was at least forty-five feet high, with formidable towers every two hundred feet. On the vulnerable western side, the city was separated from the harbor by a maze of ditches, battlements, parapets and fences, virtually impenetrable to an invading army. Seeing this, Scipio thought of the difficulty the Romans had had with the more modest defenses at Utica, and his appetite for a siege diminished rapidly.

Military considerations aside, Carthage was a beautiful, gleaming city, shimmering in the Mediterranean sunlight, and every bit the rival of Rome in architectural diversity. Scores of tall buildings, some as high as six stories, boasted columns, detailing, and form, whereas in Rome, only temples typically were given such attention.

The guide was pointing out the highlights. "There, in the center of the city, running all the way back to the slopes of the Byrsa Hill, is the principal residential area," he said, pointing to a densely packed cluster of buildings. He then swung his arm to the northwest and identified a large complex of buildings just to the north of the ports. "That," he said, "is the Forum, wherein the Council meets to govern the affairs of the nation.

"And over there," he said, pointing to what was by far the largest single structure, a dazzling specimen of construction sheathed in gold and copper, "is the Temple of Ba'al Hammon."

Scipio gave him an uncomprehending look.

"You do not know what transpires in the Temple of Ba'al?" the merchant asked, surprised. "For sixteen years you have fought this enemy without knowing about Ba'al?"

"Do not mock my ignorance about my enemy," Scipio warned the little man, irritated with him. "I have concentrated upon his methods in battle, not his religious customs."

The merchant shrank back a bit, chastened by the powerful Scipio Africanus. "Inside those gilded walls is an open air precinct, called the Tophet, which the Carthaginians hold sacred. There, on their ritual holidays, they sacrifice babies to the god. The tiny bodies are then burned, and the ashes are buried in ceramic urns."

Scipio looked at him, mouth agape.

"It is true," the merchant said. "There is a statue of the god, seated, with his arms held out, but sloping down. A fire is constructed in a pit at the feet of the god. The sacrificed infants are placed on the arms, and then roll down into the flames."

"It is said that wealthy families, to escape the levy, sometimes purchase children from the poor and offer them up instead of their own children. The priests know this, of course, but for a gift, they will feign ignorance."

At this, the city did not seem quite so beautiful to Scipio. "I have seen enough," he called to the captain. "Take me back to Tunis."

By the time he returned to Tunis, the legions had arrived and established themselves in a camp outside the city walls. Scipio was delighted to see Vibiana, whose belly was now beginning to swell noticeably, and he settled her comfortably in a small but lavish palace that had been offered him by the Tunisians. He was told that the ten envoys he had encountered on the high seas had been joined by twenty others, who had been dispatched from the city as soon as Hannibal's grim news on the outcome of the battle had been received. These latter envoys had made something of a trek through the countryside trying to catch up with Scipio's movements before joining their colleagues in Tunis.

Scipio kept the entire assemblage waiting for two days before he would see them. His delay was taken to allow the Roman fleet to arrive from Utica so as to strike further terror into the hearts of the Carthaginians. The Roman fleet duly made its appearance, jamming the whole harbor with its mass.

The fleet brought with it an item Scipio did not want to see: another scroll from Marcia. He was at a loss over what to do about it, and so he put it away, unread.

The Carthaginian envoys were paraded through the Roman camp so that they might acquire an appreciation of the strength of their adversary's arms, then were ushered into the palace, to a room carefully chosen to afford a full view of the harbor. Scipio, clad in his most formal consular garb, stood before the window, against the backdrop of dozens of scarlet sails festooned with golden braid. He had at his side Lucius and Massinissa, the latter swathed in the regal purple robes of royalty. The supplicants were ushered in for an audience.

Their entreaties were piteous, and Scipio nearly drove them to despair when he announced that there was considerable sentiment among his council for the complete destruction of their city. He had no such intentions, of course: the siege of Utica had proven difficult enough, and the thought of besieging so great a city as Carthage, equipped as she was with stout fortifications and considerable resources, was quite beyond his immediate resources. However, the envoys were utterly cowed by the show of Roman military might, and begged him only to state his terms.

"Having been put to a test of arms upon the field at Zama," Scipio said coldly, "Rome can hardly be expected to make the peace on so generous terms as Hannibal himself rejected."

"Africanus, I am Ilderim, and upon my unhappy shoulders has fallen the heavy ignominy of begging for peace," said the lead Carthaginian negotiator, a distinguished-looking man with a long white beard. "You have only to name your conditions."

Scipio first repeated the terms he had laid down to Hannibal: recognition of Massinissa as king of Numidia, the destruction of the Carthaginian navy, and the enormous reparations.

These provisions, especially the huge indemnity, brought cries of anguish from the envoys.

Scipio then demanded that all the war elephants in Carthage's possession were to be surrendered, and no more were to be trained. Furthermore, all Roman deserters, runaway slaves, and prisoners of war were to be handed over immediately. The deserters would face the harsh retribution of Roman justice: citizens would be beheaded, all others would be crucified.

"Most importantly," he then stated, "Carthage has proven herself to be untrustworthy. Accordingly, never again shall she be afforded independence of actions in dealing with the nations of the world. Carthage shall swear by sacred treaty never again to make war against anyone outside of Africa without first having obtained the permission of Rome."

Many of the envoys were now weeping and tearing at their garments as the full extent of their shameful defeat made itself known. But still Scipio was not finished.

The Roman leader's eyes narrowed in a hard gaze. "Your great general Hannibal has proven completely unworthy of our trust, or our mercy. I demand that you turn him over to us, to be taken to Rome, where he will face the judgment of our Senate."

To a man, the envoys cried out in dismay.

Their spokesman looked grave. "Africanus, Hannibal is like a god to us. He is our only hope to lead our nation to recovery from these harsh terms."

"Precisely so," Scipio snapped. "That is why he must not be allowed to remain as a threat to the Roman people. You have my terms. You may return to Carthage and present them to your Council. I shall expect an answer within the fortnight. But I admonish you most severely: either accept our terms in full, or the misery and calamity you have suffered to date will pale in comparison to the vengeance I will visit upon your unhappy heads."

He turned his back on them and looked out over the harbor, a rude dismissal.

When the wailing and lamenting envoys were gone, he turned to his colleagues and grinned. "Well?" he said.

Lucius looked pensive. "I approve of everything except your requirement concerning Hannibal. I cannot believe they will surrender him."

Scipio mulled this over. His demand for Hannibal was part of a plan he had devised to mollify the Senate over Vibiana. Surely, he thought, if he could deliver so undeniable a prize as Hannibal himself, they would grant him a pardon for her. He glanced at Massinissa.

The African kept his face impassive.

Scipio was concerned that they thought he had gone too far. "We shall see," he said, a little irritably.

XVIII

ROME

202 BC

LAELIUS HAD MET WITH bad weather during his voyage back to Italy and was blown far off course by a powerful storm. The foul weather left him with a severe case of seasickness and, accordingly, he arrived in Rome having lost several pounds and feeling entirely miserable. Even worse, his ship had arrived days after the vessels bearing the lavish spoils from the battle of Zama, and after a second dispatch from Scipio, which had related the details of his demands upon Carthage. And so Laelius found the city in the midst of wild celebrations. Everywhere he went, he was mobbed by hordes of admirers pressing him for details concerning the battle. He resolutely put off all these requests and made his way straight to the Forum to deliver his report.

Even though the senators had by now gotten most of the story from the sailors who had beaten Laelius back to Rome, their reaction to his account of the battle of Zama was completely predictable: the senators cheered wildly, slapping each other on the back and clasping their arms about one other, as if every one of them were personally responsible for the glorious outcome. The chamber was taken over by a mood of euphoria, and several resolutions were offered and passed unanimously. These variously proclaimed a weeklong celebration of games in Scipio's honor, and called for lavish sacrifices in gratitude for the blessing of the gods.

Then a motion was proposed to authorize Scipio to make whatever peace he saw fit. Regarding this matter, Cato rose to speak. This brought forth a murmur from the group, for Cato had been relatively quiet since Scipio's successes in the field had put to shame Cato's decision to abandon the campaign. Scipio had been right: there was no thought now to challenge the costs of the adventure, given the monumental results.

The senators noticed that for some odd reason, Cato was holding the folds of his toga in a peculiar manner, as if to form a sheath to conceal some item.

"My friends," Cato said, his powerful voice echoing off the marble columns, "I offer my congratulations to the noble Scipio Africanus upon his victory over Hannibal at Zama. And I am proud to have played a part in the organization of the effort."

Laelius barely was able to restrain himself at this brazen attempt to rewrite history. Several of the senators loyal to Scipio hissed at the lanky plebeian.

But Cato continued, "Now I rise to address the question of peace with Carthage."

He released the folds of his garment that he had gathered up in his hand, and there fell to the gleaming floor a half dozen figs. "These fruits come from Africa. I purchased them myself only this morning, on the way to the Forum," Cato said. "You may inspect them yourselves, and see that they are still fresh. So close is the continent of our enemy that the produce of their gardens can be transported to your feet before it can even spoil! And just as quickly, my friends, can the Carthaginians recover from the beating we have given them! No terms of peace will protect us, however harsh they may be. We are dealing with an enemy that has proven, time and again, that it will break a treaty whenever it finds it expedient to do so. No, my friends, Carthage cannot be permitted to recoup her losses, and make trouble for our grandchildren. No Roman child will ever sleep safe in his or her bed so long as the Punic flag still flies."

He paused for dramatic effect, then shouted, "I say to you, Carthage must be destroyed!"

The Senate broke out in an uproar, and it was several minutes before order could be regained. During this time, Laelius pondered Cato's motives: undoubtedly he realized that Scipio, upon his return to the Capitol, would be feted as the greatest man in Rome. Perhaps he meant by this demand to keep Scipio far away for the years it would take to reduce the city by siege.

Laelius' fears were soon enough put to rest by Fabius, who spoke briefly against the proposal. The Roman people were weary of war, he said. It was time to enjoy the benefits of such peace as Scipio in his judgment might make.

Quintus Valerius Caldus got up and added his support, indicating that the members of Marcinius' faction should fall into line. Scipio's allies joined in, and the original motion to authorize Scipio to make peace at his discretion was passed.

The Senate then turned its attention to the matter of Antiochus III, king of an assemblage of territories loosely referred to by the natives as Syria, but known to the Romans as Asia. This character evidently fancied himself another Alexander, even to the point of referring to himself as "Antiochus the Great" in his formal communications. He certainly had the territorial ambitions of Alexander, for he had set upon a methodical program of annexing territory to his kingdom.

Throughout the last few years of the war with Carthage, Rome had monitored the activities of Antiochus with an increasingly nervous eye, but the Carthaginian drain on her resources had been too demanding to permit anything other than an occasional note of protest addressed to the Asian potentate when he added another territory to his dominion. Now, however, with Carthage apparently vanquished, it was time for Rome to turn her attention to the east, and to the riches that lay there.

Quintus Valerius Caldus had been designated by Marcinius as the spokesman regarding the question of Antiochus. His remarks were short and to the point. "Our friend and ally Attalus, who has been steadfast in his support of our cause, who has for years prevented Philip's efforts toward Roman soil, now calls upon us for help," Caldus told the Senate in his deep voice. "We cannot call ourselves men and yet turn a deaf ear to our friend in Pergamum, where Antiochus makes hostile advances by the day. I say that we must dispatch a delegation to Antiochus, and instruct him to cease and desist in his aggression against our ally, lest he make himself the enemy of Rome."

Laelius watched with dread as Caldus' resolution passed without a dissenting vote. One war barely finished, and already they were inviting another! Perhaps, he thought, if some of these windbags had to do the fighting, they would not be so eager to send others to do so.

As the senators began wending their way out of the hall, Fabius caught Laelius' attention and directed him to a small anteroom off the main chamber. The unfortunate death of Silanus had deprived Fabius of his advance notice of the events in Africa. This did not sit well with the old general, whose power in part depended on possessing superior knowledge regarding events. He had learned of the circumstances surrounding Silanus' death from one of the first ships to arrive bearing tidings of the battle of Zama, well before Laelius' return. Fabius was absolutely mystified at Silanus' behavior: his instructions were to report on Scipio's behavior, not challenge him. Why would Silanus have risked his life, challenging Scipio to a duel? Marcinius professed to be baffled as well. Fabius decided that something was wrong, and he was determined to get to the bottom of it.

Laelius found himself cornered by Fabius and Marcinius in a small, empty room, used chiefly for caucuses between factions of opposing senators. Fabius pulled the stout door shut behind them as they entered. Once inside, they pressed him for more details than Scipio had related in his formal dispatch.

Laelius managed to maintain his composure, answering Fabius' pointed questions concerning the meeting between Scipio and Hannibal with a reasonable degree of truthfulness, but avoiding the part about Hannibal's demand for the return of Vibiana. Fabius wanted to know the specific term upon which the negotiations had broken down, but Laelius feigned ignorance, claiming he had not heard the entire conversation because of the blowing winds, and Scipio had refused to tell him. He made a mental note to relate this story to Scipio, so that his story would be corroborated. Fabius then began asking about the specifics of Scipio's tactics for dealing with the charge of the elephants, when Marcinius, who was more interested in other things, interrupted.

"Enough of this military talk. Why has Scipio failed to write anything to Marcia?" he demanded of Laelius.

"Clearly," Laelius said uneasily, "he has been terribly busy: meeting with Hannibal, the preparations for the battle—"

"Don't insult my intelligence," Marcinius snapped. "I am aware that he is carrying on an affair with the widow of Syphax. What are his intentions with respect to my daughter?"

Laelius glanced at Fabius, who seemed quite agitated with Marcinius, and wondered whether Fabius was in on Marcinius' plot to kill Scipio.

"I must know," Marcinius pressed him, "whether he intends to honor his pledge to my daughter."

Laelius was unsure how to respond. "I cannot say. You'll have to discuss that with Scipio himself."

But Marcinius would not be put off. "It is said that this woman of his was formerly a captive during the campaign in Spain, and that she escaped her captivity by murdering her guard, a Roman soldier."

"That is so," Laelius acknowledged.

"Then her life is forfeit, and I will demand that she be punished to the fullest extent of the law. You are Scipio's closest confidant. How does he intend to explain himself? Victor over Hannibal or not, his behavior toward my daughter has been abominable!" Marcinius was growing apoplectic.

Laelius had had enough. "That accusation, sir, is most unseemly, considering the actions you yourself have undertaken in connection with it."

This retort set Marcinius back. "I—I don't know what you're talking about," the senator stammered, his entire face flushing red.

"Does the sum of ten million sesterces refresh your recollection?"

The color drained from Marcinius' features and he now turned white as the snow atop Vesuvius.

"What are you talking about?" Fabius demanded.

Laelius leveled his gaze at the portly senator. "You two are close allies. Let him explain it to you."

"I'll not be a party to any such interrogation, not when I am the one who has been wronged!" Marcinius said with as much pomposity as he could summon. He stormed off in a huff.

"What in blazes is going on?" Fabius demanded again. Then, seeing Laelius did not intend to answer, said in exasperation, "I was afraid of something like this. You must return to Scipio, and explain to him that his disgraceful behavior toward Marcinius' daughter must end. He must not bring this girl back with him. It would undo all the glory he has managed to win for himself. Surely he would not throw away all he has earned over this mere trollop."

But Laelius did not respond, for under no circumstances would he tell Fabius just how far Scipio was prepared to go to keep Vibiana at his side.

After managing to excuse himself from Fabius' oppressive presence, Laelius made his way through hordes of well-wishers, heading for the luxurious baths lying just below the Temple of Apollo. Bone tired and still a little wobbly from his rough voyage, he was determined to take in a few of Rome's pleasures before returning to the harsh routine of campaign living. The signs of celebration were everywhere: bright banners proclaimed the news of Zama, and people were behaving as if the war was already over.

En route to the spa, he stopped briefly at the Macellum, the expansive open-air marketplace lying at the bottom of the Capitoline, and basked for several moments in the aromatic diversity. *For too long,* he thought, *have I been eating camp food!* He purchased a cooked sausage and ate it on the spot, the rich juices dribbling down his chin. He washed the spicy meat down with a small carafe of sweet wine. He then found a tasty flour cake, glazed with honey, and sampled several fruits, including an exotic-looking date that the purveyor insisted was imported fresh from Egypt.

One corner of the Macellum caught his eye and he wandered over to investigate. A thriving commerce was being carried out in slaves, whom Laelius recognized from their attire as captives from the African Expedition. He watched as a distraught pregnant woman, evidently far advanced in her term, was hauled up on a small wooden stage and exhibited. There was no way of knowing the identity of the father, of course, as the woman might have been taken dozens of times during her trek from Africa to the auctioneer's block. At the shouted request of several bidders, she was roughly stripped so that the spectators could verify her condition. Laelius had never seen a pregnant woman naked, and he was fascinated at the huge mound her ripe belly formed beneath her engorged breasts, so completely out of proportion to the remainder of her slender figure. The bidding was brisk, for, given her state, the buyer would soon have the woman's offspring as a return, so to speak, on the investment. Laelius recognized the auctioneer, an agent handpicked by Scipio. The man skillfully manipulated the bidding, bringing a winning offer of fifty sesterces. Laelius could see from the long line of captives, chained to posts and available for inspection while awaiting their turn on the block, that Scipio was going to have more money than he would know how to spend.

The woman was barely off the block when the next unfortunate was hauled up. This individual was a superbly built African, whose hands were kept chained behind a back marred by severe scarring. As he was hoisted onto the platform, he seemed a mass of muscle, which, with his movements, swelled and knotted like kinking cords. The auctioneer announced that this prisoner had proven very difficult to manage and been sternly disciplined with whips, which accounted for the ravaged condition of his backside. The nude African was turned slowly on the block, and Laelius, like others in the audience, gasped at the sight of his manhood, enormous even in its flaccid state. Several ribald remarks greeted this spectacle, and the bidding began. The information concerning the man's bad temper dampened the enthusiasm of the buyers, who realized they would have their hands full handling this fellow. Bidding was light, mostly coming from a few farmers who could make use of the African's apparent strength. The maximum bid was twenty sesterces. Offered only such a pittance, the auctioneer pulled the man off the block. He would bring more on the wharves, where his brawn would be attractive to the galley captains, who would make short work of breaking his spirit. The African, who could not understand Latin, was led away, oblivious of the terrible destiny to which he was now consigned. It was regrettable, thought Laelius, that so marvelous a specimen should be dispatched to so slow and horrible a death.

Laelius quickly grew bored with the slave auction and decided to move on to the baths. He rounded a corner and paused before a bustling construction site. Scores of workmen scurried about, carpenters and stonecutters, surveyors and masons, laborers and overseers. In an instant, he realized that this was Scipio's enormous temple to the honor of Neptune. The construction was well into its second year, and already the outlines of the massive edifice were clearly discernable. The footings had been dug and heavy limestone blocks set in place for the foundation, to support the imposing structure, along with the bases for dozens of Corinthian columns, planned to hold the ceiling and roof. A number of the columns themselves were scattered about the site, having been dragged up the hillside on pallets from the River Tiber. A huge crane, bigger than any Laelius had ever seen, was hoisting the columns into place. This machine was comprised of a massive wheel beneath a tall tower. Thick ropes were tethered to the wheel, which—when turned by dozens of slaves—had the desired effect of lifting the heaviest stones. Laelius moved closer, and he could see that the portion of the terrazzo floor already in place held a phenomenal block of marble shrouded with scaffolding.

He wondered for a second what purpose the block of marble was intended to serve, and then understood that from this raw material the sculptor would conceive the deity. The sculpture was intended to be so large that the temple would have to be built around it, while it was being carved.

Laelius spent a few moments taking in the sight, and concluded that all the wealth he had witnessed being amassed on Scipio's behalf at the slave auction was being expended only a stone's throw away.

Finally, he came to the baths. Ah, what a sweet relaxation came over him as he entered the facility, unquestionably the finest advancement of civilization yet offered by Rome to the world. On arriving, he disrobed in the clammy dressing room and made his way to the unctarium, where the attendant gave him a slow, luxurious rubdown with fine-smelling oil. The attendant was strictly professional, and Laelius knew he would have to look elsewhere for companionship. From there, he went to the gymnasium, where he had a brief bout of exercise, more for the purpose of assessing the other participants who were, like himself, completely nude, than for the need to stretch his own muscles. It didn't take him long to link up with Patroclus, a distinguished-looking, middle-aged Roman who, he knew from past experience, shared his own preferences. Patroclus was a little thick around the middle, but Laelius knew him to be versatile in his lovemaking, and so he accepted the man's invitation to dinner following the bath.

Laelius and his friend put in a leisurely appearance at the tepidarium, where they lazed around in the warm-water pool, chatting with various admirers who were still agog at the triumph of the African campaign. He told the story of the battle of Zama over and over again until finally he could not bear to repeat it. They then took a dip in the caldarium, reveling in the hot and steamy atmosphere while attendants brought drinks. Dripping with perspiration, Laelius got to his feet and stood patiently while a body servant scraped him clean with the curved strigil. Finally, Laelius and Patroclus plunged for a few moments into the cold bath of the frigidarium. Thus invigorated, Laelius and his friend dressed and adjourned to a nearby tavern, notable for the towering jug of wine painted on its stone walls, to celebrate the success of the war against Carthage.

After a few hours of listening to—and participating in—dozens of toasts, Laelius was quite inebriated and so was entirely agreeable when Patroclus suggested that they remove themselves to his insulae, not far away. Patroclus was prosperous: his brick apartment building was massive, comprising some six floors. Of course, Patroclus lived on the most desirable ground floor—the higher one went, the less attractive the space became.

It had been weeks since Laelius had left his young slave behind in Africa, and he was hungry for the delights of love. It was not necessary to waste time on preliminaries: Laelius and Patroclus were very quickly lost in the pleasures each could give the other.

Marcinius, in the meantime, was finding anything but pleasure as he returned to his mansion atop the Palatine. Judging from Laelius' remarks, somehow the officer knew about his offer to Silanus. Perhaps Silanus had been foolish enough to disregard his suggestion, contained at the end of the letter, to destroy the evidence. *Yes*, Marcinius thought glumly, *it would be like Silanus to expose himself and everyone else to danger.* As he huffed and puffed up the steep slope of the Palatine, his mind groped for a solution to the dilemma. Had Laelius told Scipio of the plot? Evidently not, for no challenge had been forthcoming from Scipio. What then, was Laelius' game?

Even worse, he knew that Marcia would be frantic for information, and he had nothing good to tell her.

He had hoped to slip into the house unnoticed, but Marcia was far ahead of him. He had barely made his way up the broad marble steps and onto the spacious portico when she swooped out of the structure and confronted him.

"Well, Father?" she asked plaintively. "Is there any news about Scipio?"

The innocence in her lovely face absolutely crushed him. Dozens of times, he had resolved to tell her the truth about her fiancé, but now, seeing her rapt eagerness, his determination failed again.

"No," he said, shaking his head sorrowfully, "not really. He is well, of course, and completely immersed in the details of concluding the peace now that he has won his long-sought victory. He is a soldier, my dear, and for him, duty comes first. I am sure that is why you have not heard from him."

She was crestfallen, and tears welled in the corners of her eyes.

"But why, Papa, does he not respond to my letters? Did you ask Laelius about that?"

He sighed and took her into his arms. "Now, now, little bird, you know how I hate to see you cry. I am sure Scipio thinks of you often.

You must be patient, though. First, he had to fight Hannibal. We waited sixteen years for that victory, so you can appreciate how hard it was to come by. He is presently engaged in making the peace with Carthage, and making peace is even more difficult than making war. Do not trouble yourself. He is now the greatest man in Rome, and when he returns, you will be the most famous couple in the city."

She looked up at him and smiled a little. "Oh, Papa, I do not care about fame. It's just that I miss him so much. You never should have made me wait until he gets back to get married!"

This hurt Marcinius more than she realized. Perhaps, he thought ruefully, if Scipio and Marcia had been wed before his departure to Sicily, he might have honored the marital vow. Marcinius put his arm around her, and they walked into the house. He managed to get her dispatched to the kitchen to check on the evening meal.

They ate in silence, Marcinius absentmindedly picking at his broiled pheasant. Marcia could see that her father was preoccupied with something, but after he had fended off several inquiries with vague replies, she gave up.

Marcinius retired to his bedchamber and tried to settle into a fitful night's sleep. After a lengthy period of tossing and turning on his wool-stuffed mattress, he gave up and went into his study.

Although he had been careful to conceal his true thoughts from Marcia, Marcinius seethed with anger at his prospective son-in-law. He paced back and forth across the intricate marble floor. The pattern was a series of squares, each set within another. Some craftsman had spent months piecing it together, like a mind-bending puzzle. *Indeed,* Marcinius thought, *what to do with the puzzle of Scipio?* He pondered his course of action, considering and rejecting all nature of wild schemes to take his revenge. Finally, in exasperation, he plunked himself down at his fabulous desk, took up a stylus, and began writing a note, inviting Laelius to a parley the next day. He finished in a few moments and rang for a servant to act as messenger.

"But where, my master, might I find this Laelius?" asked the sleepy servant, a short Celtiberian named Berningsus.

"I do not know," replied Marcinius. "He was headed for the baths when we parted company. Start your search there. But find him, or I will stripe your backside with a horsewhip."

———

Given so extreme an injunction, Berningsus wasted little time dressing and hurrying to the baths to take up the hunt. They were closed for the night, of course, and so Berningsus had to present himself at dawn when the facility reopened. He had little difficulty in tracking Laelius to the insulae of Patroclus. So terrified was he of the threatened penalty that Berningsus refused to leave the message with Patroclus' own body servant. Instead, he waited patiently in the small dining room of the apartment until Laelius, wrapped in a sheet, ventured forth to receive the message in person.

Laelius read the note in a few moments, and gave it back to the anxious Berningsus. "Tell your master," he said, "that I will visit him this afternoon."

The slave bowed deeply from the waist, relieved that he had escaped punishment under the lash, and excused himself to return to Marcinius' mansion.

Laelius watched him go. Then, hiking the sheet up, he returned to the waiting Patroclus.

———

Laelius had a stop to make before he called on Marcinius. With both of her sons away from home, Pomponia had taken up residence in the city, to be close to the temples so that her daily ritual of prayer could be more easily observed. Laelius insisted that the servant not

ANTHONY R. LICATA

announce his presence, for he wanted to surprise her. He crept into
the atrium, concealing himself behind the colonnade, and found
her busily planting flowers around a statue under a well-manicured
and vine-wrapped pergola. He considered the sculpture for several
moments before the trident gave it away: the figurine was—who
else?—Neptune. But it was a likeness such as he had not seen before.
The god was usually depicted with a thick, curly beard, whereas in
this treatment, he was clean shaven. And even more peculiar, the god
was much younger than one might expect for so ancient a personage,
rather more like the dashing Apollo than the grizzled lord of the seas.
And the god was tightly posed, his weight delicately balanced on his
right foot while the left was tilted at a suggestive angle. Even more
shocking, the god was not draped in the customary modest loincloth,
but was completely nude, his muscles rippling as he stood with his
trident poised against some unknown foe. It was a highly sensuous
pose, even erotic, more fitting for the bedchamber, thought Laelius,
than for a garden.

He turned his attention to Pomponia herself and studied her for
a moment before revealing himself. She was older now, a little bent
and withered. She had not borne the burden of her sons' absence at
all well.

He stepped out into the sunlight bathing the garden and let her
gradually realize he was there. She gasped at the sight of him, and
then a broad smile swept across her face. Laelius winced, for he could
see that her teeth were going bad, a common ailment among elderly
Romans.

Wiping her hands on a small cloth, she rushed to hug him.

"Oh, Laelius," she said lightly, "how good of you to visit. If only
you had brought my boys with you! How are they?"

Laelius' grin matched her own. "They are both fine. And if you
saw them, you would not think of them as boys," he said. "Lucius,
especially. He has grown into a man. But neither of them would be

pleased to find you working in the garden, like a common slave."

She wagged a grimy finger at him. "Now, now, Laelius, don't you go criticizing one of the few things that give me pleasure." Pomponia looked suddenly sad. "Isn't it odd, how one can be so lonely in the midst of the most crowded city in the world? The only visits I receive are occasional letters from Lucius, the only one who writes to me. Why does Scipio never write?"

"He is very busy. It took tremendous concentration to overcome Syphax and then Hannibal."

"Well, at least my younger son has not forgotten me. I did not want him to go, you know."

"Yes," replied Laelius. "But he has served well, and will be recognized for his exceptional contributions to the victory. You can be very proud of him."

"Tell me," Pomponia asked, "when will they return?"

Laelius shook his head. "It is difficult to say. I understand that Carthage has again asked for terms, and Scipio has made them a harsh offer. If they accept it, the war will be over. If they do not, a siege will be necessary, and that could take some time."

She squinted at him, and he realized that, like the rest of her body, Pomponia's eyes were probably fading, too.

"A siege of Carthage? That could take years!"

Laelius thought of all the difficulties they had encountered at Utica, and realized she was right. Carthage could hold out indefinitely.

"I think that is unlikely," he said, trying to allay her fears. "They are quite exhausted by the war, and with Hannibal defeated, they have no realistic hope of success. I believe they will make the peace."

"And then Scipio will return to be married to the daughter of Marcinius," she said, a note of skeptical disapproval in her voice.

Laelius was surprised by her tone. "Surely you are anxious to have grandchildren?" he asked.

"If I were certain he'd be happy with the daughter of Marcinius, I'd be pushing him to the altar. But I'm not convinced he's gotten over that first girl."

Laelius blushed. He had not known that Pomponia had been aware of Scipio's relationship with Vibiana in Spain. Thankfully, at least, she did not appear to know that the romance had been rekindled.

She gave him a knowing look. "Come now, Laelius," she admonished him, "you of all people know full well how a general might carry on when he is on campaign."

Laelius was speechless. Had Pomponia known all along about his relationship with her husband? But how? What were the implications of her knowledge?

Pomponia seemed pleased by his reaction, as if she had somehow settled a matter that had been pending for many years. Feeling there was no need to prolong his discomfort, she moved on to other things. "Look here," she said, pointing to the statue of Neptune.

"It is a likeness of the god I have never before seen," Laelius said, still reeling from her remarks.

"It is an early model of the statue being carved in Scipio's temple," she said proudly. "The sculptor gave it to me as a gift."

She gave him a wicked look. "Does it look at all familiar?"

Laelius laughed, then realized she was quite serious. "I do not understand what you are getting at."

"It should look familiar to you. Scipio posed for it before he left."

Seeing Laelius' jaw drop in shock, she cackled with laughter, almost like an old hen. "It's true," she said.

Laelius glanced at the statue, intrigued. The artist had taken liberties, to be sure: the finely defined rib cage was rather more pronounced than Scipio's in reality, and Laelius was certain that the sculptor had been generous in addressing the genitals. But now that he was in on the secret, yes, he could definitely see the likeness, particularly in the manner and bearing of the god.

"How will the people react to the idea?" was all he could manage.

"If the people find out that Scipio sat as the model, they will throng to the temple, for he is their hero now. Have you noticed? Ever since word arrived of the victory over Hannibal, the common men of Rome have taken to shaving off their beards, in honor of his victory."

Laelius had in fact observed that an uncommonly large number of men in the streets were beardless, but he had not bothered to inquire as to the cause. "I am sure," Laelius said politely, "that Scipio will be honored by the custom."

She took him by the arm and led him out of the sun and into the cool shade underneath the colonnade. They sat down on a wicker bench.

"Tell Scipio I am concerned with the cost of the temple. They seem to keep adding to it. If he were home, he could watch over the construction."

"I visited the site yesterday, and share your concern," Laelius agreed. "Although I think that Scipio's winnings in Africa will more than cover anything the architects come up with."

"When do you return to the campaign?" she asked.

"Tomorrow."

"So soon? Will you join me for dinner?"

Laelius considered it for a moment, but he would soon return to camp and longed for another night in the company of Patroclus. "No, thank you," he replied politely, "I have other commitments."

"Well, then, thank you for coming. Please tell Scipio and Lucius that I am praying for them every day. May the gods give them safe passage home."

He bowed his head in reply and turned to take his leave.

With tremendous emotion in her voice, Pomponia spoke quietly after him. "And Laelius, thank you for everything you've done for my son. His father would have been so proud of both of you."

He nodded his appreciation for her thought, then hurried out to his meeting with Marcinius.

———

Marcinius wore a formal white toga to greet Laelius, who was clad only in the common maroon tunic of a legionnaire. The disparity of their dress accented the chasm between the two men.

Marcinius made no effort to greet the soldier warmly, knowing that Laelius would see through any attempt to be patronizing. Instead, he merely nodded as Laelius was admitted into his study, and waited as he took in the lavish surroundings.

"Do you find the setting to your liking?" Marcinius asked as Laelius marveled at the workmanship of the carpenters who had lined the room with an elaborate oak molding.

Laelius turned his attention to the corpulent politician, whose thinning white hair tumbled around his ears in a disorganized fashion.

"I find it unlikely," he said with an edge to his voice, "that you have invited me here merely to admire your taste in architecture."

Marcinius did not smile. "No," he replied.

"Then I suggest that we get on with whatever business you have in mind."

Marcinius went over to a couch in one corner of the room and stretched himself out on it. When he was settled comfortably, he said, almost casually, "It is apparent that you are aware of my offer to Silanus. What do you intend to do about it?"

Laelius thought for a moment, and told the truth. "I do not know what to do."

Marcinius rubbed his hands as if he were washing them. He wore an enormous gold ring, set with a sparkling ruby. The senator gave Laelius a shifty look, a look of which only a consummate politician is capable. "Are others aware of the contents of my letter to Silanus?"

Laelius felt his skin tingle in concern. If Marcinius learned that only he knew of the letter, the senator might well try to have him killed. "I am not going to tell you that," Laelius responded. And he added hastily, "Your letter to Silanus is in a safe place, where it will remain unless something happens to me."

Marcinius nodded, understanding the implied threat. He had not really expected Laelius to fall into a trap, but it had been worth a try. Now, he knew, he would have to make an arrangement.

"I trust," Marcinius said carefully, "that you can fully appreciate the delicacy of this situation. You certainly can make the facts known, but in so doing, you will cause a distress to the Cornelli as well as to my own family."

"That," Laelius snapped, "is an understatement. The scandal would be unprecedented. Never before has a senator of Rome tried to arrange the death of a pro-consul!"

Marcinius finally managed a smile. "Well, let us say that at least such an effort has never become a matter of public knowledge. And unless you do something very foolish, neither will this one."

This knocked Laelius back. Had such things been going on for years? He shook his head. If this was life at the upper crust of society, he had had enough of it.

"Is there a sum of money," Marcinius asked, "that might induce you to return the letter?"

"You have had too much money for too long," Laelius replied with evident disgust, "for you believe that it can solve all your problems."

"There are very few, my friend, that it cannot solve." Marcinius managed a small laugh, then tried a different tack. "I understand that Scipio insulted you in the presence of the other officers, and he subsequently apologized. Surely, there is some lingering resentment on your part."

Laelius was offended. "This situation will not be resolved by your questioning my loyalty to Scipio. He sometimes lets his passion get the better of his reason, but I am dedicated to furthering his career."

"Ah," replied Marcinius, "his passions are precisely the source of all our difficulties, are they not? You yourself knew that his relationship with this girl would cause trouble, didn't you? You even tried to warn him about it in the presence of the other officers! So surely you can understand how upset I am over the insult he has perpetrated upon my daughter."

This registered upon Laelius, for he knew Marcinius was right. He said defensively, "Scipio did not intend to hurt your daughter. When he proposed to her, his feelings were entirely genuine. He thought he would never see Vibiana again. He feels badly about the pain he will cause Marcia. But he is in love with this woman, heart and soul. Believe me, there is no standing in the way of his feelings for her."

"Vibiana?" Marcinius asked, pleased to put a name to his daughter's enemy. When he saw Laelius nod in agreement, he muttered, "What is it about her that captivates him so?"

"She is extraordinary," replied Laelius.

"Is she so beautiful that Scipio would throw away his entire career over her?"

For a moment, Laelius considered telling Marcinius the real reason why the negotiations with Hannibal had failed, but swiftly rejected it. It was too shocking—the families of the soldiers who had died in the battle would be outraged if they learned what had actually happened that afternoon on the plain outside Zama.

"Scipio is in love, absolutely and completely. If he has Vibiana, I think he cares about nothing else."

"You understand that I cannot permit this insult to my family," Marcinius said. "You must tell him that he cannot return to Rome with her."

"He is capable of being stubborn."

"So am I," Marcinius said harshly, his face stony. "If he brings her here, I will do everything in my power to have her brought to justice for killing a Roman soldier. And you can make public what you know, for all I care. Let the consequences be what they may. If he breaks my daughter's heart, I will see this woman of his burned alive. I pledge this to you with every fiber of my being."

Laelius looked away, frightened. It was a powerful oath, given by a powerful man possessing vast resources to carry out his will.

"Do not forget that your Scipio has his enemies, notably that hayseed, Cato. Cato has allied himself with a rather despicable character, a freedman named Quintio. Together they are said to be making a fortune. If the question involves embarrassing Scipio, Cato certainly will join forces with me, and together we have absolute control of the Senate, no matter how great a hero Scipio may think he is. Let him give siege to Carthage and remain in Africa, if he wishes. Let him tell my daughter that he has had a vision from the gods, requiring him to remain celibate. I do not care what ridiculous story you come up with. Only do not let him think he will live in Rome, underneath my nose, with this Carthaginian whore at his side."

Laelius had heard enough. He turned to leave and was nearly out of the room when he heard his name. He twisted his head without turning his body. Marcinius' features were contorted into a horrible visage, and he pointed at Laelius, the bulbous ruby on his finger glistening in the light.

"Tell him I will bribe the executioner. I will pay him to keep her alive, roasting over the coals, for as long as possible. Her death will be slow and hideous. Make certain Scipio understands that."

Laelius hurried out of the study, still trembling from the awful encounter. He was nearly out of the house when he heard his name called again, this time by a sweet-sounding female voice. Aghast, he turned and confronted the anxious Marcia.

"Laelius! Why didn't Father tell me you were coming?" she asked.

As she had not been expecting a visitor, she wore a rather plain, everyday dress and simple cork sandals. Her hair was not done up, but rather flowed over her shoulders. Even without cosmetics, she was a pretty girl. *Certainly pretty enough to marry*, he thought.

"That is a question you will have to address to him," Laelius said, deftly avoiding her question.

"You must give me news of Scipio!" she exclaimed, drawing closer. "I have had no letters from him, no news at all. Why can he not find time to write?"

"Well, he is very busy," Laelius found himself saying for the second time that day. Damn Scipio! "It's tremendously hard work, you know, running an army on campaign in a hostile country."

"Oh, nonsense! Certainly, in between laying waste to the African countryside and defeating Hannibal, he could find a few minutes to write."

Inspiration flared in Laelius' mind. "You should know that you are not alone in this complaint. I was with Scipio's mother just this morning, and neither has he written a word to her!"

Marcia frowned, unconvinced.

Laelius tried to change the subject. "I can assure you that he is well."

"You men are all alike," she said in disgust, "always covering for each other. Does he realize that I think of him constantly, and every night pray to the gods to watch over him and bring him success?"

Laelius felt bad for her but realized he would have to lie to her to get away. "Rest assured, he thinks of you often. But his every waking moment is devoted to ending the war, so that he can return to Rome and you at the first possible moment."

At this, she smiled. "Are you returning to Africa?"

"Yes," Laelius said, "by a transport leaving tomorrow morning."

"Wait here just a moment, then," she said. She scurried out of sight, leaving Laelius waiting uncomfortably in the foyer, hoping that Marcinius would not appear.

In a few moments, she returned, carrying a rolled sheet of vellum.

"This is another letter for Scipio," she said. "Will you see that he gets it? And, please, tell him to write back."

Laelius took the rolled sheet and bowed slightly. He then hurried out of the mansion, relieved to be clear of the place.

———

Not even the skillful administrations of Patroclus could ease the anger with which Laelius seethed as he considered the dreadful conversation with Marcinius, over and over again.

Sensing that something was deeply troubling his companion, Patroclus stroked Laelius' hair and asked lightly, "What is it, my dear? What is bothering you?"

"It's far too complicated to try to explain," Laelius grunted, through clenched teeth. "I'm so upset with someone, I could kill him."

"Oh, it would never do for you to kill anyone," Patroclus said with a chuckle. "You're much too famous for that."

Laelius snorted. "I've killed men before. It doesn't require much skill."

Patroclus gave him a sidelong look. "Why do something yourself when it's easy enough to hire someone to do it for you?"

"What?"

"You can buy anything in Rome. It's easy enough to hire an assassin."

Laelius sat bolt upright in bed. "Are you serious?"

Patroclus said cynically, "You have been away on campaigns for too many years. With Hannibal terrorizing the countryside all this time, all nature of ruffians now live in the city. You can hire anyone to do anything."

Laelius stroked his chin, deep in thought. *Marcinius had tried to kill Scipio. . . . Perhaps turnabout would be fair play.*

"The stakes would be very high," he mused. "It would require someone very reliable."

"If the stakes are high," Patroclus said as he pulled up the sheet around himself, "so would be the sum of money needed to complete the task."

A plan was forming in Laelius' mind. "Absolute confidentiality would be essential."

Patroclus laughed. "That would merely make the assassin's fee even higher."

Laelius eased back onto the pillow and turned his face to his lover. He proceeded to relay instructions, which he made very clear were not to be put into action until after he communicated an explicit authorization from Tunis. He explained to Patroclus that he was going back to Africa to try to talk some sense into Scipio. Scipio must leave Vibiana in Africa, and not subject them all to the ordeal that Marcinius had threatened. However, if Scipio refused to budge, then he must take steps in Rome to ensure that Marcinius did not follow through on his threat to ruin Scipio's reputation.

Patroclus listened patiently to the entire soliloquy.

"Everything you have asked for can be arranged," he said confidently. "But it's going to be very expensive."

"Money," Laelius said quietly, "is no object."

XIX

Tunis, Africa

202 BC

S CIPIO TURNED SLIGHTLY ON his side, stretched out on a divan, his head in Vibiana's lap, tucked beneath her swollen belly.

Scipio's motion had wakened them both. Looking out an unshuttered Palladian window, they could see a stretch of lower housetops in the vicinity, a bank of green-blue ocean beyond to the north, and the sky tinged with a fiery red as the garish sun peeked above the horizon. The last traces of the night sky, its shadowy depths brilliant with stars, were retreating before the inevitable onslaught of daybreak. The city was quiet beneath them, and only the winds stirred, rustling the light sheet that covered them.

"After I ran away at Ilipa, I remember once looking at the stars," she murmured, stroking his cheek with her hand, "and wondering whether I had erred by leaving your side."

"And what do you think now?"

"I think not."

This surprised him, and he twisted about to look into her face.

She smiled, that same radiant, warm smile that also lit her eyes and always brought calm to his impetuous nature. "I say that because I think that by losing me, you were forced to confront your own feelings for me. When I was a prisoner in your camp, it never occurred to you to contemplate life without me. When I was gone, you felt the void."

He settled back, turning this comment over in his mind. Why was it so hard to admit she was right?

"I suppose it is a failing of mine," he sighed. "I made the same mistake with my father. I rode into battle at his side, never thinking that either of us might not emerge. And when he bid me farewell as he left for Spain, we acted as if he was merely going away for a few days on a simple trip. Oh, if only I could have back those moments—and have the chance to say the things I did not say." Scipio thought of his mother, and realized that here too, he had taken things for granted.

Vibiana knew she was guilty, also. Her thoughts drifted back to the last time she'd seen her own father alive, as he climbed onto a horse, heading off to fight at Baecula the very man whose child she now was carrying. She had waved at him and wished him good fortune, without considering that she might never see him again. How odd the twists and turns her life had taken!

Suddenly she twitched and gave a little gasp. "Oh!" she exclaimed. "The baby is moving inside me—feel it!"

Quickly he moved his steady hand up to her abdomen. Beneath her light cotton shift, he felt the stirrings of the infant.

"How wonderful!" He marveled at the sensation, feeling the life he had created kicking at her insides.

"It is strong," he laughed. "Perhaps a boy!"

"Perhaps," she said impishly, knowing his desire for a son, "but perhaps as well a girl. Will you abandon us if it is?"

The baby's movements subsided, and he moved his hand to take hers. "Never," he said, intently. "Haven't I made that plain enough?"

"You have spoken words," she said softly, "but action would be more convincing."

"And what action would you seek?" he asked, suspecting the answer.

She did not hesitate. "Marry me."

"I intend to," he replied easily. "When we return to Rome. I want to be married in the temple I am erecting to the honor of Neptune.

It is by his divine hand that we have been reunited."

"But it may be many months before we return to Rome," she complained. "And if Carthage holds out, it could be years. Your child will be illegitimate."

"I doubt that," he said with conviction. "A delegation from Carthage arrived yesterday, and I have granted them an audience for later today. By nightfall, the war will be over."

This was news to her, and she thought over the implications. "It seems impossible to imagine life without the war," she said. "Ever since I was a small child, it is all I have known. So many deaths, so much destruction, so much needless suffering. Can it really be over?"

"Carthage has nothing left," Scipio said with an air of satisfaction. "Rome is ascendant. With the obstacle of Carthage removed, her power will rule the world."

Vibiana ran her fingers through his tousled hair. "The Greeks have a saying: 'Be careful what you wish for, for your wish may come true.' It may be that Rome suffers by her victory over Carthage."

This struck him as most peculiar. "How so?" he asked, puzzled.

"The rivalry with Carthage has kept both nations fit and strong. With the total victory you have given her, Rome may grow fat and lazy."

He scoffed at her idea. "Never! Rome became great by the strength of her arms, and ever will it be so."

"The world is vast," she cautioned. "Just as Carthage found a nation she could not overcome, so too may Rome."

"There is no nation that can long withstand the power of a Roman legion," he said stubbornly.

She could see that he would not hear of the possibility of a Rome in decline. So she said, "Then the war will go on. The only change will be in the identity of the combatants."

"The choice will lie with the other nations of the world. They can peaceably negotiate alliances with Rome, if they wish. But you are right—many will not. They will think their armies capable of defending them. They will be mistaken, of course, and much suffering will fall on their heads because of their folly."

She was annoyed by his arrogance, so typically Roman. "The record of Roman military prowess is not as clear-cut as you would make it out to be," she pointed out. "At least it was not before you assumed command. And the benefits of Roman rule are debatable."

"What Rome seizes with a strong hand, she also defends. In return for taxes, we will give them the safety of a *Pax Romana*. No one will dare to attack those who have given their allegiance to Rome. In time, it will be a better life for everyone."

She was not convinced. Then, struck by an alarming thought, she demanded, "Does this mean that you intend to take on further campaigns?"

He gave a little laugh. "No. I have spent most of my life away from my home, fighting and campaigning. I have done enough fighting for one lifetime. My duty to my country has been served. It will be for others to build on the foundation I have established. Lucius, for example, is anxious to make a name for himself. I intend to retire to the quiet life of a gentleman farmer. With you as the mistress of my household."

He lifted his head from her lap and edged up the divan, bringing his face close to hers. He kissed her lightly at first, then brushed his lips down her neck.

She felt him rising, and pulled the nightshirt up over her thighs. She climbed onto him, having found it more comfortable in her condition to straddle him during lovemaking. Scipio had not complained—he seemed to enjoy the position.

"How much longer can we continue this?" he asked, thinking of the infant as she lowered herself onto him.

"Forever," she gasped, before losing herself to the pleasure he gave her.

At midday, a host of Carthaginian envoys were herded into a large reception area, where they were kept waiting for many minutes before Scipio made his appearance. This was by intent, for the Romans desired that the Carthaginians should be reminded of their positions as supplicants before the all-powerful Scipio Africanus.

Finally, he swept in, carrying in his right hand the ivory baton of his imperium, escorted by dozens of officers all clad in their formal armor. The clanking of their metal garb made quite a racket as the commanders filed in behind Scipio, who took up a position behind a long table made of teak, with a polished marble top.

Scipio at once recognized the bearded Ilderim from their previous parley, and he waved the old man forward.

Befitting his role as petitioner, Ilderim, like the rest of his delegation, was barefoot and clad in simple sackcloth. From this, Scipio expected the Carthaginians to beg for relief from his oppressive terms, pleading poverty.

"So, Ilderim," he said, with all the Roman haughtiness he could manage, "you have been given time to present the terms I have dictated to your Council. What is the response of Carthage? Will it be peace, or do you choose to invite ruin upon your city, and visit more suffering upon the heads of your women and children?"

Ilderim bowed his head in submission. He responded in a deep, mournful tone. "Great Africanus, we have no choice. The Council has voted to accept your terms."

A murmur of approval rustled through the Roman officers. The war was over!

But Ilderim held up his hand in a pitiful plea for attention. He fought back tears. "I regret to inform you, however, that there is but one demand it is beyond our power to meet."

Scipio glared at the Carthaginian. "And what is that?"

"After the battle at Zama, Hannibal retreated with a small force of bodyguards to the fortress at Hasdrumentum. He has refused our pleas to surrender himself to you. Therefore, Carthage is unable to deliver him as you have demanded."

Scipio looked out over the delegation from Carthage. They were downcast, humiliated and beaten, forced to beg for mercy from an intruder upon their own soil. Their nation had been brought to its knees. But he had demanded the living body of Hannibal, to be returned to Rome for judgment. In his heart, he had planned that by delivering the greatest enemy of the Roman people for their retribution, he would simultaneously lay claim to a pardon for Vibiana. Those hopes now were dashed, and he fought to conceal his disappointment.

"I am instructed," Ilderim was saying, "to offer you instead one hundred hostages, of your own choosing, to be transported to Rome as permanent guarantors of our performance under the terms you have dictated."

"A million hostages would not be sufficient if Hannibal is determined to continue the war against us," Scipio snapped.

"Hannibal has said he will abide by the peace, and without the resources of Carthage, he will be of little threat to the power of Rome," Ilderim pointed out plaintively. "But he will not submit to the spectacle of being paraded through the streets of Rome in chains, only to be crucified in the Circus Maximus."

Scipio did not answer, for this was precisely the fate he had envisioned.

"I beg you, Africanus, do not let your thirst for vengeance against Hannibal result in the deaths of thousands more of our people." The old man now broke down, tears flowing freely down his cheeks and into his beard.

Scipio turned and looked at Massinissa, whose impassive gaze gave him no comfort. Lucius, however, had an eager look on his face, as if he were ready to celebrate the peace.

"Very well," Scipio sighed. "Our two nations have suffered long enough from this war. The offer is accepted."

The Romans gave out a little cheer, and the Carthaginians clasped each other, weeping with relief.

"You will join me for a feast tonight," Scipio said to Ilderim, "for we have much to discuss. I shall dispatch an envoy to return with you to Carthage so that the terms may be written down for presentation to the Senate in Rome."

The noble Carthaginian bowed again, and turned to gather up his colleagues to take their leave of the Romans.

After they were gone, the Romans erupted in a fit of back-slapping and congratulations. Massinissa came over to Scipio and the two men embraced.

"You will rule Numidia all of your days, without challenge from Carthage, and with the strength of Rome at your side," Scipio said, smiling at his comrade in arms.

"Only Africanus could have made such a peace," said Massinissa.

But there was little joy in Scipio's heart, for he knew that his own private battle, the struggle for Vibiana's freedom, still hung in the balance.

"Yes, my friend," he said with a thin smile, "let us only hope that we have today ended the rivalry between Rome and Carthage."

———

Just as he was capable of severe cruelty in the name of war, so too was Scipio capable of broad generosity in the cause of peace. Now that the war was over, he greeted each person attending the feast with the gift of a fine silver cup, the Carthaginians included. These cups were immediately put to good use, for the wine flowed freely, and many toasts were offered to Scipio, who in making the peace had proven himself a master of war.

A long enough table could not be found anywhere in Tunis to accommodate all the invited guests, and so several tables had been placed in Scipio's residence, forming a huge U. Couches had been set out all along the tables, for it was the Roman custom to take the evening meal reclining. Scipio was established at the center of the U, and Massinissa sat at his right hand, symbolic of the new political hegemony that would govern Northern Africa. Vibiana, noting that there would be no other women present, had refrained from attending.

The revelers were treated to an array of seafood samplings—prawns, oysters, and sardines. This was followed by a tasty salad made of greens tossed with radishes and mushrooms, topped with a spicy, flour-thickened sauce of aromatic herbs. Eyes widened as the main courses were brought on, comprised of several kinds of fish and poultry, served with an accompaniment of braised vegetables. Just when the dignitaries thought they could not possibly eat another bite, enormous platters of exotic pastries appeared. Somehow, most of the men in the room found the capacity in their bellies to sample the treats.

The feast was served by dozens of servants mobilized for the purpose by the ever-diligent Narcussa. Every conceivable need of the diners received instant attention: most importantly, the goblets were kept filled to the brim with a fine wine, imported from the Greek islands. Flies were kept off the food by a battery of servants waving large fans made from the feathers of peacocks.

"If Romans eat like this every day," Ilderim said to Scipio lightly, "they will be digging their graves with their teeth."

Scipio laughed, pleased that the wine had helped to take the sting from the Carthaginians' defeat. "Do not fear, noble Ilderim. Only the upper classes can partake of such a feast as this. The common Roman has a much more modest diet, which accounts for his strength."

"Strength alone did not give Rome its victory," Ilderim pointed out. "Fate played a part. Or perhaps it was the intention of the gods."

"Certainly," Scipio agreed, "it was the will of the gods. But never forget, it was Hannibal who earned their enmity by breaking the peace so long ago, in sacking Saguntum."

Ilderim chose not to respond, fearful of reopening the dispute.

Scipio's mention of Hannibal stirred his curiosity. "You stated today that Hannibal has fortified his position at Hasdrumentum. What will become of him?"

"I do not know," Ilderim said, munching on a broiled leg of pheasant. "But I hope he will return to Carthage. So shattered is our economy and our homeland, we will need every bit of his talent to begin the rebuilding. After all, the indemnity you have imposed is heavy, and I do not know how we are going to meet it."

"Is Hannibal alone at Hasdrumentum?" Scipio asked.

"No, he is there with a remnant of the army you shattered at Zama. It is also said that Hasdrubal Gisgo has made his way there as well."

"Hmm," mused Scipio. "Perhaps we should march there and give him a siege."

"The war is over now," pointed out Massinissa. "Let us give our attention to the future, and to the peace that will be hard enough to keep, without retribution over things that happened during the war."

Scipio lifted his goblet in a toast. "To peace. And prosperity."

They all nodded at this sage advice, and quaffed more of the grape.

The next day, the Carthaginian delegation departed, accompanied by Lucius and a handful of scribes and interpreters, to set out the articles of agreement in writing. Scipio, ever vigilant against treachery, also dispatched with them a cohort of his finest veterans to serve as a guard.

Only two days later, a large transport ship sailed into the harbor at Tunis, and Scipio greeted his loyal colleague Laelius as he wobbled down the gangplank, a little green from the tossing of the waves.

"I should think that as many times as you have sailed on a ship, you would have overcome seasickness by now," Scipio laughed, clutching his colleague happily.

Laelius, who was relieved to have solid ground beneath his feet, managed a smile for his commander. "I will never overcome it, I'm afraid."

They walked together to Scipio's quarters, and Laelius reported on the developments regarding Antiochus and Philip. "I'm not sure what will happen," Laelius said, "but if Antiochus does not back down, we may find ourselves sailing from Africa to Asia to settle the latest affront to Roman dignity."

"Is it Rome's dignity that is at stake, or Rome's appetite for conquest?" Scipio asked incisively.

"You of all people should know the true answer," Laelius laughed. "Come now, fill me in on the details regarding the peace negotiations."

Scipio did so, and by the time they reached his residence, Laelius was flushed with pride over the successful conclusion to the glorious African Expedition. Scipio took him into his study, and the two Romans stretched out on couches to continue their conversation in the leisure of comfortable surroundings.

Narcussa flitted in and out of the room, first bringing in a platter of bread and cheese, then pouring wine for both men.

Laelius related to Scipio the highlights of his trip to Rome, including his visit to Pomponia. Scipio thanked him for his consideration in calling on her and promised to get off a letter to her immediately. Laelius told Scipio about the model of the statue of Neptune in her garden.

"It will be controversial," Laelius warned. Then, with a wicked look, he said, "In particular, I am puzzled that the artist did not choose to drape his loins in some modest cloth."

"That was at my request," Scipio laughed. "I wanted the statue to be unlike any other in the temples of Rome."

From this, Laelius moved into expressing concern with the mounting cost of the massive Temple of Neptune.

"Trouble yourself no further," Scipio said with a dismissive wave of his hand. "The revenue from the sale of the slaves is more than you can imagine. And I have had a communication from my overseer in Spain. The production of silver at my mines is at an all-time high. There will be no shortage of money. I will soon enough be back in Rome, and will take the construction under my personal supervision."

At the mention of Scipio's impending return to Rome, Laelius lowered his head. Scipio could see at once that his colleague was deeply troubled.

"What is wrong, my friend?"

Laelius looked away, searching for words to break the news.

Scipio knew that something was very wrong. "You do not serve me well," he said sharply, "by keeping from me things I must know. Do not fear, for I am strong. And do not hold back, either, for I cannot overcome what I do not know."

Laelius watched as Narcussa deposited before them a tray, this one bearing a quantity of assorted fruits. And then, his head still lowered, Laelius told Scipio in a quiet voice the story of his meeting with Marcinius. He omitted, however, the details of Marcinius' offer to Silanus. And he said nothing regarding the contingency plan he himself had put in place in Rome before he departed.

After he finished with the part about Marcinius' terrible threat, he looked up. Scipio's face was drawn tight, with an ashen pallor.

"You must give this careful thought before returning to Rome," Laelius cautioned him. "I have no doubt that Marcinius was deadly earnest. Perhaps you should leave Vibiana here in Africa, at least until you can determine the sentiment of the factions in the Senate."

"Damn them!" Scipio cried, the color returning to his cheeks. "I have given them the greatest victory in the history of Rome, and they would deny me the woman I love?"

Laelius had feared that Scipio would react violently, and had carefully thought out what he would say. It was a time for reason, not passion. "Now, Scipio, do not lose your head and do something foolish. The object here is to prevail, not win a mere debating point. The fact of the matter is, you are engaged to the daughter of Marcinius, and upon this basis, he provided the support that won for you the command of this expedition. And you have not only fallen in love with another woman, but you have chosen a woman who murdered a Roman soldier. That is a very serious matter, as I have been warning you. No matter how grand your victory over Hannibal, a certain number of senators will be sympathetic to Marcinius. And he will be supported by Cato and his backers, certainly no friends of yours. Those who may support you will be easy targets for bribes."

"I too am wealthy now," Scipio said in desperation. "I can buy as many senators as Marcinius."

"We have traveled that path before," Laelius reminded him, "without success. Given the ferocity of Marcinius' feelings, I do not think your fortune, however fast it is growing, can overcome his."

Laelius waved off Narcussa, who was attempting to fill his cup with wine.

Scipio got to his feet.

"Where are you going?" Laelius asked.

"I do not know. Somewhere I can think."

Laelius rummaged through a cloth satchel he had brought with him from the ship, and produced the vellum scroll Marcia had given him. "This is another letter from your fiancée," Laelius said, handing him the correspondence. "While you are thinking, you might consider responding to her. The poor girl is beside herself with worry over why you have not been in communication with her."

Scipio, without saying a word, thrust the letter into the pocket of his tunic and walked out. Laelius, exasperated, sank back onto the cushions and looked up at Narcussa, who gave absolutely no expression at all.

Scipio, unaccompanied, made his way to a stable not far from his headquarters, wherein he knew Bucephalus was billeted. He found there a young lad tending the noble animal in a stall, brushing its flowing white mane with a long comb cut from the bone of a whale. The youth, a towheaded boy not more than ten years of age, was barefoot and clad only in the common homespun of peasants. The boy gave Scipio a stern look as he approached.

"Now look here, Roman," the boy said, recognizing only Scipio's coarse army tunic, "come no closer, for this warhorse belongs to none other than Scipio Africanus, conqueror of Africa."

"Really?" asked Scipio. "I do not believe you."

The boy pointed to the richly detailed golden armaments hung about the sides of the stall, and the beautifully tooled saddle resting on a nearby bench. "Look there. Do you think that is the gear of a common cavalryman?"

Scipio acted unimpressed. "Even if it is his horse, why should I be concerned about it?"

The boy, who resumed brushing Bucephalus' lustrous mane, gave him a skeptical look. "Come now, Roman. You know very well who Scipio Africanus is. He who defeated Syphax and Hannibal would have that smart tongue of yours cut out if he learned of your disrespect."

"He is cruel, then, this Scipio Africanus?"

"All Romans are cruel. You have seized my father's stable, helping yourselves to our barn and our hay, with nothing said about payment."

Scipio arched his eyebrows. "Perhaps you should consider yourselves fortunate to be selected to care for a great man's horse."

The boy scoffed at this suggestion. "That will not give us bread to eat. My father is out foraging for food now. We have run out of money, thanks to you Romans."

"Where is your mother?"

"She died," the boy said, matter-of-factly. "Typhoid. I don't remember her."

"How sad," Scipio said. Then, realizing that his horse should not have been left alone, he asked, "If indeed that is the horse of the general, where are his guards?"

The boy laughed. "They are in a tavern not far from here, where they spend most of their time. I don't mind, though. It gives me a chance to ride him."

Scipio's eyes widened in surprise again. This was proving to be a most informative outing. "How so?"

"Every day, I take him out for a ride to keep him fit and trim. I can ride better than most soldiers, you know."

Scipio stepped forward and patted the animal on the snout. "Is he fast?"

"Of course. Would Scipio Africanus have a slow horse? He is the fastest horse I have ever ridden."

"And what do the guards say about your riding him?"

The boy put down the comb. "They don't seem to mind. They're perfectly happy to spend the whole day over there—"

"Take me to them," Scipio commanded.

"And why should I? I am not a slave, to take orders from any Roman legionnaire who comes slithering in here."

Scipio could not help but laugh at the boy's audacity. "Very well, then. Might it be worth a Roman coin as to so trouble yourself?"

The boy's eyes lit up at the mention of money. But just as quickly, he regained that healthy skepticism. "Pay me in advance."

The boy was marvelous! "I do not have my purse with me," Scipio was forced to admit. "But I give you my word as a Roman that I will pay you."

The boy was unconvinced. "My father says a Roman's word isn't worth cow dung."

"What is your name?" Scipio asked.

"Garnesso," came the reply.

"Well, Garnesso, I will give you this as security for my payment," Scipio said, pulling off his heavy gold ring, bearing the coronet of his family.

The boy's eyes grew wide as he gazed at the ring, realizing it was worth far more than any sum he could imagine. He began to get an inkling that this Roman might be an important officer.

"That's all right," he said a little nervously, handing back the precious ring. "I trust you. Follow me."

Scipio followed Garnesso out of the dim stable and into the muddy street, stepping carefully to avoid the worst of the muck. They went over to a poorly maintained stucco structure, more of a hut, actually, than a building, with no door. Scipio stepped inside, and paused as his eyes adjusted to the dark interior. His nose, too, required an adjustment, for the place reeked of stale wine, urine, and vomit. About a dozen tables were spread throughout the room, each lit by a single candle and surrounded by a handful of men sitting on small, wooden stools. Strands of beads strung on long cords hung from the ceiling. An obese woman, naked, waited on the tables, her enormous breasts drooping nearly to her navel. Her flabby arms and legs were, like her belly, covered with thick black hair. She shuttled back and forth to a long plank stretched between two posts, which served as a bar. An emaciated man with a filthy brown beard stood behind the counter, a wary eye on his inventory. As the woman moved about, the patrons felt completely at ease in pinching and stroking her ample flesh. At the back of the room was a small, elevated platform bearing a lumpy mattress. This, Scipio presumed with revulsion, was for the comfort of patrons who desired to make use of the woman.

Two Roman soldiers were seated across the room, their backs to the door, swords resting in their scabbards on the table before them. Scipio came up behind them and waited for several moments until their intuition made them aware that someone was looking over their shoulders. One guard turned and, recognizing Scipio, nearly fell off his stool in fright. This caused the other to turn as well, and the two of them, terror in their eyes, fumbled to get onto their feet.

"What are your names?" Scipio demanded, his voice icy and his eyes fixed on the cowering legionnaires.

"Porcellus," said one.

"Drusus," said the other.

"And your centurion?"

"Bartullis, of Estrusca."

Scipio regarded them in silence for a few moments, letting them sweat in anticipation of what he might do to them. Finally, he said, "The two of you will present yourselves at once to your centurion, and then report with him to the senior legate, Garibus Paullus Laelius. You will tell him you have been derelict in your duty, and give him the particulars. Beg him to spare your lives, and let you off with a severe flogging. Your centurion is to be demoted to the rank of common soldier, for his failure properly to supervise your duty. He will lay the stripes upon your backs. I shall return within an hour, and I expect to find both of you at the whipping post, under the lash. Do not disappoint me."

Porcellus and Drusus staggered under the sentence. To be flogged by the very man whose demotion they had caused! Bartullis was a hard man: he would be brutal with them, furious over the setback to his career. Weeping at their imminent punishment, they thought to plead with him for mercy.

"Get out of my sight," Scipio barked. The men hurried from Scipio's glare. Garnesso, who had followed him into the tavern, was silent.

"Let us return to the stable," Scipio said to the boy, and this time he did not get a smart response.

Back at the stable, they found waiting an anxious-looking, stockily-built bulldog of a man.

"And just where have you been, you little ruffian?" the man barked at the boy, without bothering to regard his Roman companion.

"This Roman promised me a coin to show him to the tavern." Garnesso pointed at Scipio.

Perhaps because Scipio was backlit by the sun behind him, or perhaps because the stablekeeper's eyes were beginning to fail him, the man strode over to Scipio and thrust a stubby finger into his chest.

"Now see here, Roman. It's bad enough that you come marching in here, putting me out of business, eating us out of house and home. But I'll not have you corrupting my boy by taking him into that den of vice."

And then perhaps the light changed slightly, or perhaps Scipio turned a bit to blunt the onslaught. At any rate, the stablekeeper got a better look at the Roman in his barn, and he gasped in shock. In a moment, he fell to his knees in the yellow hay of the stable floor, while the boy looked on, bewildered.

"Oh, mercy, mercy, Master!" the man slobbered. "I meant no disrespect! I did not recognize you. Please take mercy on me. I am the only family this boy has."

Scipio looked at Garnesso. "Should we spare him?" he asked lightly.

The boy responded with a broad grin, and Scipio noticed for the first time that he was missing his two front teeth.

Scipio reached down and hauled the cowering stablekeeper to his feet. "Steady, friend, steady. Do not so humble yourself before your son."

The stablekeeper gave his boy a hard look. "Aye, has he been disrespectful to you, Lord Africanus?"

For the first time, the boy understood the identity of his companion, and he looked up in shock.

"Not in the least," Scipio replied amiably. "In fact, he has made a significant contribution to my education, for which I am grateful.

Now, if you will saddle my horse, I would like to go for a ride."

The stablekeeper stumbled over himself in his haste to carry out Scipio's request. But the boy, fearless, stood his ground.

"Hey!" he cried. "We had an agreement. You owe me a Roman coin."

The father gave his son a horrified look and started for him, fist raised, as if to clout him on the head.

But Scipio intervened, holding up his hand. "Do not punish the lad, for he speaks the truth." He turned to the boy. "Help your father with his task, and then I will take you with me."

When Bucephalus was bridled and saddled, Scipio climbed up and held out his hand. Garnesso grasped it, and Scipio with a single pull hauled the boy onto the saddle in front of him. They headed out of the barn, leaving the stablekeeper standing dumbfounded in their wake. Scipio trotted the horse over to the steps of his residence. A centurion and a dozen legionnaires, recognizing their general on the approach, snapped to attention.

"Centurion," said Scipio, "this young man and his father have befriended me, and to my embarrassment and shame, have suffered for it. Fortunately, the facts have come to my attention, and I wish to set things right. Find my servant, the slave Narcussa. Have him draw one hundred sesterces from my private purse, and see that it is paid to this boy's father for the diligent care they have given my horse. And also draw a single coin for this boy, so that I will not be in his debt."

Garnesso was astonished. He could not even comprehend so vast a sum as one hundred Roman sesterces. He felt Scipio's strong hand at his waist, and understood that the Roman wanted him to dismount. But he paused for a moment, and turned to Scipio.

"I believe what they say," Garnesso told him.

"And what is that?"

"You *are* a god."

Scipio laughed and helped the boy into the waiting arms of the centurion. "This lad is a special friend to me," Scipio admonished the soldier. "See to it that no harm befalls him on his return to his father's side."

With that, he wheeled the horse about and rode away.

———

Bucephalus' hooves kicked up a storm of slop from the muddy streets of Tunis as Scipio made his way through the narrow passageways. Small huts and commercial shops of every kind lined the avenues, many sharing common walls. The peasants and shopkeepers scurried to get out of the way of the oncoming Roman and his mount.

When finally he was free of the urban congestion, Scipio gave the charger a small kick in the ribs, and Bucephalus burst into a full gallop, hurtling over the short plain and leaping a small ravine at a bound. Scipio stormed up a near hillside, Bucephalus' strong hind legs easily propelling them up the incline to the crest, to a small clump of cypress trees and brought the warhorse to a halt before the stand. With a sigh, he slipped down and went over to take comfort in the shade of a tree, leaving Bucephalus to roam about and graze. The clouds seemed so calm and peaceful, a marked contrast to his turmoil. Lowering his gaze, he looked out over the sweeping vista before him.

Off in the distance was the Tunis harbor, still gorged with dozens of Roman warships, neatly rigged for anchorage and resting in perfect alignment. And to the left, north of the city itself, was the enormous Roman encampment, protected by the ever-present wooden stockade. Row after precise row of canvas tents lined either side of roads carefully laid out to provide ease of access throughout the entire camp.

Yes, thought Scipio, it was all so neat and orderly, so completely

Roman, and subject to his absolute command. Why, then, was his own life in such disarray? He had conquered the enemies who dared to face him with a sword—why did he have such trouble with those who stood behind his back and used only words as their weapons? Ruefully, he admitted to himself that a politician with his ingratiating words was more dangerous than all of Hannibal's elephants. And Rome was full of politicians: Marcinius, Fabius, Cato . . .

And Marcia. She too was a politician—clever and manipulative, skilled at wheedling what she wanted out of her father. Yet he could not in fairness be resentful of her. She had freely given her love, and he had rejected it. Once she learned about Vibiana, she too would join the throng screaming for Vibiana's hide.

The thought of Marcia made him remember the letter Laelius had brought to him, and he took it from his pocket.

> *My Dearest Scipio,*
>
> *If I were an orator, perhaps I could manage to express my deep disappointment at your unbroken silence in some way that might influence you. Is there something wrong? Have I somehow offended you? I can only plead with you to break the unrelenting loneliness of my days with some word of news about yourself. Surely, despite all your duties, you can find a few minutes to send me a short letter! All I have had is the official dispatches, and while I share with all of Rome in the joy of your triumphs, more than any other Roman, I long desperately for your return.*
>
> *From what I hear about your successes, we will not much longer be separated. I have been devoting the utmost care to planning our wedding, and even have allowed the seamstresses to begin work on my dress. I know you value tradition, and so I have already obtained the customary red veil. I cannot wait!*
>
> *Marcia*

He put the letter down. No, Marcia was not going to be let down easily.

He sat in the shade for a length, pondering. He could return to Rome without Vibiana, as Laelius had pleaded, and negotiate with Marcinius for an honorable end to the engagement. This was occasionally done in Roman society: a betrothed suitor could with money simply offer to buy his way out of the impending marriage. But Marcinius might say no, as he might well do at his daughter's insistence, or the negotiations could take months. He could not bear to be separated from Vibiana for so long. He wanted to be with her when the baby was born, and hold it in his arms.

He considered remaining in Africa, perhaps establishing a residence in Tunis. Spain was also a possibility. They had enjoyed their time together in Cartagena, and could presumably do so again.

But his pride rebelled at these ideas. He had conquered Carthage for his home city: was he not entitled to ask clemency for the woman he loved? Should not his child be raised as a Roman? And moreover, Rome was the center of the universe. There lay the bones of his ancestors. There was his past and his future. He could no more turn his back on Rome than he could turn tail and run before Hannibal's elephants.

Not far away, a bird resembling a quail picked and scratched in the soil. A moment later, a second bird swept down from the sky and landed near the first. Together, they spent several minutes strutting about, bobbing and pecking at unseen grubs. Then, it seemed to him that the two birds looked at each other, fluttered their wings, and took to the sky, soaring away until he could see them no more.

It was an omen, he thought, a message from the gods. The gods had brought him Vibiana, standing there in bonds on the platform that night outside Baecula. The gods had reunited them in Africa. And the gods intended that they should remain together, like the two birds that had just flown off into the sun.

He bounded to his feet and whistled for Bucephalus, who had strayed some distance. The animal pricked up his ears at the signal and came at a trot. Scipio took up the reins and deftly jumped upon his back, full of resolve and determination to confront his adversaries and prevail.

———

Vibiana heard a loud crack of leather and the anguished cry of a man in terrible pain. She hurried to a window overlooking the courtyard. There, at the back of the clearing, was a naked man, tied hand and foot, spread-eagled between two columns. Just behind him stood a sour-looking centurion, wielding a long bullwhip that played out on the gravel behind him. The angry centurion struck again with all his might. The vicious cord left an ugly, raw welt just below the kidneys and elicited another shriek. The scene was witnessed by a dozen or so grim-faced Romans, one of whom was clearly in custody and visibly upset, as if he knew he was next.

It was horrible. She flinched as the air was rent again and again by the sound of the thrashing. This was worse by far than the beating of Camarissa—they had only used straps on her, not the braided leather lash capable of slicing the skin like a knife. If they kept it up they would kill the wretch. She turned away for several minutes, unable to watch. She lost count of the blows, but soon the hapless victim's cries gave way to low grunts, and then he fell completely silent. She stole another glance and saw that the man was unconscious, sagging against his restraints, his skin carved into a bloody pulp. The centurion, breathing hard from exertion, finally paused, and the man was cut down. She could see that his front side had been given the same treatment: he would be weeks, if not months, in recovering from the severe whipping. He was dragged away, mud mingling with his wounds. It would be a miracle if a fatal infection did not set in. Then the second man, pleading for mercy, was pushed forward, made to hand over his garment, and secured to the posts.

She heard a sound behind her and wheeled to find Narcussa in the room.

"They're so cruel," she said sadly as Narcussa took up a position beside her. The first blow fell upon the second victim. "Do you know why those men are being punished?"

"Master Scipio himself gave the order," Narcussa said. "These two men were charged with the duty of guarding his horse, but chose to spend their day in the tavern, leaving only a small boy to care for the animal. The master discovered their dereliction, and pronounced the sentence you see being carried out."

She wondered at the strange combination of loving gentleness and strict harshness which she had so often witnessed in Scipio. How could the same man who had so tenderly stroked her cheek at dawn have imposed so brutal a punishment? They were unbending, these Romans, and ruthless if their discipline was broken.

"The centurion has been demoted for his failure to supervise his men," Narcussa told her. "He worked very hard to earn that promotion, risking his life in combat time and again. Now, because of their misbehavior, he is back where he started when he first joined the army. And so the master has allowed him to take his revenge."

"They are so unforgiving," she murmured.

"To anyone, no matter how powerful," Narcussa said quietly. "Do not forget that."

She gave him a sidelong look. "What are you talking about?"

"Oh, nothing."

But she would not be deterred, and grabbed the old man by his tunic. "Do not be coy with me," she said. "You are aware of the influence I have over Scipio. If I told him you insulted me, he'd have you strung up like those men down there."

Narcussa would not budge. "If he knew that I told you about a conversation I overheard, he'd do it anyway. And so if I am to be at risk for my life, there ought to be something in it for me."

"Very well," she said. "What is it you want?"

"You have, as you say, considerable influence over the master. I want my freedom. Persuade him to grant me articles of manumission."

She considered his demand. It would not be hard to meet—Scipio would do whatever she asked. "This is not like you," she observed.

"I am getting old," Narcussa said. "I was born free and grew up free, until my family was sold into slavery to satisfy my father's debts. I have been a slave ever since, waiting on Romans hand and foot. First Scipio's father and now the son. But I do not want to die a slave. You are my best hope for freedom."

"All right," she agreed after a moment's hesitation. "I'll do it."

Narcussa's eyes gleamed at the prospect of freedom beckoning before him. "I overheard them talking," he told her. "Scipio and Laelius. They carry on conversations as if I were not even present. The Roman senator Marcinius has sworn to have you burned alive if you return to Rome because of what you did to Maximillian. He is a very powerful man. I do not doubt his ability to make good on his oath."

A wave of terror swept over her. "Scipio has promised that he will obtain an amnesty for me," she cried.

"According to Laelius, that's out of the question if you return to Rome. Marcinius even promised to bribe your executioner, so as to prolong the agony of your death. I saw them take a murderer once and tie him to a spit and turn it over a slow fire. The man lasted for hours. So I have no doubt the ordeal could be stretched out—"

She cut him off. "But why? Why does this man Marcinius hate me so much? I've done him no wrong. I've never even met him."

Narcussa now gave her a sly smile. "Ah, but you have done the senator a very grave wrong, indeed."

She gave him a bewildered look.

"You have stolen the master's heart, and deprived Marcinius of a son-in-law in the process. Before leaving Rome for Africa, the master was engaged to marry the daughter of Marcinius. Now, with you back in his life, he has no intention of marrying her. And Marcinius will not stand for it."

Vibiana was overwhelmed by these revelations. *Scipio, engaged to a Roman girl? And after recapturing me, he abandoned the girl, whose powerful father is now threatening to take his revenge!* She felt the baby kick, and gasped. She staggered over to a chair, her head swimming in disbelief.

Tears began to form at the corners of her eyes. "Oh, Narcussa. What can I do? What can I do?"

"I do not know. But this much I can say, do not think of returning to Rome with Scipio, not if you wish to see your child grow."

This was too much, and he left her, head in her hands, sobbing uncontrollably, the weight of the entire world bearing down on her fragile shoulders.

———

The ravaged body of Drusus was being cut down when Scipio strolled into the courtyard of his residence. He saw at a glance that his orders had been observed, and he walked over to the throng of soldiers.

"You are the centurion Bartullis?" Scipio asked the man, who was still holding the blood-soaked whip.

"I am centurion no longer," the man replied, deep disappointment evident in his voice.

"What have you to say for yourself?"

"My duties were heavy. I thought these men reliable, so I did not check on them. Clearly, I made a mistake. I am grateful that you have spared me the same penalty these wretches have received."

"You were strict, then, in meting out their punishment?"

"Look yonder at Drussus, and judge for yourself," Bartullis said, motioning with the whip.

Two legionnaires were now dragging away the unconscious, blood-caked body of Drusus.

"Then I restore you to your rank. Endeavor to make yourself the best centurion in the service of Rome. But I caution you—do not be so casual with your command again."

Bartullis, delighted by this sudden reversal of his fortune, broke into a broad grin, and several of the other soldiers congratulated him as Scipio walked away, satisfied that he'd sent a message through the ranks this day.

From her window, Vibiana saw him enter the courtyard, and by the time he joined her, she had managed to regain her composure.

"Are you all right?" he asked. "You seem upset."

"I am fine," she said, fighting to conceal her feelings. "I'm just feeling a little out of sorts—it's common for a woman at my stage."

He was concerned, and took her by the arm and led her over to a couch. "Lie down and rest," he said. "Do not take any chances with the life you are carrying."

She managed a slight smile for him, and then, seeing he was spotted with mud, asked, "You are filthy. Where have you been?"

"Oh, I had some things on my mind and went for a ride in the country to sort them out." He went over to a table in the corner of the room, poured water into a cup from a clay pitcher, and brought it to her.

"And did you? Sort them out, I mean."

He gave her a penetrating look. "Why, yes, I believe so. I believe I witnessed an omen from the gods, and it helped me come to a decision."

"What was it that so troubled you as to make necessary a ride in the country to find the answer?" she asked meekly.

He took the tip of his index finger and ran it lightly over her lips, then flicked at the golden hoops dangling from her ears. "Why, I was just trying to decide whether to take you back to Rome before the baby is born, or to wait until afterward."

She felt her blood run cold, but kept her voice calm. "And what did you decide?"

"I do not wish to delay," Scipio told her, now taking her hands in his own. "I wish for our child to be born on Roman soil, and so as soon as Lucius returns with a signed peace treaty, we will depart at once for Rome, so that I myself can put it before the Senate for ratification. Laelius tells me that the Senate has voted to authorize me to make peace on any terms I see fit, so I imagine that they will approve whatever I give them."

Her heart began to pound. Would he really expose her to such risk? "Perhaps," she said, "I should not make a crossing in this condition."

"Nonsense," he said, in his typically Roman high-handed manner. "I will obtain for us a quinquereme, the largest and most comfortable ship available. She will have five banks of rowers, and I will have them work without stopping—we can make the crossing in two days."

She began to despair. "Did Laelius have any other news from Rome?"

For an instant, he wondered if somehow she knew. But he put the idea out of his mind—she could not possibly know about Marcinius' threat. "No, not really. He tells me the Temple of Neptune is making good progress, although the cost strikes him as extravagant."

She managed to hide her concern. "Tell me," she said softly, "what will we do in Rome?"

He looked away, a fond expression passing over his face. "Ah," he said fondly, "there is no city in the world like Rome. The buildings are immense, the architecture exquisite. There is running water, brought in from far away by magnificent aqueducts, and public sewers, so the streets do not stink like they do here! There are elaborate religious festivals. And the markets—anything you could want, from anywhere in the world, can be bought in the marketplace of Rome. And the races, games, and spectacles beyond belief . . . there is so much to do!"

He shifted his weight slightly, taking the classic Roman pose, weight balanced on one leg. "I will build you a beautiful home, situated high on one of the seven hills, high enough to catch the cooling breezes. The Palatine is the most fashionable place to live, but it is dominated already by the house of a man I do not care for. And so perhaps I will choose a different hill, possibly the Quirinal, although its proximity to the poor district may not be to your liking. Well, we'll find a spot when we get there. It will be big, so you'll have quite a task filling it with furniture and decorations. You will be mistress of the house, with slaves to meet every need. I will dabble in the affairs of state, and oversee my various interests. We will have a houseful of children."

"It sounds too wonderful to be true," she said, hoping to draw him out.

But he had no intention of giving her any reason for concern. "It will be true," Scipio said. "It will be our new life together. Now, unless you have further questions, I would like to get cleaned up before dinner. Ask Narcussa to draw my bath."

She propped her head onto her hand. "Speaking of Narcussa," she said carefully, "he certainly has been a loyal slave to you for a long time."

Scipio thought this comment a little odd, but he nodded in agreement. "Yes. He was valet to my father before me."

"He is getting old," Vibiana observed. "You might consider giving him his freedom, as a reward for all his loyal service."

Scipio was nearly out of the room, but turned back. "Well, I hadn't really thought of it before, but, yes, I might just do that—once we return to Rome."

XX

Tunis, Africa

202 BC

Over the next few days, Vibiana managed to keep Scipio in the dark about her apprehensions. On several occasions, she contrived to bring up again the question of the timing of their return to Rome. Each time, Scipio was more insistent than the last: they were going back to Rome, just as soon as Lucius returned with a signed treaty, and that was that. Once, she even dared to suggest they remain in Tunis, only to be met with a stony silence.

As Scipio became more insistent about his plans, Vibiana slipped into a deep melancholy over her prospects, endlessly turning over and over in her mind the hundred different questions the dilemma presented. *Why,* she asked herself time and again, *would Scipio subject me to such danger? Is he so proud that he believes they cannot refuse to give him his way? Having beaten Hannibal, does he believe he cannot be overcome by mere politicians?*

And more than once, she found herself wondering: *Perhaps Scipio really does not want to marry me, and by taking me back to Rome, I can be conveniently disposed of, leaving him free to marry the daughter of Marcinius!* In her troubled mind, she imagined this was his vile plan.

Then she would regain her composure, remembering again the gentle caress of Scipio's touch, the fondness of his smile whenever he looked up as she entered a room. No, surely he was in love with her, and would, as he vowed, not let anything tear them apart.

But the awful prospect remained. Narcussa's warning resounded again and again, turning her dreams of a happy life with Scipio into the nightmare vision of a slow death over hot coals.

After another sleepless night, she resolved to visit Laelius and sound him out. It was a warm, muggy day in Tunis, and she felt the drops of perspiration running down her ever-expanding belly as she ambled over to the small house in which Laelius had set up his quarters. It was built of lime-mortar and mudbricks, and was not favored by the harbor breeze. Accordingly, Laelius had recruited a slave to hold and flap a large fan, made from the feathers of some exotic bird, in a valiant if unsuccessful effort to circulate air through the small room he had made his office.

She found him hard at work going over ledgers of the accounts for the campaign, an utterly thankless task he had assumed since the departure of the quaestor, Cato. Because of his own hiatus in Rome, the accounts had fallen far behind, and since his return he had been working day and night to get things back into order. He was attended by a thickset Roman, evidently some type of staff officer. They were poring over a long vellum scroll of numbers when she entered the room. Hearing her knock, he looked up and smiled, putting down the sheet.

"Vibiana!" he said with real pleasure in his voice, delighted to have a break in the monotony of perusing the endless rows of figures. "What a pleasant surprise!"

"If this is an inopportune time, I can come back. . . ." she started to say.

"No, no, not at all. Have you ever met the master of supply for our little undertaking, the centurion Bocullus Metarrus?"

The stout Roman recognized her at once. He lumbered to his feet and bowed respectfully. He had a florid complexion, and, perhaps because of the heat, seemed to be very uncomfortable.

"Bocullus is the real reason we have prevailed on this wretched continent," Laelius said almost gaily. "An army travels on its stomach, as they say, and there is no better supply master than Bocullus. What he cannot buy or trade for, he steals."

Vibiana laughed as the sweating Roman tried to manage a smile.

"That is enough for today," Laelius said lightly to the officer. "We shall continue tomorrow. Perhaps by then you will have an explanation for what happened to that consignment of iron plates we ordered to protect the siege equipment at Utica. Now that they have disappeared, someone is going to have to tell Scipio why the final assault cannot begin for another month, and it is not going to be me."

Bocullus swallowed hard. "Yes, sir. Of course." He backed out of the room, sweating and flushed even more deeply with concern.

When he was gone, Vibiana slid into the chair the soldier had vacated and gave Laelius a mischievous look. "What do you think he did with the iron plates?" she asked.

Laelius held up his hands, to signify that he had no idea. "Who knows? He made some swap, no doubt. I know how these things happen. Perhaps someone urgently needed rope, and so he traded for it. Or possibly, someone was screaming for fodder for the cavalry horses, and it seemed at the time that the war would be over before the plates could turn up missing."

"I saw what happened to two soldiers who were a little irresponsible in guarding Scipio's horse," she observed. "I shudder to think what will become of poor Bocullus if he has delayed the siege for a month."

Laelius laughed. "Oh, nothing much will happen to him. The meanest lashing he'll receive will be from Scipio's tongue. Scipio knows how things get done in the Roman Army. If we start flogging a supply master every time he makes a trade, our domination of the world will disintegrate in a hurry."

She noticed a huge stack of vellum sheets and wax tablets piled in a corner of the office.

"What's all of that?" she asked.

Laelius' face turned glum.

"One of my duties as quaestor is to write the official account of the African Expedition for the army archives in Rome. All of that is my source material. I haven't yet begun—it will take months to write."

Vibiana gave him a sympathetic smile. Then changing the subject, she ventured, "I am surprised," Vibiana said, "that the siege of Utica continues. What military significance can it possibly have, now that Carthage has agreed to terms?"

"It has the military significance of being a burr under the saddle of a great general's horse," Laelius said irritably and not a little sarcastically. He felt safe in criticizing his general in her presence, for he knew she was discreet. "The effort requires thousands of men, working night and day, consuming rafts of supplies and equipment, and the deaths of a hundred slaves a day from exhaustion. But the general in this case is Scipio, and he is angry that Utica has refused to surrender to him. He regards it as a blemish upon the honor of the Roman Army. He is capable of being very stubborn."

"Indeed," she replied. "Utica may be the least of the monuments to his stubborn pride."

She saw that his expression was puzzled, as if he did not quite follow her.

"Laelius," she said softly, "I know that I can trust you to be honest with me. Just like at Zama."

Laelius shifted uncomfortably in his chair, leery of where this was heading.

"Scipio is insistent that we return to Rome. What is going to happen to me—and my baby—once we are there?"

Laelius sat up stiffly behind the desk, wary now. What did she know? Had she learned of Marcinius' threats? Could Scipio have been foolish enough to tell her? No, he thought, not even in the throes of an erection could Scipio make such a blunder.

"That is something," he said carefully, "you should take up with Scipio. I do not know what his plans are."

"He has made up his mind. He's taking me back to Rome with him."

Laelius' mind was racing as he thought through the implications of this news. If Scipio was hell-bent to pursue this course, Laelius would have to put his contingency plan in play. "I'm sure things will work out in the end," he said, trying to sound supportive.

"You know the political situation in Rome," she pointed out. "You were just there. I'm sure Scipio is a big hero, the only Roman to beat Hannibal. But is he revered enough to win amnesty for the murderess of a Roman soldier?"

Laelius was on quicksand, and he knew it. "Really, Vibiana, I can't imagine where you get all these wild ideas. Yes, Scipio is a hero, the greatest general in Roman history, unquestionably. There are banners hung everywhere proclaiming the glory of his name, the glory of Zama. The Senate passed a resolution giving him blanket authority to make the peace with Carthage on whatever terms he sees fit. That is unprecedented. Let him be your protector when you return to Rome. There could be none better."

Somehow, Vibiana was not convinced. "In Carthage," she said astutely, "the greater a man becomes, the more determined become his enemies to bring him down. I suppose in Rome, it is no different."

Laelius studied an insect crawling up the wall across from him. He did not respond to her comment.

His silence was like a hot knife, sealing the certainty of her fate. She could bear it no longer, and burst into tears. "What is going to happen to me?" she cried out.

He jumped up and ran around the desk to her, taking her in his arms, and hoping for all the world that Scipio did not decide to come just now for a visit.

"There, there . . ." he whispered to her softly. "Things will work out all right in the end. They always do. Scipio will not let them harm you, or the baby."

She took the hem of her garment and used it to dab at her eyes. "Thank you for being honest with me. We are all pebbles in the hands of the gods."

She struggled to her feet, no mean task given the drastic relocation of her center of gravity. As she waddled toward the door, Laelius asked, "Where are you going?"

"To find an apothecary," she said vacantly. He did not understand.

"I am constipated," she said in a tired voice, seeing his confusion. "The midwife says that the elixir of hannamon will provide relief."

He watched her go, then put his head in his hands, torn by the momentous decision pressing upon him. He wondered if he should tell Scipio of the conversation with Vibiana. He decided against it, presuming it would only make Scipio more upset and reinforce his stubbornness. *He's bound and determined to take her back to Rome . . . and if he does so, Marcinius will do everything in his power to ruin Scipio.*

He thought about Scipio's father, and how much he had loved the man. *I have spent my whole life serving the Cornelli. We have made Scipio the greatest Roman general in history. His father would be so proud of him. He will hold all of Rome in the palm of his hand. And he's willing to risk it all, for the love of a woman!*

Laelius gritted his teeth, steeling himself for what he must do. *I have tried everything I can to talk Scipio out of this insane course he's following. He won't listen. Ergo, Marcinius cannot be allowed to bring down all we have done to achieve the legend of Scipio.*

He took up a sheet of vellum and scratched out two simple words:

Patroclus—Proceed

And then, in the midst of sealing the correspondence for delivery to the next boat leaving for Rome, he was struck by an odd thought: he had never heard of a remedy called the elixir of hannamon.

———

The first passerby Vibiana encountered was able to give her directions to the shop of an apothecary. She picked her way through the muddy streets of Tunis, passing dozens of stalls at which every sort of finished goods and imaginable food could be found for sale.

In a short distance, she found the apothecary's stall, tucked away on a narrow ribbon of a side street that, because of the overhang from adjoining structures, received no sunlight. Deprived of the cleansing effect of the hot sun, the muddy lane itself and the adjacent walls smelled of mildew.

The room itself seemed to be empty. She entered the dimly lit establishment and was bombarded by the pungent odor of countless different compounds. She was able to pick out a few as she moved about the room: sulphur, magnesium, antimony, oil of vitriol, cymene, basalt, a sweet smelling benzene liniment made from a tallow base, and others. The walls were lined with shelves, containing all manner of jars and flasks, made of clay, ceramic, and metal, several of which were plugged at the bottom with a stopcock. Open bowls were filled with small piles of unknown substances, mostly ground into fine powders.

She paused before the only furniture in the space, a long table stained with years of use, on which sat dozens of scrolls and a scale, its oval metal dishes suspended by wires from a long, symmetrically carved arm. There were porcelain mortars and pestles of various sizes, several filled with unrecognizable substances. On another table, resting on a metal rack, was an alembic vessel, connected to a receiver to collect distillate.

"May I help you, milady?" a thin voice croaked from behind her, and Vibiana startled. Turning, she saw an ancient prune of a man, a walking cadaver, his features barely discernable beneath a shaggy mass of hair, white as snow, from head to chin. He held his hands before him, fingers laced together. She took note of his long, grimy nails and the discolored skin about the fingertips—to be expected in one who spent his days tinkering with all nature of potent chemicals. As he moved about, or rather shuffled, the hem of his gray robe brushed along the dirt floor, reordering the dust into ever-changing patterns.

"You are the apothecary?" she asked.

"Some call me that," he replied.

"You are old enough to have the experience I seek," she observed.

"Over fifty years in the trade, milady," he said, a note of pride in his voice. "There is no malady for which I cannot provide some relief."

"I have need of an extraordinary powder," she said.

His wizened eyes studied her carefully. "And what might that be?"

She looked directly at him, hoping that she could make her lie convincing. She said slowly, "A relative of mine suffers from the consumption. His end is slow in coming. He has lost control of his bodily functions, and the pain is terrible. He cannot care for himself. He has asked me to obtain a substance that will end his life."

The old man cocked his head, wary now. "Why doesn't he simply take his life by opening his veins? Many people in such circumstances hold a small party first, with their closest friends and relatives invited to witness the passing of the loved one."

Vibiana thought for a moment. "I do not wish his ending to be painful—I want to administer the drug, but have its effect delayed until he is asleep."

"Ah," he said sharply, "you want me to give you a poison."

"Yes."

He was not fooled by her story, and pulled on his long whiskers, deep in thought. "There is a danger for me, for a poison is not discriminating—it can be used against anyone."

He was cagey, she realized. "I can assure you, no harm will befall you."

"Still," he said, "if the poison you seek were to fall into the wrong hands, it could cause great mischief. I do not know you. The risk is too high."

Vibiana lifted her chin slightly. "I have nothing I can offer you except money. Name your price."

He rubbed his hands slowly, pondering. The woman clearly was of the noble class—how much would she pay? After several moments, he offered, "Say, one thousand Roman sesterces?"

She did not blink. "Done."

This gave him pause. Damn it all, he should have asked for more!

"For my own safety," he said, "the drug should cause a death that would not indicate that the victim was poisoned. Its symptoms should mask its application. Perhaps the poison should bring on something resembling a stroke."

"Yes." She looked away, choking on emotion. "That would be very useful."

The aged hands now came to rest atop the cracked table. "Do you have the money?"

"Not here with me, now. I shall return with it within the hour."

The venerable head nodded slowly in agreement. "Very well. By then, I shall have ready the powder you desire."

She left the old man to his chemicals and hurried back to the villa, determined to carry out her course.

———

Vibiana prepared herself carefully for their dinner. She was aware that no seamstress alive possessed sufficient skill to do anything but hide her vast, protruding belly beneath a wide swatch of cloth. No sheer silk for her tonight: she would not be able to beguile her Scipio with a scandalous dress providing a hint of her round, firm breasts or the tightness of her buttocks, as she had done so often in the past. And so she summoned a slave girl skilled in styling hair, and spent the better part of the afternoon being ministered to, having her hair washed and combed into an elaborate arrangement, a bun atop her head trailing out long, tightly wound curls all about her face. She then applied her cosmetics with a delicate attention, studying her image in the polished mirror as if each dab of eyeshade or stroke of blush were a matter of life and death. Which, most certainly, it was.

Finally, she chose her jewelry: lustrous pearl earrings set between delicate golden fronds, a matching necklace, featuring a stunning collection of emeralds, gleaming golden bracelets on each wrist, and on her left middle finger, a ring bearing a brilliantly polished diamond large enough to choke Bucephalus. When she was satisfied that she was sufficiently prepared, she removed herself to the dining room, where she found Scipio waiting, already sprawled comfortably on a couch facing the low, flat marble table flanked by elaborate bronze candelabra. He looked up as she entered, and a broad smile spread across his features. She knew at once that her efforts had succeeded.

He got to his feet and took her into his arms, having to stretch a bit now to reach completely around her. "You grow more lovely with each passing day," he murmured, kissing her red lips lightly.

"Certainly, I grow with every passing day." She laughed, thrusting her stomach against him. "I am beginning to fear it may be twins!"

"Twins!" he marveled, not certain whether she was jesting. He felt the unyielding mound with his fingertips. "It would be a blessing from the gods!"

He took her by the hand and led her to the couch opposite his own, and when he was satisfied that she was comfortably established, resumed his place. He clapped his hands loudly, and servants scurried into the room to begin the meal.

Because they were dining alone, the feast was a relatively simple one, beginning with an appetizer of fresh oysters dipped in lemon juice, followed by a generous platter of broiled lamb surrounded by boiled new potatoes, baked squash, and grilled shallots. A bowl of tossed greens was followed by a sampling of fruits and cakes.

Vibiana made light small talk between the courses, asking him about the little details of military administration and the progress of the siege at Utica.

"There is something they are not telling me," Scipio rumbled when she brought up the siege.

"What do you mean?" she asked innocently, batting her eyelids at him.

"The engineers have been building a siege tower, which is to be pulled up against the ramparts. From it, they will hoist a battering ram. They tell me that the tower cannot be finished for another month, because of the complexity of its construction. They are making excuses. I have asked Laelius to get to the bottom of it."

"I am certain he will ferret it out."

"Yes," he agreed. "Laelius always gets to the truth, no matter how painful it may be."

Nervously, she picked at the salad before her, wondering if Laelius had related to Scipio the tenor of their conversation. But Scipio seemed completely relaxed as he pulled the lamb into smaller pieces with his fingers. No, she decided, her love was blissfully in the dark.

"What did you do today?" he asked, chewing on the lamb.

"Oh, nothing much. I went for a walk through the city, and saw the most captivating little child, begging for coins in the street. She had no arms, poor thing."

Scipio frowned, uninterested in the fate of a street urchin. "You went unescorted?"

She nodded.

"I do not approve. The streets are full of ruffians of every sort, and my guards cannot be everywhere at once. Next time, find a centurion and insist that you be escorted. Or better yet, send a servant. You are soon to be a noblewoman of Rome—I suggest you start behaving like one."

She reached out with her hand and brushed it against his hairy forearm. "Oh, Scipio, you worry too much."

"Not at all," he replied. "In Rome, a woman absolutely must go out with an escort. There is no protection at all in the streets of Rome, you know. We are a Republic. If there were armed men in the streets to keep order, they might be bribed to favor one faction over another, threatening the liberty of us all. And so we have violent streets, every traveler for himself. It is a small price to pay for democracy." He smiled at her. "And a lady as lovely as you would draw far too much attention. No, I will hire a contingent of gladiators to serve as your escorts. Of course, you will not have to go out often, for the slaves will attend to your every need when we are back in Rome."

"Oh, do not talk to me of Rome," she sighed. "Not when we are so happy here."

"You only think yourself happy," he laughed. "Once you have seen Rome and marveled at what she has to offer, you will not want to be anyplace else."

"Do not be so certain," she said, a little peeved at his attitude. "We were happy together in Cartagena, and we have been happy here. Why must we tempt fate by traveling to Rome?"

He sighed wearily. "Please don't start on that theme again. I thought we had settled it, once and for all. I am a Roman. A famous one, at that. Why would I want to be anywhere else but at the center of the world?"

"Perhaps," she said tartly, "it is not where I want to be. Do my wishes count for nothing in your eyes?"

He thrust his fingers into a small ceramic bowl of water with painted flowers glazed about the rim and rinsed them. The conversation had taken a sour turn, and he wanted to return it to a more pleasant plane. "Your wishes are of the utmost concern to me," he said in an amiable tone, seeking to placate her. "But Rome is where I must be. And I am taking you there."

"But I do not want to go to Rome!"

Her eyes were locked upon him, and he met her gaze with a determined glare. "Why do you say that?" he asked. "You have never seen Rome—it is a lovely city. You will be very happy there."

"If I survive my arrival," she snapped.

"What do you mean by that?" he asked, knowing the answer.

"I am concerned about what will happen to me in Rome," she said, fighting back tears in a mixture of frustration and fear.

"Nothing will happen to you in Rome," he said stubbornly. "I am a pro-consul of Rome, conqueror of Hannibal, granted the title of Africanus. I am building a temple honoring Neptune. The people worship my name. You will be my wife—many women would die for that honor."

"I may die because of it," she said bitterly.

"What do you know?"

She remained silent.

Angry now, he leaped to his feet and grabbed her by the arms, shaking her violently. "Damn you, do not play these games with me! What brings this on?"

"The camp is full of rumors," she lied, terrified by his rage. "I have heard that you were engaged to the daughter of a senator, and that you have broken your engagement by taking me to your bed. And I have heard that her father will seek his revenge by demanding that I be put to death for the murder of Maximillian."

He released her, stunned. "Only Laelius knows about that," he said, his mind reeling. "Why did he tell you? Why? Why?"

"It wasn't Laelius," she replied flatly, her tone so matter-of-fact that he could only believe her. "There are others who know. And you do not deny it—you only seek revenge upon the person who told me."

"I will not let them touch one hair upon your head," he said furiously, drawing his hand into a fist and shaking it in the air before him. "Not one hair!"

"Oh, Scipio," she said softly, placing her hand on his shoulder, "do not try to fight them. Let us remain here. Let us go to Spain. Or even Alexandria. The world is so vast—we do not have to go to Rome."

"That," he snapped, "is out of the question."

She could see that it was useless. He was being a Roman again, proud and haughty, conqueror of the world, made righteous not by the nobility of ideals but merely by the tempered steel of the Roman short sword.

A servant entered the room, bearing a tray with two goblets and a silver decanter of wine. The servant poured the beverage into the cups while Scipio turned his back to Vibiana, lost in thought. The slave bowed slightly from the waist and withdrew. And so no one saw Vibiana's hand dart into the fold of her dress and withdraw a small clay vial. In a deft motion, she removed the lid and poured the white crystalline powder into the cup on her right. To her relief, it did not foam or otherwise give any evidence of its presence. She slipped the vial back into her dress.

It is in the hands of the gods, she thought.

After several minutes, he turned and faced her. "I love you," he said simply. "I cannot bear to be without you. But neither can I bear to forsake my country. As soon as Lucius returns, we will depart. I swear to you, no harm will befall you. Not even if I have to bribe every senator and tribune and assemblyman in Rome."

She looked down. "You would put my fate—and the fate of your child—into the hands of politicians?"

He managed a slight smile. "I have fought other battles over you. This one will not be nearly so difficult."

"Those battles were fought face to face, where the strength of your arm and the craftiness of your wiles could influence the outcome," she pointed out. "If you take me back to Rome, you will be fighting against the law. Not even you can overcome it."

"Laws are made by men," he replied softly. "And men can change them."

"Please," she whispered, "do not subject me to this ordeal."

"My mind is made up," he said stubbornly. "We leave for Rome as soon as possible."

He began to leave the room.

"Do you not wish to take any wine?" she asked feebly as he walked past her.

"I desire a clear head, for there is much to do," he said, abruptly walking out.

She considered the two cups on the tray before her. Then, with tears trailing down her cheeks, she reached out and took the cup on her right. With a sob barely audible, she held the goblet to her lips, and, thinking of the child that would never be born, drained it to the last drop.

———

He stirred at the first trace of the breaking sun, scratching himself and turning slightly onto his side. Vibiana lay with her back against him, clad in a simple linen sleeping shift.

Scipio opened his eyes. As the night's shadow slowly retreated before the persistent light of day, he studied the elaborate modillion that ran about the room beneath the ceiling, held up by a series of Doric columns, between which the stuccoed walls were set. The pattern was uniform: three square projecting blocks, then a half circle, followed by three more blocks, and another circle, repeated around the room. *How interesting,* he thought, *that the Greek influence would reach even the architecture of a bedroom in Tunis.* On a pedestal in a corner of the room was a small statuette of the god Mercury. Masterfully carved, the entire weight of the likeness balanced solely on his delicate left winged foot, forever frozen in the running pose—the expected image of the god of messages—with his right arm extended far into the sky. It was the extension of the arm, he realized, that counter-balanced the statue and kept it from tipping to the left.

More Greek influence, he thought: balance above all else, moderation in all things. How rich were the Greeks! And how pitiful that their arms had failed to keep pace with their culture. . . .

He pulled himself to a sitting position, his legs dangling off the edge of the sleeping platform. It was still cool and quiet, his favorite time of the day. He went to the chamber pot and relieved himself, releasing a long, luxurious stream into the tall porcelain bowl.

Scipio turned and glanced at Vibiana. She had not moved. Something about the angle of her recline seemed amiss, and he moved back to her side.

Her skin was cool to his touch. He prodded her gently, and received no response. He jabbed at her, harder now, with his finger in her ribs. Still nothing.

He put his hand on her shoulder and pulled her over onto her back. Her head fell limp to one side, her hair thick with sweat upon the pillow beneath.

With a jolt, he knew she was dead.

The enormity of it struck him. He screamed, long and loud, again and again.

Narcussa burst into the bedroom, his white nightshirt billowing about him. He found his master, cradling the woman Vibiana in his arms, rocking softly in rhythm with his moans, tears gushing down his face like great torrents of rain.

A moment later, two guards stumbled in, swords drawn and at the ready.

But there was no one there to fight, only a wailing man they knew as their general, victor over Hannibal, conqueror of Africa, the great Africanus.

Laelius arrived at the bedchamber shortly after the chief surgeon of the army had begun his examination, having been roused from his own slumber by an urgent notice to make haste to Scipio's quarters. The guard who brought the summons had informed Laelius of the tragedy, and so he had somewhat overcome his disbelief by the time he entered the room. He found his general perched upon an upholstered chair in the corner of the room, his eyes vacant, his cheeks sunken into the hollows of his face.

He placed his hand upon Scipio's shoulder, but received no response. The man was in shock. Better to leave him be, he thought, and went over to the surgeon, the old, reliable Demosthenes.

"What happened?" Laelius insisted in a quiet voice.

"I cannot say for sure, but the symptoms appear to indicate a stroke," the surgeon said, carrying out his duties with an air of professional detachment. "Very unusual for a healthy pregnant woman."

"A stroke?" Laelius glanced down at the corpse, incredulous. Vibiana was as lovely in death as in life. Only the absolute stillness of her features and the total absence of color in her skin gave any indication that she was dead. "How can that be? She was the picture of health!"

The surgeon gave him a critical look. "I am more accustomed to dealing with soldiers in need of an amputation than with the corpses of pregnant women. I could conduct an autopsy. An examination of her internal organs might shed some light on the cause."

From the corner of the room, a hoarse voice cried out, "No!" They wheeled and saw Scipio, on his feet now.

"Go away, surgeon. This one is already dead—you will not make her any worse."

Demosthenes was accustomed to criticism, and so he was not unduly stung by this rebuke. He bowed at the waist, and backed out of the room.

Scipio shuffled over to the bed and stood by Laelius. He reached down and arranged his love's hair about her face, trying to restore the curls she had worn to their dinner the night before.

"So lovely, so lovely," he choked.

Laelius went over to a small table, where Vibiana kept her cosmetics, and looked through her things. Nothing seemed out of place. And then he noticed a small clay vial, which he picked up. He snapped off the lid and sniffed at it—it gave off a bitter smell, and he observed that there were a few granules left, clinging to the base of the vessel. Wisely, he slipped the container into his pocket.

He advanced toward Scipio, intending to take him by the hand, when a distant trumpet, from the direction of the harbor, caught his attention. He hurried over to the arched window and squinted into the distance.

"What is it?" he heard Scipio ask dully.

Laelius instantly recognized the flag atop the graceful trireme pulling into the harbor, her oars cutting the waves with a steady, measured pulse.

"What is it?" Scipio demanded once more.

"It is Lucius' ship, returning from Carthage," Laelius said. "It is flying your battle flag, triumphant. It can only mean one thing. The peace is concluded. Lucius has the treaty in hand."

Scipio grazed his hand over Vibiana's cheek, oblivious to the news.

"Hail, Africanus," Laelius said, his voice barely audible.

———

The day, fittingly, was dark and overcast, matching the mood of the small group of Romans assembled on a small hillock outside the camp.

The corpse, wrapped in a gray shroud of woven linen, was delicately placed atop a large mound of stacked white cedar, cut into pieces roughly the length of a Roman spear.

Scipio waited until the pallbearers were clear of the pyre, and then stepped forward. He ran his fingers lightly over her face a final time. Then, without so much as a sob, he took up a torch and thrust it into the stacked wood.

The timber crackled a bit as the flames spread through the pyre. In a few moments, there was a roaring blaze.

Scipio could not bear to watch, and he staggered away, followed by Lucius, Narcussa, and several others.

Only Laelius remained behind, waiting until the others were well out of sight.

When he was sure he was alone, he stepped close to the fire, feeling its heat on his face.

He removed from his pocket the letter from Marcinius to Silanus, and the mysterious vial he had found that awful morning in Scipio's bedchamber.

Overcome with sadness for all that might have been, he hurled both into the blaze. The flames consumed them.

He paused for a moment, reflecting on Scipio's reaction to the tragedy. Lethargic, the general had barely stirred from his curule chair, where he had sat, brooding and weeping, since the terrible discovery. He had not taken up even once the treaty that would make him the most famous Roman of them all. All military matters had been referred to Lucius for disposition.

The mound of burning wood collapsed on itself, obscuring the last remnants of Vibiana's corpse in dense smoke.

For a brief moment, Laelius considered sending another letter to Patroclus, revoking his prior instruction. And then he rejected it.

Let everything, Laelius decided, *turn to ashes.*

XXI

ROME

202 BC

FABIUS, NOTIFIED THAT A swift boat had arrived from Tunis, hurried to his office, arriving just about the same time as the messenger from the docks. Hands trembling, he carefully opened the sealed scroll, sent by his replacement spy in Scipio's command.

He read it through, and sagged back in his chair, incredulous. Unable to absorb it, he read it again, and then again, finally putting the letter on the simple table that served as his desk.

"Guard," he barked to the legionnaire stationed outside his office. "Fetch Marcinius," he said slowly. "Tell him to come immediately."

———

By coincidence, the same ship that bore the spy's message to Fabius also carried the letter from Laelius to Patroclus.

Given its brevity, Patroclus hastened to get to work.

———

Marcinius, his round rump smarting from the coarse chair placed across the desk from Fabius, pored over the communication, sharing the commander in chief's sense of disbelief.

"Extraordinary," was all he could finally summon forth. "The terms of the treaty are incredible. This completely neuters Carthage.

She will be no threat to us in the future."

"No question," Fabius said with grudging admiration. "The Senate will name him the greatest Roman of all time." And then, narrowing his eyes to a squint, "They may even grant him the amnesty for that girl."

Marcinius slammed his fist on the table. "Never," he rasped, his voice almost croaking.

Fabius put his hands together with the fingers interlaced, as he was prone to do when thinking. "What if we offered him command of the campaign against Antiochus, far away in Asia Minor?" Fabius said in a sly tone of voice. "That would send him off for another five years or so. You could give him the chance to withdraw from the engagement, because he'll be away so long, serving the country. He might take that deal, and take the damn girl with him on the campaign."

Marcinius drummed his fingers on the desktop, thinking. *Perhaps that wouldn't be so bad. . . . It would no doubt break Marcia's heart, but that scenario was infinitely preferable to how shattered she would be to learn she'd been discarded by Scipio for a Carthaginian whore.*

"Let me think about it," he said simply.

"Don't dawdle," Fabius snapped. "It will require a good deal of maneuvering to convince the Senate to give the Asian campaign to Scipio. Especially with that damn Cato out there making trouble."

The two men rose and headed for the door. Fabius walked Marcinius out to the portico, neither man speaking, the wheels turning in their respective heads, until Fabius noticed: "Where is your bodyguard?"

Marcinius laughed. "Your summons was so urgent, I came unattended."

Fabius had an uneasy feeling. "This is not wise. Let me send someone with you."

Marcinius waved him off.

"Don't bother," he said flatly. "I'll be fine."

—•—

Marcinius huffed and puffed his way up the Vicus Trabonius, the narrow roadway that wound along the Palatine Hill, toward his residence. His head was so full of the intricate details of the intrigue he was plotting with Fabius that he did not notice the two rough-looking characters, clad in the common woolen tunics of construction laborers, who fell in behind him.

They reached a sharp turn in the pathway, the flanking buildings forming a natural blind spot for any onlookers.

The assassins struck with lightning quickness. The larger of the two men grabbed Marcinius from behind and forced him facedown onto the gravel, throwing up a bit of dust. Before the portly senator could even turn to see what had happened, the second man grabbed the top of his head, jerked it back, and ran a sharp dagger deeply across his throat.

Nothing but a gurgle escaped the senator's lips as he departed the world.

The two thugs waited only a few moments to be certain their task was complete, and then made sure to locate and remove Marcinius' bulging coin purse from a pocket in his toga. This was essential: the attack had to look like a robbery. They hastily grabbed all the coins, but noticed there was a single metal key in the purse.

"Leave it," one of the ruffians said to the other.

Then they ran, each taking different directions at the first intersection they reached, to prevent their being caught together.

It was an unnecessary precaution. Several long minutes elapsed before another wayfarer came across Marcinius lying in the pool of his own blood, and by then, the killers had melted into the vast teeming humanity of lower-class Rome.

———

Fortunately for all concerned, the fellow who happened upon Marcinius' corpse recognized the senator and sounded the alarm. Within an hour or so, a small contingent of soldiers from the garrison of Rome arrived at the scene. By then, a crowd had gathered, uttering all sorts of pithy lamentations for what so brazen a murder, of so prominent a citizen, must mean for the sad state of affairs in Rome.

There was nothing to be done: Marcinius was dead, no one had seen anything, and, in any event, Rome did not have any type of municipal police. Learning from bystanders where Marcinius' residence was located, the soldiers loaded the deceased onto a pallet and cursed their bad fortune at having to haul so portly a victim up such a steep hill. The commander of the detail, however, detached himself from this laborious task, and returned to the army headquarters to inform the chain of command of what had happened.

The commander of the watch, upon learning the identity of the victim, wasted no time in rushing to the office of the commander in chief to inform Fabius of the shocking development.

Fabius the Delayer, dictator of Rome, was staggered by the news, but quickly recovered his composure in the presence of the junior officer.

"I told that bastard to let me give him an escort," was all he said, and waved the man away.

———

By the time Fabius made his way up the steep slope to Marcinius' residence—accompanied, of course, by a heavily armed escort—the household was full of weeping and fearful servants. He found Marcia prostrate upon a couch in her father's office, clearly in a state of shock, clutching a leather coin purse in her hands.

Fabius sat gently beside her on the divan. He took her in his arms.

"Marcia, my dear, what a frightful tragedy," Fabius said to her softly. "I have stationed soldiers at every approach to the residence, and every door. You are completely safe."

Marcia barely moved her head in acknowledgment. He wondered if anything he said would sink in.

"I have ordered that a complete investigation be made," he said, but then added as tenderly as he could, "I am afraid, however, that there is very little to go on. Whoever did this was nowhere in sight when your father's body was discovered. And I am told that no one seems to have seen or heard anything."

He noticed the coin purse. "Was that his?"

Tears poured forth from her reddened eyes. "Yes," was all she could utter. Then, gathering herself a bit, she managed, "It was empty of coins. Father never went anywhere without money on his person. So it was a robbery."

Fabius took the purse from her. It was finely crafted leather, itself an expensive item. Hearing a soft clink, he pulled it open and took out the metal key, on a golden ring. "What is this?"

Marcia managed a small smile. "It's the key to the lockbox in father's library, where he keeps his most valuable items."

"Well, everything belongs to you now," he said, handing the purse and the key back to her. He released her from his arms and got to his feet.

"Allow me to engage undertakers to prepare your father for the pyre," he said, feeling the burden of command yet again. "The Senate will declare a week of mourning, I will see to that. And the funeral tributes will be held in the Rostrum itself. I promise you, Marcia, we will send him off with all the honors."

Before she could manage any words of thanks, Marcia, realizing the awful finality of it all, swooned again, falling back on the couch. Fabius could see that she was in no shape to do anything.

"Tribune!" he called.

An officer entered quickly, his brass body armor gleaming.

"Post a detail near her door," Fabius instructed with his customary authority. "Around the clock. Use your most reliable men. I hold you responsible for what happens here. No one is to be admitted into her presence without her express wish. Have her servants fetch for her whatever she desires. Give her no cause to complain to me about anything. If there are any problems, notify me immediately."

The tribune gave him a sharp salute and left the room.

Fabius followed him out, noticing that a number of servant women lingered anxiously nearby.

"Tend to your mistress," he told them sternly.

On his way out of the mansion, he found several undertakers hovering near the main entrance, like the vultures they all were. Recognizing one he knew to be a capable professional, he took the man aside, and sent all the others packing. He gave explicit instructions for the lavish preparations that were to be made for the funeral.

"Begging your pardon, General," the man remarked sheepishly. "This will be . . . costly."

Fabius scoffed, and tilted his head in the direction from which he had just left Marcia.

"Have no concerns about the cost," he said coolly. "The lady is now the richest woman in Rome."

———

The next days sped by Marcia in a continual blur. An endless stream of people came and went, many wanting to know what to do with respect to items of business they had pending with her father, some of them trying to gain advantage while she was emotionally vulnerable. Others were mere well-wishers, hoping to express their condolences for the passing of a great man. She was polite to everyone, but noncommittal to all. She went through the motions, numb from the horrible suddenness of it all.

The worst part, by far, was the public proceedings of the state funeral that had been arranged for Marcinius. She exhausted her last reserves of strength, enduring lengthy tributes in the Rostrum of the Senate, followed by the burning of her father's corpse on the massive funeral pyre that had been erected in the public plaza outside the Forum. Escorted by Fabius and Caldus, Marcia played the role of the bereaved noble Roman daughter perfectly, sitting stoically through the long orations, never showing a hint of the anguish she truly felt.

The embers from the conflagration that consumed the remains of her dear father were still glowing red as the senators and other dignitaries began to peel away from the scene. She could not help but notice that many of them congregated around Caldus, the obvious heir apparent to leadership of the Marcinius faction. They slapped him on the back, shaking his hand, already aligning themselves with the new political reality. Others fawned over Cato, who seemed intent on recruiting as many former Marcinians as he could. Marcia bit her lip, determined not to let them see her anger over this show of disrepect—Marcinius' ashes were not yet even thrown to the winds, and already they were carving up his pie!

If only Scipio were here, they'd show more respect, she thought. But the recollection of her missing fiancé, and his long silence from Africa, tipped her over the edge, and the tears flowed freely down her cheeks.

I am alone, she realized, *all alone.* She wobbled a bit. Fabius took her by the arm to steady her.

A few seconds later, she found the steel in her soul.

I may be alone, she determined, *but these scoundrels will not get the better of me.*

Several days passed before Marcia was able to get up the energy to tackle what she knew must be the first priority in her new life as mistress of her father's vast empire. His holdings were extensive and his partnerships almost too numerous to comprehend. Prudently, Marcinius had taken some steps to prepare his daughter, at least superficially, for the complexities of the estate she would inherit upon his demise. She knew, for example, that his will was securely locked in the metal box he kept in his library, where she had made her first advances to Scipio.

Her father's murderer had conveniently left behind the key to the lockbox in his coin-purse.

Clad in simple mourning garb of a black linen shift and a silk armband, Marcia padded through the mansion's labyrinthine corridors to the library. The thought struck her: *With Father gone, will Scipio be willing to move into this house?* She shrugged that question off—too complicated for now.

The large metal box was situated in a finely paneled cabinet in the middle of one of the bookshelves. She pushed a comfortable chair over to the shelf, expecting this to take some time, and inserted the key.

The box opened easily. It was full of documents, which she began removing and putting into separate piles on a nearby table. Each would require careful review. When the scrolls and tablets had been removed, she discovered something fantastic: ingot bars of solid gold stacked across the bottom of the lockbox, over a dozen of them. She struggled to lift one, amazed by the mass of it. This gold alone would be an enormous inheritance.

She turned her attention to the documents.

The will was easy to spot: a large vellum scroll, sealed with wax and stamped with Marcinius' individual signet. She knew very well to treat it carefully and not break the seal. She did not feel a need to read it—her father had assured her that he was leaving everything he had to her, his only child.

She spent several hours browsing through the other items, noting all manner of deeds, memoranda regarding her father's investments and holdings, certificates of ownership, and other indicia of the financial empire over which she now would preside. It was overwhelming, and she knew she must enlist someone she could trust to help her prepare an inventory and bring order to this sprawling enterprise.

And then she saw what appeared to be a folded copy of a letter addressed to her father. She glanced at the bottom, and saw that it was signed by someone named Silanus.

She delicately opened the folds, and began to read.

Minutes later, Marcia dropped the letter and put her shaking hands to her head, completely stunned by the contents of the correspondence.

This fellow Silanus apparently was an officer in Scipio's command. It seemed her father had engaged him to kill her fiancé in the event he survived the battle with Hannibal because Scipio had taken up with a Carthaginian woman captured by the Romans!

She gasped, finally getting an idea why Scipio had not written for all those months. Of course, she knew that a man at war could not be expected to go without the company of a woman now and then, but the confirmation of this activity was devastating in her already weakened state, and she collapsed, sobbing. She had lost her father, and perhaps her fiancé, all in a matter of days.

XXII

TUNIS, AFRICA

202 BC

NOT FOR THE FIRST time, Laelius marveled at how often in life momentous news arrives in batches.

Tunis Bay, glittering in the fine morning sun, was made even more spectacular by the arrival of a military courier bearing the best report they had received in months. The long-missing iron plates had finally turned up in Utica and were promptly affixed to the menacing siege towers. The city, facing the imminent breach of her walls by these fearsome machines, had surrendered. The long ordeal was at last over.

Scipio, who had gradually been showing signs of rousing from his lethargic stupor following the death of Vibiana, seemed energized by this news. Another victory!

The joyous announcement had barely been conveyed to the other members of the high command when another packet arrived on the daily ferry from Rome. The ferry had been put into service to speed the flow of men and materiel to sustain the ever-growing Roman presence in her newest province.

The senior officers had gathered in Scipio's office, in a building overlooking the bustling harbor. They were still celebrating the happy tidings from Utica when Scipio opened the second correspondence. He read aloud the news that the prominent senator Marcinius had been found murdered in the street near his residence. All the officers, save one, were shocked by this development.

Laelius, having had the opportunity to anticipate these tidings, had been giving considerable thought to what to do next. He wasted no time saying to Scipio, "You must write to Marcia immediately, bearing your condolences."

Scipio gave him a passive look. "Yes, I suppose you're right," he said at length. But his heart was not in it.

"You must get on with your life," Laelius said gently, in his most affable voice. "Tell her you still love her, and now, with the fall of Utica, you can immediately return to Rome."

Scipio spent several long minutes looking out a window, across the frantic shipping activity in the clogged harbor. Until now, he had shut out of his mind all thoughts of Marcia, or of what the future might look like. The weight of his grief for Vibiana was crushing him. He could not go on like this. He knew that Laelius was right, that he had to pick up the pieces somehow and move on.

"I agree," he said with a sigh. "If you will excuse me, gentlemen, I wish to compose a letter."

Laelius ushered the group of officers out of the room, then turned to face his general.

"I propose to deliver that letter myself," he said. "I want to go back to Rome immediately and begin the preparations for your triumphant return."

Scipio nodded, somewhat vacantly. "As you wish."

Laelius turned smartly on his heel, and closed the door behind him, leaving Scipio alone with his thoughts.

———

After several fits and starts and a number of crumpled scrolls of vellum, Scipio put down the stylus and tried to think it through.

How do I feel about Marcia? he asked himself, over and over. There was no question, he still felt a warm affection for her. He had always been content in her presence. She was pleasant and charming, and very intelligent. Witty, too. Certainly, her acute sense of politics and the devious ways of the Roman Senate left him groveling in the dust.

And she was lovely in face and alluring in body.

At the same time, he did not feel any burning passion for her. He did not have the absolute determination that he must have her, no matter what the consequences, that he had felt for Vibiana. He knew it in his heart: there could never be another Vibiana. . . .

But his love was gone, her ashes scattered to the ends of the earth.

He had to go on living. And to make a life, and carry on his family traditions, he must have a good Roman wife. Given that, there was no woman in Rome he cared for more than Marcia, or who would make a better match for him.

He took up the instrument and began again.

Marcia, my love,

The gods intervene in our lives in ways we mortals cannot comprehend.

Just this very morning, I was rejoicing in the excellent news that Utica is ours. The fortress has surrendered. Rome's hold on Africa is now secure. This event was especially happy for me, because it means that my duty here is now complete. I wasted no time in preparing for my return to Rome, and to your arms.

And then the courier arrived, bearing the awful tidings concerning your father. I am completely at a loss to comprehend this horrible event. I cannot imagine your grief. My own horror is compounded by my deep frustration that I am unable to be with you, to help you bear this staggering loss.

I have ordered my senior legate, Laelius, to leave Tunis this very day and make haste for Rome, to prepare the arrangements for my return. I expect to conclude my duties here very quickly.

I am aware that I have been terribly remiss in not writing to you over these many months. For this oversight, you have my deepest apology. Be assured that the burdens of this command have been oppressive upon my time and my energy. My responsibilities have consumed me, night and day. But consider what we have done—Hannibal beaten! Victory in this long and brutal war! Carthage on her knees before us! Rome's rule of the Mediterranean uncontested!

You and I have sacrificed our happiness to the achievement of these important goals. I know that the gods will reward us for all that we have given for the glory of Rome. I love you more than ever, and cannot wait until we can begin building our lives together.

With all my love,
Scipio Africanus

He read it over several times to be sure it was what he wanted to say. Satisfied at last with the composition, he sealed the letter and called for an attendant to take it to Laelius.

It was now all in the hands of the gods.

———

For once, the seas were calm, and Laelius made the crossing back to Rome without experiencing seasickness. He offered up thanks to Neptune as the boat put into the seaport of Ostia Antica, at the site of the Tiber River's outlet to the sea.

He wasted no time in securing a military wagon to take him and his gear inland. The road hugged the banks of the Tiber, snaking through the sprawling suburbs of the Roman metropolis, teeming with all manner of commerce. So far, at least, the consequences of peace with Carthage seemed favorable—things appeared to be booming everywhere he looked.

Laelius stopped at his residence long enough only to bathe, shave, and change into suitable formal garb. Properly presentable, he headed to the Palatine Hill.

The military guard Fabius had installed at the mansion had been replaced with private gladiators in the employ of the new mistress of the estate. Laelius was obliged to wait at the perimeter gate while a message was taken inside, requesting an audience with Marcia.

Marcia herself soon enough appeared at the entrance, and with a wave to the guards, beckoned Laelius to join her.

He was taken aback by her appearance. She had lost weight, and seemed drawn and wan, surely from incessant fits of weeping. Her eyes were still red and puffy. Not having expected any visitors this day, she was dressed in the traditional black mourning attire, and wore no makeup or jewelry.

"Laelius," she said softly, managing a faint smile.

"Marcia, my dear," he said, embracing her, "you have my deepest condolences. Your father was one of the great men of Rome. What a terrible shock this must have been."

She took him by the hand. "Come with me to the atrium." She led him to the spacious central garden, lush with its plantings and fountains. They took up seats on a finely carved marble bench, made more comfortable by satin pillows.

"I bring you what I did not have last time," Laelius said when they were settled. "A letter from your fiancé."

She did not take it. "I should suppose he is telling me that now my father is dead, he wishes to call off our wedding."

Laelius, startled by this suggestion, could only shake his head. "Marcia, why would you ever think that? I am sure that in this letter, he is full of love for you."

With a disdainful look, she took the scroll, opened it, and scanned through it. As she read, the look softened slightly to one of skepticism. She finished and met Laelius' eye.

"He says he loves me more than ever," she scoffed.

Laelius shrugged his shoulders. "Yes, of course. I am with him every day. He speaks of you constantly. He cannot wait to return and to be with you."

Then, louder, she spat out, "And what of this Carthaginian girl he took from the African king? Does he plan to keep her in a room down the hall from our bedchamber?"

In his mental preparations for this visit, Laelius had considered several possible ways the conversation might proceed. He specifically had pondered at length the possibility that someone in Rome might have told her about Scipio's relationship with Vibiana. He had his story at the ready.

"I do not know what you're talking about," Laelius said, expertly feigning ignorance.

Marcia's eyes narrowed, in the same manner as her father's famous scowl. "Do not play these games with me, Mr. Senior Legate. I have seen a report that my fiancé took the widow of Syphax—she who was the Carthaginian girl given to seal a treaty—and he has made her his concubine. I will not be humiliated in this fashion."

Laelius gave her a puzzled look and then brought forth a rich laugh. "The widow of Syphax? In Scipio's bed? Madam, you are deeply misinformed. The widow of Syphax was given to an African ally of ours, a cavalry leader named Massinissa. These reports you speak of are not true." Marcia looked at him, incredulous. She could not tell him about her father's offer to have Scipio killed, of course, but she did say, "My father was told these things by an officer on Scipio's own staff! How could they be untrue?"

Laelius' eyes gleamed at Marcia's inadvertent admission. He gave her a knowing look and cocked his head expressively. "Any chance this officer was named Silanus?"

The look of shock on Marcia's face told him he had guessed correctly.

"Silanus was a traitor," he told her simply. "He wanted to take charge and claim the glory for the success of the African Expedition.

He challenged Scipio for command of the expedition. He attempted to kill Scipio in a duel. Fortunately, he was no match for Scipio's swordsmanship."

Marcia's head was reeling. "But why all of this intrigue? How can these things go on?"

Laelius shrugged. "You of all people must know that Scipio has had, and will continue to have, political enemies. There are men who are jealous of his greatness, who envy the status he will possess for all time as the man who defeated Hannibal and brought Carthage to her knees. Powerful people in Rome have spies in our camp. All manner of crazy rumors have been spread about. They want to tarnish his legend, for their own selfish purposes, even before he can return home."

This deflated Marcia a bit. *Could it be that Father was misled? But to the point of actually trying to kill Scipio? No! It cannot be!* she thought. *Father could not have done something so vile without good reason. . . .*

Her eyes fell upon the letter again, and she re-read the words *I love you more than ever. . . .* This was not at all what she had been expecting, after so many months of silence. She would need some time to decide whether to accept his apology. Too, she would need to meet him face-to-face before she knew whether she could trust him again.

Laelius could see she was wavering. "In any event," he said in a dismissive tone, "you need not worry about that young lady. Yes, Scipio was going to bring her back to Rome, but as a trophy. She would have been forced to march in the upcoming triumphal parade—in chains. When she was informed of this, she took poison and killed herself. The lady is quite dead."

Marcia looked up. "She's dead? Truly?"

"Indeed." Laelius lay his hand on hers. "Marcia, you are engaged to be married to the greatest Roman of all time, the man who defeated Hannibal. He is returning home, to make his future here, with you as his wife. He loves you. I know that he does. Do not let these wicked trickeries deter you from your love for Scipio. Follow your heart, Marcia. All will be well."

He took the vellum sheet and rolled it. "I would like to suggest that when Scipio arrives in Ostia, you should be waiting for him. We will bring you aboard his flagship, and you can be privately reunited before the parade into Rome."

After a long pause, she nodded. "Yes," she said, her tone a little more harsh than Laelius would have liked. "I will meet with him."

———

Laelius remained in Rome, having no wish to brave another transit to Tunis.

The reception being planned for the conquering hero's homecoming was beyond the scope of anything ever seen in the city. It would make the Spanish triumph seem paltry by comparison. There was much to do, and Laelius threw himself into a flurry of activity.

He met with Fabius, ostensibly to brief him on the details of the treaty with Carthage. But in this conversation, he was able to learn that the investigation into the murder of Marcinius had revealed nothing, and had been terminated. There were no leads, and utterly no evidence. Fabius had written off the incident as an incredibly unfortunate crime, which could have been avoided if Marcinius had but taken his offer of an escort.

Fabius also told Laelius that with Carthage vanquished and Hannibal on the run, he was retiring from the army and heading for his familial estate.

Laelius then visited with the apparent successor to leadership of the Marcinius faction, the ever-astute Caldus. This meeting was taken at the residence of Marcinius, with Marcia in attendance. Laelius, as Scipio's representative, assured Caldus that Scipio would rely upon him in the years to come, forging an alliance against the dour but wily Cato. Rome would be in steady hands.

Caldus' first act in this new role was to shepherd through the Senate a resolution approving the treaty with Carthage. There was only one addition by the senators: they appended a clause naming Hannibal Barca to be a sworn life enemy of the people of Rome, and establishing a fabulous bounty upon his head to anyone who could deliver it to the Senate. This assured that Hannibal would spend the rest of his days as a fugitive.

Correspondence with Scipio was required, of course, to alert him to the cover story Laelius had given Marcia. And as an added measure, he instructed Scipio that Narcussa was never to be allowed near the bride—he should be given his freedom and sent to Spain in retirement.

Scipio's reply was but three sentences: *Narcussa off to Spain. I gave her to Massinissa? Why him?*

Laelius wrote back: *Who will ever go to Numidia to verify the story?*

Ever cautious, however, Laelius did send word to the new king of Numidia informing him of the delicate situation and asking him for his cooperation. In due time, Massinissa sent a letter, saying, in part:

> *Though I am saddened by the loss of my concubine—the woman Vibiana, niece of Hannibal, who has taken her own life rather than be paraded in chains before the Roman people—I have already found a suitable replacement for my harem.*
>
> *I wish the great Africanus every happiness in his forthcoming marriage.*

Laelius provided a copy of the letter to Marcia, which helped to further soften her resistance to the impending reconciliation with her fiancé. All of this was just housekeeping, in Laelius' mind. What truly gave him joy was being back in Rome, free of army routine and discipline, and savoring all of her culture and her diversions—in particular, one by the name of Patroclus.

In the days preceding Scipio's return, despite the swirl of activity and the frenzied preparations for the epic celebration, Marcia continued to agonize over the meaning of the letter she'd found in her father's papers, particularly its revelation concerning Scipio's relationship with the widow of Syphax. *How could Father have been wrong?* she asked herself, over and over again. And then she would remember what Laelius had said about the rumor-mongering by those jealous of Scipio's burgeoning fame and power, she would reread the letter from Massinissa, and she would start all over again with her brooding.

Another letter arrived from Scipio, this one even more romantic. He begged her again to forgive his failure to communicate during the long months of the campaign, and professed his love for her, even expressing intimate thoughts about their being together. It only added to her inner turmoil.

I do love him, I really do, she thought over and over again, *but if he loves me, how could he have done this to me?*

One of her slave attendants, perhaps her closest confidante, made a suggestion. "You struggle because you have no mother or sister to share this anguish, or give you advice," the girl said. "Perhaps you should take counsel from the person who loves him as much as you do."

Marcia gave the slave girl an odd look. "What do you mean?"

"Why not talk to his mother?" the girl said with a sly smile. "Surely she must know how he really feels about you."

"That is preposterous," Marcia said, unwilling to consider discussing so intimate a topic with her possible mother-in-law. She stalked away in a huff.

But it was not preposterous, and after sleeping on it, the next morning Marcia sent a messenger to Pomponia, asking if she might call on her that afternoon. As was to be expected, the reply was gracious and welcoming.

Accompanied by her ever-present cadre of gladiator bodyguards, Marcia made her way over to Pomponia's residence, bearing a gift of a glittering golden brooch.

"Marcia, my dear, what a lovely surprise!" Pomponia said, greeting her son's fiancée in the foyer with a warm embrace. "You are always welcome in the home of the Cornelli."

Marcia handed her the brooch. "I brought you something that might show my warm feelings for you."

Pomponia, who of course was at a point in life well beyond caring for material baubles, nonetheless took the gift humbly and gave thanks for Marcia's thoughtfulness.

"Come with me, my dear," she said, and led Marcia to the comfortable and well-lit sitting room, where Pomponia often worked on her sewing.

They reclined opposite each other on finely padded couches, and after a servant brought wine and a platter of fruits, engaged in light conversation about the upcoming parade and the lavish spectacles planned to celebrate the end of the war.

After some minutes of this small talk, Pomponia gave Marcia a perceptive look. "Glad as I am to have you as my guest, something tells me you did not come all the way over here, bearing an ornate gift, to talk of these trivial matters."

Marcia wrung her hands and studied the floor. "Am I so transparent in my intentions?"

Pomponia could see the young woman was carrying some heavy burden and needed to unload it. She leaned over and took Marcia's hands in her own. "You are to be my daughter-in-law. I care for nothing but your happiness with my son. Tell me what is troubling you."

Marcia looked away, but Pomponia waited patiently. Finally, fighting back tears, she screwed up her courage and managed to get out, "I have heard vile rumors that Scipio has been with another woman while on the campaign in Africa. I don't know what to do!" It was as if a dam had broken, and the tears gushed down Marcia's cheeks.

Pomponia's maternal instincts took over, and she took Marcia in her arms, holding her until the weeping subsided. She brushed away Marcia's tears and looked in her now-swollen eyes. "Marcia, do not bother yourself over whatever vicious things you might have heard. I have spoken with Scipio at length and questioned him closely. He has told me repeatedly that he loves you, with all his heart, and there is no reason he would lie to me about that."

Marcia sniffled a bit, trying to clear away her tears. "But you have not spoken with him since he went to Africa," she argued. "What if he has been dallying with another woman, behind my back?"

Pomponia now grew stern. "Marcia, you are a grown woman," she said firmly. "Our men go off to war for years at a time. They risk their lives for us, to make Rome stronger, and protect us from danger. Even if what you have heard is true, what of it? The important thing is that he's coming back to *you*, and he wants to marry *you*."

Marcia shook her head. "Easy for you to say. You have not been so betrayed."

Pomponia drew back, suddenly aloof. "You forget, madam: my husband was a general, too."

Marcia gave her a stunned look. "And did he—"

"It does not matter," Pomponia said, her voice turning cold. "My husband was a great man of Rome. I was privileged to be his wife. All that matters is what he did when he was with me. What these men do in some remote military camp is irrelevant to their love for us."

Marcia pondered this.

"We are women of Rome, Marcia. Our men do their duty, and

we must do ours. And let us not forget, my dear, that information held in your heart is always at hand should you ever need to use it." Pomponia looked pointedly at Marcia, waiting for her to begin to understand the power a woman might hold over her husband, if she remained quietly wise to his ways.

As Pomponia's words sank in, Marcia felt herself strengthening. "I suppose. . . . Well, perhaps you are right."

Pomponia handed Marcia the goblet of wine she had left on the small table separating the couches. "Open your heart to his love, my dear. He will make you happy all the days of your life."

Marcia nodded, and they drank.

XXIII

Ostia Antica

201 BC

THE ENTIRE OSTIAN HARBOR was decked out in festive banners. Trumpeters were stationed on many of the ships at anchor, blowing a raucous greeting as the sleek trireme flying Scipio's battle standard was rowed to a pier at the center of the bay. Hordes of people lined the quays forming the breakwater of the harbor, and even more thronged to the wharves on the river side of the bay. All of them were cheering, waving colorful cloths and Roman imperial flags.

Old Neptune had come through for them yet again: the god had provided a cloudless blue sky and a cool breeze off the water, so that everyone taking part in the festivities might revel in the gorgeous weather.

The three legions that Scipio had led into Africa had already disembarked; they formed an honor guard lining the road the entire distance from the port to the gates of the city. The plan called for Scipio to pass through them, riding on a parade-style chariot, freshly painted in the bold red and gold of the Roman Army. The chariot was to be driven by his brother Lucius, and the soldiers would then fall in behind him as he passed. Scipio would lead the entire contingent over the parade route, through Rome and past all the famous landmarks, including a brief stop at the nearly finished Temple of Neptune. Ultimately, he would arrive at the Forum, where he would be feted by the Senate.

By prior arrangement, Marcia, Laelius, and Pomponia were waiting at the shore edge of the pier. They would board Scipio's flagship when it was secured and take a private visit with the mighty Africanus before he would show himself to the masses eagerly awaiting his arrival.

The plan went off smoothly. Laelius was the first in to see Scipio, thus assuring them a private opportunity to make sure their stories were aligned. Pomponia, and then Marcia, would next be reunited with him.

Scipio was resplendent in a new suit of ceremonial armor, all glittering gold and silver, the entire complement a gift of the grateful Senate and people of Rome. He was carefully barbered and had never looked more handsome. He lingered only briefly with his mother, who rejoiced, of course, to be reunited with both her sons. Following their heartfelt embrace, with much shedding of tears by Pomponia, Scipio gave her a special gift. He removed from a large silk bag his father's cuirass, carefully repaired to eliminate all traces of the gash from the awful blow that took his life. Pomponia, overcome by this relic of her long-lost husband, had to be propped up by her loving son. Still weeping, she was shown to an adjoining cabin, where Lucius awaited her.

Marcia had chosen to dress herself demurely, seeking to present to the people of Rome the somewhat matronly image of a loyal bride-to-be, who had waited faithfully while her fiancé was off conquering Rome's enemies. She wore a silken peach gown, flattering to her figure without making any controversial display of her womanly charms. Her makeup and her jewelry, like her gown, were modest. There was to be no ostentatious show of her exceptional wealth to the masses of common Roman citizens.

Yet hidden in a pocket of her undergarment was a folded scrap of parchment. It was the letter from Silanus. After many days of agonizing, try as she might, Marcia had been unable to reconcile herself with Pomponia's advice. Maybe the simpler Roman girls could turn their heads and pretend not to know what their men were doing behind their backs—but not Marcia. She intended to confront Scipio with her awareness of his alleged infidelity and have it out with him. If he tried to deny it, she would thrust the letter into his face. She would not live her life as a colossal lie—if he did not truly love her, she was determined to end their relationship then and there, the crowds of admirers be damned.

Laelius could sense her tension, but he knew that Marcia's actions were far beyond his control. Pity Scipio—facing Hannibal was child's play compared to this bubbling volcano. He smirked as he led her to the door of Scipio's cabin. He paused and glanced upward. *Dear Neptune, if ever you truly favored him, let it be now.*

She drew herself up, took a deep breath, and nodded to the senior legate. He opened the door and she stepped in. Laelius gently closed the door, leaving them to their privacy.

Marcia had been steeling herself, anticipating and dreading this moment, rehearsing over and over in her mind what she would say, how she would confront him, admonish him, and lay down the law for their future days together.

She was quite unprepared, however, for his aura.

At a glance, she realized he was enormously changed from the young man she had last seen those many months ago. Certainly, he still had his rugged good looks and that captivating smile, but she now saw before her a man whose face was etched with stress borne of the countless horrors of battle, who had led so many men to their deaths, and others to victory. She looked beyond the fabulous armor into those penetrating blue eyes and found a maturity that had not been easily attained, and yet a tenderness that outshone the armor. She felt her resolve begin to ebb.

Summoning all her willpower, she held her ground and said to him, a little more sharply than she had intended, "Do you truly think I am so naïve as to believe that all those months in Africa you could not find time to write even a single line to me?"

Scipio, not at all surprised by this onslaught, shook his head. "I can honestly say that there has not been a day that we've been apart that I have not thought about you. I realize now that I let the situation get the better of me. I can only pray that you forgive me."

He's become a better politician, she thought ruefully. *His answer has a kernel of truth, but evades the real issue.*

"Can you not see that what has happened makes me question whether you truly love me?" she flared. "Why should I not believe you used me as bait to lure my father into giving you the votes you needed to launch your grand campaign and go do whatever it is you've been doing?"

Scipio reflected for a moment and then, drawing on the power of his piercing stare, looked deep into her eyes. "If I were the crass manipulator you seem to think I am, I would have ended our engagement immediately. After all, with your father dead, there is nothing further to be obtained from him—or you. No one in Rome would have questioned my decision had I renounced our contract. But instead, I hastened home to be with you. Perhaps, my love, you have spent too much time surrounded by all those rascals in the Senate. You cannot believe anyone is sincere because you have been witness to so much devious scheming."

This resonated with her, but she launched a final volley. "How am I to overcome my fears for what happened in Africa?"

Scipio gave her an even more potent look. "I went to Africa for Rome. I came back from Africa for you. Because I love you."

He said it so simply, so easily, so much from the depth of his heart, she could not deny him.

After a few moments of looking at him somewhat skeptically, all her preparations evaporated like dew in the morning sun. She rushed into his arms, kissing him and weeping.

———

When the couple emerged arm in arm, both smiled broadly. They walked a few steps to the side of the ship, into the view of the people massed along the shore. Scipio gave them a wave of his free arm. A huge roar erupted, followed by prolonged chanting of "Africanus! Africanus!"

After a few minutes of this adulation, Scipio took Marcia's hand and carefully led her down the gangplank to the pier, to the waiting Lucius and the chariot, pulled by four magnificent black stallions. Laelius was waiting alongside. The faithful Bucephalus, also adorned in a new set of gleaming armor, waited nearby. He would parade behind the chariot. Everyone along the route would wonder about the identity of the young lad riding the now-fabled warhorse, but Scipio had insisted that Garnesso accompany him back to Rome to participate in the triumph.

It had been planned that Marcia and Scipio would split at the foot of the chariot. Scipio was to climb aboard; Marcia was to be escorted by Laelius to a waiting carriage and taken to a viewing stand.

Reaching the chariot, Scipio saw that its sides had been decorated with elephants, carved out of ivory, symbolizing the historic victory over Hannibal. He laughed, slapped Laelius on the shoulder, and pointed them out to the crowd. This produced another roar of adulation.

While Scipio was acknowledging the cheers, his back to Marcia, she deftly pulled the parchment note from her undergarment and slipped it to Laelius. "Do with it as you will," she whispered to him. "What is in the past shall stay in the past."

"I must go now," she said to Scipio, seeking to release her arm.

But Scipio held her tight in his grip.

"No," he said in his most commanding voice.

"But why?" she asked. "You are to ride in this parade!"

Scipio put both his hands around her waist and hoisted her onto the floor of the chariot.

Marcia was nearly speechless. "What are you doing?"

Scipio stepped up behind her, and took her in his arms again, giving her a long kiss, producing yet another roar from the crowd.

"Ride with me," he said.

"All of Rome loves you," she said, putting her arm around him for support.

Scipio smiled. "The people of Rome love victorious generals. The Senate is a completely different matter."

Marcia shook her head. "If you lead them, the people will follow you. And if you have the people, the Senate must fall in line."

Scipio reflected for a moment, and laughed. "Well then, together let us see where we shall take them!"

And with a nod to Lucius, they were off.

———

Laelius waited until they were safely out of sight, then opened the sheaf of parchment. He was enormously pleased to realize what it was, and what it meant for Marcia to give it up.

He walked the short distance back to the edge of the dock and faced a line of soldiers waiting to fall into place for the parade. He pointed to the centurion. "Which of your men can throw a spear the farthest?" he asked.

The centurion, a scarred and crusty veteran of the campaign, pointed to a powerfully built legionnaire. "That one," he said with a grin.

Laelius motioned for the soldier to hand over his spear. He pushed the paper over the point and down toward the shaft. Handing the spear back to the soldier, he pointed to the water and said, "Make your best throw."

The soldier dutifully complied, and launched the spear far out into the bay. The trajectory was flat, and the point did not penetrate the water. Instead, the missile lingered on the surface for a few seconds.

And then the great god Neptune, ever protective of Scipio, pulled it under the gentle waves and tucked it close to his breast, there to remain forever.

EPILOGUE

ROME

200 BC

L AELIUS WATCHED WITH SOME concern as the team of slaves struggled to carry the heavy wooden crates through the musty corridors of the Roman Army headquarters. His sweating crew muscled their cargo down several flights of narrow stone-cut stairs, ultimately reaching the subbasement safely. He followed along behind them, carefully watching his boots to make sure he did not take a tumble in the dim light provided by the occasional torches.

He reached a long counter staffed by a couple of clerks, pasty white in complexion from their long years in this subterranean service.

One of them gave him a steely look. "And you would be?"

"I am Garibus Paullus Laelius," he said sharply, "senior legate to Scipio Africanus, commander of the African Expedition, and quaestor thereto. It is my final duty as quaestor to deliver to you for permanent safekeeping the relevant records of the African Expedition."

He pointed to the boxes. "It's all there. Every invoice, every payment record, every journal entry, every payroll register, down to the last sesterce. Oh, and as many of the dispatches and written orders as we could assemble."

The clerk's expression turned sour. He could see that putting all these records into the archives of the Roman Army would take months, if not years. With a heavy sigh, he began to write out a receipt for the various materials.

"Most important of all is this," Laelius added, handing over a thick stack of vellum sheets. "It is the official report of the quaestor on the entire history of the campaign, from the first departure to Sicily, to the triumph accorded to Scipio Africanus by the Senate."

Laelius had personally dictated the entire record, and read every word of the scribes' transcription. He was determined that the Massinissa version of the story of Vibiana and her tragic suicide would be the one that survived throughout history. He knew full well that within two generations, there would be no survivors of the actual events to contradict the official record. For all time, people would believe that Vibiana had been given to Massinissa and then killed herself rather than be exhibited in Rome. He had even included the correspondence he had received from Massinissa, confirming these events.

Without looking up from his writing, the clerk said, "This is quite some piece of work. The triumph was over a year ago."

Laelius acknowledged this fact with a grunt.

"I understand Africanus is a father already," the clerk said, scratching away on his pad.

This brought a smile to Laelius' face. "Yes. Scipio and Marcia were married only a week after the triumph, and they wasted no time making a family. Once again, we have a Young Scipio."

"And Africanus has retired?"

Laelius nodded. "From the military, yes. But he is quite active in politics." *And Cato is proving to be more challenging an adversary to Scipio than Hannibal was*, Laelius thought.

The clerk handed him the first page of the receipt form. "Rumor has it that his brother Lucius is trying to secure command of the new campaign against Antiochus."

Laelius was growing weary of this gossipy clerk. "I wouldn't know about that," he said evenly. "I only know that under no circumstances will I be taking the field ever again."

"Can't blame you there," the clerk remarked. "Can you believe that Hannibal was caught trying to sell his services to Antiochus?"

Laelius nodded. Rumors were swirling that Hannibal, trying to escape the long arm of Roman justice, had gone to Syria to offer his services to Antiochus in the coming war.

The clerk handed him the second and final page of the receipt. "All done. You have officially completed your duties. That receipt will serve as your formal discharge from the Roman Army."

"Thank you," Laelius said, and turned to go.

"One last question, if I may?"

In exasperation, Laelius faced the clerk.

"How was he, really, to serve under? Was he a bastard, like most of these generals?"

Laelius put the receipt into his tunic. "No, my friend." He paused for effect. "Not a bit. He was the greatest Roman of them all."

AFTERWORD

Hannibal's Niece is an historical novel. Like any historical novel, it takes a series of established historical events involving actual individuals and spins a story for which there is no established documentary record.

When considering matters regarding Ancient Rome, it is important to recognize that there are *no* actual documentary records extant regarding the events covered by this novel. The accounts written by the well-known historians Polybius and Livy were in fact penned many years after the fact.

The romantic story line of *Hannibal's Niece* is an amalgamation of two historical sources.

First, an account by the Roman historian Valerius Maximus, written three hundred years after Scipio's death, includes a tale that Scipio's soldiers presented him with a beautiful woman captured at Cartagena, who turned out to be engaged to a local tribal chief. According to Valerius, Scipio returned the woman to her fiancé, virtue intact.

Second, there is the better-known story of Sophonisba, who was, by most accounts, Hannibal's niece. She was married off to Syphax to seal the alliance between Numidia and Carthage against Rome. She was subsequently captured after the Romans defeated Syphax, and ended up with Massinissa, who married her. However, Scipio rejected the marriage, and insisted that she be brought to Rome to be displayed in his triumphal parade. Rather than submit, she committed suicide.

My Vibiana is the fictional merger of these two reports. In writing the book, I agonized long and hard over whether to call her Sophonisba, for the actual personage. In the end, I simply liked the name Vibiana better and stuck with it.

There are many other actual historical figures who are aggressively blended with totally imaginary characters. Fabius, Cato, Laelius, Lucius, Hannibal, Hasdrubal Barca, Hasdrubal Son of Gisgo, Syphax, and Massinissa were real; Silanus, Massiva, Quintio, Narcussa, Demosthenes, and Caldus invented. Bucephalus, of course, was the name of Alexander the Great's famous mount; the historical accounts don't tell us about Scipio's horse, but it seems reasonable to suggest that Scipio would have named his horse in Alexander's honor.

There are other instances in which I've borrowed well-known names. Laelius' co-conspirator, Patroclus, for example: the name is that of Achilles' lover in *The Illiad*. We have a guard named Polybius, in a salute to the early historian by that name. There are others, but I will leave it to eagle-eyed readers to spot them.

The historical accounts tell us that Laelius was in fact a highly skilled military officer who was instrumental to Scipio's success, although in real life, he was closer to Scipio's own age than to his father's. I have enriched this character with an alternative sexual preference and the completely fictional account of his relationship with Scipio's father.

Scipio married Aemilia Paulla, the daughter of a former consul who perished in the disaster at Cannae. My Marcia, and her wealthy father, Marcinius, are total fiction.

Probably the most outrageous license-taking in the book is the suggestion that Zama was fought over Scipio's refusal of Hannibal's demand for the return of his niece. The historical accounts of Livy and Polybius are clear that they in fact had a parley before the battle, but their accounts are unsatisfying in pinpointing the reason for the breakdown of negotiations. In my treatment, Scipio fights his great nemesis because of his love for a woman. I hope readers will agree that it makes for a great story.

Professional historians will spot lots of other anomalies. The descriptions of the buildings, the food, the weapons, the ships, the baths, and the clothes come largely from various sources describing such items which are actually from periods later in time. The historical timelines have been altered, various battles are omitted, and other details are substituted. The strict historians can nit-pick all they want—it was all done in the name of readability.

In any event, I have given myself an ironclad defense: there's no doubt that Polybius and Livy would have relied on the archives of the Roman Army for basic source material. In my version, the crafty Laelius has stacked the historical deck with his account of the campaign—and more importantly, the tale of Vibiana.

Acknowledgments

I am deeply grateful for the insightful editorial assistance of Maya Myers. Her patient tutorials in the Chicago Manual of Style have produced a text hopefully tolerable to professional proofreaders everywhere.

I wish to thank G. A. Beller, who, after reading my manuscript, generously provided guidance and support. It was at his suggestion that I submitted my manuscript for grant consideration through GABE Advisors, LLC. In addition, he introduced me to Vivian Craig of G. Anton Publishing/Chicago, whose many suggestions improved the text markedly. I couldn't have gotten it done without them.

I'm grateful to my daughter, Haley, whose good behavior, educational achievement, and career success have given me nothing to worry about over the years, freeing me to spend time on this quest.

Finally, my dear wife Susan suffered through the hundreds and hundreds of hours I spent laboring over this book, which became something of a hobby to me. She read the text repeatedly and made lots of comments—and I actually included some of them in the final product!

ABOUT THE AUTHOR

Ever since seeing the movie *Spartacus* as a kid, Anthony (Tony) Licata has been hooked on the Roman Empire—reading and studying Roman history and following it in the popular culture. Throughout his career, Tony has been a committed student of European and American history as well. These interests, coupled with several visits to Italy and Spain, led to his desire to write the historical novel *Hannibal's Niece*.

A graduate of MacMurray College and Harvard Law School, Mr. Licata has built a successful law practice specializing in commercial real estate. He is Partner-in-Charge of the Chicago office of the law firm Taft Stettinius & Hollister.

Tony lives with his wife in Highland Park, Illinois, and has a daughter living in Chicago with her husband.

www.ingramcontent.com/pod-product-compliance
Lightning Source LLC
Chambersburg PA
CBHW020502020726
47493CB00001B/148